ELECTRIC ORANGE

A NOVEL

TJ POORTINGA

PEEP STONE PRESS
LOS ANGELES

PEEP STONE PRESS FIRST LOOK EDITION 2025

Copyright © 2025 by TJ Poortinga

This is a work of fiction. Names, characters, places, and incidents are products of the author's imagination or are used fictitiously.

Library of Congress Control Number: Pending
BISAC: FICTION / Literary. | FICTION / Psychological. | FICTION / Satire.

Paperback ISBN: 979-8-9998824-0-0
eBook ISBN: 979-8-9998824-1-7

Cover design concept by TJ Poortinga
Interior design by Chicken Scratch, LLC

Published by Peep Stone Press

Los Angeles

Printed in the United States of America

For the one who got away.

1

Pieter Verboom paced the studio, whispering fragments of an alibi. His pockets, stuffed with snacks swiped from the lobby, crinkled with each step. Coming to a stop in the greenroom, he placed his right hand over his neck.

"Heart racing. Ears ringing. Vision narrowing..." Verboom listed symptoms like a textbook entry, his panic-stricken eyes betraying his monotone voice.

"No one's ever died of stage fright," said his publicist, Ella Walker, who was leaning against the doorway. She glanced up from her phone and forced a smile, then looked down at his pants and frowned. "You can't go on camera with that bulge. You'll start a new rumor."

The low shag carpet silenced her heels as she closed the distance between them.

"Why are you hoarding junk food like a student?" Ella asked Verboom while motioning toward me with a flick of her head.

"They told me to help myself," Verboom said. "I couldn't help myself."

She then dug into his pocket and pulled out a mini chocolate bar. "It's already melted along those hulking thighs," she teased, pinching the candy.

"In Friesland, Grandpa was a speedskater," Verboom lamented. "Better those frozen canals than this frozen swamp."

From the same pocket, Ella pulled out a pouch of mixed nuts, a swollen bag of potato chips, a few loose pretzels, and several peppermints. She passed me the stash, then emptied the other pocket—a handful of teabags.

With the precision of a TSA agent, she patted his pants, working her way up his inseam to the top, where she paused with a grin. "Let's save *this* treat for later."

The flirtation was lost on Verboom. Now, with both hands on his neck, he croaked for water and could barely swallow once I brought him a cup.

"Breathe," I said.

He inhaled sharply, then let it out.

"Wiggle your toes," I suggested—an old trick to fight off anxiety.

He closed his eyes. His brown Oxfords bulged and flexed.

After another deep breath, a producer steered the reluctant psychologist toward the host, Jonathan Kuiper, who was seated behind the set's desk.

After a few hesitant steps, Verboom froze, his gaze fixed on the shadow beside the stage wall, as if he hoped to dissolve into the darkness.

The producer tugged on Verboom's tweed jacket, coaxing him forward.

"You know there's an 'I' in my name, *ja*? It's the Dutch spelling of Peter, but students prefer my last name—two O's, you know?"

Verboom had crossed the Potomac in obscurity, but now his influence seemed to loom over the capital as critics blamed him for the president's sagging popularity. A commentator on ANN even dubbed him "a ruthless Svengali." Ever the fixer, Ella secured a spot on WNN's *Hot Button Science with Jonathan Kuiper*, hoping to turn the tide.

With thick brown hair cropped tight and dressed in a snug navy-blue suit, Kuiper looked into the camera and introduced his guests: a theologian preaching Christian Nationalism, a historian pushing pluralism, a political scientist exposing spin, and Verboom—staring at the red light, his plump lips moving soundlessly. Whether argument, prayer, or gibberish, his words evaded capture.

"Professor Verboom, sources inside the administration claim you told the president to 'get God out of government,'" Kuiper said, his tone neutral, his face quizzical. "And to 'build a wall'—a wall of separation between church and state."

Verboom mouthed the word "God," punctuating it with an air quote, then raised his hands to shield his eyes from the glaring studio lights.

Kuiper repeated the allegation, his gaze steady, and for a moment, the two men locked eyes.

The other guests leaned forward.

Verboom wiped his brow, as beads of sweat had broken through his stage make-up. Then he closed his eyes and said matter-of-factly, "If God is truly God, how could we get such a Being *out* of anything?"

The white-bearded theologian straightened up to speak.

Verboom sprang to his feet. "Let '*God*' answer the question," he growled like a surly prophet, air-quoting 'God' again before throwing his hands skyward, as if tossing confetti.

Arms still up, Verboom stormed off the set, passing through the greenroom and outer lobby, then down the hallway bathed in fluorescent light.

"Stop!" Ella yelled. She hurried around and planted herself in front of the 6'4" psychologist. "Look at me—I worked so hard to land this booking. You're here to clear your name, not spout riddles. Now turn around and give America some *breaking news*!"

The words 'breaking news' shot through Verboom like an electric charge. With a manic gleam, he bolted back to the set.

"The Union Must And Shall Be Preserved!" Verboom howled at the ceiling before his gaze darted to the camera. His eyelids snapped back feverishly.

"Professor!" Kuiper exclaimed. "Did you tell the president to build a wall?"

"Don't Change Horses Midstream!" Verboom bayed, running circles around Kuiper and the guests. He yanked the lapels of his tweed jacket over his blond hair and looped the anchor's desk like a headless horseman, shouting more historic slogans. "A Chicken In Every Pot! The Buck Stops Here! All The Way With LBJ!" He neighed like a feral stallion. "It's The Economy, Stupid! Ross For Boss!"

He stopped, squared up to Kuiper, and lowered his jacket.

Verboom glanced side to side, then asked the host in a whisper: "*Yes We Can?*"

"*Can we*, professor?" Kuiper demanded. "Can we build a wall between church and state?"

Now trotting in place, Verboom chanted boldly: "*Yes We Can! Yes We Can!*"

"There's never been a wall!" scoffed the theologian.

"There's a wall higher than any ladder!" the historian shot back.

Verboom flung his arms wide and sang, "*Ain't no ladder high enough! Ain't no pundit low enough! Ain't no angle wide enough. To keep me here talkin' with you.*"

Then he galloped off stage, through the greenroom, down the hall, down the emergency stairs, and out through the exit door onto the frigid streets of Capitol Hill.

I kept pace with him, but Ella had fallen behind by the time we reached his hotel room, just a few blocks from the studio. Once inside, he slammed the door shut and slid the chain lock into place.

"Don't let her in, Santo! She'll drag me in front of the cameras!"

The electric lock clicked with the swipe of a card key. The door cracked open a few inches before the chain caught, and Verboom sprinted from the entry.

"Open up! We need damage control," Ella said sharply, then

softened her tone. "Are you there, Santo?"

I eased the door forward and unhooked the chain.

Eyes flickering with gratitude, she stepped inside and kissed me on the cheek. Then she wrapped her arms around herself, drawing her shoulders up.

"Where's that draft coming from?" she asked.

I glanced down at her black skirt. "Do you ever wear pants?"

"My leggings are warmer than your jeans—what's your point?"

Leaving the suite's foyer, she strode into the living room.

The balcony curtains were drawn but swayed with a gust of wind. She marched to the sliding doors, yanked the curtains apart, and followed the faint wail of sirens out onto the balcony. It was empty.

"*Keep Hope Alive!*" echoed from the sidewalk, two floors below. I leaned over the railing and spotted the professor.

He shouted the slogan again as he turned a corner.

Ella sighed, creating a mist in the January night air, then she sank into the cushions of a lounge chair and looked up at me.

"What's wrong with him?" she complained.

"Verboom hates cameras. How did you ever talk him into that?"

"He wanted to help the administration."

"He's the one who needs help."

She reached into her black clutch. Out came a hardtop pack of menthols, which she snapped open and gave a practiced shake. A single filter rose above the rest, and she brought it to her lips.

Her eyes squinted with the first drag. She began nodding and then said with an exhale of smoke, "I've *got* it."

The next day, a honking horn echoed through the hotel's rotunda, pulling me out of a plush seat in the lobby. I'd been trying to read a journal article but was mostly people-watching.

I put on my black peacoat and walked through the entrance to find Verboom in a gleaming full-size pickup, engine revving, while circling the fountain at the center of the roundabout. Symphonic music blasted from the open windows as he leaned on the horn.

When he spotted me, he brought the truck to a stop.

"Your chariot awaits!" he announced with frenzied eyes.

"What happened to the rental car?"

"This one's ours to keep! We're going back to Michigan in style. All aboard!" He blew the horn with boat-like toots.

"Where'd you get this beast?"

"Followed the billboards straight to the dealership!"

"You *bought* it?" I thought he'd merely upgraded our rental sedan.

"When negotiations hit a wall, the rep asked: 'What's it going to take to get you in this truck?' The answer came naturally, '*The Flying Dutchman* on surround sound.' So, the guy ran to a music shop and came back with a version on CD."

"*Flight of the Valkyries* would've better set the mood."

"Woulda, coulda, shoulda!" He threw up his bare arms, pretending to conduct an orchestra of what-ifs.

Despite his long legs and the brutal winters of Grand Rapids, Verboom stubbornly clung to an early model hybrid hatchback. When I reminded him of this fact, he quickly offered me $5,000 to take the old car off his hands. After I declined, he countered, "Make it six!" But as his most devoted graduate student, I didn't want to further complicate our relationship.

"Let me get Ella," I said. "She's trying to book you on ANN, claiming your meltdown last night was actually a gonzo denunciation of the media's absurdity..."

"Dunce indeed! Pass me the coned cap!" he barked. "*Wait, wait, wait!* Did you say, ANN? American News Network?"

He threw the truck into reverse, adding an ear-piercing beep to the thunder of opera music.

"Hold on!" I pleaded. "She's saying you'll reveal the story behind the story."

"What story?" he mumbled.

Foot still on the brake, he put the truck in park and stared through the windshield to a distant point, weighing his options and their implications.

"Before you take off, we need to check out," I said.

"*Check out!* That's it! I'll check out from the entire spring semester!"

"A leave of absence?"

"An emergency sabbatical! I'll jump in with both feet—take the plunge headfirst!" He pressed a hand to his chest. "But I'll let the heart lead."

"Lead where?"

"*Thumpity thump*! Ask my heart!"

His delivery wasn't sarcastic or sincere—it was something stranger.

Being called up to the capital earned Verboom clout at home with the university, but he never made it clear if his so-called emergency sabbatical was a simple rescheduling of his courses or a form of medical leave. Whatever the arrangement, Verboom asked me to "mind the shop" in his absence. Then he riffed on his immigrant father confusing the words '*mine*' and '*mind*,' musing on whether the paternal error primed the son for cognitive science.

"Along those lines, please *mine* the shop while you're at it—dig around, take whatever you please." He winked with joyless energy, then added, "I may never come back!"

With that, he took a bow and left his office.

A few weeks later, still reeling from his televised meltdown, he showed up on campus. He wore a tweed driver's cap, a lavender scarf, and D-frame sunglasses. Said he needed career advice—and would only talk to me.

Though still in the early stages of development, Ella had a proposal for a comeback. This time, radio. No cameras.

Despite his recent meltdown on WNN, Verboom was surprisingly receptive to the idea. Alone now for days on end, he was restless. His insatiable need to talk had combined with a dwindling circle of friends, and he had come to depend on the classroom as an outlet. With the classroom gone, he realized a sabbatical was the last thing he wanted.

He needed my help because he refused to be in a room alone with Ella.

"Like a philandering evangelist who can't be reformed, I may cave to her sensual beckoning. Will you stand by me, man?"

"She's still looking for a Dutch treat?"

"More than that, I need your advice. You have good *taste*."

After enlisting my help, he dialed Ella from his office phone and confirmed his meeting with a production company based in Chicago.

Two days later, we met the producers at a coffeehouse near campus, and they presented the concept: a call-in radio show, with a Q&A format, one hour, five days a week.

"Too much," I objected.

"No classes to prep for, no tests to grade," Ella said. "The professor will have plenty of time."

"Five hours a week." Verboom nodded hyperactively, looking eagerly from person to person. "That should take the edge off."

Of course, the producers wanted to be realistic. There would be the travel time to a Grand Rapids studio, some pre-show prep, and some promotion, but they assured us with a list of success stories. The production team would handle "all the heavy lifting"—an odd choice of words as Verboom was by far the strongest person in the room.

"Just show up and be you." Ella offered Verboom a pen.

Her silky-voiced pitch made me shudder.

"Do I have to pay for this? Like an infomercial?" The professor reached for his wallet.

"No! Of course not, we'll be paying you," the senior producer answered.

"Only a modest stipend, I hope. If I'm paid too handsomely, who would trust my motives?"

"Would you prefer to volunteer your time?" the junior producer asked.

"Yes. Just cover gas and parking." Verboom nodded.

"Would free coffee make you uncomfortable?" joked the senior producer.

"Not if it's fresh!" Verboom sung.

The junior producer pushed the document forward.

"A deal is a deal," Verboom chanted as he signed.

Ella grinned. "You have a face for television," she added, "but your mind is made for radio."

"A longform Longfellow, and you know it!" Verboom gleamed.

I shook my head. "Who's backing this? Did they see his WNN appearance?"

"That's exactly it! We want a contrarian, not your typical professor," the senior producer said.

"What WNN appearance?" Verboom asked, passing back the pen.

"*Hot Button Science*. Recorded at their DC studio," I reminded him.

"I only remember putting on my suit and following the signs to the Dodge dealership—where I got a *helluva deal!*"

I studied their faces; they must have known that the man needed rest?

"No need to remember it, my dear professor," Ella said. "The smoke has cleared. My story stuck."

The junior producer pushed forward *The Wall Street Journal*: "Showboat Sinks: Kuiper Drowns in His Own Spectacle."

"A show like that isn't an honest forum. And the article explains how you rubbed Kuiper's nose in it," the senior producer summarized, then smiled.

"Kuiper seems fair to me," I remarked.

"Most people think Kuiper is a smug know-it-all," the junior producer claimed.

In a punch-drunk stream of consciousness, Verboom rambled on, as if he still needed to audition his gift of gab.

Impressed by his willingness to pontificate on any topic—expertise be damned—the producers reassured him that a radio show was the obvious next step for a budding public intellectual.

"Just don't call me a 'national treasure,'" Verboom quipped, wagging a finger with giddy exaggeration, "or someone will steal me!"

Then they indulged him with laughter and promised to deliver the audience he deserved.

"What will you call the show?" Ella asked.

"Ask the professor," the senior producer replied with a deferential smile and raised eyebrows.

Verboom pounced on the words, tapping a finger to his nose.

The call-in show *Ask The Professor* was born. Regular folks could learn on their lunch breaks, in their cars, or on a walk. After failing with the DC elite, he could speak directly to the people. There was so much promise, and so much *promised*.

Verboom's impulse buying followed him to Michigan. Most notably, he developed a fixation with seersucker fabric. In what he declared a "stroke of genius," he repurposed the material for his so-called "fighting rehabilitation." Not only did he claim to invent the seersucker karate suit, but he also rushed them into production.

I was unaware of his creative leap until he arrived at the radio studio wearing three seersucker *karate* jackets and his seersucker karate pants tucked into enormous snow boots.

Ebullient and jittery, his eyes darted around the studio as we prepped with practice questions. Despite his theatrical gestures, Verboom answered like a man droning through the encyclopedia, his dynamism flattened into a monotone info dump.

A few weeks later, the show went live. At first, he remained clinical in word and monotone in voice, even as callers unleashed torrents of rage.

However, show by show, his reactions shifted from detached to paranoid—understandably so. The calls railing against the administration and its experts didn't let up. For these callers, Verboom seemed to be a proxy—a punching bag—for every teacher, preacher, boss, doctor, principal, or president they'd ever resented.

Ella was sure the rabid callers would move on, and the audience the professor longed for would soon find him.

"The only thing shorter than the American memory is the American news cycle," she said.

The initial chemistry between Ella and Verboom simmered for weeks before bubbling over. Ever the strategist, she struck when lust and familiarity peaked. I found out about their encounter the next day, as the professor slumped into a chair at his favorite diner.

"My publicist," he muttered, voice laced with disgust, "has become my paramour." Staring out the window to avoid eye contact, he tightened his lips into a grimace. Then he let out a sigh like the universe had just blindsided him.

Afraid he'd launch into an epic overshare, I didn't ask for details, but I did have a theory: Ella had plateaued in Grand Rapids. Her PR agency represented the university's account, and when Verboom was invited to the President's Emergency Conference of Scholars for winter break, Ella zeroed in on him. Her regional client was suddenly becoming a national one. She was eager to see Verboom's star rise. While their chemistry seemed genuine, her decision to act on it felt calculated.

Verboom, on the other hand, had reached that point in life where he failed to see social signals in the noise swirling around him. He was like a man half-watching a TV drama, his mind drifting and missing clues—only to pester others with questions about what happened. In that sense, he probably was blindsided.

His growing social blindness was part of why he'd come to rely on me. Though he was my academic mentor, I had become his fixer—a role Ella was now eager to take. Hoping to be a hands-on talent manager, she badgered his literary agent and took an active part in the radio production.

In our quiet battle to be his confidant, she had the upper hand, save for one glaring disadvantage: Verboom couldn't handle romance. He wasn't intimidated by a woman at work, in a park, or in a parking lot, but if attraction set in, lust utterly derailed him.

Caught in a loop of restraint and release, he tightened up on-air even as he unraveled everywhere else. By smothering his wild streak for the sake of the show, he somehow perfected the role of an overly self-conscious academic—save for the seersucker karate suit.

Once the broadcast ended, he would zigzag flamboyantly from evolutionary psychology to Old Testament ethics—part armchair philosopher, part street preacher. One moment he was swept up in desire for Ella; the next he recoiled in outlandish Sunday school prudery.

Mocked and taunted show after show, he soldiered on through early spring—until a second nervous breakdown erupted live on air. Uncorked by exasperation, he dared the country's extremists to practice what they preach.

"Quit calling my show *just* to bash the government! Put up or shut up! If you really want to put the whole damn thing out of business, then *do it*—and quit whining! If 'big government' is so 'godless,' why not replace it with 'big church'? Trade *policy* for *purity*!"

He went on like that, mocking his audience with an ironic plea for theocracy.

But as the teasing tirade wore on, his slaphappy delirium curdled into rage. Off-the-cuff, he laid out a playbook on how to dismantle the federal government, sneeringly calling it *Final Freedom*. The rant ended before the show, and he stomped out of the studio with dead air in his wake.

He went missing for two days, only to resurface with a call from a payphone in Grand Haven. Eerily jolly and predictably verbose, he pitched the idea for a trip to Arizona like an adventure vacation, his words tumbling out in the easy rhyme of a children's book. Like a schoolboy dodging the truth, he danced around the real reason. There were clinics near home, but Verboom chose Flagstaff for one reason: its distance from Ella, who would be six states away. For his sake, I let him explain how the drive would supposedly benefit me. He needed more than a favor; he needed me to have a good time.

"Flagstaff is so much more than a gateway to the Grand Canyon.

It's the world's first International Dark Sky City! They're saving the *night* from the pollution of *light*. You'll see all the milky milk in the Milky Way! Consider it a chance to clear your head full-of-hair in the high desert air—a chance to get out of Dodge in a *Dodge*. And of course, absence is the mother of disappearance."

"Absence makes the heart grow fonder," I corrected.

"Indeed! Slip out of town, and your lover will pine for you like a lumberjack. Now please come fetch me, I'm doomed on the dunes... The tourists are coming!"

Later that day, in the cool lakeshore evening, I found Verboom pacing circles around Grand Haven's south pier lighthouse, its fire-engine red paint radiant in the dusk.

"House of light, house of light..." he murmured into the lake breeze.

I called his name once. Twice. The third time, he stopped mid-stride and looked at me.

"Red and white, day and night, standing is the house of light," he intoned. Then he nodded, as if confirming he recognized me.

At a gastropub near the pier, he ordered a double cheeseburger with sweet potato fries but showed little interest as the server set the food down. Between bites of my club sandwich, I asked the following questions:

Did he remember his radio rant? *No.*

Did he remember hosting a radio show? *Yes.*

Did he remember hooking up with Ella? *Yes—more than once.*

Had he eaten? *Not sure.*

How did he get to the lakeshore?

He climbed onto the back of a milk truck south of downtown Grand Rapids, rode it to its destination in Norton Shores, then walked three hours south to Grand Haven—where he'd "been working on some philosophical loose ends while marching around the beachhead."

"Beachhead?" I asked.

"The territory seized by tourists," he said matter-of-factly.

"And the philosophical loose ends?"

"The one and the *many*. The many and the *one*."

Seeing my blank face, he provided a disjointed analysis of Western philosophy as a search for universals amidst the particulars. About twenty minutes later, as I finished my sandwich and he his lecture, I asked if he'd found the solution.

He opened his eyes and said, "To *what*?"

"The one and the many!" I yelled, drawing looks from our fellow diners.

His eyes lit up with recognition. In fact, he had seen the light... or was it the lighthouse?

I let him go on, connecting thoughts by rhyme, color, and shape, until he finally ran out of steam. Then I asked, "So this is how you came up with Flagstaff, the absence of light?"

"No, I asked a local librarian to help me find a sanitarium in a warm climate, not too humid, and not too expensive."

"The *clinic*?"

"Call it what you like. They have an open bed. Plus, the tools to nail down the loose ends in my thinking, something like pinning the tail on the donkey. You still up for a drive?"

When I didn't answer, he asked why I'd been so hard to reach lately.

"You're right here, Santo, but you are so far away. There's a word for that, *ja*?"

"Preoccupied," I said.

Finding the right word mattered more to him than knowing the reason. If he had asked me about the cause—or if I had chosen to tell him—he would have learned that while he was in the throes of his midlife crisis, I had endured the worst heartbreak of my life..

Two days later, well before sunrise, Verboom rumbled up to my apartment building in his Dodge pickup. As the truck idled, he poured coffee from a steel thermos into a small cup, which looked comically undersized in his hand. As I walked toward the passenger side, he stopped me, asking me to drive. He had spent the night making circuitous routes to ditch anyone who might be tailing him—Ella in particular—and now he needed a break.

Though I dismissed his talk of a tail, it occurred to me that a sleeping professor might be preferable to a speaking one. I took the wheel.

South of Gary, Indiana, we passed a billboard that said, "FINAL FREEDOM NOW." The words were hand-painted in black on a whitewashed board, and I heard Verboom mumble each one.

"What's that all about?" he asked.

"Remember your dare?"

"*Dare*?" He shook his head. "You've seen my personality assessments, I'm highly agreeable!"

"Let's go back to the last radio show. Tell me what you recall."

"Mean caller after mean caller... Ella tantalizing me with her beauty... then... *nothing*."

"You've always told me you have 94% recall accuracy."

"Only blackness."

"After the blackness?"

"Hitching a ride to the lakeshore so I could see the light."

"The lighthouse?"

"Right."

"You don't remember rolling out a sarcastic plan for theocracy?"

"Far too reckless for my taste. See my assessments. Perhaps we'll have my records sent to the clinic? Give them a better idea of who they're dealing with."

"Do you remember enough to be sure the dare didn't happen?"

Caught off guard, he worked through the question a few times. Finally, he conceded the point. He wondered aloud if his blackout might be contagious—if it might spill over, wiping his entire brain clean.

"Like a virus corrupting a hard drive?" I suggested.

"Keep your technology out of my psychology!" he feigned offense, then launched into a canned sermon on the difference between mind and machine. "Remember, Santo: all artificial intelligence is artificial."

"You've written it down somewhere."

"But will I remember where?"

"Does it matter?" I asked.

He shook his head with a wry smile. "No, it doesn't."

"As you've said before, 'human intelligence requires human viscera.'"

"Et cetera, et cetera..." he trailed off.

The car ahead of us on the freeway had a bumper sticker: HONK FOR FREEDOM.

"Hands off the horn, Santo. No telling what kind of freedom they're after."

To shut down his running commentary, I flipped on the radio and landed on NPR:

"From Washington, the president refuses to comment on Final Freedom or distance himself from E.C.S. fellow Dr. Pieter Cornelius Verboom. Our sources, speaking only on background, disagree as to whether the Final Freedom movement is a serious political force or a

stunt for the attention-starved. Some see Dr. Verboom as the master-mind of a revolution; others, as an accidental prophet whose message was taken..."

"Back-asswards," Verboom said, reaching over to mute the radio.

"Isn't the phrase ass-backwards?"

Without answering, he switched the audio to CD. The opening strains of *The Flying Dutchman* filled the truck, and he let it play through without another word about politics.

A day later, as our chariot rolled into the high desert city of Flagstaff, Arizona, I asked Verboom how long he planned to stay. He laughed—sharp and unhinged, like a man in need of medication—then mumbled something about Jonah in the belly of a whale.

"My father can name every kind of tree," he said, gazing up at the mountain slopes.

"Mainly ponderosa pine, some oak, a few juniper."

"Let's not get into the particulars until they've got my mind universalized."

At the clinic, he scrawled my name on the intake form, listing me as his emergency contact and labeling me *student.* Then he frowned and tore up the form.

He asked for a replacement.

The second time, he wrote *son.*

I'd like to say the title meant nothing to me, but I can't.

My girlfriend believed I'd become so obsessed with Verboom that he was taking advantage of me. When I told her I was simply following my interests and had genuine respect for his research, she scoffed. She insisted I was shopping for a surrogate father—my mind colonized by his influence and the whole of Western Civilization. Then she would twist the knife and describe his overwhelming manliness.

"He must have great physical *prowess*," she would marvel, "in addition to his blind obedience to capitalism."

To my knowledge, Verboom had no commitment to a grand economic theory, but her point was clear: the fact that I so deeply admired a middle-aged Dutchman meant I had failed to see his true nature.

As for my dedication to the man, my motives weren't *mixed* but *many*—not a conflict of interests, but a confluence. He was someone I wanted to help, *and* he was my cover story to get out of town. My quarterlife crisis paired with his midlife crisis. For a few days on the open road, I could escape the heavy clouds of Lake Michigan and my heartache, narrowing my role to that of a getaway driver.

Once in Flagstaff, I decided to stay at a hotel near the clinic to make sure Verboom got settled. After three days, with my duty complete, I packed for home. Before bidding farewell to the professor, I received a text message. No greeting, no affection—just a blunt declaration: "We should see other people."

My heart pounded hard three times, heat rushing to my face. Embarrassed, I didn't write back. I'd been saving for a ring, debating whether to surprise her with one or to let her choose. She chose: none of the above.

On our first date, she told me I was too diplomatic—the only time she was polite about my politeness. A few months later, she met my mother, who, though frail beneath a wig, summoned the strength to give her approval with awkward gusto.

And just like that, a year had passed. Now I was six states away with my mentor—America's most notorious social scientist. Not famous for research, but for being the first man in history to have a nervous breakdown on live television, followed by a radio encore that ended with a roadmap for dismantling democracy.

Since my coursework was complete, I could write my dissertation anywhere. Why not stay in the high desert? Already sick with grief, and now unceremoniously dumped, going back to campus felt impossible. Instead of hiding in my apartment, I decided to stay in Arizona until Verboom checked out.

Clearly in need of a long stay, we had Verboom's mail forwarded to the clinic. His case manager suggested I screen my "father's correspondence" for anything triggering, so I intercepted Ella's letters and stashed them in a size-thirteen shoebox. Once the shoebox filled, I put her letters in a beat-up plastic milk crate I had found behind the clinic's cafeteria. Some of the envelopes felt like they held Polaroids and pamphlets. I had the nerve to run my fingers over them but not to open them.

In addition to Ella's envelopes, I held back a slew of speaking invitations. On the heels of his dare, fringe groups and fanatics flooded Verboom with speaking requests. The sarcastic screed born in madness was metastasizing. As a swelling congregation of zealots clamored for Verboom to lead them out of the wilderness and into the corridors of power, the media took notice again.

The New York Times picked up the *Final Freedom* story, calling his immodest proposal "an ironic rant taken literally by literalists." And a leading WNN pundit fumed, "Verboom crashed our last dance with democracy."

More troubling than Verboom's unraveling was the country's willingness to embrace a delirious dare. People on the Left understood the rant as irony—which it was. People on the Right took the rant as an invitation to man up.

The provocation became a watershed moment, a defining plot point in the media's election year melodrama. Verboom had baited the American fringe, and they had taken it as the Lord's Supper.

As the spotlight intensified, he sank deeper into denial, refusing any discussion of politics or the press. He began to see the clinic not as a place to heal, but to hide. And yet, even as he closed his eyes and shook his head, his thought experiment took on flesh—and dwelt among us.

2

Behold! I send you out as sheep among wolves, therefore be as shrewd as snakes and as innocent as doves!" Verboom recited from the Gospel of Matthew, lying in his bed at the clinic, staring at the ceiling.

By the end of our first week in Flagstaff, Verboom spent large chunks of time testing his memory by recalling poems and proverbs from childhood. While I saw decline in his judgment, I observed no change in his memory; in fact, his still seemed better than most—except for *Hot Button Science* and *Final Freedom*.

After citing the verse from Matthew, he went on lamenting. "If only we had a transcript of everything. A way to check the record." He clutched the linens, as if trying to grip his slippery mind.

"All your work on radio and TV is archived," I reminded him.

"I want real life! I don't care about show biz."

"Your memory isn't a problem."

"It's *the* problem. Can you please help me one last time?"

Annoyed, I sighed.

"Could you record everything I say?" He paused looking for affirmation. "At least when we're together. Perhaps a content analysis could figure out what's wrong with me?"

With sympathy clouding my judgment, I caved.

While easy enough technically, I forgot to capture a few conversations. So, I began tapping the record button on my phone as soon as I left my room each morning. For a mic, I used my earbuds, which I fed under my tee shirt then out over the collar. It became one more habit, like patting my pockets for keys and wallet.

I thought the recordings would be a nightmare to track, but he didn't ask for playback. He only checked for the red light. He would nod in a way that indicated relief and gratitude. It was all there—somewhere.

Our clinic routine developed for the next few weeks: I'd sleep in, while he did his morning meetings and appointments, then I'd stop by his room before lunchtime.

Most days, I'd find him reading Dutch language novels, his voice rising and falling, then breaking into laughter. As we waited for lunch, he'd go on reading, while I scrolled the news.

Preoccupied with grief, I embraced the responsibility of supervising Verboom's convalescence, while trying to create one of my own.

Four weeks had passed since our arrival in Flagstaff, and our routine persisted.

One late morning, I needed a break from Verboom's throaty Dutch, so I sat in the clinic's lobby, waiting to meet him for lunch in the cafeteria—where he always ladled up enough food for both of us, a "two-for-one special," he called it.

But before Verboom arrived, Ella burst through the clinic's front doors. Though I sat next to the entrance, it was like I didn't exist. She marched straight to the reception desk.

"Who are *you*?" the receptionist asked, put off by Ella's direct manner.

"I am Dr. Verboom's *fiancée*."

"One moment." The receptionist studied her screen, then opened the drawer with Verboom's hardcopy documents. "You're not on file. We'll need approval from the patient."

"Call his room," Ella insisted.

"Where's your ring?"

"Where's your supervisor?"

Verboom didn't pick up the call, so the receptionist paged a medical tech to check the room.

Curious to see the security screens, I stepped over to the front desk, where Ella continued glaring at the receptionist.

The cameras showed the medical tech entering Verboom's room. Moments later, Verboom burst out the door in his bespoke karate suit—orange belt cinched tight—and sprinted down the hall toward the back exit.

In four-inch heels, Ella tore off after him, sprinting on the balls of her feet.

Another security camera caught Verboom descending the back stairs.

"Stop!" Ella's voice boomed, travelling down the main hall, reaching us in the lobby.

A split second later, the camera showed Verboom freezing like a criminal who's just realized there's no way out.

Ella descended deliberately, seized him by the belt, and towed him up the steps.

A camera in the hall caught her dragging him into his room.

Jogging down the hall, I heard shouts and furniture sliding.

Outside his room, I noticed a slipper wedged between the door and the floor, the tip just poking past the threshold, an improvised wedge acting as a lock.

"*Gawd*, I've missed these ostrich eggs," Ella growled.

"'Can a man scoop fire into his lap without being burned!'" Verboom quoted Proverbs 6:27.

"Take off your jacket," Ella commanded.

"Save me, *O God*!" Verboom hollered. "I sink in the miry depths, where there is no foothold."

After hearing 'save me,' I rammed the door with my shoulder and stumbled in to see Ella's right hand buried in Verboom's seersucker pants like a magician reaching for a rabbit.

"Stop squirming and let me..." Ella's voice trailed off with my entrance. She turned and scowled.

Her shirt and jacket lay on top of a desk stacked with dog-eared novels. Hair pulled back into a knot, she stood in black heels, a snug knee-length forest green skirt, and a lacey bra with one nipple free, looking ready to breastfeed.

After freezing for a moment, I hurried back to the lobby and paced a few circles across the fake wood floor, laid in vinyl strips. A diffuser filled the air with a eucalyptus scent, and the decor featured Southwestern colors applied to clinical furniture forms.

"Should I call security?" the receptionist asked, looking up from her display screens.

I paused before answering. "He's in capable hands."

Then I found the tallest yucca palm and sat next to it.

The end table had a stack of magazines. *Righteousness*, a glossy quarterly publishing the most prominent right-wing essayists, included a piece by Solomon Krebbs, who argued for the total deregulation of drug pricing. Be it insulin, antibiotics, or antivirals, the capacity to save a life is the ultimate market advantage. Krebbs' case failed to distract me from the thought of Verboom's room: Ella had spoiled our hideout.

"Is that really his fiancée?" the receptionist whispered.

I kept my eyes down and pretended to read.

About ten minutes later, as I skimmed the quarterly's cover story—a plea for arming schoolteachers—Verboom came toward the lobby. With the light behind him, he looked like a giant walking down the hall. As the lobby's glow transformed him from a silhouette into a full-color creature, I could see red lipstick on his right cheek above his golden-brown beard, like he'd turned away from a kiss. His *seersucker karate jacket* hung open, revealing a lean stomach and muscular chest; his *pants* were about to fall from his hips.

Hesitant, he asked me to update Ella's status with the clinic.

"Since you're standing in as my son, I ticked a box and signed some extra forms giving you some kind of medical guardianship. I forget the term, but you can make decisions for me, like 'pulling the plug.'"

"She's not your fiancée, is she?" I whispered.

"Perhaps it's another event I've forgotten," he said. Then he turned and shuffled back toward his room.

Blocking his request seemed more complicated than granting it—Ella was already here. As his next of kin, I made the arrangement and continued playing the role of son.

Since the clinic banned overnight guests, any sensual encounters—what Verboom called "Biblical relations"—occurred during regular visiting hours.

On my way to check in with Verboom the following day, I cautiously approached his room, hoping to find the door open. But before I reached the threshold, I heard a commotion.

Like a monk stumbling into sin, Verboom was once again quoting scripture to draw strength against temptation, but the more he resisted, the more titillated they both became.

A new patient walked by with her family, so I headed to the cafeteria.

Checking back the next morning, I heard Verboom quoting St. Paul's Letter to the Romans: "I do not understand what I do. For what I want to do, I do not do, but what I hate, I do." However, all Ella seemed to hear was *do, do, do.*

From what I could gather from the hall, Verboom rejected Ella's advances all the way through climax.

After a few days of these antics, I stuck to the lobby and cafeteria, staying clear of more melodramatic love scenes.

With Ella in Flagstaff for a week, I got restless loitering in the lobby, so I popped into the dive bar across the street.

The bar's owner and operator, Adam, was an Ogden Nash fan and had "candy is dandy, but liquor is quicker" printed at the top of each menu.

We were off to a good start.

"Nash is the only poet I liked in high school," Adam said, watching me study the laminated beverage list for the first time.

I nodded and ordered. He turned to get my beer.

"*Fleas!*"

"Excuse me?" Adam asked, looking back.

"'Adam. Had'em.' Isn't that the poem 'Fleas' by Ogden Nash?"

"Not Nash—but a good guess." He grinned. "Maybe you can figure out how I named my bar?"

"Haddit's. Short for... *Adam's Had It!*"

He nodded with approval.

After our introduction, I scrolled through my news feed, then cracked open a book by Evan Heidkamp, a psychologist writing for a general audience about how moral reasoning shapes our political divides. It was the kind of clear, stripped-down research that turned scholars into public voices—the path Ella had planned for Verboom.

Though Haddit's was a dive bar, Adam kept his prices high enough to keep away the daily daytime drunks. His business was for students and working people—and an after-work hangout for the clinic's staff. Spending a month hanging around the clinic, I'd overheard folks joking about having "a case of the Haddit's."

"More often than not, employees complain about management and pay," Adam explained. "But if you perch yourself on a barstool just after a shift change, you'll hear some wild stories about patients. In fact, there's some giant manchild over there who keeps trying to avoid intimacy with his fiancée. Fends her off by quoting scripture, like she's some kind of demonic temptress." Adam shook his head, the hint of a smile forming. "Am I making you uncomfortable?"

"It's his publicist, not his fiancée."

"You know them?"

"Long story."

A nurse from the clinic walked in, ordered a glass of wine, took a sip, then gave Adam a nod, like a signal for a standing agreement.

Adam sauntered to the sound system and put on a track; it began with acoustic guitar. A familiar song that I couldn't quite place.

"'*A Mi Manera*,'" Adam said, returning. "Sinatra's 'My Way' in Spanish. After any patient moves on, she sings it."

"Did someone just *die* over there?"

"Probably not. Most don't. It's a tribute to anyone moving on. She can't bear the thought of people living—or dying—in regret."

The bar didn't have a proper karaoke machine, but Adam allowed requests and sing-alongs, using a microphone and amps set up for trivia night and the occasional singer-songwriter. In the back corner of the bar, a set of stairs came down from the office and hit the main floor. The landing near the bottom step acted as a small stage.

Thin but not frail, somehow regal in her teal scrubs, the nurse's eyes grew teary as she sang, pulling her thick brown hair out of its bun between the first and second verse.

Adam came by with a glass of water for me.

"Does she always sing with so much feeling?" I asked him.

He nodded. "For of all sad words of tongue or pen... the saddest are these: it might have been!"

"Keep at it with all this poetry, Adam, and someone's gonna fall in love with you."

"Still surprises me that somebody with this tender outlook can work in the medical industrial complex."

"Some people feel best when they're helping others," I suggested.

He raised his brow. "Or making money."

After a small speech on human nature, he asked, "What brings you to town?"

"I brought the giant manchild."

"Oh yeah? How'd you two meet?"

Smiling politely, I had a flashback to my first encounter with Verboom during the university's preview weekend. He had said, "I was a psychologist while still in swaddling clothes." A rather odd comment to make, as I was just a visitor. But now years later, I still couldn't shake the image.

Adam asked, "You okay?"

I exhaled. "Lost in thought."

"Beer can help with that. So, the *guy*?"

"He's my professor. 'A psychologist while still in swaddling clothes.'"

"He put that line on his business card?"

"No. It's what he said the day we met."

"Good to know your fate."

As the nurse's song wound down, a customer walked through the swinging doors.

"Let me know when you're ready for another round," Adam said as he moved down the bar.

My flashback to the university preview visit continued:

I asked Verboom why, specifically, he'd become a *social* psychologist, expecting something more nuanced than simply being born that way.

"Termites. Witchcraft. Electric shock," Verboom had said.

Just four words, and I had no idea what he meant, or that the man who was to become my demented mentor and pretend father was prone to trances and flights of fancy.

At the university's preview reception, Verboom cradled a paper plate of cheese cubes—each pierced with a toothpick—and a clear plastic cup of apple cider in the same large hand, explaining the words in reverse order.

Electric shock. The trauma of World War II snaked through the Verboom family like the sins of a father. In turn, Verboom's parents taught him to see signs of creeping communism wherever he looked.

Then he said with a tortured twinkle in his eye, "As a student of history, you'll find my forebears' preoccupation most odd. Call it the ultimate case of confirmation bias. Even though fascists occupied their homeland, they worried about communists."

"Did your grandparents lean fascist?" I had asked him.

"*Nay, nay,*" he said in Dutch. "They were 'conservative' before that word came to mean reactionary. They had conservative personalities and traditional beliefs. As rural people, they detested the city and questioned the sanity of anyone who would live in such dense environs." Then he stopped himself and apologized. "You're here to learn about our program, not my heritage."

"And the electric shock?"

"Indeed! Let me tell you about Stanley Milgram, the man who shocked the world!"

I knew about Milgram, but I listened along.

"Milgram wanted to understand how the Nazis took power. With an audacious experiment in 1961, Milgram showed that *three out of four people would discharge a lethal electric shock* when the orders came from a man in a white lab coat. While most had mixed feelings, they did it anyway—though a small group seemed to enjoy it." He grimaced.

"But the participants were Germans?" I had asked Verboom sarcastically, feigning ignorance. Only our first meeting, I wasn't yet clear on his personality.

"*Nay, nay, nay!*" he continued. "These Americans were as American as Dutch apple pie! Milgram showed that it could happen here, there, *anywhere*. And there was no ambiguity! To emphasize the death potential of the situation, the recipient of the fake shock—the confederate, an actor, in on the experiment—claimed to have heart disease as he pleaded for his life!"

Termites and *witchcraft* referred to an episode described by an anthropologist living with the Zande people in central Africa. After a hut collapsed, word swirled, as the villagers guessed at what the crushed people inside the fallen hut had done wrong. There had to be a witch's curse at work. Smug or not, Verboom didn't know, but the anthropologist had suggested that the accident was simply due to termites eating timbers.

"Well of course the Zande people knew about termites—*duh*!" I remember Verboom bellowing at the university's preview reception. "They wanted to know why the structure fell while *these* people were inside *that* hut. They were victims of a plan, not dumb luck!"

Verboom went on, "It's not natural to be a naturalist, and it's not normal to resist norms. To be a scientist and a dissident is as weird as it gets!" He put his free thumb to his chest.

Then it dawned on Verboom that I was only a prospective student, and not yet part of his inner circle. He apologized for his compulsive alliteration and asked me not to worry, assuring me that his inner dissident had been quelled along with the completion of his Ph.D.

As a non-partisan independent, he claimed to be as neutral as humanly possible, and despite its inevitability, he loathed tribalism—"*my* tribe especially!" He was so attuned to bias, that his only bias was believing everything was biased. He laughed awkwardly, his tone impenetrable. Then reassuringly, he claimed total contentment studying why people made poor choices without trying to correct them.

Now, years later in Flagstaff, I wasn't just in his inner circle—I was his rehab chaperone, his next of kin, his supposed son. I shook my head, chugged my beer, and set the glass down a little harder than I meant to.

Adam returned. "One more?"

"Why not."

Adam put my empty pint glass in the sink and reached for a chilled glass in the fridge.

As I watched the frosted glass fill, I thought back to something Verboom said on our drive to Flagstaff. He'd begun reminiscing freely, like a man on his deathbed, as we crossed the Texas Panhandle. In that tangle of memory, he recounted an eerie moment from long ago—he was still a student then—when he suddenly found himself in a seminar room, with no memory of how he'd gotten there. It was as if he'd been teleported: a stranger dropped into strangeness, birthed into the moment without context. He studied the white room and its bizarre rituals. The other students seemed alien; everything had "a certain un-realness." Then he looked down at his arms and was struck by their raw animal power.

"Those arms, resting on the seminar table like found objects—tools suddenly there for me to use!" he recalled. "Then it crossed my mind, Santo. A most ugly and intrusive thought: I can bring it *all* down."

He dropped his head at the recollection. "A terrible notion, of course, an intrusive idea inspired by the myth of Samson pulling down the Philistine temple. The Bible is such a violent book, Santo."

As he made the comment in the truck, he flexed the muscles of his upper body, spine erect, then he exhaled, bearing down in his seat.

He did look the part—if not a Samson, a forlorn hulk, a philosophical farm boy who'd drunk too much milk. Then he relaxed his posture and took a long pause before adding: "It could all be otherwise, my dear Santo. It could all come to an end."

He checked the buckle of his seatbelt then closed his eyes. "I take no joy in such thoughts. Not then. Not now." He opened his eyes and looked over to me. "Humans have said 'the end is near' for thousands of years. Some even predict exact dates. Inevitably the day passes, and the group will be proven wrong, and then they'll say, 'Our faithfulness has spared the world of God's wrath! *Whoopee*!'"

"Surprisingly, humans refuse to reject all prophecy out of hand," I had said, staring down the freeway over the steering wheel.

"But eventually, one of these assholes will be right. Don't give him credit. It's just the luck of the last asshole standing. And I'm going to tell you something, Pieter Verboom is *that* asshole!" He was perhaps confusing the end of his career with the end of the world. "Pieter Verboom is *that* asshole!" It had become his mantra as we drove west.

Adam cleared his throat, his eyes locked on me. "It ain't getting any colder."

My attention came back to Haddit's.

I took a sip and swallowed slowly. "I'm having flashbacks of flashbacks."

Adam frowned. "Playing through old stories in your head?"

"The professor's stories."

"Maybe you should check on him?"

After settling up with Adam, I gulped down my beer and walked back to the clinic.

The receptionist assured me that Ella had left, so I went back to Verboom's room, where I found him sitting cross-legged on the floor.

He looked up at me and smiled.

"Hey Santo, you know the best thing about this joint?" he asked with a genuine chuckle. "It reminds me that I'm young for an older guy." He crossed his thickly muscled arms and smiled like a satisfied child swaddled in cotton.

Then a call from the front desk spoiled his contentment. Without warning, Arizona's junior senator had arrived for a favor.

3

Senator Arlen Hesse, a prayer-meeting zealot, had pursued Verboom in DC. Although Verboom had many social blind spots, he could still sniff out the gospel agenda, describing the senator's manner as stinking of the "make-a-friend-for-Christ" thing.

"Let Jesus make his own friends!" Verboom had griped in January, days before appearing on WNN.

In Arizona, the senator didn't explain how he found us at the clinic, but Verboom allowed a meeting provided I could attend.

The three of us sat cramped in Verboom's room, and I relished my decision *not* to tell Ella about the senator's surprise visit.

"Appreciate your time today," Hesse said warmly.

"Time is all I have," Verboom countered.

"Those PJs look comfy."

"It's a *gi*, as the Japanese call it. A suit for the martial arts, specifically *karate*." Until then languid, Verboom abruptly stood up and pulled his top down with a snap.

The senator's conventional black suit hung as loose as Verboom's *gi*, but Hesse showed no interest in flattening its folds. Wearing a red tie even more saturated than Verboom's orange belt, he had impressively thick silver hair and extra white teeth.

"Let's speak off the record," Hesse said.

Verboom didn't look at me or mention the recording.

"Your comments at the E.C.S. didn't escape notice," Hesse continued.

"Whoopee," Verboom exhaled flatly.

"Afraid you've formed the wrong impression of us."

"Do you not operate a DC dorm house for your boys' club while claiming the building is a church to avoid paying taxes?"

Hesse maintained a toothy smile without answering.

Verboom continued, "But that's a petty complaint compared to your global theocratic scheming. Do you even believe in democracy?"

"Despite your suspicions, I can assure you that we want to work with the president—*all* presidents for that matter."

"You're establishing a puppet government with big church and big business pulling the strings."

I wondered why Verboom hadn't put it so clearly on his radio program.

"We're a fellowship doing God's will," Hesse said comfortably.

"All men, I notice. Even in name: *First Brothers*. But your theology is worse than your chauvinism; why would an Almighty Being need workers?"

"God appointed men to fill these roles. Though that may not meet the ideals of a professor in his ivory castle..."

"Tower," I corrected.

"We influence the influential," Hesse continued. "Think of Joseph working with the Pharaoh in ancient Egypt. And Ephesians tells us to reveal the wisdom of God to 'the rulers and authorities in the heavenly realms.'"

"You view politics as spiritual warfare?" I asked.

"'Warfare' is a strong word. We seek mutually beneficial opportunities."

"Why not work out in the open then?" Verboom asked. "Get business cards and pay taxes! Why run this secret gambit on the government's dime and time?"

"Working for God and the American people go hand-in-glove."

"You must mean *hand-in-hand*," I blurted.

"The way to make this world a better place is to fellowship with those in high places, and the leaders of this world prefer privacy in spiritual matters."

"You mean political matters," Verboom said. "Quick! Get this man a copy of *Tautology*."

Hesse frowned. "Come again?"

"It's the title of Verboom's only general-interest book," I explained.

"The people want what the people want," Verboom sighed.

"Listen, professor," Hesse went on, "in all things, there's only one person we're trying to please..."

"Fritz Hearn?" I interrupted. America's most popular AM radio host and right-wing flamethrower.

"Jesus," Hesse said, heavy with S-sounds. "We're simply followers of Jesus," the senator exhaled the last three words in a whoosh and then leaned back in his chair. "He meets us where we're at."

"Why not focus on the unhoused?" Verboom asked with irritation.

"Change comes from the top," Hesse responded.

"You've got the formula backwards. Listen to scripture," Verboom growled. "'Whatever you did for the least of these, you did for me.'"

"Professor, we do something better than giving a man a fish. We're going to make everyone a fisherman and bring back *The* Fisher of Men."

Here Verboom counted on his fingers. *Fish. Fishermen. Fisher of Men*. Then he asked, "What kind of bait ya' casting?"

"Something irresistible."

"A wiggling worm on a barbed hook?"

"Relationships anchored in love." Hesse interlocked his fingers.

"If you have a yacht!" Verboom howled, then laughed in disgust.

"We're building a network of leaders who are faithful to God."

"Faithful?" Verboom snorted. He stretched his neck forward and cupped his hand behind his ear—ready for God's voice.

"I won't try to explain the ways of God to a professor." The senator leaned forward. "But I hope you'll take a step back and reconsider. We're not the bad guys. Think of the alternative: a godless nation runs amuck."

"Like Sweden?" I teased.

"Get to know us; we're not so bad. Here's my card." Hesse extended his arm.

Looking ready to eat his words, Verboom reviewed the card. Then he grinned.

"This card is for your office as senator of Arizona, paid for by the people. Don't you have something with a First Brothers' logo?" Verboom held the card up and turned it to review the back. "Or is there invisible ink?"

"Let's not trade anymore jabs out in public. If you've got a problem, come talk to me." The senator patted Verboom on the thigh. "*Boy.* You've got some meat on them bones!"

"Grandpa was a speed skater... When he wasn't hiding from Nazis."

Then Hesse pulled a folded sheet of paper from his jacket and passed it to Verboom.

"While I got you here, would you mind signing?" Hesse asked.

"As long as it's written in the language of The Lowlands," Verboom said as though it might be a possibility.

"I mentioned this in Washington. Here's a pen."

Before the fancy pen set Verboom off, Hesse claimed it was a gift from his wife.

Verboom stuck it behind his ear and with less than a passing glance flung the paper in the air. It fluttered between the two men, caught a slight breeze from the open window and arched back toward Verboom. Somehow Verboom snatched the paper with his teeth. He bit down on it for a moment and then took it from his mouth.

"You have my fingerprints, saliva, and dental imprint, so you may as well have a writing sample." Verboom slammed the document down with his thick hand, scribbled a signature, and demanded the senator leave his room. Before the senator could reply, Verboom hit the nurse request button.

"Yes?" a nurse rang back.

"Please come at once. My head hurts!"

Hesse left the room with his pen and paper in hand.

4

As we sat in the clinic's cafeteria for dinner, Ella clenched her teeth and attempted to disguise her irritation with being left out of the Hesse meeting. Aiming for aloofness, she landed closer to sulking.

No music played, and there was very little conversation in the dining hall.

Too manic to eat, Verboom built a mashed potato lagoon for his gravy.

"Are you still trying to be his publicist?" I asked. "I thought you were his fiancée."

"What red-blooded American wouldn't want to meet a senator?"

"It was a *spiritual* conversation, no women allowed. First Brothers' rules," I said like a Boy Scout.

Verboom surrounded his gravy lake with broccolini trees.

Pretending to scold, Ella said, "Come on, Pieter, if you're going to play with something, play with me."

Sensing what would happen next, I excused myself and walked to my motel.

The room had low ceilings without a fan, just an all-purpose heating/air-conditioning unit under the only window. I pulled up a journal article online, but before reading, I studied the floor, clean but synthetic. Surveying the room, I concluded that the banana sitting by the sink was the only natural object—besides me.

Unable to get through a single paragraph, I closed my laptop, left the motel, and meandered around town before landing at Haddit's for a second visit.

Surprised to see me twice in one day, Adam poured me a beer. After a second, we talked through my situation.

"Great having you in town," Adam concluded. "But it sounds like three's a crowd. Maybe it's time to head home?"

The next morning, Ella pounded on my motel door. At some point during the night, Verboom had vanished without a word. No one had noticed his absence until her visit for breakfast.

We returned to the clinic to meet with their chief administrator, who promised to notify us if Verboom showed. However, she emphasized the voluntary status of his stay and made clear that her organization had no legal responsibility for the AWOL professor.

Ella and I returned to my room at the motor inn to make calls. She sat on the bed, wearing a variation of her unofficial uniform: a deep royal blue skirt cut just above the knee, matched with nude suede heels. Her creamy white V-neck shirt had a collar but no buttons, wrinkles, or lint.

We phoned the city police to ask for help and were politely asked to call back when our concerns made more sense. Not under a conservatorship, Verboom was still a citizen in good legal standing and could travel as he pleased.

"He left without saying goodbye, yet you don't look worried," Ella said. "His pipe is gone. His running shoes are gone. His hip pack is gone. Only the Dutch novels are left, and what, a dozen pairs of karate costumes!"

"He ran out the back door the day you arrived," I said.

She frowned.

"Something will show in the security footage," I said.

"The clinic's administrator didn't seem eager to keep me in the loop..."

"Maybe the senator can find him," I suggested.

"Maybe the senator *disappeared* him."

"Sounds like blame shifting." I grabbed my keys and walked straight to Haddit's. Ella followed without my invitation or consent.

Now midafternoon, we sat at the bar. Adam poured me a pilsner. Ella ordered a stout and spun her barstool 180 degrees to face the rest of the saloon. I drank my beer, staring straight ahead into the bottles of spirits as we sat shoulder-to-shoulder aimed opposite directions. With just a few ounces left in the mug, I felt my brain unlock and asked, "So what do you *really* want with him?"

"To bring him to the world," she said. "I believe in his talent."

"And screwing the old guy's brains out is going to accomplish that?"

"He's only 47, and he's got incredible genes. He looks 37. He just needs to recover from... from whatever this is."

"At the risk of sounding like a literalist, why would someone hiding from the public need a publicist?"

"We've been mapping his comeback."

"By drawing your index finger through his chest hair? I've overheard a few of your vigorous planning sessions." I put my hand up. "Before you pretend to be offended, just come clean. I thought it was only a fling?"

"It's more, Santo."

Adam refilled my glass as I held it. Once he finished, I spun around to reverse my view, but with my pivot, a few dollops of froth flew off my glass and landed on her bare forearm.

Without hesitation she put her arm to her mouth and licked the suds clean in one pass. Ella's hands were delicate, but her classic style of dress presented an athletic build.

"Someone's watching you," she said and spun around to face the bar. "Wait a moment, then spin back, and as you do, glance over at the woman a few seats down."

I followed Ella's instructions. It was the "A Mi Manera" singer.

"What do you think?" Ella asked.

"She's a nurse. I think we're safe."

"Don't you see it?"

"See what?"

"She's into you."

Before I could say more, Ella invited her over.

The nurse walked around Ella and sat next to me, introducing herself as Anna.

"You must be worried sick about your dad."

"Technically, he's not my father..."

"They look nothing alike," Ella interrupted.

"But you both have green eyes," Anna said. "They're so rare..."

"Millions of people have green eyes." I brushed the notion aside.

"Nose, hair, skin... They look nothing alike," Ella repeated.

"I see a lot of green." Anna smiled.

"The professor wanted to make sure I could act as his 'next of kin,' though he usually calls me 'the left brain.'"

"Oh, so you're a progressive?" Anna asked and looked over her shoulder.

"It's my analytical rigor; he likes having a rationale for giving me tasks. It's kind of a left-brain/right-brain thing, if you're into that kind of thing."

"As a nurse, I'm comfortable with anatomy." She winked.

"Well, one afternoon Verboom pronounces, 'If you're doing the work of my left hemisphere, then you should have half the earnings.'"

"Sounds like he made you a partner."

"When I declined, he took offense, saying the decision was 'the undeniable conclusion of an inescapable formula.' He added, 'You could've taken more than half without me knowing... or even *wanting* to know. Don't give me any credit! I take credit for nothing but my sin!'"

"*Sin*?" Anna asked. "What did he do?"

"Verboom's people are Dutch Calvinists. God gets all the glory and humanity gets all the blame. He calls it 'a stacked deck.'"

"Sounds like a tough game."

"The professor is one of America's foremost public intellectuals. You may have seen him on WNN," Ella added.

"Not a news watcher," Anna said flatly.

"*The New York Times* ran a frontpage story: 'Professor Blacks Out Seeing Red,'" Ella continued, "and *The Wall Street Journal* ran 'Professor Provides Performance Art.'"

"Ella's still trying to spin Verboom's televised meltdown as a gonzo critique of politics—a creative use of facts."

"A strategic use of facts," Ella pronounced.

"Are you familiar with *Final Freedom*?" I asked. "Maybe you've seen the flags?"

"No, I haven't. But try not to worry. He'll show up soon," Anna assured me.

"Let us know what you hear," Ella pressed. "Hand me your phone. I'll give you my contact info. My last name is Walker."

Anna hesitated then handed Ella her phone, and the conversation stopped.

Adam replenished Anna's sauvignon blanc and poured me another pilsner, but Ella covered her glass with her right hand.

"I'll leave you two to get better acquainted," Ella said with a wink.

Anna blushed, and I tried not to smile. Looking down at the footstep below the bar, I noticed Anna's clogs and socks.

The next morning, I woke with my head under a pillow but could still see Anna from the thighs down, stepping into her clogs. She walked over to the bed, patted my buttocks, and left my room.

Once Ella left Haddit's the night before, I'd stopped my recording—but I remembered everything Anna told me. She'd been a nurse since her mid-twenties and had lived in Flagstaff for nearly a decade. She went to community college while caring for her grandmother, then started at the university. When her grandmother's health declined, Anna left school for two semesters to care for her full-time. After her grandmother passed, Anna returned, finished her degree, and became an RN. She told the story without drama, like it wasn't a big deal running hospice for her beloved matriarch, but I was touched by her steadiness.

After her biography, she put her hand on my thigh as we sat at Haddit's, then she said, "How about you?" I said something like, "You want to take care of me too?" She smiled. I ordered another round, saying something like, "It's the least I can do for all your help."

From there, it's fuzzy. Some flashbulb memories, then morning.

Before leaving the room, Anna had pulled back the blackout curtains, but I kept my head under a pillow.

Through the privacy curtains, I saw a sedan with Michigan tags pull up and park directly in front of my room. Ella made no attempt to hide, staring at me through the small part in the curtains, her blue eyes judging me. She repeatedly claimed to have 20/10 vision, even proving it a few times, reading things I couldn't with 20/20.

The AC hummed for hours as I laid there. The phone never rang.

Shortly after noon, I left the room, patted Ella's rooftop, and we walked to Haddit's. Adam poured us both a coffee as we sat down.

"So last night was fun," Ella said.

"What did you do?" I asked, disinterested.

"Went back to my place, got comfy on the couch, and watched the feed from the camera in your room."

I coughed up the hot coffee. Adam poured me a glass of water. After a few swallows I looked over to her—my nose, throat, and eyes burning.

"You can't hide him from me," Ella said coldly.

I ran back to the motel and bounced through my room like a hockey player throwing body checks into every wall and piece of furniture, hunting for the device. Nothing. She had only been teasing me.

Exhausted, I plopped into a chair and looked up. In the wall-mounted lamp over the desk, a camera the size of a chickadee was perched in the frame of the shade.

Though too large to flush, I dropped it into the toilet and made the water spin. The water slowly refilled the bowl, and the camera submerged. I poured the two remaining motel shampoos on it and searched the room for other devices, then went back to the toilet and pushed the lever a final time to work up lather.

Back at Haddit's, Ella sipped a mineral water and smiled at my return. In an overly cute voice, she asked Adam for a lemon wedge as I sat down next to her.

"That's why you asked for the Wi-Fi password," I grumbled.

"Poor cell reception. I needed to check my email." She smiled. "You spend a lot of time in the bathroom."

"I'm a thorough hand-washer."

"Don't forget to moisturize. Let's keep those hands soft."

"I leave tomorrow."

"Where are you taking him?" she asked, restraining herself.

"Just follow the tracking device on his truck!" I roared with a sarcastic sneer, then wondered if it might be true.

"Keep your voice down, Santo. Tell me where he is, and you have nothing to worry about."

I stood up.

She stood up and patted me on the rump like Anna had earlier that morning. Then, Ella grabbed both of my arms and pulled me in.

"He's *mine*," she growled, as much declaration as threat.

5

That evening, I milled around town, taking in the architecture, the trees, and the surrounding peaks, washed in the soft light of golden hour. Verboom called it "orange hour," the time of day "when you couldn't stop wondering if you'd be hauled off in a straitjacket."

Sentimental and eager for company on my last evening, I popped into Haddit's as the stars came out. Unfortunately, it was trivia night, and the scene was raucous by the bar's low-key standards.

As I moved from the entryway to the bar, a student asked in a hushed voice, "What's the national debt?"

"Around 30 trillion," I answered.

He spun around to his team, whispering, "It's D. 33 trillion."

Each table had an empty deep-dish pan on an elevated pizza stand. All competitors had to place their smart devices on the tin and keep their hands visible, like playing poker in the Old West.

"Join us," the young guy said, pointing to a full pitcher.

I sat on the open barstool at the team's high-top.

He poured me a beer with a big head of foam and introduced me to the team. Then, with a poor cowboy accent, he said, "Okay now pard'ner, kindly place your six-shooter on this here pedestal."

I obliged, setting my phone down on the tin.

The woman sitting next to me asked about my course of study.

"ABD in Social Psych."

"Is that like a doctor?" a guy with a neckbeard asked.

"All But Dissertation. I have writer's block."

"It's psychology," the woman said. "It's not a matter of inspiration."

"The answer is D. 33 trillion!" the trivia MC broke in for a moment.

"What's your area?" I asked her.

"Creative Writing MFA at NAU."

"You don't think a social scientist can have writer's block?"

"Is an ABD really a scientist?"

"Almost."

"You don't want to do the work. It's understandable. You're probably measuring stress hormones in rat pee."

"*Next question*," the trivia MC boomed. "Put your hands where I can see 'em! How many Americans have a license to carry a concealed firearm? A. 600,000. B. 6 million. C. 16 million. D. 660 million. Or E. No such licenses exist."

"Sixteen million," I said without missing a beat. "The population is under 350 million, and we have a lot of guns. That's the highest possible number."

No one else volunteered an answer.

The creative writer studied my hands, which were sitting on the table like awkward paws.

"It's C," I said to her. "Bet you a shot."

A moment passed as the answer sheets were collected and reviewed.

"*The answer is C!* Roughly sixteen million Americans have a license to carry concealed firearms."

When she returned with shots, I raised my glass: "I only regret that I have one liver to give for my country."

As she squinted at my poor choice of words, I threw back the tequila.

"Next question!" the trivia MC hollered. "Hands where I can see 'em! How many times is the word "God" used in the Constitution? A. Three. B. Seven. C. Twelve. D. Over twenty times. Or E. Not at all."

"This is a trick question," the team scribe guessed. "The founders were hifalutin. They probably wrote 'Creator' or 'First Mover' or…"

"Seven," said the wrangler.

"We all *know* this is a Judeo-Christian country, so I think it's probably only three," the red-hat-and-neckbeard guy said.

"E. Not at all," I said.

"No," the wrangler shook his head, "that option is added just to mess with skeptics. The kind of people who think, 'Yeah man, this could all be, like, a dream, man.'"

"Your stoner impersonation is terrible," the scribe complained.

"Not a stoner. A surfer who's sniffed too much lacquer repairing boards."

The writer nudged me with her elbow.

I looked her in the eye and could feel how close we were sitting. I don't think she drank tequila often.

"What's the answer?" she whispered.

"E."

She bit my shoulder through my t-shirt, not hard enough to break skin but enough to bruise. I pulled away from her and rubbed the bite.

The team scribe watched from across the table, wrote "E" on the small square paper, folded it in half, and turned it in for collection.

"The answer is E," the trivia MC announced a moment later. "God as word or concept is *not* mentioned in the Constitution. It is, in fact, a godless constitution." He went on to run down each team's score.

"We're in first, thanks to the ABD," the wrangler chirped. "The prize is ours!"

"What is it?" I asked.

"A leather holster, handmade," the wrangler answered.

I shook my head. "You're kidding?"

"Haven't been here for trivia?" the neckbeard asked.

"Not a trivia fan."

"Adam buys things from Coconino student craft and shop projects," the wrangler said.

"The prize inspires the questions," the team scribe injected.

"He goes to garage sales, too," the neckbeard added. His arms were crossed, and he leaned back in his chair with his chin up, his lips pursed.

"You seem surprised," the writer observed.

"Sorry. Tell me your name?" I asked.

"Jacqueline." She sighed like it was poor word choice. "It's the name they gave me."

"*They*," the neckbeard said with air quotes.

"*Next question, campers*! Half of all civilian guns in America are owned by what percentage of the US population? Now, most of you are smoking weed, living with mommy, and playing video games all day, so let me repeat this question slowly: Half of all civilian guns in America are owned by what percentage of the US population?"

"Do you mean legally?" someone yelled.

"It's from a survey. We don't have a gun registry—*yet*," the MC quipped.

"Do *you* own a gun legally?" a heckler yelled.

The MC slid off his stool and spun around to reveal a tiny handgun clipped onto his belt like a bowtie above his flat ass. "The answer options are A. 3%. B. 17%. C. 42%. D. 50%. Or E. 75%."

"Even as a progressive," Jacqueline said, "I love the gun range."

"That holster is yours," I said.

"Thanks, but I don't own a gun. I borrow from the range."

"The answer is A. 3% of citizens own 50%," I said. "Firearm

inequality. Gun collecting. Survivalist hoarders. Militia folk. Plus, the answer is more startling if it's only 3%."

The scribe handed in my answer, and we chatted about how to outsmart multiple-choice questions.

"Okay, listen up now, the correct answer *is* ... A. 3%! That puts Flowers for Algernon up by two points. They'd have to choke to lose now."

"That was rude," I said.

"He's an ornery, washed-up comic," Jacqueline said.

The scribe added, "He went to Chicago as a springboard to New York, but he never got any bounce."

"A few weeks ago," the wrangler jumped in, "he went on a rant about Liberals ruining his career with political correctness. He said, 'Straight white males aren't allowed to be funny anymore.'"

I started laughing.

The wrangler frowned. "That wasn't the joke."

"The trivia master is a joke," Jacqueline said.

"Breaking PC rules is central to the enterprise," I said.

"Maybe you just can't do comedy as a good ol' boy," the wrangler countered.

"Anyone can do comedy," Jacqueline corrected. "You just have to be funny."

"I'm not saying he's a first-degree racist. Maybe he just wants to use a certain word that starts with an N because he *can't* say it?" the wrangler mused. "Isn't that how the argument goes? If you can't say every word that starts with N, are you *truly free*?"

Jacqueline turned to me. "So, where you from?"

"Not a very creative question," I said.

"On an empty stomach, I have low tolerance for booze and bullshit."

"*Okay, cow-pokers*, here are a few fun facts. *Fact*: There are more guns in America than people. *Fact*: We are making more guns than babies! *Fact*: Americans make up 4% of the world's population, but we own half of the entire global stock of civilian firearms! Can I get a *U-S-A*?" The MC put a hand to his ear. "Another *fact*: We own at three times the *rate* of Canadians. '*O Canada! Our home and native land*!'"

The crowd booed.

"Are you booing me or Canada?" the MC cackled.

The response was mixed with *you*s, *boo*s, and *Canada*s.

"Don't boo, *reload*!" he squawked. "In fact, under this Liberal regime, gun sales have tripled! You kids think you've won with this guy in office? Wait and see! This Volvo-driving, basketball-playing, college-lecturing, hip-hop-loving president has awakened the silent majority."

After staring at the pizza tin for a few moments, the scribe pointed at my phone and bellowed, "What's that red light? Are you *recording*?"

"Who cares? We're in public," Jacqueline dismissed.

The neckbeard narrowed his eyes at me. "You some kind of government agent?"

"They don't care about who sucks at trivia," the wrangler said.

"They can record all this chatter without this dissertation-less dill weed," the scribe said, arms folded. He had thick glasses and wore a *Thelma & Louise* t-shirt.

"Recording for a friend," I said. "Worried he's losing his memory."

"So where is he?" Jacqueline asked.

"He lost us."

"Then why are you recording?" the neckbeard asked.

"He could show up at any time," I suggested.

The wrangler looked over his left shoulder toward the main door, then back at me. "How will we know it's him?"

"Think of a sasquatch in a karate suit."

Before I could stop the recording, the scribe lunged for my phone and flipped the tin over, spilling all the devices across the table and onto the floor.

I grabbed my phone and walked to the bar.

Adam looked at me with the wry grin of a mind reader.

"Six shots of your worst tequila."

"Coming up."

"Have you seen Ella?"

"Not since this afternoon, but it looks like *you're* on a roll: the singing nurse last night, and tonight, this beauty's nibbling on you."

Jacqueline slapped my arm. I didn't realize she'd followed me.

"I thought you were a respectable almost-scholar," she teased.

"You're the one who bites."

She bared her teeth. Then she laughed and slapped my arm again. "I'm here to carry drinks."

I reached for my phone to stop the recording.

"Leave it," she said. "Keep drinking at this rate, and you won't remember your trivial brilliance."

"Please don't trivialize my brilliance," I said solemnly.

"How old are you? It's hard to tell. You're aloof and knowledge-able. Wrinkle-free but prone to fatherly wordplay."

"Twenty-seven."

She laughed. "And you still haven't finished your dissertation!"

"Finished my B.A. in three years."

"I'm teasing. Who gets a Ph.D. in their twenties? It's too earnest."

"And you?" I asked.

"I'm twenty-six. Went to Mexico City after college, then I took a year to apply to schools and save money. Now that I'm here, I'll finish on time."

"You'll be a fine artist."

"By degree, at least. Listen, I can help you write."

"Okay?"

"*Write*. You just have to do it."

"So why are you in a writing program?"

"You're around other people doing the same thing. You read each other's work. When you spend too much time alone with a story, you lose track of what's on the page and what's only in your head. Let me look at what you have, even if it's just about rat piss."

"In the sciences we call it 'urine'."

"What's your throughline?"

"I have a thesis and finished the research ..."

"But your rats want more cocaine. Now you're selling plasma to keep up with their nasty habit."

"Reading more articles instead of writing, I don't want to miss anything." I didn't tell her that my mother had succumbed to breast cancer three months before, at only forty-two, and I hadn't been able to string two thoughts together ever since.

"For being so good at trivia, you're not so confident," she said.

I shrugged.

"Meet me for breakfast tomorrow at the Spotted Owl." She smiled for a moment, then added, "Keep meeting interesting people like me, and you might turn your recordings into a passable memoir."

Then, with her right hand, she patted my crotch twice like a bully in a locker room and walked away.

I froze.

"Quite a farewell, Santo. You won't want to miss breakfast," Adam said from behind the bar as he poured the last shot.

My cheeks were burning. In a mirrored beer sign, I checked my hair.

"Looking good, Santo," Adam confirmed.

"Shots are a bad idea," I said.

"Apparently, they're good for your balls."

I shuttled the shots to the table.

"So, what's our answer?" the scribe asked.

"What's the question?" I asked.

"Since 1999, what constitutional amendment has been proposed most often?"

"The answer is A," the neckbeard said. "Not campaign finance, school prayer, term limits, or even a ban on same-sex marriage."

"What did you do to Jacqueline?" the wrangler asked.

"The correct answer is *A*!" the MC broke in again. "Balanced budget amendments are by far the most common type of amendments proposed in the last twenty years. And so, according to my tally … Flowers for Algernon take the prize!"

"Okay for me to grab it?" I asked.

No one smiled, but no one objected.

Dank cannabis funk and dry tobacco smoke wafted in from the side door near the bar, which opened to an alley where folks puffed on their vices.

"The questions tonight, I didn't know you were so … *political*," I said to Adam, who was washing beer pitchers in the small sink behind the bar.

"You prefer to discuss decision-making and bias, but it's all technique and no content—interesting, but a narrow scope."

"You said 'scope' because of …" My voice trailed off, and I nodded toward the holster.

Adam handed it to me.

"You're not a gun nut, are you?" I asked.

"I'll be ready when the real nuts crack."

"Think the rallies will turn ugly?"

"Think your professor's dare caused it all?"

"He was joking," I said. "It was a movement in search of a slogan."

"The rally boys have better gear than the police, but I'll be ready."

"Ready with what?"

"Ammunition."

"Wow. Thought I had a better read on you."

"I think you mean 'bead,' schoolboy. Listen, you're young. You've probably never seen a backlash."

His seriousness made me nervous.

"Being a bartender is like being a cop. And I've done both."

"Why didn't you say anything?" I asked.

"Don't want to upset my clientele, but since it's your last night in town ..."

"Trivia is the only thing upsetting me."

"Humanity is terminally flawed. Give up on its perfectibility, and you'll be a happier man, Santo."

"Sample bias," I replied. "You see the worst of the worst."

"The bias is in your psychology department. You test middle- and upper-class kids between eighteen and twenty-two. You don't think that's weird? But me. I've seen the best and the worst—and a lot in between. And what about you? You've become my number one customer."

"That does set the bar high."

Adam tilted his head, studying me intensely. "If you really want to learn about humanity, you ought to join law enforcement. That's where the rubber meets the road."

"You mean where the rubber bullets meet the protesters?"

"You could make detective," Adam said. "They're looking for people like you."

I shook my head, trying to chuckle, but I couldn't.

"Unless you're the kind of doctor who can do plastic surgery, cure cancer, or make hair grow," Adam lifted his cowboy hat to show his balding scalp, "then I'm afraid your time at the university may be wasted."

"Harsh."

"Like I said, come to trivia night; you might learn something."

"Last question: should I be worried about Ella? She accused me of hiding Verboom, but I think she's losing her grip on reality."

"Are you hiding the professor?"

"How could I?"

6

Just after 8:00 AM, I arrived at the Spotted Owl. The aromas of bacon, coffee, and French toast swam through the old school diner, but I was too wound-up to feel hungry. I took a booth and ordered coffee—a dark roast, freshly brewed.

The server was pouring my second refill when Jacqueline appeared at the door. She gave me a slight nod of recognition and walked to my booth, sliding into the seat with a casual ease as if we met there every morning.

Reaching into my backpack, I pulled out the holster. Extending my arm across the narrow table, I set the leatherwork at her elbow.

"Thank you. I'll be sure to wear it with pretentious irony."

"Is there any other way?"

The server came by with a cup of coffee for Jacqueline.

"The usual?" he asked.

She nodded.

"I always have too much," Jacqueline said to me. "Let's split them."

"Buckwheat pancakes coming up."

"And a side of bacon," I said. "Extra crisp."

Jacqueline frowned.

"You'll wear leather but won't eat bacon on a special occasion?"

"This is a special occasion?"

"You're going to set my pen free."

"Awkward phrasing," she said.

"I should warn you..."

"Hook up with another woman last night?"

"Too much caffeine."

"Great, I'm still waking up. You do the talking. Start by explaining why you'd record a trivia night for your mysterious friend?"

"He might show up any moment." I paused. "Are you comfortable with me recording now?"

"Sleepy, but comfortable."

"Like you said, one day some of this might be interesting."

"I am good material," she said. "How would you describe me?"

"Slender and stylish..."

"You start with my figure? Put your gaze away, man."

"At this point, could I describe you spiritually? How about 'raven-haired know-it-all?'"

"Before I *caw*, tell me about the mysterious professor losing his memory."

"Pieter Cornelius Verboom."

"What a strange name."

"It's Dutch. Lots of vowels. He was my faculty advisor, and it grew into something unorthodox."

"Santo, I know the pecking order. Even now, you're recording *just in case* he shows."

"You don't like your advisor?"

She shrugged, her face conceding my point. "So, you're at the university? You have a distinct look. Surprised I haven't notice you."

"We're visiting from western Michigan. If I'd ordered a pop..."

"Michigan? You know what I'm asking next."

"He needed to get out of Grand Rapids and asked for help with the drive. But once we got down here, he seemed too emotionally fragile to leave. He checked into a clinic voluntarily to prevent an involuntary situation."

"Like a 5150?"

"His moods are severe."

"In your memoir use 'mercurial.' How else would you describe him?"

"He's socially awkward yet magnetic. Like a dairyman who's drunk all the milk and mainlined bovine growth hormone. My ex always mentioned his intense physicality, a raw animal appeal…"

"I like 'raw animal appeal.' Why did you choose each other?"

"Common interests and backgrounds. We're both the first in our families to attend college or grad school."

"The latter requires the former, you only need to say college."

"It's not fair to grade on an empty stomach."

"But it's primal, right? Bond with the biggest ape."

"Is that what you do?" I asked with uncertainty.

"Switch to decaf."

I took a pronounced sip and exhaled with satisfaction. "He pulled me in on a study that earned public attention and earned our department funding."

"He's a cash cow."

"You said 'cash cow' because I described him as a dairy farmer."

"He brings in the cheddar."

I looked at her deadpan.

"And you're milking him."

I threw my napkin on the table as she continued.

"Now you're out on the high plains exploring your manhood with an older gentleman who provides funding. Is he asking for any *favors*?"

"Just the usual babysitting," I said.

"How sick is he?"

"Seemed to start with a public meltdown on WNN's *Hot Button Science*."

"'Don't Change Horses Midstream!' That was Verboom?"

"He claims no memory of it, but the legend of his antics snowballed and earned him a baby cult following."

"A baby cult following?"

"A small but avid following."

"'The Avid Baby.' That could be one of your chapter titles."

"Do you follow politics?"

"Santo, baby. *Everything* is political."

"You're saying 'baby' because I said, 'baby cult.'"

"Now that you've tasted the limelight of media and politics, you can't go back to your rodents. You're fame adjacent. It's where you got your swagger."

"A baby portion."

"And it's adorable. But how could Verboom forget his TV performance?"

"A fugue, I think."

"A *fugue*? Sounds so Victorian."

"A dissociative state that can last for hours, days, weeks, even months. You forget your personality and biography."

"You mean like a zombie? He was out there like a *zombie*?"

"His skin didn't rot; he wasn't hissing, growling, or limping. It was like..."

"A *trance*."

"Something broke. His biographical memory is back, but his executive function is gone."

"Meaning?"

"He can't prioritize or regulate his emotions. He gets lost in his own arguments. Right after the WNN appearance he bought a new truck, and he talked the whole way from DC to Grand Rapids. After a few addled weeks, he seemed more himself. He took an 'emergency sabbatical,' but before getting much rest, his publicist got him a radio show. After a few months of taking crap from callers, he lost his mind again and dared the haters to put the government out of business. Of course, it wasn't meant *literally*."

"But the literalists took it literally."

"Oh, you read *The Times'* piece?"

"Maybe?"

"The rant, what he dubbed *Final Freedom*, caught on with the ultras."

"*Wait*, Verboom's responsible for all these rallies? I've seen a few *Final Freedom* flags. They're worse than zombies; they're jackals! No wonder he's gone into hiding. What an asshole!"

"'Pieter Verboom is *that* asshole.' If I'm still permitted to quote him."

"Did he give the president any good advice?"

"He called for an all-out rhetorical assault on politicians who belong to a secret fraternity called First Brothers. They're a clique in government tearing down the wall between church and state."

"*Opus Dei*? I've already seen this movie."

"Bigger. Just a few days ago one of their members visited the clinic. You know Senator Hesse?"

"Enough not to vote for him. Never heard of First Brothers."

"The establishment press doesn't know how to handle them."

"So, what about Hesse?"

"When we landed in DC, Hesse invited Verboom out for coffee—schmoozing for the Lord. Verboom was already a bit addled, perhaps manic, but I thought it was just the jitters of being in DC. Whatever it was, Verboom recoiled to the invitation like it was an insult to his honor, telling me afterword that he was going to 'out the brotherhood!'"

"What did they do?"

"First Brothers has a dorm house on C Street that's registered as a church to avoid taxes. The members, mostly elected officials, pay only a nominal rent. Interns do all the cooking and housework."

"Imagine the outrage if a crew of Muslim congressmen lived in a building designated as a mosque to avoid taxes?"

"Verboom claimed their prayer meetings are only a front. The real purpose is brokering backroom deals at home and abroad, using political influence for Jesus."

"So, what happened?"

"Anyone listening said he was grasping at straws. But online, I found a shadow network of religious nationalists, who want to establish a nation 'governed by the Bible and godly men.' First Brothers is the fraternity holding all these groups together."

"*Theocracy is an inside job*," she said gravely. Then laughed. After pausing, her face grew stern. "So, you've been chasing conspiracies instead of writing your dissertation? Don't tell your mom."

I winced, then went on. "The media didn't want the story. First Brothers only made news with a sex scandal—a member cheated on his wife with his best friend's wife. The Brothers tried to buy off the cuckold with cash and a new job."

"Why not throw the adulterer out of their pious group?"

"They're traditionalistic but not moralistic. Any moral passion they have is for loyalty to the organization."

"Maybe the press simply respects their religious freedom to seize government." She smirked.

"Attacking 'faith groups' makes you sound like a devious secularist."

"What about the religious dimension with the 'war on terror?'"

"The president separates terrorist acts from religious labels. He calls terrorists criminals not martyrs. They don't stand for true religion."

"But *they* say they're religious," Jacqueline said. "Isn't that a designation they should make for themselves?"

"Under that logic, we should call Klansmen 'Christians.'"

"You said it."

"Verboom advised the president to expose First Brothers during the State of the Union Address, labeling them 'theocrats hiding in business suits.'"

"Don't remember that line."

"Verboom hoped the speech would start a new Red Scare, but his suggestions didn't make the cut." I sipped my coffee and reflected for a moment. "They sent me down a rabbit hole."

"Who did?"

"First Brothers."

The server came back to refill our coffee mugs and set down my side of bacon. I quickly bit into a slice.

"Your story's got potential," Jacqueline said. "Your lips are shining."

I tucked in my lips.

"It's the bacon," she whispered.

"So, what do you think?" I wiped my mouth with a napkin.

"You've got great lips."

"This isn't *a story*, it's the collapse of democracy."

"If the theocrats were zombies, you'd get a week's worth of headlines," she said.

"You really know how to punch up a plot."

"So, now that we've got your story on track. What about home? What about all your friends? Your *ex*?"

I looked down at my coffee.

"You don't have to answer," she said tenderly. Then she returned with her red pen: "You're an introvert, despite your gift of caffeinated gab. You really don't have many friends of any type. You just need that one daily relationship, and now you're fully wrapped up with your mentor—all others be damned."

I folded my arms.

"Do you play any sports? Your arms are so veiny."

"I'll put on my jacket," I said.

"What were we talking about? I got lost in your arms. Oh yes, your *story*. How you became the professor's butler. Hey! That's a good title for your book!"

I chuckled defensively.

"Let's proceed, and I'll figure out how you landed in Flagstaff and became: *The Professor's Butler*."

"My mom died of breast cancer a few weeks before we left for Arizona. I didn't want to be at home."

"God, Santo. I'm so sorry."

"I'm getting distance. Verboom pays for the motel and gas, but not my time."

"With grant money?"

"No. Publishing royalties."

"You said 'ex' earlier?"

"She left me a few days after I got to Flagstaff. She'd wanted out for a long time but didn't have the courage."

"How could you know that, Santo?"

"A direct confession. A few months before my mom passed, my ex got pathetically drunk and admitted she wanted to break up but couldn't bring herself to do it while my mom was dying."

"What did you do?"

"She didn't remember the confession. A total blackout, she's prone to those the way some people are, and we just went on."

The server set down a stack of buckwheat pancakes. The syrup and silverware were already on the table. Jacqueline cut the pancakes in half and used her fork and knife to push the halves apart. Then she spun the plate 90 degrees.

"Your side. My side. Don't let your syrup cross the line." Then she spoke like a Valley girl, "I *loathe* soggy pancakes."

"The halves and the half not," I said, too pleased. "To half and to hold."

"Wouldn't working on your dissertation offer a distraction from your…"

"Mourning," I said.

She took a bite.

"My dissertation is on parenting."

"Probably no rats then."

"Nope."

"Can you take bereavement leave?"

The server came by to fill our cups. A thermos in one hand, a pitcher of ice water in the other. I took a long drink of water and put my glass down.

"What's your plan post-MFA?" I asked.

"Let me ask the questions."

"The Grand Inquisitor!" I grinned.

"Funny you say that? Dostoevsky means a lot to me."

"Are you Russian?"

"One hundred percent *Chicana, guey*."

"*Que bonita!* But I have to admit…"

"What?" Jacqueline asked quickly.

"I don't know Dostoevsky. Verboom just says that when I ask too many questions."

"'The Grand Inquisitor' is a parable within the larger story of *The Brothers Karamazov*. Jesus returns during the Spanish Inquisition, and the lead inquisitor doesn't want him back. It messes up their operation, so they put him in jail."

"Jesus puts the Grand Inquisitor in jail?" I asked.

"No. The Grand Inquisitor puts *Jesus* in jail."

"Well, for Verboom it was only word play. His mind works on

alliteration, allusion, rhyme, onomatopoeia, and a jumble of non-se-quiturs he calls 'creative leaps.'"

"What's he doing in science?"

"Going mad as a hatter."

She raised her eyebrows, then looked down at the pancakes and ate.

I sipped coffee silently, determined to stop oversharing.

When she finished her half of the stack, she pulled pen and paper from her satchel and drew the outline of a pistol, writing her email address down the barrel. Then she slid out of the booth, pinched my right bicep like it was a child's cheek and walked away.

I waved, but her back was already turned to me.

No one came by with a check, so I went to the cashier's stand.

"Bea has a tab. She's got it."

"Who's Bea?" I asked.

"Beatriz."

"*Huh*?"

"Your breakfast buddy."

I went back to the table, took another swallow of coffee and put five dollars under my mug. I didn't know how well Jacqueline, or Beatriz, tipped, and I had five cups.

As I walked back to the truck, I called the clinic. Still no update. I felt clear in my conscience to head home. The rationale for my stay in Flagstaff had evaporated, leaving only a big white truck and a stalker behind.

With my backpack sitting in the passenger seat, I set out for the interstate.

For distraction, I flipped on the radio and scanned the FM dial—three seconds of rock, three of R&B, then soul, cumbia, ranchero, a shock jock, and finally, NPR. Switching to AM, I landed on firebrand preaching about the flag and the cross—the nation belongs to God, apparently. I let the sermon play until the broadcast cut to a news update about a *Final Freedom* rally in Phoenix.

I sat in silence with my painful thoughts.

Despite the thrill of meeting Jacqueline, my mind kept drifting back to my ex. For the first time since leaving Michigan, I called her. It went straight to voicemail, and I hung up before the beep. A text followed almost instantly: "Can't talk now, but I never loved you. Felt stuck in your kindness."

I pulled onto the shoulder and read it again. Then I changed her name in my contacts directory to first name: NEVER CALL. Last name: DON'T PICK UP.

Not far from Flagstaff, I took the next exit and headed west for Haddit's.

Adam looked both pleased and surprised to see me back. After finishing my second beer, I broke down and told him about my mom, my ex, my academic dead end, and the video with Anna. He listened without interruption, his eyes steady, quiet with understanding. When I finished, he poured me a glass of water.

He offered to call his police friends about the missing professor and speculated that Ella's camera might have been a prop. Even if it wasn't, the footage was probably grainy. Either way, he thought it best to let it rest and keep my distance. As far as he could tell, Ella was only interested in Verboom. If I stayed away from him, I could stay away from her.

Sensing how shaken I was, he didn't argue when I floated the idea of a tracking device on Verboom's truck. Perhaps out of pity, he even offered to sweep it, though he doubted there was anything to find. He also suggested parking Verboom's truck outside his bar for a few days—his security cameras would catch anyone snooping. Then he ordered me a club sandwich from the diner two doors down and picked it up while I sat nursing a cup of coffee.

He offered a loaner car, but I stuck with my ten-speed, which I had brought from home. It was one of the few possessions I truly cherished. With all my gear in my backpack, I pedaled out of downtown toward the university. After a slow tour of the campus, weaving through pedestrian-only zones, I shot off the grounds and found a motor inn near the freeway. The clerk could accept an open-ended stay and was happy to have a cash deposit.

Where my last motel had been all new vinyl and synthetic sterility, this place was frozen in the 1970s—except for the flatscreen TVs and Wi-Fi.

At the desk in my room, I emailed Jacqueline to let her know I'd be in town longer than expected. She replied immediately, inviting me to breakfast the next morning.

My grandmother called, but before I could answer, Ella called. I froze and let them both ring through to voicemail. Ella called back three more times. Each voicemail simply said: "Call me."

I ordered a Hawaiian pizza for delivery and went to bed early.

The next morning, I biked around campus for exercise, then zigzagged my way to the Spotted Owl. This time, Jacqueline was already sitting in a booth.

After a smile to acknowledge me, she jumped right in.

"Tell me more about *the missing professor and the stalking publicist*. You've got a solid hook, let's flesh it out."

"You want to turn my predicament into a pitch?" I asked.

"I've been thinking about your situation. Since you're so committed to these recordings and your unravelling mentor, why not turn this escapade into a personal narrative?"

"A *memoir*?"

"It's a slim timeframe, so 'personal narrative' makes more sense… some kind of creative nonfiction. Maybe a long magazine piece? A ride-along monograph, perhaps? Follow the story."

"I'll keep a lookout for zombies."

"Seriously, you could write about being embedded with America's second most cited social psychologist."

"You looked him up?"

"Yeah—*wow*. His appearance on WNN was prophetic."

"Let's not make him a prophet."

"Did you know some guy named Paul Heitinga wrote a book on him in the 90s? There's precedent. This could be the bookend on his career."

"So I can transcribe and edit the recordings?"

"You've got to tell the story from your point of view. If you want people to read the book, it's got to be immersive. We need to know about *you*."

"That's a tall order."

"You'll want to avoid cliches."

"So, some kind of Hunter S. Thompson gonzo journalism? What's his famous quote? 'When the going gets weird, the weird turn pro.'"

"Yes! But I think you're more of a Tom Wolfe."

"I don't know. The recordings were his idea…"

"But it's become *your* compulsion."

"I'll admit it." I adjusted my earbuds, looking so innocent on the table.

Jacqueline tilted her head, studying my fingers. "How often do you wash your hands in a day?"

"Depends on what I'm doing." I did a quick tally. "Today? Five times."

"It's 9 AM, Santo. Your skin's too dry."

"The pace slows down, but by the end of the day somewhere between twenty and thirty times. I didn't think to count until you asked."

"When did this start?"

"Not long ago. I've been reading too much about infectious diseases."

That was the truth, but not the whole truth. It started when my mom began chemotherapy, and I didn't want to kill her with a virus because I was too lazy to wash my hands after touching a doorknob.

She studied me for a moment. "You're holding something back."

"Good hygiene is highly rational. I use my elbows to push elevator buttons and my feet for toilet levers. What else do you want to know?"

"You don't want to lose anything. Even *words*."

"Especially words," I admitted, my shoulders dropping.

"What happened?"

"My cell reception was spotty around Flagstaff, so I switched carriers and upgraded my phone." I stared out the window, inhaled, and tried to clear my mind.

"You lost all your voicemails."

"Hundreds from my mom. All gone."

She reached out for my hand, but I pulled my arm back, grabbed my glass, and took a sip of ice water.

The deep roar of a revving truck came through the diner's open windows. Then another. A third. A fourth. I stopped counting. A caravan of pickups with flags.

"Looks like you have a lot to write about," Jacqueline said after the last truck passed.

"I'll send you the rough draft."

"The sooner, the better."

7

After a few days of holing up in my new Flagstaff motel, cabin fever hit hard. Strangely, the more restless I became, the more I hunkered down.

Through the university's library portal, I could access virtually every publication from my laptop. But instead of going back to my dissertation, I read more on Hesse and First Brothers, then searched for links between Verboom's radio rant and the rally guys.

As a firsthand witness to the delirious challenge, I doubted its potency, but down the rabbit hole I went, chasing the ever-elusive question of *who really controls America's politics.*

On edge, I cleared my browser history and considered using a VPN. But could I trust the VPN host? After reading several articles on digital security, I glanced outside. A truck, neither old nor new, with tall tires and a stretched suspension, was parked outside the motel. A giant Confederate flag waved, mounted at the rear of the bed. Visible through the cab's back window was a gun rack, fully loaded.

The last bit of information Ella and I received from the clinic concerned their closed-circuit security video. Although we couldn't view the footage, they would summarize it for us. Verboom was last seen walking the hallways at 2 AM the morning of his disappearance. Oddly, the exterior cameras failed to record his departure.

I couldn't believe that someone so large could evade the surveillance cameras. An image came to mind of Verboom hiding in the clinic's rafters like a colossal squirrel.

"Perhaps he's still on the premises somewhere—a storage room?" I asked, only to be gently told such a thing was "impossible." Then, like Verboom, I muttered, "You mean *implausible*."

Ella kept calling and leaving messages, insisting we meet. I refused to engage, then she sent a screenshot of a woman straddling a man on a bed in a budget motel. Though fuzzy with pixilation, the scene was unmistakable. I replied, "Who are these people?" If she named them in her response, I could use it as evidence of extortion.

She wrote back: "You tell me."

Rather than escalate with more texts, I offered to meet her at a downtown brewery that Friday.

With 48 hours to kill, I stocked up at a natural foods market—hummus, pita, string cheese, sparkling water, apples, and cheap table wine. I'd stopped watching TV as a college freshman—not as a moral crusade, I just didn't own one and was too busy reading.

In the new motel room, I folded a blank sheet of paper into a name card for the TV: *Media Studies 305*. A joke to myself—a reminder to keep things from getting too weird as I spent the next two days watching television from bed.

WNN covered the president's meeting with American faith leaders—an event he convened—as he tried to win back the God-people. In the report, a news analyst cited Verboom's "call for a wall" as a turning point at the E.C.S. last January, blaming the professor for the president's continued loss of support among religious voters.

Later, ANN ran clips of Fritz Hearn sneering at the gathering, "The president's extending his fig leaf as an olive branch." Aligned with Hearn, the most conservative clerics rejected the invitation, but their absence barely made headlines. Instead, the focus landed on a single misstep by the Commander in Chief.

Using his lofty tone—or "soaring rhetoric" as the press liked to call it—the president praised the clergy standing behind him, but something came out wrong. When he referred to them as "faith leaders," it sounded an awful lot like "fake leaders." Worse, he kept repeating the phrase: "Every single faith leader in this great country," or... was it "every single *fake leader* in this great country"?

While WNN framed the story as a comical mishearing, ANN insisted that "fake" was both said and meant. ANN commentators expressed outrage, speculating that this would permanently sour any goodwill from the religious right.

Of course, there was little evidence that such goodwill had ever existed, even as the president's first term began. On inauguration day, Fritz Hearn openly declared, "I hope he fails." That same day, the House and Senate minority leaders met to plan total obstruction of the executive branch. Their top *legislative* priority was to make the president a one-termer. Ironically, that wasn't something they could legislate.

Of course, the president regretted not articulating his *th* more forcefully. Hinting at an apology, he spelled out the word he actually used: *F. A. I. T. H.* Late that night, satirists joked that he lost the American public after just three letters. But as it often turns out, laughing at American ignorance was an ignorant thing to do.

The crowded downtown brewery had exposed brick walls and high ceilings, the music was guitar-driven, and the air smelled of hops and yeast. Dressed in jeans and a tee shirt, I grabbed the only available two-top in the back. After I ordered, Ella walked in wearing a black knee-length skirt, a black long-sleeve shirt without a collar, and black pumps. Her hair was pulled back into a sleek ponytail, her lips painted red. Heads turned, eyes lingered. She commanded the room without a word.

Black widow, I thought.

She dragged a heavy wooden chair from the table and sat down, waving off a man who tried to help her.

"I don't know where he is," I said, my voice firm, final.

Ella studied me, poker-faced. Then, with her back to the room, she glanced over her shoulder, sensing the lingering eyes. Slowly, she turned back, locking onto me with a glare.

I slid a menu across the table. She didn't look at it. Instead, she stood. The chair scraped along the hardwood floor with a screech. Without another word, she walked out, every set of eyes in the brewery following her exit.

My tasting flight arrived. Before ditching Verboom's truck at Haddit's, I took the last issue of the *Grand Rapids Gazette* from his correspondence stash. With Ella gone, I unfolded the paper and settled in like a gentleman enjoying his drinks. Finally out of the house, I crossed my legs, leaned back, and glanced over the pages while casually people-watching. I wasn't a creep. And I didn't want to look like one.

After the third taster, the weight of isolation rolled off my shoulders. I turned the page and started the next story.

Direct Democracy Movement Establishes Camp at Grand Circus Park, Detroit

"We're participants, not a party. We're a movement, not an organization," a protester said, giving the name Jane Doe. When asked if she planned to vote in the upcoming national election, Ms. Doe replied, "I believe in direct action, not in

a false choice between bad-faith politicians in a republic for patriarchs." Similar gatherings had cropped up in East Lansing, Flint, Grand Rapids, Kalamazoo, Lansing, Muskegon, Traverse City, and Ypsilanti.

My ex and her crew must have attended the Grand Rapids event, probably handing out fliers written in theoretical rhetoric impenetrable to a reader outside of Ph.D. work. Further down the page, a headline from the Pacific Northwest caught my eye.

Prayerful Protest on the Burnside Bridge

A group of men gathered in Vancouver, WA, and took a chartered bus to downtown Portland, where they assembled on the Burnside Bridge, blocking traffic in both directions. As law enforcement arrived, the men knelt in prayer. A witness reported that their words were drowned out by a chorus of honking horns. However, police allowed them to finish their prayers before ordering them to clear the bridge. No arrests were made.

Did they think prayer was more effective from a bridge? More potent in Oregon than in Washington? I smirked, then frowned. Verboom's voice was echoing in my head.

A shadow fell over me. A large man stood at my table.

"Mind if I have the paper when you're done?" he asked. "I like the crosswords."

"All yours." I folded the *Gazette* in half and passed it to him. He glanced at the paper, then looked at me.

"You visiting from Michigan or *Michoacan*?" He wasn't looking for an answer.

With a slight nod, he grabbed the paper and returned to his table, where five men sat wearing mismatched military fatigues, each carrying a sidearm strapped to his thigh. At ease, they leaned back in their seats, beer glasses half-emptied, relaxed as their presence threatened.

Tasting flight finished, I bought a six-pack and left downtown on my bike, heading away from campus. With enough distance from the brewery, I looped around to the eastern edge of the city and then cut south, winding through the part of campus closed to motor vehicle traffic before taking a direct route to the motel.

The next afternoon, Adam called. Ella had just stopped by Haddit's, asking about me and the truck. Adam said he played dumb with Ella, and then reviewed his security footage after she left.

"Didn't see anything sketchy," he said. "No Verboom-like or Ella-like characters snooping around the truck. Ella says she's heading home, leaving for Kalamazoo tomorrow morning," Adam added. "Tomorrow evening might be a good time to move the truck."

"You need the parking?"

"Anything left in one spot too long becomes a target."

"How can I be sure she's leaving?"

"Ella thinks the professor's already back in Michigan. Says the clinic's a dead end, she's been all over town with no luck, and it makes more sense to go home."

"You believe her?"

"Seemed honest," Adam said with confidence. "I asked her to send a postcard."

"Really?"

"She thinks she's got me wrapped around her finger. Her charm doesn't work on me, but I let her believe it does."

"Were you a detective?"

Adam chuckled. "So, what's the plan now that you're out of hiding?"

I hesitated. "Think it's safe to take the truck? I wouldn't put it past Ella to have planted something."

"You mean a tracker?"

I exhaled, embarrassed about my next request. "Can you sweep the truck?"

Adam let the question hang. "Looks like you *do* want to be a detective."

"Can you?"

"Sure. Anyone else have a key?"

"No, he left both with me at check in."

I holed up in the motel for two more days, avoiding Adam and Jacqueline, venturing out only for food. After baring my soul, I opted for silence.

The mini fridge buzzed incessantly.

Moving to the bed, I grabbed a pillow with each hand and pressed them to my ears, like a monkey with cymbals. Clutching them tightly, I finally found quiet. Lying flat on the mattress, I thought about my next move.

Working on my dissertation was out of the question; the focus required a clearer mind than I could currently muster. Both sullen and restless, I needed to move—to see things, feel, think, drink. Academic work seemed futile. The thought of being in Grand Rapids was unbearable.

Despite having a pal in Adam and an infatuation with Jacqueline, I was staying in a junky motel six states from Grandma. My only family was in Michigan. Eventually, I'd need to head back, but at what point would it be fair to leave with Verboom's truck—and what about *Verboom*? His undoing could jeopardize my academic future.

Jacqueline's suggestion to write about Verboom crossed my mind again.

As I relaxed my grip on the pillows, the rhythmic squeak of bedsprings from the next room broke the silence. I tightened my hold again, eventually falling asleep.

My phone slid off the nightstand and continued buzzing on the floor. Releasing the pillows, I scooped it up.

Verboom was on the line, manic. I switched on speakerphone, sat at the desk, and started recording the call with my laptop.

"...Tinsel twinkles in the starlight!" he bellowed. "The stars have spoken! We're going back into the cosmos! The show must go on!"

His idea for a radio comeback had struck after seeing a man on Hollywood Boulevard holding a handwritten sign: *I kick you in the ass. $20.* Verboom couldn't believe his eyes—until he saw a customer.

It was after observing this bizarre exchange that Verboom called me from a payphone. As an aspiring Luddite, he kept phone numbers and aphorisms in a pocket-sized address book, which was always on his person. For hours, he wandered along the Walk of Stars on Hollywood Boulevard. "A grand circus of humanity" he called it, and I endured several celestial puns and scriptural citations.

"I'll provide more details after you collect me."

"Have you spoken to Ella?" I asked.

"A dream, perhaps. You know that I'm open to panpsychism. But that's beside the point. We're going back into radio! A new show!"

"You have a working title?"

"*The Dutch Uncle.* I'm convinced human beings crave a certain level of abuse. Out here in California, consumers are paying hard cash to be kicked in the ass!"

"*Abuse?*"

"A kick in the pants! But it's more than that, I've kicked the concept into a new dimension. We'll pants the public, cognitively speaking. Strip them bare of their prejudice! Hell, let's pants the entire English language, *ja*!"

"*The Dutch Uncle?*"

"My philosophy professor used to say it all the time. But it turns out he was a Scot, though not a Scottish Common Sense Realist, as you may have guessed. Everything was a language game for him. 'Philosophy is conceptual clarification and analysis,' he liked to say. He left metaphysics to the theologians."

"You lost me in the stars."

"To my professor, a 'Dutch uncle' was an irritating know-it-all who rained on your parade. I asked one of my actual Dutch uncles— he'd never heard the phrase."

"But he was Dutch?"

"It's an old *British* euphemism—like 'Dutch courage' (drunken bravery) or 'Dutch treat' (a booby-trap) or 'Dutch nightingale' (a frog). And now, *Dutch uncle*—one who delivers blunt, unsolicited advice. Ha! That's it! There's our show! It'll be easy. All my uncles are Dutch!"

I sighed.

"Now. If it's not too much to ask, could you pick me up in the pickup? Soon but not too soon. I've found *her*."

"Ella?"

"*Genevieve Van Diest*. We're meeting for a consultation."

"Let's fly you home. I can pick you up at Gerald Ford."

"My license is expired."

"Where's your passport?"

"Let me stop you now. I can't rent a car or take a train or a bus without acceptable ID. But let's get to the heart of the matter: I'm aviation averse."

"It's safer than driving."

"I don't fit on planes."

"First class. Expanded leg room. Wider seats."

"Don't be gauche, Santo."

"If it's practically required, then it's not luxury."

"Once you're in the sky, you *can't get out*! I'm claustrophobic!"

"You've never been on a plane?"

"Correct," he confirmed. "Make sure you use my gas card! You shall bear no expense other than your *invaluable* time!" Then he rattled off an address in Venice Beach. "Oh, and one last thing. Let's keep Ella in the dark."

8

At the corner of 4th Ave and Rose Ave in Venice Beach, Verboom sat in a laundromat. His deep tan surprised me—flattering, but his cheeks were too thin. Without offering a hug or handshake, he simply said, "*Goede dag*," then slid into the truck's passenger seat, fixing his gaze on some distant point. He didn't look like a drifter, but his seersucker *gi* was heavily wrinkled.

He ran a finger along the truck's dashboard, inspecting for dust.

"You must know, Dutch immigrants in America are obsessed with cleanliness."

"Like most people groups."

"But my people have an extra ferocity—caused by sexual repression and theological oppression. You're too young to have seen the severe brand of caustics sold as Old Dutch Cleanser. That didn't happen by chance."

"Are you clean?"

"Every morning, I wade into the Pacific fully clad, rinse off at the public beach showers—still clothed—then I air-dry my duds over a bench."

"What do you wear while your clothes dry?"

"My birthday suit," he said matter-of-factly.

"You sat *naked* on a bench every morning while your clothes dried?"

"I kept my legs crossed."

"How modest."

"The water is cold. The air is cold. The skies are dark. 'Fun in the sun' is a myth in this gloom! But I'd bear any shame or inconvenience to stay clean."

He elaborated on this morning routine, saying the process left his clothes starchy stiff and his tan without lines.

Verboom had always prioritized comfort over style in footwear. His extra-wide, size-thirteen orange running shoes remained a constant—his only eccentric fashion choice until he snapped on WNN and graduated to karate suits.

"Glad you still wear shoes," I said.

"Van Gogh said, 'Orange is the color of madness.' And Van Gogh would know! Just follow his ear!" Verboom howled.

"Colors are just colors. Van Gogh had the madness."

"Deutschland, Deutschland Uber Alles? No, no, dear friend, 'tis Comfort, Comfort Uber Alles! Verily, I say unto thee: Comfort, Comfort Ye My Phalanges."

"I packed fresh socks for your phalanges."

"Since escaping the clinic, I've wandered Los Angeles nonstop. It's electric! The ambition, the energy of these young actors!"

"You went to the theater?"

"Nay, nay, nay! I stand at the edges of sidewalk cafés, watching them hustle and smile between tables, performing their biggest parts—until I get shooed away. It's a real talent! Always on."

"You're too big to sneak up on anyone."

"Au contraire, mon frère! When you're homeless in Los Angeles, it's like you don't exist."

"You're a giant. They're avoiding eye contact."

"*Nay*, Santo. I haven't existed for days. The experience has been exquisite."

"Still reading without glasses? Still continent?"

"Don't diminish my prowess! I'm a hound and a hawk rolled

into one big farm boy."

When he wasn't lost in thought, Verboom's senses were over-tuned. He could hear, smell, and see better than anyone I knew. Especially smell.

"Your sniffer is quite something," I acknowledged.

"But if I get too old, Santo, all I'll have left is my smell. I'll just be a nose. A giant, squinting nose-man—all bones and papery skin, unable to do anything but smell!"

"It's true, the human nose never stops growing."

"Hey, Pinocchio—before we leave town, I want to show you the camps."

For the next few hours, Verboom spoke nonstop, giving me a guided tour of LA street life—pointing out the conspicuously wealthy, the decisive weirdness of weirdoes, the grit of immigrants, the garb of Hasidic Jews, and the food and fashion of Little Armenia, Koreatown, Japantown, Thai Town, Chinatown, and the togas of the last remaining Hare Krishnas in Venice.

"For two quarters, you can take a city shuttle to Griffith Observatory and gaze over the city—an oasis and a junkyard!"

He spoke of Los Angeles like he was in love, and he had to count the ways.

"You know, Santo, people blame 'Hollywood' for moral decay. Historically, it works as shorthand for the entertainment industry, but most of the major studios have long since moved north to the San Fernando Valley or west to Culver City and Santa Monica."

"You're telling me Tinseltown isn't made of tinsel?"

"For years, the district of Hollywood was derelict, unglamorous, and only now is being refurbished. How's that for an emblem? Most of the east side is still working-class. 'Hollywood' says more about the ruthless machinations of late capitalism than it does about cinema."

"What *are* you, a Marxist tour guide?"

"People wander the streets like they're in another dimension. They don't ask for money; they speak to the air. They look right through you, like *you're* the air. Maybe I'm moving into the next dimension myself. Think I'll fit in?"

"Careful. Conservatives believe all behavior is a free and punishable moral choice, and Liberals think it's rude to be fascinated by abnormalities—unless that abnormality is conservatism."

"Good one, Santo! I'm glad you're recording everything."

"Actually, 'abnormal' is out. 'Psychopathology' is in."

"What do they call a guy like me these days?"

"You're a special case."

"*Aha*! This is how we save your career! Write me up as a case study. Give my condition a grandiose name. You'll be known as the guy who came up with... Well, you'll think of something."

"How would you feel about someone writing a book on you. Not just your 'condition' but the whole of you?"

He thought for a moment. "Sounds like a poor use of time."

"But would you mind?"

Again, he thought for a moment. "As long as I don't have to read it."

In the truck, he yammered on about the political forces of the '70s and '80s that delivered tax cuts but led to budget shortfalls, which reduced public services. Then the '90s brought tough-on-crime politics and three-strike laws—passed by both parties. Prisons replaced social services. There was heroin, crack, meth, opioids, and heroin again.

"Where'd you get all this?"

"The library, of course." He didn't own a smartphone—not even a dumbphone. "And I may have spoken to a few people. Frankly, I've been eavesdropping a tad. But I don't consider myself a spy—more of a gadfly."

"So you've figured out homelessness."

"When a person doesn't have housing, they're unhoused. Give them housing, and they're not unhoused."

"My aunt came back from California saying big-city Liberals caused homelessness. I told her it was Conservatives cutting social programs."

"The rent is too damn high!" Verboom interrupted.

"She blamed the coddling mayors who let the sidewalks become free campgrounds."

"Did she pitch a tent? Everyone loves a government freebie!"

"I told her about the *LA Times* series on homelessness, how LAPD's gang task force set up surveillance cameras around Skid Row and caught something unexpected—police cruisers and ambulances from surrounding communities 'dumping' unhoused people downtown. People discharged from hospitals or jails with nowhere to go."

"What did she say?"

"Even with video proof, she couldn't believe the police would do something inhumane. But you know what she said?"

"The wheels on the bus go 'round and 'round?"

"She said, 'Agree to disagree.' She smiled, but her eyes were angry."

"Sounds like a polite lady."

"My aunt married a country-club guy and found their ways agreeable. Funny thing is, as a young woman, she was a hippie."

"Ever been to a country club, Santo dear? Personalities *in* situations. There are no personalities in the abstract—unless, of course, you're speaking in abstractions. But that's just words."

"How'd you ever get a teaching job?"

"*My height*, obviously. Sure, I have the credentials and whatnot, but there's just so much positive bias for the tall." Then he leaned over to me, a wild glimmer in his eyes. "Now, Santo, back to the topic at hand."

"What's the topic?"

"The streets of LA, of course! There's a man who circulates around La Brea Boulevard and Sunset Boulevard. He doesn't have hands. I saw him three or four times. Both arms end at the wrist! Try to picture that for a moment."

"Why are you telling me this?"

"Tell me why that man doesn't have hands."

I focused on maneuvering the truck through tight traffic.

"You know, Santo, there are two exotic dance clubs in that same neighborhood."

"So what?"

"Remember that Sunday school song, 'O Be Careful, Little Hands, What You Do'?"

"'O be careful, little mouth, what you say' was the next verse."

"I'm talking about Old Testament justice here. A paw for a paw."

"Probably an accident with heavy machinery," I said.

"Maybe gangrene... I can't get the image of the man's missing hands out of my mind. One afternoon, we got on the bus together. The sight was too pathetic to put into words. His clothes didn't fit; he couldn't provide his pass or money. Before I could help, the driver waved him onboard. His beard was wild. His hair was wild. His eyes were wild. I went to the back of the bus and wept."

"Where did you stay all these nights?"

"The canals of Venice, of course. I slipped into an abandoned canoe each night and paddled under one of the large bridges. First, I tried camping on the beach, but the police clear the sand every night. I only need a few hours of shuteye, anyway."

I never got a clear answer as to why he fled Flagstaff for LA. Maybe it reminded him of his first burnout (see Paul Heitinga's *A Theologian East of West Hollywood*). Maybe it was just the first train out of town. Or maybe he had dumped his own humanity onto the streets in an act of solidarity.

Skid Row was a city unto itself. People filled every sidewalk, every block. At first, Verboom seemed devoid of sympathy, but then I realized—he wasn't observing with so-called objective distance, he was identifying with them.

After viewing several camps, he directed me with a few more turns.

"Where we going now?" I asked.

"Genevieve Van Diest's."

"*Now?*"

"Almost forgot." He handed me a 104-page manuscript detailing how he met Genevieve. The first draft was written in pencil, traced over in ink to make it permanent.

"The working title is *Almost Amsterdam*. Wrote it in a rundown coffee house on California and Abbott Kinney. The coffee's cheap, and with enough cream and sugar, it's like a meal. They let me sit in there all day, no hassle. They even have a bathroom."

"I'm driving. Give me the gloss."

"She runs a self-realization center on the Eastside. I went there." He paused. "She left Christianity because it's too political."

Unable to contain himself, he went on. Verboom had never heard of Genevieve until one afternoon in Venice Beach, when he sat along a concrete wall at the edge of a parking lot and heard her voice coming from a car. The car sat there for hours, as the driver binged on a series of Genevieve's teachings. Verboom listened along, captivated by her voice—serene, composed, the rare mix of erudition and warmth.

"And sitting on the wall," he continued, "I was thrown into a rapturous state, as if I existed just for that—for the wisdom, for the kindness. *Hyper unitary awareness*, Santo. The sun broke through the clouds. I went outside of space and time."

After that oceanfront revelation, he had gone straight to a library in Santa Monica, combing through everything he could find about her.

"Strangely, so many of her critics comment on her appearance," Verboom said.

"Isn't that beside the point?"

"Exactly! They reduce her to her beauty. And of course, I knew nothing of that. All I had was her voice. It was all I needed." He exhaled, irritated. "Someone even called her a Jezebel! It's sexist and incoherent! If she were just conventionally attractive, she'd be just that—another beautiful woman. But she's a profound teacher, an empath, a clairvoyant! Her mind is magic. Her voice is hypnotic. I'll never understand why people say, 'Oh, so-and-so just got this job because they're good-looking.' It's absurd. If all people needed was a beautiful face, they could just flip through the JCPenney catalog."

"So, she knocked your socks off."

"Right off!" He clapped his hands, then looked at me. "You'll see for yourself."

9

Genevieve's right-wing detractors also fixated on her status as a single divorcée. For nearly two decades, she had endured the same judgment: Where was her husband? Who fathered her child? Why did she need to preach? Couldn't she accept the roles God had ordained? These questions weren't concerns for her community or for three-quarters of Americans, but they mattered deeply to those casting stones from the rightmost flank. And that quarter of Americans who did care? They made up half of all voters—the ones who now called themselves *Conservatives*.

What political scientists called "The Great Sort" culminated after the president's historic election. The Right scrambled to rename and rebrand. Their two-term president had embarrassed them—bungling speeches and botching wars in the Middle East. Rather than expand the tent, they zipped it shut. Showing little interest in preserving the status quo, they sought a radical "return" to a "past" that never existed. No longer the party of Abraham Lincoln, they officially renamed the party *Conservative*. Even though the name no longer fit in any literal sense, it sounded better than the alternatives.

Riding high on electoral success, the other party decided to embrace the Conservatives' name-calling and "own" the label of "liberal." The speaker of the house said in a disjointed fit of glee: "You want to call us liberal; fine, we are proud to be the *Liberals*." She said "the Liberals" like a ghost going *BOOO* on Halloween.

Why not be proud? The president was a gifted speaker and writer.

He could sink a three-point shot in street clothes without warming up. His coalition was broad, and his success historic. Though not an official name change, the label became ubiquitous. Party strategists knew the label stunk, as their ranks held conservatives, moderates, liberals, and progressives alike. But Madam Speaker had misspoken. After the midterm election, she became Minority Leader.

While reviewing Genevieve's biography and philosophy, Verboom delivered a sermon of his own as we drove. Most of us, he argued, find it easier to feel the love we give than to believe in the love we receive. And if the divine could accept you, maybe you could accept yourself.

"It's like trusting big data not to extort you," I said, trying to summarize while we drove.

"Keep your technology out of my theology!" Verboom declared in mock outrage, once again clutching imaginary pearls. "Say, do we have any snacks? Perhaps chocolate in peanut butter!"

"Does Genevieve do religion or self-help?"

"How would you draw that line?"

"Does her program require God?" I asked.

"If God is in fact *God*... Then what does that *mean*?"

"Since Genevieve isn't here, I'm asking you."

"God is God. There is no pronoun, not even a noun!"

"You ready for a quiet contest?"

"Speaking of nouns, the guy who taught Modern Theology at my college didn't *get* Hegel. Can you believe that? That's like trying to milk a cow without knowing what an udder looks like." Verboom shook his head. "I must confess that I don't get Hegel either—but I sure do love his way with words! He said, 'Only one man ever under-*stood* me. And he didn't under*stand* me.' What a goofball, playing around with time and tenses!"

"Shall I turn on the radio?"

"And time, Santo. Time! In my forties, I find myself returning to childhood again and again. Those years are more alive to me than my twenties and thirties."

"That must be helpful professionally."

Verboom described to the spiritual experiences of his teens—altar calls that made his spine shiver as he met divinity through the preaching of the holy word. In his denomination none of the stodgy Dutch ministers, the *dominies*, called anyone down to the front of the sanctuary, unless they'd been busted for adultery. But at weekend youth retreats, the pastors took a page from their more flamboyant brethren in other sects, summoning the young lambs down to the chapel's stage for a frenetic rebirth.

"Come. Come! COME down to the altar to meet your God!" Verboom hollered a reenactment.

And there, at the front of the chapel, stood Verboom with his big Dutch head in a sea of other Dutch heads. They were American kids, but they also thought of themselves as Dutch, even though, like Verboom, they understood little of the mother tongue.

When I asked about his first altar call, he said he'd been born again—even though, apparently, he'd already been predestined for salvation. Then I asked about the second. He said it would be too embarrassing for me.

"For *me*?" I asked. "It's *your* altar call..."

"I asked to be healed of compulsive masturbation."

"You're right. I'm embarrassed."

Hardline, not mainline, the church of Verboom's youth was traditionalistic and fussy about doctrine. "Sophisticated fundamentalists," he called them. They argued about *infralapsarianism* versus *supralapsarianism*—real words, though they sound like nonsense sung by Julie Andrews in *Mary Poppins*. Divorce was rare, even as the national rate hovered around 50%. Members tended to marry within the church, either by meeting in the church's singles groups or attending one of the denomination's colleges. Verboom described it as a "successful breeding program," then corrected himself: "successful *inbreeding* program."

In Verboom's youth, men smoked pipes, even in the church parking lot. Drunkenness was frowned upon, but alcohol wasn't considered inherently evil, as it often is among evangelicals. Though some members upheld Puritan-like piety, they remained a minority. According to Verboom, the church's defining spirit was an obsession with the purity of belief and a deep antipathy to all things *liberal*. "Reformed" was the most sacred label—provided it was understood in the 16th-century sense. Verboom's church followed the paper papacy of John Calvin. He gave me the whole story once again in the truck.

"How important is this?" I interrupted.

"It affects us all *today*! For the heirs of Calvin every aspect of life must be brought under God's control. They claim each 'sphere' of life is 'sovereign' and contained by its own rules, but in practice, all the rules are found in the comprehensive worldview of Calvinism. While it's not spelled out as totalitarian, in practice, every thought and act must be submitted to God's law. Tell me how that's not theocracy?"

"We can't let you back on the radio."

"Not to worry, Santo. A groovier thinker will come up with a better name than *Sphere Sovereignty*, maybe like the *Five Pillar Mandate*—a whole guidebook on how to take control of society. Some kind of catchy blueprint for how God's people can command the commanding heights."

"*Spear Sovereignty*? Why does this sound so familiar?"

"*Sphere Sovereignty*. I repeat myself. A family curse."

"That's it! Your *Final Freedom* rant! *You're the one who made it groovy!*"

"Man-o-man." Verboom slapped his forehead. "Glad I wasn't there—consciously speaking—when it happened!"

"All those decades of fundamentalism came pouring out in your rant. No wonder it felt so fluid, so natural. You were uncorked!"

"Oh Santo, in my tribe, you'll find the most sophisticated schemers for theocracy. They never say the word directly, the craziest might say *theonomy*, but usually they use words like *reconstruction* and *transformation*. And what they mean here is making every aspect of culture and society obedient to God!"

"You still don't remember *Final Freedom*?"

"I saw the billboard, what else is there?"

"You handed America a blueprint for theocracy!"

"Thought you said it was ironic. Good old sarcasm, like when you have students chatting in your class instead of listening to your talk, so you subtly work your way over to them, then turn on them theatrically and say, 'Please speak up so we can all hear you! In fact, let *me* be quiet! I wouldn't want to interrupt your thought. *And* let me turn up the lights and turn off my slides! I want to make sure you can see each other!' Don't all teachers do that when they get low blood sugar?"

"This wasn't a classroom. You did it on live radio!"

His eyes were closed, still thinking of childhood. "My people didn't even believe in free will. Some even mocked our lot as the frozen chosen. Because God chose who was saved from hell, you didn't hear talk about 'having a relationship with Jesus' or 'asking Jesus into your heart' like all these evangelicals today—not until you got to high school youth group retreats, where the theology loosened up in the collective overload of virgin pheromones."

"I can see why one part of your radio audience thought the whole show was a parody, and the other God's honest truth. *Pacific*

Monthly says you've become an 'accidental prophet.'"

"Like all young prophets, I had *massive* libido. As a student, moderation did not seem possible. My size made me awkward, even among tall Dutch girls. And though more extreme, abstinence seemed more practical. Conveniently, church dogma stated that sex required marriage."

"Enforced pair-bonding. I get it. Would you *really* prefer to talk about your childhood than this political movement? The movement running truck convoys with *your* slogan on their flags?"

"When I lost my baby fat and became the blonde swan chased by the girls at church, I took no joy in it. I'd already been conditioned to fear unsanctioned acts of breeding—simulated or otherwise."

I reached for the radio. "NPR or jazz?"

"Without stain, Santo. I wanted to be without stain. And now it sounds like I'm hocking laundry products."

"Enough about cleanliness."

"It's lunchtime, Santo, have you made a decision for *rice*? Do you have *rice* in your heart?"

We pulled off Sunset Boulevard for gas. Verboom lowered the sun visors and asked to stay in the truck, requesting potato chips and an iced tea from the gas station's mini-mart. Then he handed me a hundred-dollar bill from his fanny pack.

"Thought you invited rice into your heart?" I asked.

"Too many security cameras. I'll stay in the cab."

After gassing up and buying snacks at the edge of Thai Town, I hopped a low wall made of blocks and popped inside a family-run restaurant to grab pineapple fried rice for Verboom.

"The Venice Canals remind me of my twenties," he said. He refused to use the plastic spoon provided and scooped the fried rice with potato chips, continuing his story with food in his mouth. "That's when I dubbed myself 'The Last Flying Dutchman,' brooding alone in my boat, endlessly in search of my better half. Not a damsel, but my *Self* in the World behind the world. The *Self* as described in the letters of the saints and the martyrs—the good and eternal and definite essence—without ambiguity and contradiction. I was a man without a home, Santo. No place to place my wooden shoes."

"Have you ever owned wooden shoes?"

"Of course not, I'm speaking *cosmically*."

"You mean *culturally*."

"I sailed so far and long that I'd become fully absent from my flesh. This ability to separate mind from body probably came from being a chubby kid—*no better preparation for Dutch Calvinism*! I despised my appearance and felt perpetually embarrassed for simply existing in public. Then I'd feel guilty for *feeling* bad about my appearance. The superficiality of it! So, I'd take a trance to nowhere. I couldn't hide, mind you. I was plump *and* tall. At least until I turned fifteen—then the whole *swan* thing." He paused, then smiled. "But forget all that. We're here!"

Genevieve's self-realization center was an old A-frame building painted pure white. Formerly a Presbyterian church, the cross on the steeple had been replaced by a metal peace symbol—welded together from scraps, its seams and rust plainly visible. The campus included a mid-sized educational building, a broad parking lot, and a wood-shingled bungalow surrounded by large leafy trees.

"Is she expecting us?"

"She has a 'public' ministry. Are we not the public?"

10

The parking lot was empty. Verboom stepped out of the truck. I followed him around the old church building to the security gate outside of Genevieve's bungalow.

He pushed the buzzer.

"Come in, Pieter."

The gate lock clicked open.

"How'd you know it was me?" Verboom asked.

"There's a camera, darling."

He flinched and instinctively raised an arm like the sun was in his eyes.

"Come around the back," she said.

Genevieve opened the door as we approached. She wore a white A-line gown, adorned with delicate beading, its cape sleeves draping fully over her arms. Her eyes were bright, her hair thick and wavy.

"You're ready for an *appearance*!" Verboom marvelled. "Where is everyone?"

"I'm meeting a reporter in our sanctuary, so I decided to go with my Sunday best."

"We won't keep you," I said.

"Let's have a quick cup of tea," she offered.

I expected more of an earthy guru vibe, but Genevieve carried herself with a 1920s aristocrat's elegance—classic style, exquisite textures. Not a frumpy intellectual, not an over-primped televangelist, she appeared young, but her serenity felt too seasoned for someone looking so young.

We sat in her kitchen nook while she heated water in a copper kettle on the vintage stovetop, and prepped mugs and tea.

"I'll take black tea. As long as it's not *English* breakfast," Verboom requested.

"For you, Santo?"

I hesitated. "How do you know my name?"

"You're almost all Pieter talks about."

Before I could respond, Verboom pushed back his chair. "May I use the restroom?" he asked, already walking away.

Genevieve watched him disappear, then quickly sat down beside me, leaning in close. "The man has a big bladder, but we don't have much time."

"Okay..."

"Are you worried he's gone mad?"

"Are you?" I countered.

She exhaled softly. "I see no signs of physical illness, but I think..."

"*What*?"

"A spiritual crisis." She studied me. "When he left the church, he thought he'd freed himself."

"That was decades ago."

"Yes, and in that time, he's put himself in a new set of constraints. Liberalism is a godless Protestantism. He's replaced 'God' with 'Truth.' And now he's finally coming apart."

"*Coming* apart? So, he's getting worse?"

"You'd be a better judge. I've only been with him a handful of times."

I sighed. "He's gone from eccentric to goofy. He's a scientist, but he quotes scripture before sex."

She gave a knowing nod. "He wants to be carefree but doesn't know how. He's mired in regret."

"Regret?"

"I hear the plumbing." She glanced toward the hallway, then lowered her voice. "Could you take a small detour? Let him follow his fancy a bit longer? He needs space to be free before he can be truly free. He needs someone to believe in him."

Despite wanting to be polite, I sneered. "A gigantic Dutchman with a Ph.D. and cash falling out of his fanny pack needs to be *believed in?*"

"He's tender but repressed."

"His chatter is too much."

"The new show would help with that."

"No way the producers will take him back."

"It's not about the audience. It's the format that matters. And I may have a solution: go DIY."

"He's a virtual Luddite—still prefers pencil and paper."

"The technical part would be your contribution. Someone on my production team can help set you up. Pieter said you wanted to make documentaries in high school. And in a way, aren't you already doing that with your audio recordings. Why not test that early interest? What's the worst that could happen?"

"Verboom blacks out and starts another fanatical movement."

"I find it hard to believe Pieter inspired those men."

"You're not seeing the convoys?"

"A show provides the structure he needs to talk—to free his mind."

I shook my head. "He's 47 years old, he should have figured things out by now."

"That's what *he* thinks. And that thought only makes him feel worse. Spiritually, he's a child. Remember that when you look at him."

"A gigantic, bearded, lumbering child who's hellbent on giving lectures to people who don't want them."

Verboom sauntered up to the kitchen table.

"Pieter, I was on the verge of telling Santo about the spare apartment in Seattle. It's yours to use—stay as long as you like. Plenty of space to start your new show!"

"Just want to see the Space Needle," he said matter-of-factly.

"So you can feel like a child again, full of *wonder*."

"You *are* clairvoyant!" Verboom reveled.

"You mentioned it before."

"We can't keep Santo from his girlfriend—a pretentious Neo-Freudian in the English department, who lectures on depth psychology without knowing a thing about the scientific method. Sorry, Santo, just calling balls and strikes."

"It's good to voice your opinions," Genevieve said. "Even if they're negative."

"That was my dad's job in our house," Verboom said.

"In Seattle: my apartment, my rules. You'll always be free to speak your piece." She grinned and rose to her feet.

"Some coffee, some donuts, the Space Needle... maybe a night or two. Then we're back to Michigan. Santo must miss his lady friend."

Genevieve glanced at me. "I'll call ahead to the property manager *and* my production team." Her expression asked, *You're okay with this?*

"A bit more than I expected, but it sounds nice." It didn't, but I was still keen to avoid Grand Rapids. Verboom didn't know that my mom had passed or that the Neo-Freudian was now my ex. Most of the time, I appreciated his disinterest in my personal life, but occasionally, his obliviousness hit a nerve.

"The reporter will be here any moment." Genevieve said as if a timer had rung.

"Why the interview?" I asked.

"Other than the Pentecostals, our church is the only one in town that's growing."

"So you *are* a church?" I said with a *gotcha* tone.

"A fellowship without dogma."

"A self-realization center?" I asked.

"It's a lot easier to say 'church.'" She smiled without reservation. "Perhaps you'll walk me over."

"Genevieve has helped me realize I'm not self-realized," Verboom submitted.

"That's the first step, darling."

The way she said *darling*, I caught a trace of a Southern accent.

She led us through the house to the front porch. The home was filled with green plants and black-and-white pictures of her daughter. At the front steps, she offered us each an arm. Verboom still wore his crisp *gi* and orange running shoes, while I had on a white tee shirt, distressed jeans, and classic sneakers.

We escorted her to the church building. The news van had arrived, and the cameraman hoisted his camera to record our approach. I glanced over at Verboom, his eyes were closed, savoring Genevieve's hand on his arm

"Are these your bodyguards," the reporter asked, extending her mic.

"More like guardian angels," Genevieve said.

Verboom kissed Genevieve's hand and stayed bent forward so she could kiss his cheek.

I nodded a bit awkwardly, almost bowing.

Then Verboom spotted the camera. He threw up his hands and bolted for the truck.

Still locked, he hopped up into its bed and laid flat, out of sight. He hollered something in Dutch. I jogged over and unlocked the truck. He slithered out of the pickup's bed and into the front seat, slouching low as we pulled away.

"Good thing we didn't stay any longer." Verboom exhaled dramatically.

"They won't show your face on the news," I assured him.

"Another ten feet with her hand on my arm..." He ran a hand through his beard. "I could barely fight off my arousal."

"I assumed you were exaggerating about her... her whole *being*."

"You never use 'being' as a noun! You *are* impressed!"

"You're rubbing off on me."

"I'm *clean*, Santo baby! Nothing to rub off!"

"I'll take your word for it."

"So, can we make Seattle in two days?"

"It's eighteen hours of drive time. Then a few nights at Genevieve's, and back to Michigan?"

"Let's not wear out our welcome."

"How did she get the place?" I asked.

"She's a modern thinker with roots in fundamentalism. Her views reflect 19th-century German theologians like Schleiermacher, the guy who said religion is the 'feeling of absolute dependence.' She also likes that 'ultimate concern' guy—another German, this one from the 20th century... What's his name? *Tillich!*"

"That's not what I asked."

"According to these theologians, you meet divinity through experience."

"Isn't that how you meet anything?"

"Careful what you call a *thing*, Santo! Genevieve emphasizes the intuition at the seat of knowing. Something you can testify to, but not demonstrate."

"So, she admits that she can't prove her beliefs..."

"How could she? She voyages mysterious mysteries, not the

yucky legalisms of political ideologues and moral purists." Verboom beamed. "A sparse intro, but what do you think about her thinking?"

"Sounds like she's tried to find the nice parts of western religion. And you're implying that her theology is why she's well-loved, and why someone would give her an apartment."

"If you say so."

"Can't you give me a clear answer?"

"She may have mentioned that a distant aunt left it to her. A rental property, something about 'passive income.'"

"That makes sense."

"I laughed so hard when she said 'passive income' that she quit talking."

As we reached the Grapevine—a steep, winding stretch of Interstate 5, climbing the Tehachapi Mountains—Verboom tried to describe Genevieve's charisma. He took a breath, gazed through the truck's moon roof for a moment, then leaned in close like a drunk.

"She makes you feel like you're on drugs—like everyone's on drugs—but nobody's on drugs."

"There's palpable chemistry between you two."

"I wonder what's wrong with her."

"Why do you say things like that?"

"'Let me offer you a reading,' she said the first time we met. 'I have a way of cutting to the quick—quickly. Now, close your eyes and tell me: what do you *want*?' 'Payback,' I said. But after I said it, I was surprised."

"You're not so dispassionate after all."

"'Revenge?' she asked. 'You want revenge?'"

I shook my head, listening to his reenactment.

"And again, I answered without thinking. '*Yes*.'"

"You gave her a one-word answer? She *did* cast a spell on you."

"So, Genevieve asks, 'Who?'"

"Well, *who* is it?"

"'The callers mocking me,' I said to her. Then she asks 'How?'"

"And?"

"You already know. She blessed the new show as a way of doling out revenge."

"I thought the project was self-realization."

"It's not mutually exclusive, Santo. Did you ever take a philosophy class?"

"Her *reading* sounds like a series of open-ended questions."

"She read me like a beat-up pamphlet on the death of the Enlightenment."

"Thought the stars of Hollywood Boulevard inspired you?"

"She laid bare my unconscious motivation."

"With your head in the clouds, how do you see the stars?"

"Don't know if I'm 'lost at sea' or 'out to lunch.'"

"You're out-to-sea losing your lunch," I said.

"So you *do* get Hegel!" Verboom beamed.

"You should have stuck with philosophy; its fuzzy wordplay suits you."

"So much *BEING*, so little *TIME*!" he howled and banged on the ceiling.

In psychology you learn that the best way to extinguish a behavior is to ignore it. I stared ahead silently.

"As a man of science, Santo, you'll appreciate the naturalistic turn in my conversation with Genevieve. She says, 'Since I advised you, would you offer me a consultation?' I say, 'Tell me how!' Now listen to *this*—she drops the robe off her shoulders and stands up. 'Tell me honestly,' she says, 'do I look like a 42-year-old woman?' Santo, she asked me for a forthright assessment of her earthen vessel!"

"Nothing under her robe?"

"Nothing but epidermis!"

"I don't want to hear more."

"Though given modest breasts, she has a wildly curvaceous set of upright buns—exceptional skin tone. She's ageless!" Verboom fanned himself like an old lady in church. "You know, in the early grades, we sang a ditty about what girls were made of: 'Sugar and spice and everything nice.' Then the boys: 'Snakes and snails and puppy dog tails.'"

"And what did that song teach you?"

"Rhyme."

He hummed the song through a few times before clamming up. Then he broke the silence.

"I always took words too seriously. I wanted to know their deeper meanings," he said, his voice thick with eerie earnestness. "My obsession with the precision of language made me an outcast..."

"Wasn't it your gigantism?"

"Now I'm lost in qualifications. Lost and found, lost and found... The words are here, then gone. Then they mean too much. Then nothing."

At this point, I didn't want to use any words.

"Thinking about the word 'God' got me in the most trouble." He shuddered. "Just saying the word—good thing I'm sitting. I'll do my best to tell you this story without actually thinking about it." He took a deep breath, looking out the side window for a moment.

"You thinking about jumping?" I asked.

"In high school, I wanted to understand the meaning of divine omniscience. I think most kids were happy with the definition: 'all-knowing.'" Verboom clap-wiped his hands. "Done and done."

"Textbook."

"To get to the real *meaning*, I started reflecting on the complexity of my mind."

"Thinking about thinking."

"Exactly. Then, I imagined another mind—just as complex. Then a third mind, a fourth mind, all simultaneously. While trying to inhabit them at once, I added a fifth super-mind, one that could judge the previous minds with even greater awareness and feeling." He exhaled sharply. "Well, somewhere in there, I fainted."

"Like fell-on-the-floor fainted?"

"*Ja*. My brother Willem found me after hearing the thud. Said it took a few minutes for me to come to."

"What did the doctor say?"

"*Doctor*? Good one, Santo. My dad gave me a tongue-lashing for thinking too much. Said I should spend my energy on real work... A fair point."

"He wasn't worried?"

"He never expressed empathy. Only directions."

"Had a few coaches like that."

"I still get woozy flashbacks whenever I slip into deep contemplation of divine knowing."

"Maybe you confused knowledge with consciousness. I know a lot of words, but I'm only conscious of a few at a time."

"Watch it, Santo. I feel my *being* tipping back, like a teeter-totter that only goes one direction. Like a Ferris wheel spinning backward and down. Like I did that time in high school. Like I'm going to fall into the black forever and ever and ever and ever..."

"You mean faint?"

"Maybe I'll just close my eyes."

Looking over, I saw the color had drained from his face. His expression rested in agony.

Coming down The Grapevine, Verboom opened his eyes, returning from his fall into oblivion. He leaned across the center console, his voice barely above a whisper.

"I tell you too much. It's unseemly. Don't tell anyone. They'll hate me for being so ungrateful. I grew up on the farm with milk, eggs, and pork, while some people didn't even have a pot to piss in." He sighed, shivering at the thought. "It's just that when I look into your green eyes, I feel like you understand. But then, you must also see how selfish I am. Forgive me. It can't be easy to know your advisor is always on the verge of tears."

"Haven't noticed."

"Tell me when people start catching on. This will be our secret."

"What secret?" I said, winking in assurance.

"It seems I'm coming apart at the seams," Verboom muttered.

"I'm not acknowledging the secret—I'm keeping it so well."

"If Ella saw me like this, she'd never jump my bones."

"I don't think anyone has said 'jump my bones' since the '80s."

"And Genevieve... she's got a heart of gold, but seeing a man in this state—*gaaah*. All she'd have left for me is pity. I've been told by modern people that women love sensitive men as consorts, but I don't believe it."

"If by sensitive, you mean blubbering about the cosmos, probably not."

"What else does sensitive mean?"

"Aware. Caring. Alert to others' feelings. Sharing your own, too."

"Make sure no one finds me! I can't keep my private thoughts private anymore."

11

As we traveled north, handmade political signs lined the freeway:

CONGRESS CREATED THIS DUSTBOWL

NO WATER / NO JOBS

FOOD GROWS WHERE WATER FLOWS

WHITE HOUSE MAKES BROWN FIELDS

IT'S CALLED 'THE WHITE HOUSE' FOR A REASON

FINAL FREEDOM NOW

"Do you have a can of spray paint?" he muttered. "I'd like to revise these signs."

"Fresh out."

Verboom leaned back in his seat. "So, how's it going with the recordings?"

"Still rolling."

"And the content analysis? Am I a promising case study for your next big paper?"

"It's only been a few hours since you asked. I still haven't listened."

"*Really?* How will we know what the words add up to?"

"Want to take over?"

He scoffed. "A hill of beans. That's how my mother would've described it. She loved American clichés. They sounded so strange to her Dutch ear. In fact, she once bought a book just because the title made her laugh so much."

"What was it?"

"*If Life Is a Bowl of Cherries, Why Am I in the Pits?*"

When he ran out of ideas, he read aloud every road sign and bumper sticker as though a blind man was driving him north. With nothing but the expanse of browning fields and the drone of Verboom's voice, I gave the radio another try—this time FM. We picked up an NPR broadcast from Bakersfield.

> *In a major setback for US counterterrorism efforts, a leaked report suggests that a covert operation to capture OBL has been compromised. According to sources within the Pentagon, two Black Hawk helicopters carrying an elite Navy SEAL team departed from an airfield in Afghanistan shortly after midnight, flying low to avoid detection as they entered Pakistani airspace en route to the compound of the world's most wanted man. However, during the assault, one of the helicopters reportedly clipped a security wall while deploying troops, forcing a crash landing and turning the mission into a high-stakes rescue operation.*
>
> *The incident forced an immediate shift in strategy, with SEALs from the second helicopter providing cover for their stranded teammates as gunfire erupted between US forces*

and armed security within the compound. A third helicopter was dispatched to extract the downed team members.

At this time, it remains unclear whether there have been any casualties. The White House has declined to confirm or comment on the details of the mission, and the Pakistani government has yet to issue an official response. A statement from the US president is expected later this evening...

I clicked the 'seek' button. The radio cycled through stations, pausing briefly—three seconds of static-laced voices, then moving on. Every station carried either commercials or urgent updates on the failed mission. Hoping for a reprieve, I stopped on an advertisement, thinking music might follow. Instead, the broadcast returned to breaking news.

REPORTER: *Reactions are pouring in as the world absorbs the news from Pakistan. We now go to downtown Tucson, where Sheriff James Kroes—one of the president's most vocal critics—is addressing a self-styled "patriot rally." Let's listen in live:*

KROES: *Fellow patriots, as the sheriff of Pima County for almost three decades now, I thought I'd seen it all. But today—this happens. The so-called president gets some of our finest boys shot-up and humiliated! If the president knew where America's most wanted man was hiding, there was just one thing to do: drop a warhead on that rat's nest and be done with it! No helicopters, no risky nighttime raids—just good old American hellfire!*

Now, I've never been one for politics. Never thought much about sitting in the Oval Office. But I'll tell you this: if I were commander-in-chief, this would have been over on day one. Jim would get him!

CROWD: *GET HIM JIM! GET HIM JIM! GET HIM JIM!*

KROES: *Talking about OBL? Or the president?*

CROWD: *GET THEM JIM! GET THEM JIM! GET THEM JIM!*

KROES: *...Now, now. You know that I'm a lawman, not some greasy politician. I've got no appetite for the spotlight. And with this so-called president welcoming every gang-banger from Panama to Mexico, there's plenty to do here on our border...*

CROWD: *RUN JIM, RUN! RUN JIM, RUN! RUN JIM, RUN!*

KROES: *...I hear you, fellow patriots! And I'll tell you what—if you love freedom, if you want a real leader in the White House, then you're gonna have to draft me. I don't play the DC game. If you want me, if the votes are out there, I can promise you this: Jim will get them!*

REPORTER: *All right, we're going to pull back from Tucson, where Sheriff James Kroes—hailed by supporters as "America's toughest cop"—delivered what sounded like* *the opening salvo of a presidential bid. While speculation around Kroes has swirled for years, most analysts dismiss his chances outright. Beyond his incendiary rhetoric, his record is filled with deeply controversial policies. He famously limited prisoners to two meals a day and forced inmates to wear purple uniforms. His infamous Tent City—where temperatures inside the canvas structures soared past 130 degrees—was later described by Kroes himself as a "concentration camp." He also introduced the nation's first chain gang for incarcerated women, earning national outrage after quipping, "It's the kind of feminism I dig." But perhaps most alarming to civil rights groups, he deputized a private militia to detain suspected undocumented immigrants—justifying his actions by invoking the Second Amendment.*

"Think I'll get blamed for the SEALs too?" Verboom asked.

"Did you ever talk foreign policy at the E.C.S.?"

"*Nay*. Just the contours of *theological incorrectness*. The greatest threat to our democracy."

"Missing OBL and losing the SEALs is going to scramble the election. Can Kroes still get on the ballot?" I asked.

He answered flatly, staring out the window. "Fifty states. Fifty sets of rules. Each state has different deadlines."

"And signatures, it takes hundreds of thousands."

"I'm not an expert, Santo, but it's important to remember that electoral requirements vary from state to state. However, with a third party in the race, remember: under the winner-take-all system, a candidate doesn't need a majority to win a state's Electoral College votes—just more than anyone else. Kroes could win a state's Electoral College with well below 50% of its popular vote. There's even a scenario where Kroes could become president with around 30% of the national popular vote, depending on how votes are distributed across the states."

"Sheriffs are elected, right? They run for office just like a governor. He's as much politician as lawman." I shook my head. "And he sounds nutty enough to run as a publicity stunt. He's terrible."

"Not to a third of America," he said, still staring to the side. "Playing his speech is free advertising."

"But if they don't cover him, then he may..."

"*What*? Sneak up on us?" He turned toward me. "No! He should be totally ignored, like I'm trying to do now."

And there it was. I finally found the one topic to shut Verboom up: James Kroes.

Deep in the endless flatlands of the Central Valley, the interstate stretched arrow-straight, flanked by fields of corn, almonds, pistachios, cotton, and wheat. Verboom claimed he could distinguish each crop by scent, but all I could detect was a dank funk wafting from the open-lot dairy farms.

My phone wouldn't stop buzzing, cutting short Verboom's lecture on the varieties of manure odors. He groaned and shot me a look. "Can you silence that thing!"

I flipped it over. Another missed call from Ella Walker.

"Your fiancée," I said wryly.

Verboom yanked his *gi* up over his head, like he'd done with his jacket on WNN's *Hot Button Science*.

"I'm not here," came the muffled reply.

"Ignoring her hasn't stopped her." The phone beeped with the arrival of another voicemail. We better hear what she has to say."

I pressed play.

"Santo, I know you're upset. After Flagstaff, I wouldn't trust me either. But you have to understand—the professor is like no one else, and I must have him. He feels the same way, I know it. Attraction this strong can't be hidden. I'm going to find him. Let's do this the easy way. Tell me where he is."

Verboom burst in: "You *can't* tell her, Santo!"

"Do you think I *want* to see her?"

He squinted. "Wait. What happened in Flagstaff?"

I exhaled. "She turned the camera on me."

Verboom blinked. "You better get a disguise."

"What's your plan?"

"Plan?"

"What are you going to do when she finds you?"

"*When?*"

"*If.*"

He shrugged. "Depends on the circumstances... Can we talk about something else? I'm feeling faint."

He lowered his window, letting in a warm blast of farm air.

I raised his window and hit the child lock, then scanned the local stations until finding a clear signal.

The local host teed up the next program: *The Fritz Hearn Show.* Though Hearn grated on me, I couldn't deny his talent as an entertainer.

The station ran an ad for a chain of regional pawnshops, followed by spots for a truck dealership, a bottled iced tea brand, and a "male enhancement" supplement. Then, one final pitch, a sausage producer was now selling an instant coffee, "perfectly paired" for their microwavable breakfast sandwiches. The show returned.

Let's thank the renowned economist Bill Willingham for filling in on the show last week. No working economist does a better impersonation of the president. And no working economist has so deftly dissected this president's lousy impersonation of being a president. And before you Libs lose any more of your marbles, please note that Professor Willingham is, how should we say, well he is of the right complexion, even under the most censorious political correctness, to make such pantomime. Other talkers on the Right denigrate academia, but I think we should cherish the few gems we have. While 90% of professors are raging Liberal blowhards, if not full-blown Communists, we still have some wonderful exceptions, like Dr. Willingham. So, let's not throw out the baby with the BONG WATER!

Here in the mists of Manhattan, I see things as they truly are, and today I tell you: the time is now. The convoys. The rallies. Our grand demonstration of political force is working. Freedom is within our grasp! We cannot take our foot off the gas. This so-called president must resign or suffer the consequences. This isn't a realignment of American politics; it's the last gasp of liberalism!

"But Fritz, you can't threaten the president," Hearn said in a fake, high-pitched whining voice.

I'm not threatening, folks. I'm just offering some free advice: Leave. For the good of the Republic. As I've said from day one, the man is incapable of leading the free world. And now? Now we have the ultimate proof. Instead of executing the mastermind of 9/11, he's given us a masterclass in failure.

You can't surrender our SEALs to the terrorists and expect to patch it up with an eloquent speech. You can't juke the press with a crossover dribble and pretend it never happened. This isn't a game. There's nothing more to say. No time for impeachment. We're making our case in the streets.

Now, your friends or neighbors may not share our patriotic spirit—they may think the president simply got some bad luck, a gust of wind at the wrong moment—so remind them of what we already know:

One, he will not wear the flag pin. He disowns the flag every day he goes to work. Where does his allegiance lie?

Two, he will not refer to America as a Christian Nation; in fact, he thinks religion entered politics to manipulate the masses! He claims your pastors have brainwashed you into doing the will of corporate fat cats. Sure, he's for "Main Street not Wall Street." He pretends like he gives a rat's ass about small business and 'genuine spirituality,' but it's all pandering.

Perhaps I could muster an ounce of respect for the man, if he'd come clean and say what he means. If he'd come out of the closet and admit he's a full-blown Marxist.

"Fritz! You've gone too far. He seems like a decent man! He's got a beautiful wife, two nice-looking kids," Hearn said in the same fake, high-pitched whining voice as before.

Do you think the devil comes as an angel of darkness or as an angel of light? Pardon the confusing metaphor, folks. Listen, it's no accident that the man looks good on TV. I'll give you that. He is telegenic. But since when has looking good on TV qualified someone to be president?

Three, he will not say "God bless America." He'll only say, "May there be peace on earth." He's trying to talk like he's Jesus, but he doesn't even believe in Jesus.

Four, and it's plain and simple folks, he's a wolf in sheep's clothing. A big phony shilling for the internationalists, the globalists, and all the other pompous elitists. America is NOT first in his heart. His border policy is an open-door policy. He'd rather bow to foreign dignitaries than fight to ensure your freedom. He wants red-blooded patriots replaced with immigrants who will make America last. He's made America a doormat for every "refugee" who wants to take your job.

Sheldon says, "We don't have enough Volvos!"

Sure, he may attend a Chicago church spouting a radical social gospel with preachers screaming damnation for America, but that's not true religion, that's the hateful speech of the Radical Left. And think, folks, really think. Just look at him. That smug know-it-all smile! Do you think this is a man who humbles himself before God? Think he's ever asked God to forgive a sin? This man does not love God and country, and he only pretends to love golf! FORE! He better duck. There're a lot of little white balls headed in his direction.

Sheldon says, "But he loves his wife!"

Do you think he has a choice? Do you think he even wears the pants in his own family?

Sheldon is screaming from the other side of the glass, "Yes, he does! Mom jeans! MOM JEANS!"

Indeed, my dear Sheldon, it could not be more apropos, more emblematic. The truth has a way of revealing itself, and sometimes that truth will be in acid wash!

Do not be fooled by this man's actions, his faithfulness to his wife and his loyalty to the Chicago White Sox are only part of his con! Of course, his biggest con is his claim to be a Christian! There's a reason we don't have OBL and the other terrorists—they're all brothers in the worship of Allah!

Now, before we go to break, let's take a moment to review what happened in the media yesterday. While the so-called president was busy handing our SEALs over to the jihadis, real patriots made history—taking it to the streets! And how did liberal media react? Pure meltdown. Let's roll the clip from WNN last night, so you can hear how the 'flyover' media is absolutely losing it:

RODGER: With demonstrations intensifying in every metropolitan area, it's hard to see how the president will be able to move on. Armed protesters are demanding the president leave office. Here in New York, I've seen vintage pistols, modern handguns, assault rifles, shotguns, hunting rifles, vintage grenades, and what looks like a World War II era flame thrower. In fact, the man's tee shirt says: "SCORCHING FLAMING LIBERALS."

RACHEL: Shocking. Just shocking.

RODGER: Sizzling, indeed, Rachel. Now without further inspection, I can't confirm if this mechanism is an actual flamethrower, but by golly, it sure does have the appearance of one, though it may be a prop...

Stop it! Stop it right there, Sheldon! Did you hear that, folks? Another hack journalist cannot believe what his God-given eyes are telling him. You know folks, if you don't accept the God who gives you those eyes then perhaps you can't actually see. Okay Sheldon, let it play.

RODGER: With this many guns, you'd think someone would've squeezed a round by accident, but nothing so far. There are thousands of men, marching with what appears to be thousands of firearms, but I have yet to hear one shot, only the sound of boots marching. Rachel, I must say, the sound of these boots on the street, almost in rhythm but not quite in rhythm, somewhere between a Russian ceremonial detail and an old-fashioned American mob; well, forgive me, but I must tell you, it's enthralling. I think we've underestimated the movement's discipline and organization.

RACHEL: What are they chanting?

RODGER: They're saying:

YOU...

CANNOT...

REPLACE US!

RACHEL: In Houston they're saying: NO YOU CAN'T! In San Francisco: HEY-HEY! HO-HO! THIS FED'RAL GOVERNMENT'S GOT TO GO! In Portland: SHUT IT DOWN. We'll continue to keep our viewers updated on more slogans as they emerge. And we encourage you at home to submit any protest-related video through our WNN portal, as you help us investigate who's behind this ominous group of protests.

Stop it there, Sheldon! WHO'S BEHIND THIS, Rachel? I'll tell you! Patriots demanding freedom! It's not a Super PAC, or some think tank, or the shock troops of some billionaire oil tycoon. Rodger is surprised by our 'discipline!' He's astounded that they're so well heeled. Meanwhile he can't hide his titillation for the sound of boots marching. Now folks, there were good patriots out there in running shoes too. Sneakers. Hell, maybe even a few pairs of loafers like we had down there in Miami-Dade for the so-called Brooks Brothers Riot of 2000! But they say "boots" because the word scares the tar out of Liberals! Men who wear boots work and fight.

"Mob," Rodger says. "An old-fashioned American mob!" Do you think he'd call a group of angry feminists marching on the Washington Mall a 'mob?' Would he call bra-burning feminists 'arsonists?' Do you think he would compare a group of Black Panthers to the North Koreans? Well of course not, and surprisingly the president has yet to give the Panthers a nuke, since he's all but handed one to North Korea.

And there you have it, the 'flyover' media besides itself in smug condemnation. Running from rally to rally—aghast, dismayed, afraid... The 'flyover' media needs to fly home. And the man occupying the White House must go home too—to his real home.

Hearn cut to a commercial break. The first advertisement hawked precious metals with a tone of urgent conspiracy: "The FED can't be trusted; inflation will quickly wipeout your hard-earned wealth. Act now! Secure your financial future with gold before the FED prints more worthless dollars and turns your hard-earned cash into toilet paper..."

Feeling a surge of annoyance, I turned the radio off. Though usually quick to offer his two cents, Verboom remained silent, his stillness mirroring the sudden quiet in the car.

An hour north, we pulled off Interstate 5 at a truck stop, its sun-baked lot shimmering with heat mirages, making the asphalt look wet in the distance. Inside the mini-mart, rows of glistening hotdogs spun lazily on their rollers, filling the air with the smell of saturated fat. One aisle overflowed with CB radios, charging cables, roadside repair equipment, hunting equipment, and camping gear. Another aisle had racks and racks of jerky, nuts, trail mix, chips, pretzels, sour gummies, chocolate bars, and other sugary items sure to rot your teeth while keeping you awake on the road. Two of the four walls were nothing but refrigerators, humming as they chilled an endless selection of beverages from energy drinks to French water.

I pre-paid for gas with cash and picked up a few essentials: aviator sunglasses, a bandana, and a trucker hat that read, "Don't Blame Me, I Voted for Willie." When I stepped back outside, the heat hit like a wall.

Back at the truck, Verboom was gone.

I scanned the lot while pumping gas but didn't spot him. The pump clicked off, and I holstered the nozzle, twisted the gas cap on, and slid into the driver's seat, which was now scorching from the sun. Still no sign of him.

While I eased the truck toward the street, he emerged from a small patch of trees, tying up his orange belt as he ambled.

"What were you doing?" I called out through the open passenger window.

"Irrigation."

"They have a restroom."

"And security cameras."

As the truck came to a stop, he yanked the door open and dropped into the seat. I let the truck roll forward before he could close his door. Once he buckled up, I handed him the trucker hat, held upside down like an offering plate with the bandana and sunglasses inside. He slid them on without hesitation.

"Who are Rodger and Rachel?" he asked.

"They do the *R&R* show on WNN."

"Too many letters."

"That reminds me. Grab that bag behind me."

Verboom reached back and ran his hand over the old canvas bag. He tugged at the zipper slowly, as if something might spring out. Once it was clear that nothing would pounce, he pulled the duffle bag onto his lap.

"By gummy!" he hollered. "A cache of correspondence!"

"No need to read any of it, just confirm your reception."

He leaned toward my mic. "Confirmed."

Taking an envelope by its corners, he gave it a shake. Then, retrieving the Swiss Army knife from his fanny pack, he flipped open the smallest blade and sliced through the fold. Slipping out the cover letter, he cleared his throat and read aloud:

> *How could you vanish without a word? Do you have any idea what you've done to me?*
>
> *I've retraced every conversation, trying—and failing—to understand how we got here. The last time I saw you, you stood before me stone-faced. And when I begged for the smallest scrap of sentiment, do you remember what you said? "My feelings are my feelings, and that's that."*
>
> *THAT'S THAT?*
>
> *Tell me something real, I'm asking you again. At least tell me where you are! I am worried sick. Come home, before I come looking for you...*

"It goes on like that," he said.

"Like a *telenovela*."

Studying the envelope, he said, "If we can trust the postal mark, it was sent after we left Grand Rapids, but before she located us in

Flagstaff."

"She delivered on her threat."

"Indeed. She delivers," he murmured, the words hanging there.

He took the Polaroid clipped to the back of the letter and placed it on the consol, studying the photo without comment. Ella was dressed in white shorts cut higher than her dresses, a snug white polo shirt, and a white cap.

"Tennis?" I asked.

"No, it's nautical. She's on a yacht still in harbor."

"Looks like you might be missing some fun on the high seas."

"Oh, that's not a sea. I'll bet you a *stroopwafel* it's Macatawa Bay!"

"Holland?"

"Holland, Michigan! I knew it! The Dutch mafia!"

"Walker doesn't sound Dutch."

"Perhaps it's been Anglicized from Van Wagoner."

"She's a natural on that yacht," I observed.

"Dare you say *leagues* out of my league?"

"She's objectively more attractive than you."

"Proof of the Dutch Mafia's hand at work! Now we must figure out if it's the soap people or the trash people?"

"Trash people?"

"The Dutch farmers who immigrated to Chicago slowly took over the trash business. Those husky boys didn't want to work in factories, and they couldn't afford farmland. Over generations they created the biggest private refuse company in the country, worth billions and billions. They got into car sales and VHS rentals, all kinds of products and services; they buy up companies in sectors that are small and local and then make the company national, even international. They've got people in auto parts, coffee, concrete, oil… got their hooks in almost everything."

"Proud of your cousins?"

"These people are dumping those billions into right-wing campaigns. Instead of giving it to the church, they're giving it to politicians and dark-money propaganda outfits. Think of it! They could feed the poor and provide medicine for all, but they'd rather buy off politicians to avoid taxes. They're savvy, by the way; for every million they donate to a politician, they save three million in taxes…"

"So, by 'mafia,' you mean businesspeople funding politics?"

"*Organized* Dutch Americans who mix hardline religion with hardline politics: ending public schools, social security, all social welfare programs… the opposite of Franklin Roosevelt, who ironically was of Dutch heritage. It's coordinated, Santo. They even want to privatize the military."

"Ella's a PR agent with Klinefelter and Klinefelter—clearly a German group. I don't think she's working with the Dutch mafia." I suppressed my laughter.

"She mentioned an internship with the soap people's marketing department."

"Remind me who the soap people are?"

"Santo, you live in Grand Rapids. Their names are on half the buildings in town."

"*Soap people?*"

"We're recording, don't make me say the names. Now they're into vitamins, nutritional supplements, and beauty supplies. But in the beginning, they sold soap! Lots of soap! They ask you out to coffee or grab your arm in the church parking lot, trying to sign you up as the next soap seller, and then you're supposed to do the same! The soap isn't the product, you are!"

"Your concern?"

"Ella is pregnant. She obviously doesn't love me, and now there's a *baby*! The poor child will be leverage. I'll be a suburban cuckold, while she *hastens the coming of The Kingdom of God for the Dutch*

Mafia!" he hollered.

"She's not pregnant, I just saw her."

"What did she wear? A mumu? Sun dress? Overalls?"

"Mid-length skirt, shirt, heels. All black."

"Black is slimming! Hiding the bump."

"You're way ahead of yourself."

"Santo, if the university takes me back, the student activists will make my life hell—I'll have to walk around in a slicker and goggles with all the vegan eggs they'll throw at me. I'm an accidental pariah..."

"*Prophet*. This morning *The New York Times* called you 'the accidental prophet of...'"

"And I deserve the vegan eggs and rotten tomatoes, my *getter* is in the gutter."

"Is that Dutch?"

"*Nay, nay*. I lost the thing that says you're getting it. *Get* it? The module in my brain that says 'aha' doesn't work anymore!"

"You sure it ever did?"

"Do *you* get me, Santo? If you don't, I don't know who will." He looked on the verge of tears.

"Now look. Both *The New York Times* and *Pacific Monthly* are calling you a prophet. You'll be fine, even if Ella is pregnant."

"If she is, I'll have to become a provisioner."

"You mean *provider*? She seems perfectly capable."

"*Provisioner*. I will need to *provision* valuable resources, like protein. Meat. That's the law of nature. I'll have to go work for the soap people as a market researcher, conducting focus groups and consumer interviews. '*Lavender or lemon*? What does *clean* smell like *to you*? How *foamy* do you like *your foaming* soap?'"

"*Meat* is not a law of nature."

"Santo darling, when you've got a family, you can't say 'no' to financial security. I'll be up to my ears in soap people while surrounded by trash people! Mowing the lawn, raking the leaves, *call me Sisyphus*!"

"You'll be rolling a giant meatball up a hill."

"Good one, Santo! Maybe you can do the new show?"

"Since your *getter* is in the *gutter*, let me tell you what I'm getting. Ella wants you. Bad. It's crystal clear. And it looks like she'll do just about anything to get you."

"Get *me*? Why?"

"You heard the voicemail. She needs you. No mystery. It's just not clear to me how far she'll go... Maybe you should see what else is in the envelope?"

He flipped through the contents. "There's a whole packet of news clippings. She typed a table of contents for her research, like we're still doing *Ask The Professor*:

Religion Predicts Voting Behavior More Than Economic Class

78% Of Americans Do Not Own A Gun

7 Journalists Killed In Baltimore Newsroom Massacre

Gun Sales Spike After Mass Shooting

Annual Gun Deaths in US Eclipse 33k

Annual US Deaths by Foreign Terrorist: 7

Annual Deaths by Domestic Right-wing Extremists: 42

> **36% of Americans Believe Natural Disasters Evidence of End Times, 6% Unsure**
>
> **Largest Christian University Opens Gun Range For Student Phys. Ed.**
>
> **African Nation Paid 220k To Meet President At National Prayer Breakfast**

...I'll stop there. Boy, she has a knack for finding strange stories." He took a deep breath.

"Ever heard of 'man bites dog'?"

"Well, I can't believe that would ever happen. Why not *'cow milks man'*?"

"The news is biased for the sensational. It's the business of human interest."

"*Huh*? Sorry, I was lost in thought. Trying to picture how a cow could milk a man—I mean, a man biting a dog is straightforward... Anyway, what were you saying? Looks like she's picked up my beat on theocracy, *ja*?"

"These stories..."

"*Ja*! She's helping me see the country for what it is. She even caught one on the First Brothers' breakfast."

"The president never showed," I reminded Verboom. "A bait and switch."

"Did you ever read *The Cross and the Switchblade*?"

"Never heard of it," I said.

"My sixth grade teacher read it to my class. He'd lost the tip of his left ring finger in a meat grinding accident and held his chalk in between that short ring finger and his middle finger, like it was a cigarette. He had an odd lisp and thick white hair. One day he gave us a *Reader's Digest* career quiz—we'd call it an *assessment* nowadays. Want to know my results?"

"Jester?"

"*Jeweler.*"

The Polaroid of Ella fell from the console, landing face down.

"What's written on the back of that picture?" I asked Verboom.

"'Macatawac Bay. April 22.' You owe me a *stroopwafel.*"

"Whose boat?"

"No idea. She told me not to ask about her personal life."

"You do whatever she says?"

"I can't say *no*, Nancy Reagan!" He flipped the picture around. "Which is why I must flee temptation! Sometimes I suspect her prowess is preternatural."

"I'm more of a natural man myself."

"She's uncanny," he said.

"Certainly canny. I understand that part, but why is she so hooked on you?"

"Thought she just had bad taste in men. But that's not very specific, so I asked her directly." He folded his arms.

"What did she say?"

"She said quit being so insecure."

"Do you trust her?"

"Of course not! I don't trust any woman who pretends to like me! Why do you think I fled Flagstaff? *Oh dear...* I hope you didn't take my departure personally."

"Think she's dangerous?" I asked.

"She wants me back on television to beef up my provisioning capacity. Now that we have a child on the way, she's trying to make me *America's Number One Social Psychologist.* More status. More meat."

I waited for him to ask my opinion of Ella, but the question never came; he stared out the window, lost in thought.

From the freeway, the oil fields stretched out, scores of pump-jacks nodding like thirsty birds dipping into the earth.

Verboom's hair was slicked back, hiding his thinning crown, but when he bent to pull up his socks, it was visible. He caught me looking.

"'A busy road gathers no moss,' as *pakke* Dijkstra used to say." He ran his hand over the top of his head, from back to front.

"You're thinking your hair off?"

"The thinning area is hotter than the rest of my scalp."

"You still have most of your hair. Then you must be using a very small part of your brain."

"The crucial work happens right here!" He smacked his forehead with his palm. "Feel the heat of my pre-frontal cortex! Never a hair there! Here's where all the abstractions are abstracted!"

"You may have confused the symptoms with the cause."

"Oh Santo, I just love anatomy. Takes your *brain* off your *mind*."

"Other than the Thai food, what did you eat the last few weeks?" I asked, pulling into a travel center.

"*Hmmm*. Any lamb on the lam? I can't say. Don't even remember tying my shoes. Buy me some slip-ons! I've gone off a cognitive cliff!"

"Better pull the ripcord."

"Fasting clears the mind. A requirement for all mystics."

"If your mind's so clear, why can't you remember what you ate?"

"Been dwelling on eternal verities, not mundane munchies! By the way, on my last exam at the sanitarium, the nurse said my body fat was 9%."

I chuckled. "Why would they tell you that?"

"Maybe rich folks can write off weight loss as a tax exemption."

I put the truck in park, stepped out, and started pumping gas.

Verboom, opened his door and stood next to me.

"*Tax exemptions*," he repeated. "Get it?"

"Next you'll be telling me the rich are losing weight so the hordes won't eat them."

Verboom snapped his fingers. "Exactly! If they stay lean, they're less appetizing. No marbling."

"Should I take you back to the clinic?"

"It's as though my failure to be a boring bump on a log has led you to conclude that I have the sanity of a hog."

"Easy on the hogs. Tell me more about LA."

"Genevieve will look you in the eyeball until you get uncomfortable."

"One eyeball?"

"One eyeball at a time."

"And..."

"She has a firm grip."

"And..."

"You know I carry stress in my shoulders."

"And..."

"She has incredible skin tone."

"You mentioned that."

"She came twice before penetration. Sexually, she's on a hair trigger." He paused. "It's the books. You should have seen her face when she saw the length of my bibliography. Sorry, am I out of bounds?"

"Where were your hands when all this happened?"

"'When you give, do not let your left hand know what your right hand is doing.' The Gospel of Matthew, Chapter 6."

"You don't know how she climaxed?"

"I ejaculated before penetration. It's a problem I have. Upside: technically, we did not fornicate—at least according to the narrowest definition. You're not going to tell Ella about this?"

"She's not your fiancée. She made that up to get past the receptionist."

"With my fugues, I thought she'd slipped it past me. I'm still a bachelor?"

"Yes."

"Hotdog! I'm still a bachelor. I've broken no oaths!" He sighed with relief. "Speaking of titles, Genevieve thinks we should use an alias for the new show."

"For safety?"

"No. She asked me what I wanted to be."

"What did you say?"

"Someone else. Said I wanted to be someone else. 'Why not try it out?' she says! So now I just need to think of a name for my new persona. Come to think of it, I'm perfectly suited to be a medicine man, a specialist only loosely affiliated with a tribe. Somewhere, my peculiarities would be appreciated," he mused.

"Perhaps a cupbearer to check for poison and spoilage."

"Yes! I have powerful senses of taste and smell—my palette is so *dependable,* and my being is so *expendable.* In fact, dear Santo, I smell a touch of fungi. Have you been changing your socks?"

"You wreak like a bear foraging on garlic and onions. And you think you can smell a pair of socks, which are currently in a pair of shoes?"

"I'm used to my smells, but I'm clean, Santo. It was all that raw garlic and fresh fragrant herbs. Genevieve says food is medicine. Apparently, the best medicine is raw vegan."

"So, you do remember what you ate."

"Yes, now that you've brought my aroma to our attention."

"How many times did you visit her?"

"A gentleman never tells."

"Okay, so your new persona? Medicine man? Crime dog? What's

your angle for the new program?"

"Why don't we do a podcast? Students don't even go to lectures anymore, just 'get me the podcast' they bellow!"

"You wanted a call-in audience. Said you needed 'fresh meat.'"

"I once saw a sign for a butchery that said, 'Our Meat Can't Be Beat.' Now back in my time, that was one *double entendre royale.* Our pastors preached the very same message!"

"I wouldn't use French words on air."

"How about *Air on the G String*? So tell me again, Johann Bach, why are we going to Seattle?"

"Want me to play the recordings back? Your roots!"

"*Ja jonge! Mijn bollen!*"

"Hopefully, Genevieve's place isn't in a tall building. I've been reading about the Big Pacific Quake..."

"When did *that* happen?" Verboom yelled. "I *am* losing my memory!"

"It hasn't happened yet, but the once-every-300-years shaker is due. Will be worse than anything predicted for California."

"Dispatches from the frontlines of urban chaos!" His mind reeled.

"They can't predict when it's going to happen exactly."

"Then how is it *due*?"

"Patterns. The tension builds. Inevitably, the tectonic plates shift."

"Sounds like prophecy. Get your language right, and eventually the event will happen, and you take credit. Just have to avoid being too specific."

"The longer we stay, the greater the odds."

"*Noted.* True *underground* work. You know, sometimes I get that Dostoevsky fever," Verboom said.

"I may have fallen for a Dostoevsky scholar..."

"*Who?*"

"Met her in Flagstaff."

"Going out behind my back? *My heavens!*"

"Did you read much Dostoevsky in school?"

"Only the short ones." He was about to laugh. "I feel like I'm going to pop!"

"Perhaps we can find one of those truck stops with showering facilities. I've got quarters."

"I can wait for our destination. Bye-bye polar bears, hello sunny Seattle! That's a climate crisis joke."

"Some things aren't funny."

"Just laugh, you sourpuss... I'm working on my *persona.*"

"Your alias?"

"If I can be funny, no one will ever confuse me with Professor Verboom the cable news choke artist. *Hey.* Maybe I can do a Canadian accent too, *eh?*"

"If you can't make it in the States, we'll ship you north."

"Canada is no refuge from the Dutch Mafia."

"So, what's your persona's POV? Anarchist?" I teased.

"As long as they don't make me follow their rules."

"Might have to stay in the states then. No one in Canada is dumb enough to be an anarchist."

"Which is where I'll come in, *eh*! Now, Santo, what I'm going to do is take a giant dump on the restorationists, the dominionists, the reactionaries, the nihilists, the theocrats, and the secretly sinister First Brothers..."

"That's a long list."

"Got a label to capture them all?" he asked.

"How about the *Christian Nationalist Movement?*"

He shook his head. "Too many syllables."

"*Christian Supremacists?*" I offered.

"Six syllables. And American Christians are *very* sensitive to criticism"

"Okay…" I thought for a moment. "What about *Pious Gangsters*?"

His eyes lit up. "Only four syllables! You may be onto something there!"

I leaned down to the mic dangling over my shirt. "For the record," I said dryly, "most of these folks hide under the party label of 'Conservative.'"

"My persona will return the world to the world it was before Verboom ruined it!" he howled.

"Better take a nap."

"I'm wild. I. Am. A. Wild. Man. There's a long line of wild men in the Verboom family. They tend toward Jesus or the jug, and quite often both!"

He had traced his ancestors back through the Netherlands to the 16th century. He knew their names, where they had lived, how old they were when they died, and even their causes of death. He had the entire books of Verboom and Dijkstra memorized.

In Michigan, he'd shown me the genealogical books—one *stamboom* for each family line—a family tree. After studying them, he concluded: without some kind of intervention, he would live to 94 and then "croak of old age."

"Did you know in Dutch 'Verboom' literally means 'of' or 'from' the 'tree'?"

"It's a fun name, *Ver-BOOM*."

"Sounds more like *fur-BOMB* in Dutch."

"Everyone at the university has been calling you *Ver-BOOM*!"

"Not to worry, Santo, we're in America, and *Ver-BOOM* is how the English see it."

"Ever notice that you're the only professor the grad students call by last name?"

"I thought that was just because of the other Peter—no *i*—in the department."

"We like your last name for the *boom*. Now it's a *bomb*."

"Funny how letters can add up."

After fourteen straight hours on the road, we reached Grants Pass, Oregon, just after dark. I found a tree-lined, three-star motel along the Rogue River. Verboom sat in the truck while I checked in. When I returned, he was drumming out a war rhythm on the dashboard with his meaty hands.

"You'll deploy the airbag, Dr. *fur-BOMB*!"

"Is there a swimming hole?" he hollered.

"Pool in back."

"I'm headed downtown for provisions!"

Fifteen minutes later, he returned with a paper shopping bag tucked under his arm. He sat down at the desk in our room, opened the bag, and pulled out a plastic package. After folding the paper bag, it sprang back into shape, so he folded it again and wedged it under the desk lamp. Then, using the little scissors on his Swiss Army knife, he snipped open the plastic packaging.

Earlier that day, he told me about getting the knife on a family trip. His father said, "A man should always carry a knife." He'd long since lost the tiny toothpick, but the tweezers remained intact. He pulled them out to demonstrate their pinch and proudly claimed 21 sliver removals.

Inside the plastic package was a florescent orange air mattress made for pools. He grabbed it by the corners to wave out it's folds and began blowing it full of air, checking several times to make sure it was taut. Then, stripping down to his hip pack, he spun the pouch around and fished out a pair of swimming trunks only slightly larger than bikini briefs. After stepping into his swimwear, he collected the raft and marched toward the door.

"Your attire is rather... *European*," I quipped.

"Don't tell the nationalists."

"Take your key."

"I'll knock."

"I'll be asleep!"

He whispered, "I'll knock softly."

12

The sky was already bright at 7 AM. I strolled to the lobby, poured a cup of coffee, and headed to the pool. There, Verboom floated on his orange air mattress, a dry fanny pack resting on his belly. His palms were pressed together, his arms raised straight, and his fingers pointed skyward as he sang the chorus of "Hurdy Gurdie Man."

"Always wanted a waterbed!" he exclaimed, seeing me. "It's a thing rich people used to have!"

"Go take a shower and meet me at the diner across the street in ten minutes."

He paddled to the tiled coping, pulled himself along to the ladder, and set his fanny pack on the pool's edge. Gripping the railings, he climbed out, then grabbed the inflatable mattress and placed it beside the pool. From his pack, he pulled out the pocketknife, flicked open the small blade and punctured the head pillow chamber—then the body. The plastic collapsed without a hiss. He rolled it tightly, forcing out the last bit of air, folded it in half, and dropped it into the trashcan two feet away from me.

"*Time*?" he hollered.

"Ninety seconds. You didn't have to ruin it."

"It wouldn't fit in my hip pack."

"Leave it for someone else."

"These things are drowning hazards. Best gotten rid of immediately."

"How could something that floats be a drowning hazard?"

"You get a little guy on that thing, his caretaker steps away to use the restroom, the little guy unwittingly drifts out to the deep end, slips off, can't touch the bottom, swings for the mattress but it bobs away from him. Not knowing how to swim, he panics. He splashes frantically, inhales water, lungs fill up, he sinks. When the grownup comes back to the pool, the little guy is at the bottom."

"You've got eight minutes."

An RV rumbled out of the lot as I crossed the street to the diner. The parking lot had a few sporty station wagons with mudflaps and mountain bikes strapped to the back. There was one weathered red pickup, its bed full of carpentry tools.

Inside, a group of guys—roughly my age—clustered in a corner booth, talking low over half-empty plates. At the bar, a grizzled sport fisherman sat hunched over his coffee, his fingers wrapped tight around the mug.

The air carried the rich weight of griddle grease, and the chalk menu board touted fresh cinnamon rolls for the breakfast special and chicken-fried steak for dinner. The walls were decorated with faded photos, a mounted trout, old beer ads, and a giant saw blade.

I took a large round table by the stone fireplace, unfolded the local paper, and skimmed through the back pages of international news: "Second African Nation Passes Death Penalty For Sodomy: Despite Ties, US Conservatives Deny Involvement"

While religious nationalists hadn't yet managed to make biblical dictates the law in America, a group of congressmen and senators—all members of First Brothers—had played a role in establishing budding Christian theocracies in Uganda and South Sudan.

Verboom plopped into the booth as I checked my wristwatch and nodded with approval.

"You smell fresh," I said.

"*Dank je!*"

"Citrus and lavender?"

He looked at me like I lacked the most basic human judgment.

"*Cedar* and *sandalwood*. The bar was unwrapped, but I think the fragrance is synthetic... a little too on the nose."

I shook my head and went back to reading the paper.

"Thanks for laying out a clean *gi*," he added. "We could sell a boatload of these puppies, a fusion of style and performance. Maybe as separates?"

"The clinic insisted that your 'son' take your stuff," I said. "Kept your clothes, but the Dutch novels went to a thrift shop."

"*Bedankt.*"

"Hope you're hungry. Ordered you a Denver omelet."

"*Eggggsss*-cellent. The city's a mile high, and no flying required."

"For your new show, we could pick a few articles, and you add commentary..."

"Set the table, as it were."

"Then take live callers..."

"Then—boom—you pop my persona into the universe!"

I slid the newspaper toward him. "Here's the kind of story we could use to open the show."

He squared it neatly, planted his elbows on the table, and leaned in, cradling his bearded jaw in his palms, plugging his ears with his index fingers.

"Calling the act 'sodomy' is a branding disaster," he said, lifting his head.

"How so?"

"Sodom and Gomorrah! Don't you know your Hebrew literature? The word is loaded with judgment. The theocrats won the language war before the legal battle. But all these holy rollers fail to mention the entire story of Sodom. Abraham's brother, Lot, offers his virgin daughters to the randy mob to quell their lust and spare his strange male visitors from, well... *penetration*. How's that for hospitality!"

"You're ruining my appetite."

"It's in the Bible. *Jeez*, Santo. Look it up. I'm not the one with the twisted mind."

"You do know the Bible better than the Christians I know."

"Biblical literalists tend to be biblically illiterate!"

"That will be the lead quote on Professor Watch List."

"Is that something you made up to keep me in line?" he asked.

"Look it up."

He pushed the paper back to me.

"It's not reported here," I tapped on the article with my index finger, "but First Brothers is behind this. They run the same prayer breakfast thing in Africa. The cell groups, too. I found leaked documents online. Their leader, Frank Fowler, holds up Hitler, Mao, and Stalin as examples of organizing genius."

"Why would anyone go for that?" Verboom asked.

"Because they're doing it for Jesus."

"The ends justify the means," Verboom mused. "As long as it's not rear ends."

"They say you must love Jesus more than your father, mother, wife, children, brothers, and sisters—even more than your own life."

"That's Luke 14:26," he muttered.

"Their strategy is to place 'key men' in governments everywhere. In DC, I thought your concerns were paranoia, but you may have undersold it."

He bellowed with outrage, "They're exporting theocracy!"

"Hesse admitted viewing politics as spiritual warfare."

Breakfast arrived. I cut into over-medium eggs and dipped my sourdough toast into the yoke.

"For seventy years, First Brothers wouldn't admit the existence of their organization," Verboom continued. "Meanwhile, they took donations, owned properties, paid out salaries, and dodged taxes by posing as a church. On moving to DC, Fowler called the new headquarters 'God's embassy in Washington!' The nerve! The blasphemy! Why would *God* need an embassy? If only the president had demonized them instead of isolating himself. Perhaps, I can move the story forward with the new show. Name names. Point pointer-fingers."

"They're congress members, lobbyists, mega-church pastors, and titans of industry."

"To know them is to know them..."

"How did you catch onto them?" I asked.

"They recruited me."

"A coffee date with Hesse?"

"*Nay, nay, nay.* Long before. A college friend invited me to the presidential prayer breakfast my senior year. But I was no longer the praying type."

"You could have met so many hotshots."

"You think I should've gone to *network*?"

"More like gawk."

"At first, I thought the fancy invitation was a joke. How did I get invited to a meeting with the president? Little did I know, only a few decades later I'd be ruining a different president's presidency."

"Their whole operation avoids paper trails. Why would Hesse have you sign that document?"

"Don't care. They're a bunch of jocks-for-Jesus. And they haven't the wits to abuse me anymore than I abuse myself."

"Clearly you haven't been around many jocks."

"None as strapping as you, Santo! But the more I think about it, naming names might not work. These guys brag about their faith.

Their National Prayer Breakfast is basically a red-carpet event for early-bird Jesus Freaks. It's virtue signaling. It's a *pious* front." He leaned in on my mic. "Their religion isn't the secret—*it's their political agenda!*"

The young guys in the other booth looked over at us.

Verboom went on in a whisper. "Their tentacles wriggle through the halls of power, propping up foreign strongmen and scratching the backs of big business instead of protecting the little guy."

With my napkin, I wiped yoke from my chin. "You goaded the president to pick a fight with them as part of an 'enemy within' strategy. And you were right. There's a shadow network of fundamentalists who reject democracy. Rebrand them—make *theocracy* the new 'Red Scare.'" As soon as it was out of my mouth, I regretted it.

"And how do *you* know so much about them, good sir?" he asked.

"Killing time online during your clinic stay."

"What about your dissertation? Don't let me ruin your career before it starts."

"Producing your new show will give me technical skills," I said, wondering if I was really going to play along. "We'll go DIY, like Genevieve suggested. One of her IT guys is going to show me the ropes."

Verboom inhaled slowly. "You two conspiring?"

"*Producing.* It's your vision. We're just helping with the execution."

His eyes widened. "Hot damn, Karl! We'll own the means of production. Let's throw my entire publishing fortune into this!"

The young men looked over again.

"If the show catches on…"

"Corporate sponsorships?" Verboom interrupted.

"Subscribers." I was surprised to hear my own enthusiasm for his daycare project. "Supposedly, that's the best way to monetize podcasts and webcasts."

"Until the media giants buy it all up and start running ads!" he shouted.

At this point, the guys at the other table stopped looking at Verboom.

"But folks will have to pay for the show?" he asked. "Rude!"

"The show is a loss leader. You make money on bonus content—special episodes, a newsletter..."

"What newsletter?"

"The one you'll write. Premium content for subscribers only."

He scoffed. "People would rather pay to get me *out* of their ears."

"It's not *you*, it's your persona. Pleasantly irritating. Acerbically honest."

"For this newsletter, let's use the subtitle: 'WARNING: Do Not Read Aloud.'" He cut into his omelet with the edge of his fork. "Remember when Jesus performed the miracle and told people, 'Don't tell anyone'? And what did the people do? They told *everyone*!"

"*Do not read aloud*. Sounds like a spell."

He grinned. "We'll conjure up the curse of Truth! The people don't want a professional analysis; they want a sensation! And what could be more sensational than walloping theocrats who cloak their vulgar politics in genteel spiritual language and business attire?"

The question hung in the air as Verboom turned his attention to his giant omelet.

Leaving the restaurant, it seemed best to let Verboom drive. His face lit up when I held out the key and dropped it into his hands—but

any sense of triumph was short-lived.

There was a gnat in the truck.

Verboom could barely keep his eyes on the road. He needed to kill the gnat before moving forward with the rest of his existence.

After the truck jerked and swerved a few times, my stomach turned.

"I'd say this gnat is driving me mad, but I'm already there!"

"You're making me sick," I groaned.

Without warning, Verboom hit the brakes and yanked the truck into a parking space. I braced for the sound of bumpers colliding, but somehow, he parallel parked perfectly, without even hitting the curb.

He turned off the truck, pulled out the key, and dropped it into my lap.

"It's either me or the gnat." He stared straight ahead.

"If I get it out of here, can we proceed?"

"*Ja.*"

I lowered the window, grabbed a banana peel from the cup-holder, and held it near the open air. The gnat hovered, intrigued. I extended my arm out the window, letting the scent lure it away.

It zigzagged out.

I dropped the peel, quickly shut the window, and set the key on the dashboard.

Without a word, Verboom turned the engine over and whipped the truck out of the spot as smoothly as he'd parked it.

Continuing north toward Seattle, Verboom remained silent—but flinched at every buzz and chime from my phone.

As we approached Portland, a digital road sign flashed: "Street Closures Downtown – Expect Delays."

Interstate 5 spans the Willamette River just south of downtown, and from the bridge, we had a clear view of McCall Waterfront Park, which stretched for over a mile along the west bank.

A large crowd had gathered, waving signs and flags.

To the north, a smaller group—fewer than two hundred—stood dressed mostly in black.

To the south, a vast crowd in red and military green stretched down the park along the riverfront in a dense, shifting mass.

Drawing parallel with the rally from across the river, I flicked on the radio to see if we could get the story:

> *Protesters and counter-protesters continue to gather in downtown Portland. So far the event has been peaceful, though tensions are building. Ultra-Right activists organized the event with a litany of complaints. We've struggled to summarize their movement, but the protestors are unifying around a newly minted acronym: O.F.A.M. To find out more, we're going live with Ron Jeffries, who's at the protest with one of the organizers.*
>
> **RON:** *Thanks, Ted. I'm here with Caleb. Out of concern for safety, he will not give his last name.*
>
> **CALEB:** *Nice of the flyover media to stop by, but this isn't a zoo, Ron. We're not animals to ogle.*
>
> **RON:** *I live three miles from the park. Can you help our community understand your cause?*
>
> **CALEB:** *We're Off'em. O. F. A. M. Old-Fashioned American Mob.*

RON: *Old-Fashioned American Mob?*

CALEB: *Watch TV much, Ron? Rodger Hedges on WNN called our freedom-loving movement an "old-fashioned American mob."*

RON: *What do you stand for?*

CALEB: *A better question is: who do we stand with? We've got the makings of a second revolution. The Portland siege is just one of hundreds of cities.*

RON: *What's your message?*

CALEB: *We're tired of being shit on by the media, the film industry, and worst of all, these corporate Liberals who've got a chokehold on the federal government.*

RON: *Why the guns?*

CALEB: *Just told you this is a revolution. Like Fritz Hearn said, this guy pretending to be president needs to exit the scene muy rapido! See: no puede!*

RON: *Listeners, Caleb is pointing to his tee shirt, which says 'no puede' printed on the silhouette of an M-16. Now, Caleb, if this is a peaceful protest, why are you carrying an assault rifle?*

CALEB: *Look at those anarchists with their helmets and clubs. They think we're Neo-Nazis. They love filming a guy* *with a nice haircut getting punched in the face just for speaking his mind. Like it's some kind of sport. Tell me, Ron: does a white man not have the right to get a nice haircut and speak his mind without getting punched in the face?*

RON: *Are you asking me if Neo-Nazis have the right to speak in public?*

CALEB: *We're not Neo-Nazis! We're Off'em. We'll defend ourselves from anarchists looking for internet glory.*

RON: *Do you stand with Neo-Nazis or white nationalist organizations?*

CALEB: *Would you ask Paul Revere if he was a Neo-Nazi?*

RON: *I'm not prepared to answer that hypothetical.*

CALEB: *You should be. Now listen. You can't take our money, our children, or our guns.*

RON: *Who's doing that?*

CALEB: *Don't play dumb to the Left's extreme agenda.*

RON: *Thanks, Caleb, I have to send it back to the studio.*

CALEB: *Oh, and Ron, just a fair warning. Since Rodger can't believe his own eyes, we'll see if he believes his ears.*

RON: *What does that mean?*

CALEB: *A shot will be fired.*

Verboom looked at me with big eyes. "We must defend our people from these bullies!"

"What people?"

"The anarchists, of course! They're outnumbered and soon to be outmaneuvered."

"Your persona is the anarchist, not you."

"The persona will only work if I'm fully committed! Take the next exit to the other side!"

Watching the spectacle while listening to the radio, I'd almost come to a stop on the freeway. We were just north of the Burnside Bridge and the famous white stag sign, so we exited and crossed the river via the NW Broadway Bridge. We passed through the edge of the Pearl District and parked near the Lan Su Chinese Garden. Against my better judgment, we walked a few blocks through the Portland Market toward the park. Verboom ran ahead to a flower vendor. Before I could stop him, he purchased two dozen white roses, leaving the change.

As I caught up to him, he ran around one end of the siege line and into the O.F.A.M. ranks. The police had their backs to O.F.A.M., facing the counter-protestors. Wearing a seersucker karate suit, no one knew his team membership, and he squirmed to the midpoint of the line and positioned himself between O.F.A.M. and the police. Facing the mob, he grabbed a megaphone from the man beside him. It squawked when he pulled its trigger, then he yelled through it to O.F.A.M.:

"Come now, let us reason together! Though your shirts are like scarlet, you are white as snow; though your hats are red like crimson, you are pale as wool!"

The self-dubbed patriots began to murmur, shifting uneasily as

Verboom launched into a fervent riff on the prophet Isaiah, cradling his roses like an infant.

"Your princes are rebels, friends of thieves. They grow rich on soaps, and refuse, and raked leaves. They bribe you with the lucre of sweet mammon, only to leave you orphaned and abandoned. But rebels and sinners shall be shattered together. You'll be ashamed of your idolatrous blather! You will blush for the gardens you have chosen! You will be like an oak whose leaves wither once frozen!

"*Now.* Listen unto me! I am the far and distant tree! I have seen your folly from across the river bend. I know of your poor spellings, and I forgive them! *If* you want to celebrate white, celebrate white! If you want to celebrate might, celebrate might! Now accept these thorny stems of peace, with each petal colored like a swan. Again, I say to thee: *how much longer can this go on?*"

The megaphone squawked again.

Verboom paused, letting the moment hang.

O.F.A.M.'s grumbling swelled, a low rumble of unease.

Then, Verboom went on:

"Read my lips and point at me with your gun tips. And into your barrels I will stick my peace! There's only one thing more to say, *accept this rose and go away*!"

Before Verboom could go on, a guy about thirty feet away from him yelled, "Shut up, you giant doofus!" And within a few seconds the crowd chanted.

SHUT HIM UP!

SHUT HIM UP!

SHUT HIM UP!

Then Verboom placed a rose, stem-first, into a protester's muzzle.

The man froze, eyes wide as the rose slipped neatly into the barrel of his assault rifle.

Verboom scanned the crowd wildly, searching for more receptive guns, gripping the next stem like a dart—but before he could make his next move, an O.F.A.M. protester drove the butt of his rifle into Verboom's gut, knocking the wind out of him.

The megaphone hit the ground with a squawk, like a Canadian goose in distress.

Verboom remained crouched, gasping for air. Then, with a giant exhale, he let out a guttural groan—and in one sudden, explosive burst, he sprang to his feet, arms flung skyward, launching roses in every direction.

"*The petals fall, but the thorns remain!*" Verboom bellowed.

He looked into the sky and pleaded, "Lord, come quickly..."

Another man jabbed Verboom in the ribs. He dropped to his knees, wheezing.

A police officer raised a canister and blasted Verboom directly in the face with pepper spray. Verboom yanked his open *gi* top over his head, his body hunched like a retracted seersucker turtle.

Then a handful of self-styled patriots descended on the blinded professor, boots stomping, fists hammering. Helmets on and visors down, the police pressed forward with riot shields up, forming a semi-circle around Verboom, walling him off from the mob.

As the police held back O.F.A.M., the counter-protesters in black spotted a gap in the police line and rushed through. They carried no guns but wielded clubs, bats, and air horns. Many wore skateboarding helmets, black flags whipping above them as they charged into the fray, shouting slogans at the blue shirts and red hats.

I followed them in, reaching for Verboom, trying to yank him to his feet—but I only managed to pull off his *gi* top.

Cursing mightily, I hooked him by the bare arm and hauled him up.

We pushed through the scrum, dodging wild shoves and swinging fists, slipping free as black clashed with blue and red in a chaotic tangle.

Blinded by pepper spray, Verboom let me steer him forward, his voice soaring over the chaos: "Mine eyes have seen the glory of the coming of the Lord; He is trampling out the vintage where the grapes of wrath are stored!"

A tall young man—wearing a denim shirt, blue jeans, and leather clogs—stood on the corner, cupped his hands around his mouth, and shouted: "Put a sock in it, *Steinbeck!*"

After gaining a safe distance, I dragged Verboom into a liquor store.

"Where are we?" he asked, eyes pinched shut and streaming tears.

"Getting milk to wash the pepper out of your eyes."

"Make sure it's lactose-free!"

The store attendant took one look at the shirtless, red-faced Verboom and jabbed a finger at a sign: "No shoes, no shirt, no service!"

Oddly enough, the sign said nothing about guns, knives, grenades, or flamethrowers.

I grabbed a jug of whole milk, threw a five-dollar bill at the counter, and pulled Verboom back outside.

"Get on your knees and look to the sky," I said. "It's going to hurt, but you have to open your eyes."

"Into your hands, I commit my seeing!"

Despite his best efforts, he couldn't keep his eyes open, so I pried apart his right eyelids with one hand while tilting the milk jug over his head.

Suddenly, he opened his mouth.

"What are you *doing*?"

"I'm not letting any of that precious moo-juice go to waste."

A quarter gallon of milk cascaded down his face. Most of it

missed his mouth, after splashing around his eye socket, and instead soaked into his beard, matting down his chest hair and splashing onto the pavement.

I repeated the process on his left eye, dousing him with the rest of the jug.

Verboom blinked. Squinted. Blinked again.

I led him back to the truck and shoved him into the passenger seat.

Sirens wailed and more squad cars barreled toward the park. An ambulance sped past us.

We drove north along the Willamette, cutting back to Interstate 5 via St. Johns Bridge.

Then I heard a pop.

Verboom had cracked open a can of cola from a previous pit stop. He took a long sip and exhaled with satisfaction.

"There must be a ballgame on," he mused, half-blind, fumbling with the radio.

I intervened after his wandering hand accidentally switched on the windshield wipers.

Another pop.

He lowered his window just a crack and, barely above a whisper, murmured, "Told you, lactose-free."

After fifteen minutes, we crossed the Columbia River, leaving Oregon behind.

"Open your eyes. Can you see?"

Verboom squinted against the light. "Oh *say*? Is this the state of my birth? Land that I love!" With renewed gusto, he belted out: "*Stand beside her and guide her! Through the night with the light from above! Land of apples, land of coffee, land of airplanes... flying LOW!*"

"Do you really want to get back into radio?"

"Did someone back in Portland really call me Steinbeck?"

"Yes."

"*Hot damn*! Things are looking up!"

"Genevieve said you need to let off some steam, but this is a bit more than I imagined." I sighed. "Before you get back into radio, you should hear what you did the first time. Let me play it."

Verboom cocked his head. "The first time?"

"Ask The Professor, where you issued *Final Freedom*."

He mulled that over, then shuddered. "Sounds like something carved into the wood frame of a guillotine. Let's save that for later. The less my persona knows about Verboom, the better."

"Do you know what that rant let loose?"

"A long-necked goose?"

"Your fiery tirade is traveling the fringes of American culture."

Across the interstate divide, a truck flying a *Final Freedom* flag drove past us headed southbound. I pointed, then went on. "Preppers, fake patriots, reactionaries, wannabe revolutionaries, and a whole hodgepodge of crusaders. You've thrown gas on the flames."

"Are you saying some kooky radio professor has stirred up social upheaval? Wouldn't his profession void his authority? Ever heard the figure of speech 'it's all academic?'"

"Do you remember why you went to the clinic?"

"To hide from Ella, obviously."

"What did your form say?"

"Nervous exhaustion, I believe."

"Think there may have been a psychiatric incident?"

He fanned himself. "A Victorian prude living in Babylon—you don't think someone like that might need a respite?"

"You're no prude."

"So, you think the meds are causing my spontaneous erections?"

I squinted. "What meds?"

"Well, if I had a psychiatric incident, wouldn't I be getting medicated?"

"Did your parents ever discipline you for being silly?"

"Oh Santo, I *was* silly. I would laugh myself silly, to no one's delight. I was so chunky—I hated the way I looked. I had to laugh, had to tell jokes, had to get them all laughing *with* me by laughing *at* me. A laugh is a laugh, Santo. If you're not laughing, you're crying. Don't get me crying. It's not a good look. And to think I could be a person so saddened by appearance... by *my* appearance! The superficiality of it disgusts me! You want a dare? How dare I have the nerve to feel sorry for myself!"

"Being a silly, guilt-riddled kid doesn't exempt you from igniting political chaos."

"No way I lit the match on this inferno."

"It's you."

"The self is a fiction, a pretended whole made up of parts that don't add up. If we're doing fiction, let's at least have some fun!"

"You're hard to follow."

"Don't follow me—I'm following you!"

"You lost me."

"The void in me bows to the void in you," he declared, dipping into a dramatic bow and smacking his forehead against the dashboard with a thud.

He didn't smile, but he didn't frown either—just looked ahead.

Sitting shirtless, with both hands on the dash, his bulging muscles bounced along with the truck's movement.

Then he sang, in a whisper, "I Love To Laugh" from *Mary Poppins*, wiping his wet cheeks with the back of his hand. "Must be the pepper," he added, after finishing the tune.

13

Just north of the Columbia River, we traveled through lush green hills and long stretches of forest, dotted with bustling farms and weathered barns. After miles of uninterrupted splendor, we pulled off the freeway for gas.

The sprawling truck stop was a kitschy yet endearing spectacle of roadside commerce. Inside, stark fluorescent light shone on the linoleum floors, well-worn from the passage of countless shoppers. The building included a cafeteria with chrome-edged tables and vinyl booths. Shelves brimmed with an assortment of items—from auto essentials like windshield wipers to a surprising variety of local homemade jams. Truckers and tourists could pick up anything from a "World's Best Dad" keychain to a Big Foot mug. The scent of grease from a deep fryer mingled with the acid tang of over-heated coffee.

With Verboom waiting in the truck, I meandered past an extensive section of DVDs, from blockbuster hits to obscure B-movies, and approached a section with coolers filled with sodas, energy drinks, and an impressive selection of local craft beers. Each corner of the shop offered a sensory feast—both alluring and jarring after the expansive views from high in Verboom's truck.

While waiting in line to pay for gas, I impulsively grabbed jerky, nuts, chocolate, and bottled water. A small TV near the newsstand flashed headlines on ANN: "Debacle in the Desert," "Three SEALs Stuck," and "Crashed Copter Plunges POTUS," accompanied by stock videos of helicopters and Navy SEALs.

A rack next to the register showcased "Save The SEALs" bumper stickers and T-shirts for $5 and $25 respectively, their printing slightly askew in generic block letters.

"New product?" I asked the cashier.

The clerk, around twenty years old and markedly disinterested, replied, "Arrived this morning."

"How they selling?"

With minimal effort, she shrugged. Observing her, I heard Jacqueline's voice asking for a description. Pale, with ears pierced from lobe to apex like bedazzled elfin bows. Her hat, perched high on thick, wavy brown hair, looked new—the mesh still sported creases—likely a freebie snagged from an employee lounge giveaway, a perk from the alcohol distributor. She wasn't jaded or hungover but seemed to have left her spirit at home, placed in a jar after applying lip gloss. I thought about the many road-weary older men who had tried to chat her up.

"You get tired of guys trying to make conversation while you ring up their crap?"

"Anything else?" she deflected.

"A hundred on pump nine, please."

"You don't look like a guy with a truck."

"What do I look like?"

"Fixie. Maybe a crotch rocket." She handed me the change. "Wear a helmet." She didn't smile, but her eyes brightened just perceptibly.

When I returned to the pickup, Verboom had emptied the duffel bag, organizing its contents into piles on the tailgate. A large pile contained letters from Ella; a medium pile held envelopes from his health insurer and utility companies; a small pile came from the university. A book-sized parcel sat alone. He told me that all the speaking invitations had been trashed.

"What's in the box?"

He pulled it open and removed a cover letter with a handwritten note. He read it aloud: "Dear Prof. Verboom, My memoir of the White House will be in bookstores next month, but I thought you should hear from me first. Please find an advanced copy enclosed so you can prepare for any fallout. I know you meant well. No hard feelings. Sincerely, Bill Blankenship."

Verboom looked at the front cover, and then held it up below his chin for me to read. *Friendly Fire: How a Team of Well-Meaning Intellectuals Ruined a Presidency.*

"At least your face isn't on the cover," I said.

Handing me the book, he quickly repacked the letters into the duffel bag and returned it to the cab.

Then, like a valet, he held the passenger door open for me. After I sat down, he closed it gently, then raced around to the driver's seat and hopped in.

"Can you see through your tears?" I asked, in a tone betraying some concern, though not enough to take the wheel.

"I have the vision of a prophet!" he shouted.

As we merged onto the freeway, I read from the liner notes: "We had the opportunity for a historical presidency..."

"*Ahistorical?*"

"...but an intransigent opposition party combined with key communication missteps led to the second coming of Jimmy Carter..."

"Come quickly!" Verboom interjected, hopeful.

"It continues, 'We elected a virtuous man, but bad circumstances and poor strategy would keep us from policy breakthroughs.' *Hmm.* He included transcripts in the appendices... even your session with the president and the speechwriting team."

"Let's hear it! I only have the foggiest of recollections."

"No way I'm reading all this, let me just skim through for the highlights." I skimmed for a moment. "Okay, to set the scene, you and a few other folks on the E.C.S. are meeting with the president and his writers to work on the State of the Union."

"The fact that I had the audience of the president shows you how precarious our system is! Next thing you know, Fritz Hearn will be getting the Medal of Freedom," Verboom mused.

"To summarize, you told POTUS that speeches rarely change perceptions, and you launched into a lecture on evolutionary psychology. The president said he was 'looking to brainstorm, not to unravel the mysteries of humankind.' You challenged the effectiveness of brainstorming, citing a 1958 Yale study revealing its limitations, and then you dove deeper into cognitive science. To quote you: 'Throughout history, social encounters occurred face-to-face; we were part of small hunter-gatherer bands; community life was localized and understandable; our genetic ancestors had intimate knowledge of each other and their environment; we cared for our kin and punished cheaters. Now, if you still intend to deliver a national speech, you must define "kin" and "cheaters"! A more effective strategy would focus on your audience *within* the congressional chamber—those physically present—not the viewers at home. Capitalize on this opportunity to inform allies and independents about the threat from the First Brothers within their ranks, who aim to replace democracy with *theocracy*!'"

"Sensible." Verboom affirmed, nodding along.

"Then the president asked you to skip conspiracy theories, which set you off. 'Clearly my reputation does *not* precede me. True conspiracy is impossible on a large scale. *Conspiracy*? I'm talking about human indifference to relevant information that's publicly available! *Mein Kampf* was published in 1925! There are no secrets, only indifference!'"

"Did this Verboom guy raise his voice? Sounds like you're

reading this in all caps."

"It was exclamatory. You went on to say: 'My specialty is the human constitution, not the American Constitution. Which is why I'm here, *ja*? And that's a Dutch *ja,* not a German *ja*. Now, the American people can be forgiven for ignoring these Christian Nationalists in congress—but not you, Mr. President!'"

"So glad we relabeled Christian Supremacists as Pious Gangsters," Verboom injected from behind the steering wheel.

"Then Blankenship says, 'For the last time, we're not going to alienate the biggest religion in America.'"

Verboom shook his head rapidly and asked, "Did Blankenship get away with that comment? Most Christians don't want theocracy! Knowing the Gospels quite well myself, I can tell you there's nothing Christlike about First Brothers' politics. As *Jesus* said: 'My kingdom is not of this world!' Sure hope POTUS got his terms straight for the big speech! We're not attacking Christianity; we're attacking theocrats!"

"I'm right here," I said. "You don't have to raise your voice."

Verboom squinted as I continued reading.

"Speechwriter Jon Silverberg asked you to zoom in from theory to the number one threat to Americans. 'Let's speak to their need, not their worldview,' he said. And then you sounded off once again: 'If you want to stay blind to the history of the church shilling for capitalists—turning people against the New Deal for a *raw deal...*' Then Silverberg interrupted you, said, 'Most Americans don't know what the New Deal is.' *Raw deal*. That's pretty good marketing," I said reflectively. "The Oligarchs are trading the *New Deal* for a *raw deal*!"

"Who's yelling now?" Verboom asked. "I've lost track."

"Silverberg. And I can see his point," I said. "For the State of the Union you suggested, quote: 'A cabal of ultra-conservative masterminds has duped the American voter. This radical cadre of theocrats—propped up with money from big tech, big oil, and big pharma—will replace doctors, lawyers, teachers, and scientists with puppets controlled by preachers! With their toothy smiles and glad hands, their velvet revolution is ringing in the American Dark Age.'"

"Poetic!" Verboom beamed, as he tried to focus on the school bus ahead.

"Next you critiqued the administration's 'rational actor theory.' Blankenship said, 'I'm an administrator. I don't have theories.' Silverberg told you that Americans aren't hunter-gatherer people, that they grew up with television, and your case is beside the point. Then for several paragraphs, you tried to convince the team that our mental architecture for detecting cheaters exceeds our logical reasoning; consequently, POTUS really needs to name free riders... Wow, I forgot how badly this went. You continued, '*Demonize*! Our inferential systems naturally seek a scapegoat. We don't want to trace a convoluted network of over-leveraged asset-bundling and inflated property values. Mr. President, you've become the face of these elaborate sets of causes. Although people can understand intricate systems, it demands that we suppress our more instinctual responses...'"

"Maybe we could turn this transcript into a TV drama?" Verboom interrupted.

"Silverberg said, 'We need a compelling narrative, not dark musings from a professor.'"

"*Dark Musings*! That's the show's title!"

"Hire Silverberg to write it," I said.

"Let's hope he still has four more years of work." Verboom crossed his thick fingers.

"You wouldn't stop. You turned your focus to the National Prayer Breakfast, adding, 'The human mind defaults to an insider-outsider dichotomy. You must tell your colleagues about the *outsiders* pretending to be *insiders*. Prayer is only a cover story. The National Prayer Breakfast is a perfect front, a ploy of piety! They use elected offices to advance religious agendas! They ignore the separation of church and state and neglect the duty of their office. Double *cheats*!'"

"Boy oh boy, this character really knows how to beat the proverbial dead horse."

"Then Blankenship objected, saying everyone from both parties goes to the prayer breakfast. You told them to fight fire with fire. 'Punish them as *freeloaders* not faith-holders. They take the office for a salary and with a set of responsibilities but work instead for their alternative agenda. It's like a guy collecting unemployment while he works off the books!' Then POTUS said, 'We can be strategic without rank psychological manipulation.'"

"Pass the turkey jerky," Verboom said. "*Say*? Is this why Hesse came by the clinic?"

"The conversation really soured when you said that regardless of the arguments made in the speech, the administration will inevitably get blamed for the economy. As the president rose to his feet, Blankenship recognized the signal to end the meeting."

"What about the other so-called scholars?" Verboom asked. "What did they have to say?"

"A different meeting was scheduled without you."

"That's polite," Verboom said sincerely.

"As everyone walked out, you made your final plea, 'Expand your party membership via face-to-face interaction! Act locally within the chamber while you broadcast globally.' Blankenship dismissed the idea, said it's a speech for the entire world. Then you countered: 'Viewers at home will feel like they're getting behind-the-scenes access, like some kind of gauche reality TV show, which is what the American audience craves!"

"Wow, that teriyaki flavoring has got me in its grips. Water, please. I've had more sodium than I can stand!"

I handed him a bottle. "My mouth is dry too. I conclude our reading."

He took a long chug and exhaled hard. "Did Verboom really say all that?"

"It's from a reputable publisher. You don't think they'd do a fact check?"

"There was no need to fact check *Tautology*. Every statement is true by definition!" Verboom smiled, satisfied. "Any more juicy bits from Blankenship?"

"How are your eyes doing?"

"Check our record from yesterday. I'm a hawk and a hound, rolled up into one big farm boy. Read the newspapers, I'm a prophet!"

"Okay, I think I have your naughty bits. From page 173."

> *While Professor Verboom's off-putting manner disqualified his suggestions in my mind, unfortunately, I cannot say the same was true for the president. A few days after their meeting, the president was won over—at least in part. He pulled me aside and said: "Look, I know he's odd, and I don't agree with his theory, but I believe he's right about building the wall—the wall of separation between church and state. Folks in office are getting too friendly with the zealots... In the State of the Union, I'll announce my withdrawal from the National Prayer Breakfast."*
>
> *Of course, I objected strenuously—even within the E.C.S., Verboom was considered too strange to be taken seriously. I explained that the breakfast is only a social gathering. Then*

POTUS interrupted me: "So you don't believe in the power of prayer?" We chuckled. Then he said, "Listen, while I'm in office, attending the breakfast sends a confusing message." I countered, saying the meeting helped to build goodwill among partisans, but his mind was made up.

Since the president had finalized his decision, I argued for a discreet release of the news that Friday at 5 PM, but he argued the opposite. He wanted to send a message to America and the world. The action was meant to be both substantive and symbolic. "The government works for all people, not just the privileged sects. That's important in both appearance and fact."

Unless you're reading this memoir in the far future or have been living under a rock the last few months, you'll remember what happened next.

Merging into the fast lane, Verboom snorted, "Quite *vague* for a cliffhanger."

"You still under that rock?"

"Stoned by the press!" he shot back.

"NFWF Rallies. Does that ring a bell?"

"Seems I've got gravel in my ears."

"The first 'No Freedom Without Faith' rally happened in DC the Saturday following the president's prime-time announcement to withdraw from the breakfast."

"NFWF? Sounds like 'nuff 'wiff? Like an *enough-with-this* rally?"

"More like a precursor to O.F.A.M...."

Verboom groaned. "*Blast it*! These acronyms are driving me nuts!"

"Whatever you call them, they tried to plant a thirty-foot cross in front of the White House..."

"That's not what Jesus would do."

"I remember my mom gave me a WWJD bracelet back in junior high..."

"*Aha*! So, you're the acronym expert!

"What would Jesus *really* do with America?" I mused aloud.

"*With* or *within*? Please clarify, Santo."

"Let's consider the humbler scenario. *Within.*"

"Well, if we were to take his words as attributed in the Bible..."

"Why not."

"He'd be healing the sick, feeding the hungry, and chasing the grifters out of church."

14

Genevieve's apartment wouldn't be ready until the next day, so we opted for a budget hotel in Pioneer Square. Verboom was enamored with the area's brick buildings and voiced his regret for not becoming a mason.

"Speaking of masonry, you know about the William Morgan Affair in the early 19th century?" he asked.

"The banker?"

"The anti-Mason who the Freemason's kidnapped and perhaps killed. He published a book on the order's secrets, *posthumously*. The book, *Freemasons Exposed*, inspired so much rage, a new party formed: the *Anti-Masons*. They were absorbed by the Whigs, who fizzled out as their main impulse was the hatred of Andrew Jackson. Animus for one man can only take you so far."

"Can't we just talk about architecture without historical wordplay?"

"Bricks and Masons? Secrets revealed? *First Brothers and me...* You don't see the parallels? Hesse came to my room. I've struck a nerve!"

The hotel room had emerald carpet and burgundy drapes and bedcovers. The centerpiece: a television. It felt wrong to be in that kind of room during the daylight, so we stepped out for an early dinner.

After walking three blocks: *CRACK*! A gun shot. I crouched. Verboom stood erect, going up on his tiptoes, looking off into the distance as if he could spot the shooter.

I jogged back to our room and flipped through the channels until finding the local news. The Old-Fashioned American Mob delivered on their promise at 6 PM Eastern Time, so the local affiliate was ready to run with the Pacific Time activity. News came in from Boise, Portland, and other cities in the Pacific Northwest. Surprisingly, Los Angeles and San Francisco reported shots too. Looking for national coverage, we flipped to WNN, which ran a segment titled "Shots Heard Around the World." The report claimed O.F.A.M. had coordinated single shots gathering-to-gathering, city-to-city. "The timing was remarkably precise," the host said.

"Even with poor taste in politics, they can still tell time! *Geez*! By personality type, right-wing authoritarians score high on the need for order." Verboom stared into the TV, shaking his head.

The garb of the rallying men varied in the news footage. A small handful wore tri-corner hats, mostly senior citizens, who were so out of touch with youth culture that they called themselves "teabaggers." Some of the young guys wore Hawaiian shirts over their flak jackets, ready for a luau with target practice. Like we observed in Portland, green and red dominated the pallet of rally colors. Reporters noted message hats and tee shirts, some hand-scrawled with "Draft Jim" and "Get Him Jim" and in block letters: "James Kroes For President."

After working as an international journalist, Jonathan Kuiper had become WNN's featured news presenter and head anchor—the face of the network. He questioned why local police hadn't taken each city's shooter into custody. Did they look the other way? Were they complicit? Were they overwhelmed? Isn't it illegal to fire a weapon inside city limits? *Where did the bullets land?*

"Jonathan, as political statements, these shots are protected by the First Amendment," the Conservative pundit said confidently.

A Liberal analyst on WNN repeatedly referred to a sign that read

"Keep Your Guv'ment Hands Off My Medicare." Unable to contain his mirth, he giggled at the contradiction. "Surely, these folks are too poorly informed to be a real threat." The president's administration, while diverse in appearance, was entirely Ivy League except for the vice president. Certainly, they could outfox poor spellers in a war of words.

"Their signs do indicate certain conceptual deficits," I remarked to the flatscreen.

"*Wait*, what does that guy's sign say?" Verboom said, leaning toward the TV.

"Save the SEALs," I said. "The last gas station sold the hostage merch."

Still a farm boy, Verboom could drive a tractor, castrate a bull calf, and repair a barn door; he expressed no fear of guns or stocky rural men—or suburban men aping the look. In fact, he showed a sympathetic understanding with almost everyone, to the best his damaged components would still allow. As the boundary of his identity had become porous, he spoke to the TV with a hearty work-ingman's friendliness jumbled awkwardly with a social theorist's detachment.

"It's the Fifth Great Awakening," Verboom said to the TV, sit-ting on the bed like a kid seeing his first cartoon. It was still bright outside, but I wasn't ready to leave the room.

"You mean a fifth column?"

"This is the Fifth Great Awakening of Christianity in North America. Only this time folks are armed to the teeth!"

"But it's a political movement..."

"And so much more! Look at the fella there... his sign says: 'GOD + GUNS = WE WIN.' I see flags and fear. Ritual. Faith. Ceremony. What else do you need to call this *religion*? Look, there's another one: GOD, GUNS & GUTS MADE AMERICA GREAT. The brand hierarchy seems clear. It's the Fifth Great Awakening. 'God' is written everywhere, and there again: Jesus and the cross too!"

Kuiper had to ask again: "Where did the bullets land?"

"Can't we have a normal day when the world isn't ending?" I said to myself.

Verboom turned to me. "Shall we grab a hamburger?"

"Swinging Richard's?" I suggested.

"That's the one. People just love that Swing up here. A local classic."

"Think it's safe?" I asked.

"*Safe*? Of course it's safe. These men are cowards." Verboom laughed deeply.

"We'll erase that from the recording."

"That would make *us* cowards."

"Don't know why I asked a man with a death wish if the world is safe."

"Santo, does your mother know where you are? Does she know about *this*?" He swirled his arms like eggbeaters.

"Staying in a cheap motel with a bearded giant who's wearing a seersucker *gi* and orange running shoes? No, my mom's main interest was my dating life." The past tense slipped out.

"She doesn't ask anymore, now that you're with the Neo-Freudian lady?"

"You've never asked about my mom."

"I'm sorry," he said, crashing from his news-addled heights. "Thought those questions were out of bounds professionally, but here we are, the Fifth Great Awakening, everything's about to change, she must be worried..." He looked at me. "Did you just say '*was*?'"

"She passed in March."

Verboom dashed into the bathroom and slammed the door shut. He quickly turned on both the faucet and the fan. Minutes later, after flushing the toilet, he turned off the running water and loud fan, then swung the door open. His eyes were bloodshot, yet he flashed a smile. With the dramatic flair of a stage magician, he turned off the TV.

"Burgers?" he asked, his voice a bit high.

As we met by the room's door, I could see that his cheeks were still damp around the eyes.

"Only going for burgers, you didn't need to wash your face," I said, unsure if I was taking a dig or offering him cover.

He looked at me, saline forming across his lower eyelids, and he said just audibly, "I'm sorry." His voice caught. "Wish I could be of better service to you."

I held the door open, and he walked through, pausing to wait for me instead of moving ahead. As I joined him, he extended his arm for a handshake. He didn't release my hand but continued shaking it, tears starting to well up. His hand was warm and callused, his grip firm. Covering his eyes with his left arm, he finally lowered it just enough to reveal his eyes and said, "Forgive me, I never learned to hug."

We drove up to Capitol Hill for burgers at Swinging Richard's, and then we strolled over to a bookstore on 10th Avenue. It seemed like a regular bookstore on a regular night. Everything seemed normal except that for the first time in five years, my advisor asked about my mom, and a man in every American city had fired a shot at the sky.

After parking at the hotel, I tried to pull Verboom into a pub next door, but he'd forsworn all "saloonery and tomfoolery." So, I grabbed a Rainier tallboy from a corner store and poured it into my stainless steel water bottle. We walked in concentric loops out from Occidental Square, making it as far south as the giant stadiums and as far north as Pike Place Market. No flying fish, as the fishmongers had already closed shop. All seemed calm, as we arrived back to our room. Verboom unplugged the TV with another grand gesture.

"Got anything to read?" he asked.

"We *just* left a bookstore!"

"All English."

I walked over to the closet and grabbed the green duffle bag of correspondence and pitched it toward his bed. It spun about 180 degrees and landed near his pillows.

With the corner market only a few blocks away, I marched out for another beer.

It was the middle of the week, and the streets were quiet. A few people watched the home team's away game at a sports bar, and I peeked in on the game through the larger exterior window outside. After a long moment, I looked down and saw a couple of women sitting below the TV at the bar who imitated my pouty face. Then one of the women put her hands to her eyes and wound them, like a crying baby. Readjusting my focus, I caught my reflection in the exterior glass of the window. I *was* pouty. I pulled the bell-strewn door open and walked to the end of the bar and ordered a beer. When it arrived, I took two straws from the server station, put one in each side of the pint glass, walked down to the women, and set the beer between them.

One of the women grabbed my arm, but I eased away from her grip without a word and continued to the market, where I bought a six-pack, a bag of potato chips, and a *Pacific Monthly*.

As I reached our hotel room door, I grabbed the magazine from the shopping bag so I could throw it at Verboom once in the room, but the smell of coffee surprised me. All the lights in the room were on, and I dropped the magazine next to the TV, before switching off the overhead light to mellow the brightness.

On his bed, Verboom had re-piled the contents of the green duffle bag, this time arranging everything by size. On the upper left corner of his bed, he'd stacked seven or eight Polaroid pictures. On the top of that pile sat another image of Ella formally dressed, attending some kind of fancy event. Folded glossy pamphlets sat next to a pile of cover letters and a stack of envelopes. The newspaper clippings presented a problem for his dimension-matching method.

"Did you just make coffee?" I asked in disbelief.

"It's only 9 PM. Want a cup?"

"Find any patterns?"

"Everything has a date written on it, even the pictures and the pamphlets. And of course, the envelopes came postmarked."

"Maybe she's creating an alibi."

Verboom continued to arrange the news clippings.

"All from Michigan?" I asked.

"Ella's envelopes are postmarked from Kalamazoo. The university's from Grand Rapids. All sent before she got to Flagstaff. Most of the pamphlets are from retirement communities and investment properties."

"Think she knows about your publishing money?"

"Like she's going to give up yachts on Lake Michigan to live with a jobless kook."

"What does she have to say?"

"Listen to this letter: 'I know it's crazy, but I can't stop thinking about you.' Then this one: 'I've never known a man with testicles such as yours.'"

"Maybe she hasn't seen many testicles?"

"She probably doesn't know what she's missing. The Dutch Mafia is *repressive*."

"Hand that over," I said.

Verboom handed me the letter.

"It says '*tendencies*.'"

"You turned off half the lights!" Verboom took the letters to a lamp. "Okay, what about this: 'Even if you can't commit to me, I'm committed to you. Let's go away together, you and I.'"

"Are they dated from the 1930s?"

"This year. Dates clearly marked, Santo."

"Maybe she wants to spend the rest of her life with you?"

"In a retirement home reading newspapers as we welcome the Apocalypse?"

"She followed you to Flagstaff and stayed in town after you 'escaped.' She's all in."

"*Nay, nay.*"

I felt the impulse to elaborate on Ella's surveillance of my motel room in Flagstaff, but I was still figuring out her angle and was unsure of how he would react given his broad paranoia.

"Perhaps she wants to use me for breeding and then dump me at one of these old folks' stables in ten years. All these pamphlets and so-called love letters are *subterfuge*! But why all the research?"

"That's what you bonded over. It's something to talk about; it's mostly arbitrary," I said. "The news is an excuse to talk."

"How come she never says any of this lovey-dovey stuff when we're together? Do you think someone is writing these letters for her? That's it, *they're forgeries*!"

"It's her handwriting. Her style is distinct. Now can we have a few beers and watch a movie? Maybe *Fatal Attraction*?"

"Before you open those chips, look at this one. I wanted to keep it under my hat, but I'd better let the cat out of the bag."

He handed me a letter in which Ella claimed to know the identity of my father. However, she held back his name and identifying details, fearing it might prompt Verboom to start investigating.

"If she doesn't trust you with the name, then why would she

even bring it up?" I asked and opened a beer, swallowing too much too fast, my eyes watering.

"At the clinic I pretended you were my son, so they wouldn't keep you away."

"That was just paperwork."

"She's driving a wedge between us. Step back and see the big picture: She wants my seed, and you're my chaperon. A classic reproduction gambit!"

"You are so weird about women. Is this why you're not married?" I looked down at the floor, regretting my frank question.

"My romantic forays go up in flames," he said. "It's true."

"But you do like potato chips?"

"The farmer eats what the farmer grows."

I handed him the bag of fried potatoes.

"I apologize for my incompetence as your professor," he said.

I opened a beer for him, but he wouldn't drink it, so I put it back in the fridge. It was the type of hotel that had a refrigerator yet no minibar offerings.

"Let's read for a while," I said. "I'll turn out the lights when I hear you snoring."

He handed me the Blankenship book. I handed him *Pacific Monthly*.

We both settled into our beds, propped up with pillows to read. His feet hung off the end of his mattress. I thumbed through *Friendly Fire*, starting at the back, looking at the index, then the notes, then the acknowledgements, where two surprising names appeared. Blankenship lavished some of his most effusive gratitude on Frank Fowler, longtime head of the First Brothers, and Fowler's protégé, senator Arlen Hesse.

15

Up with the sun the next morning, we packed, grabbed coffee from the lobby, and drove to Genevieve's rental on Capitol Hill, just north of downtown. Though only a short trip to Pine Street and 15th Avenue, I flipped on the radio out of habit. The broadcaster was midsentence:

> *Last night the president commended the bravery of our SEALs and promised to pursue any and all means necessary to secure their release...*

I quickly turned the radio off before Verboom could grumble.

As we drove along Pine Street, we noticed protest signs attached to the fencing around Cal Anderson Park. Groups of young people dressed in blacks, greys, and greens were setting up tents and shade covers on the artificial grass, right at the edge of the park's boundary, which was lined with maple trees. With the windows rolled down, I heard sounds of basketball games—balls bouncing, shouts echoing. A few blocks past the park, we turned left off Pine onto 15th, and just a few doors down, we spotted Genevieve's building. Verboom made a quick U-turn and expertly parallel parked in front.

"Brick and wood. My favorite materials," Verboom said. "Thank you for getting us here. I'd still be in the mucky canals of Venice if it weren't for you and Genevieve."

I buzzed the property manager, Stanley, who escorted us to the top-floor unit and handed me the keys. Inside, a leather couch and a matching loveseat faced a fifty-inch television, which appeared somewhat small given the room's twelve-foot ceilings and broad windows. The apartment also featured a cozy dining area with a round wooden table and four chairs. Down the hall was a modest kitchen with a built-in breakfast nook. From there a small bathroom, a compact bedroom, and a master bedroom with a private bathroom.

"Don't know how long you're staying, but try to give me a week's notice. The furniture is all high quality since the last tenant forfeited her stuff in lieu of back rent. We probably got the better end of the deal, but for some reason, there aren't any curtains or blinds in the apartment. And if you wouldn't mind, please don't put towels or cardboard up in the windows to block the light. We don't have a policy about that kind of thing. Please don't make me write a policy."

Verboom insisted on paying the utilities. He could accept Genevieve losing passive income, but he couldn't accept her money being actively spent. Despite our being guests of the owner, the property manager wanted a full application and a damage deposit, which Verboom paid immediately by peeling off twenty hundred-dollar bills from his roll.

"Sorry about the paperwork, I fear Genevieve's optimism makes her vulnerable to scammers," the property manager said.

"Don't worry, I'm a born pessimist," Verboom replied.

Catering to Verboom's paranoia, I filled out the application.

My mom put me on a track of good credit at the age of twelve; she even sat in on my job interview to be a paperboy. Her attendance must have helped my overall presentation, as she had the best style of any woman in Western Michigan, plus conversational polish and a dignified vibe. By sixteen, I was working in restaurants, and by eighteen, my mom helped me get my own credit card. I diligently paid off the balance each month ahead of time, reported steady income, and maintained excellent grades. She wanted me to own a house by age thirty.

"Well, with that," Stanley said, collecting the form, "I'll leave you to it."

"Let's celebrate!" Verboom said. "I saw a fancy donut shop a few blocks away."

Now just after 9 AM, we walked a few blocks south and spotted a gathering of pickups in a triangular parking lot between Pike Street, 14th Avenue, and Madison Street. The midsize lot belonged to a national bank. Most of the rigs were equipped with floodlights, spotlights, oversized tires, stretched suspensions, and ram bars.

"You know what they call those bars in Canada?" Verboom nudged my arm with is elbow and pointed at the frontend of the nearest truck.

"Of course not."

"A *moose bumper*!" Verboom chuckled. "I've got cousins up there. After a post-war bumper crop, America got its fill of Dutchies, so we started filling up the provinces to the north," he said.

The rally garb looked like the garb in Portland and on the news: red hats and shirts, camouflage hats and shirts, and full military fatigues—some faded with wear, others still crisp. Vehicle stickers and magnets showed athletic, political, and religious affiliations. Handwritten signs declared loyalty and outrage. A breeze came through, lifting their flags to make them legible:

COME AND TAKE IT

DON'T TREAD ON ME

GOD GUNS GUTS

DRAFT JIM

FREEDOM FIRST

FINAL FREEDOM

The American flag was certainly the most popular, and, fortunately, Verboom didn't notice the *Final Freedom* flag, which he would've likely seized. Instead, he reached for a set of ram bars, grabbing them with both hands and then pulling to test their stability.

"Where you guys from?" Verboom asked the closest man.

"Where do you think?" he said matter-of-factly.

"Where you going in those pajamas, chief?" another man asked Verboom.

"Donuts! You want in?"

The rally men didn't know what to make of Verboom's appearance and chipper mood. Wary of an oversized man in a karate suit offering baked goods, they declined. I edged down the sidewalk, not wanting to linger. Inevitably, the shock of Verboom would wear off, and they'd ask about my origins. Verboom caught up to me, closing the distance quickly with long strides.

"Those guys creep me out," I said.

"*Ja*! Who turns down donuts?"

"Do they know you're an anarchist? What's their hesitation?"

"I try not to guess at people's motives."

"But reasoning is a *motivated process*. You're a social psychologist!"

"Hunger for knowledge motivates my reasoning."

"Why?"

"Do you think I can know the motive behind my motivation?"

"My ex can tell you. If you're curious, I'll give you her number."

"Some of us are drawn to general insights, while others are more interested in maintaining party loyalty. Hey, are you recording me? I'm going to look like a disconnected elitist!"

"With your cognitive decline, these recordings will be all we have left of your thought."

"Don't forget about my eight published books... *Hey*, I just realized that my parents never congratulated me for earning a Ph.D. They just asked how much it cost."

"Did they read your books?"

"Beats me. I sent them unsigned copies—for them an autograph would be braggadocios and *not* supercalifragilisticexpialidocious. They displayed them on their bookshelf, next to their modest collection of Dutch theologians, but I never asked if they read them. English is their third language. Didn't want to put them on the spot."

"*Third*?" I inquired.

"Dutch, German, English."

"They never asked about your writing?"

"I was content seeing my books on their shelf, which proves that they remained unread. If read, my father would have fed them to the goats."

"What do you talk about with your parents?"

"The weather. Livestock. Family. Food."

"No sports, politics, art, history, or religion?"

"*Nay*. When I came up to visit my folks after finishing my M.A., we got to talking about politics after a few beers. So much of what my father said offended me, but I saw him as a figure of authority— and of course I was in his house—so I kept my mouth shut, except to drink more beer. Well, he went from chumming the waters to throwing bait, and once I got good and loose on that lager, I went full Socrates. I attacked his premises and logic but never advanced ideas of my own. This of course irritated the old fart, and he finally blurts out, 'You have all these fancy degrees, but all you can do is *ask questions*!' By the time he says this, I'm fully drunk and secretly fuming, suppressing my anger for hours, days, months, years… I blew the air horn of reason right up his asshole. I would not let him hide and did something worse than yell: I smirked. I unleashed an avalanche of words with which he could never compete. It was a childish use of ruthless sophistication. I got too drunk. Too…"

"Honest."

"Haven't had a drop of alcohol since then."

"None?"

"Frankly, I prefer being bottled up."

"How did you patch things up?"

"Unable to sleep, I left for California around 4 AM."

"You didn't say goodbye?"

"Left a note. The entire drive home, I pledged never to carve anyone's sacred cows, ever again. To keep that pledge, I could not drink, ever again," he said resolutely. "Let's press on for those apple fritters, the morning is getting away from us. Flour, sugar, and butter are still fair game!"

"What happened with your parents?"

"I pass through town once a year during the holidays but always make sure my brothers are around."

"Safety in numbers."

"Santo, I want to please my folks. I'm as compliant as can be—that's part of my nature. But I'm also a freethinker, and I can hold several opposing thoughts in my head. I'm drawn to new ideas and enjoy the work of thinking. Conclusion: I'm socially agreeable but intellectually contrarian. I'm averse to groupthink *and* rebellion. So, my parents have my books. If they want to know what I think, they can read them. But I believe they prefer to judge me by *my* cover; I look just like them."

"How do you know what *they* think?"

"I'm their dutiful eldest child, and they're immigrants. Again, English is their third language. From an early age, I followed their words closely and finished their English sentences when they got stuck. I lived in their world, but they haven't lived in mine..."

"What would your dad say now?" I asked.

"Quit farting around with donuts and get a gun."

"And what about your mom?"

"She'd say, 'Did you ever hear the story of the boy who saved an entire country by putting his finger in a dike?' Then she'd put out her index finger."

"I know that story. *The Boy Who Held Back the Sea*. Takes place in Holland. My mom wanted me to learn about Dutch people, since there's so many of them lumbering around Western Michigan."

"Well, besides being total nonsense on its face, it turns out the whole lineage of that story is British—my mom made fun of it. Like a 'Dutch uncle,' it isn't part of Dutch culture. So anyway, what do you think? Old-fashioneds or apple fritters?"

"Maple bar."

"Still thinking moose bumpers, *eh*?"

"You're not going to slide these donuts over their gun barrels, are you?"

"They can stick 'em wherever they please."

A small TV mounted on the wall behind the donut counter looped a rough cellphone video of Verboom placing a white rose in the muzzle of an assault rifle, getting jabbed in the ribs, crouching down, and then throwing the remaining flowers in the air. The title was "Coming Up Roses." The news ticker read: "Man described as 'Portland Rose Giant' wanted for questioning."

With his gaze fixed intently on the donut case, Verboom remained oblivious to the TV. Meanwhile, the baker, with his back turned to the screen, missed the chance to identify the Portland

Rose Giant.

"One maple bar, one apple fritter, and a baker's dozen of glazed old-fashioneds—a baker's dozen is twelve plus one. Like Jesus and his twelve apostles, and an apple fritter and a maple bar. That makes fifteen," Verboom said like he'd solved the equation for general relativity.

He reached into his fanny pack and peeled off a large bill. Gleefully in possession of the box, he left the change.

"That's some good cake right there, Santo! Feel the weight of this box. *Heavy dough.*"

He handed me the box, just long enough for me to gauge its heft, then took it back with glee.

Though I hoped to steer around the rally lot on the return to Genevieve's flat, Verboom was intent on making his delivery. Before getting too close, he opened the box of donuts so I could take my maple bar, then he pinched his apple fritter between his thumb and index finger, careful not to touch anything else. He closed the box and resumed walking. Seeing the two O.F.A.M. guys he'd spoken to earlier, Verboom sauntered up to them cheerfully.

"Man shall not live by bread alone," Verboom said, handing over the box of donuts, which was accepted silently. "Baked this morning! *Enjoy!*"

The man opened the box and looked inside.

"Let me take one so you know I stand behind the product." Verboom delicately reached into the box and removed one donut—again careful not to touch the others. He bit off half like a frog then smiled. Barely able to speak, he said, *"Heb melk?"*

The guy holding the donuts shook his head while Verboom chewed.

"So, you guys are going to run up quite a parking bill ..." Verboom coughed.

"Siege Captain covers it," said the man holding the pink box.

Then he stepped back to avoid Verboom's donut droplets.

"Come again?" Verboom asked.

"We've been flooded with donations. They're catering meals and paying parking."

"Who's donating?"

"Fellow patriots," the other man said terminally.

"Isn't that nice," Verboom said genuinely. "Well, enjoy your protesting."

"It's a *rally*. 'Protesting' is what those punks in the park do. We're *protecting* our rights."

As we walked away, Verboom endured a few more taunts about his pajamas.

Once we crossed Pike, an attractive woman in her late thirties, heavily made up with makeup and dressed in a trucker hat and white tank top, asked us to sign a petition. She introduced herself as a local "Draft Jimmer" urgently working to get Kroes onto the Washington state ballot as time was running out.

"Mademoiselle," Verboom declared, "as the future radio voice of anarchy, I refuse to recognize government authority."

"I don't believe in *this* government either, that's why we need Kroes," she insisted.

Verboom nodded once, his smile serene.

"What are *you* looking at?" she snapped at me.

"Are those real?" I blurted out, eyeing her necklace. "The diamonds on your cross?" The naked hypocrisy was too much to ignore.

"None of your business," she shot back.

"My mistake," I replied, my tone far from apologetic.

"It would be a mistake not to sign," she countered. Her eyes were combative, but she forced a smile. "Why not give the people a choice? Time's almost up."

"How many signatures do you need?" Verboom asked.

"Ten thousand signatures gets him on the ballot. We've got Jim's back, and he's got ours."

"They're real," Verboom said, studying the diamond cross suspended just above her cleavage. "According to *Reader's Digest*, I should have been a jeweler."

"If you like authentic goods, sign for Jim," she suggested with a wink at Verboom.

A news crew was setting up for interviews across from the rally parking lot when a man on a motorcycle with broad handle-bars roared in. He was clad in a sleeveless "Bikers For Kroes" vest, and his helmet was painted to resemble the General Lee muscle car from the iconic 1970s show. He parked his bike directly in front of the camera—only a narrow street between them—then revved the engine, creating one more crackling rumble before turning it off. He pulled off his helmet to reveal a meticulously waxed mustache and a mischievous grin.

The professor needed coffee to wash down his second donut, so we made our way down Pike Avenue. Drinks in hand, we walked to Pine and settled on a bus bench where we could take in the scene at Cal Anderson.

"From parking lot to park, a study in contrasts," he said as he sipped his steaming black coffee.

Though free of motor vehicles, Cal Anderson was bustling with tents and tarps, where a volunteer busily watered a flowerbed that had been transformed into a community garden.

Verboom looked over to me, a hint of approval in his smile. "All the phenotypes of the rainbow." Then he started reading the protest signs.

PEOPLE BEFORE PROFITS

ARREST WALL ST. BANKERS

ONE NATION UNDER GREED

MAKE JOBS NOT WAR

PATRIARCHY IS FOR DICKS

Verboom stood up and leaned forward with a squint. "What's this one? FREE...? FREE...?"

As Verboom leaned out too far off the sidewalk, a car blew its horn. The honk drew the attention of a small group across the street.

"Hey, you're the Portland Rose Giant!" a young man dressed in black yelled. "Saw the video on Twindle! Way to stick it to 'em."

Verboom laughed anxiously, unable to lie.

"You're that rose-ramming dude! Incredible work down there!" a second guy added.

"Let's go," I urged calmly.

"No judgment, but what's with the pajamas?" the man in black asked as he crossed the street, heading toward us.

"It's a *gi*," another guy said, following him across. "What's your school?"

"Goju-Ryu at the YMCA every Saturday for three years," Verboom responded, placing his left hand over his right fist and bowing respectfully.

"We'll see you this evening! Bring more flowers."

"Afraid they don't work," Verboom lamented.

"Get some goggles and a mask."

"Not sure the boss will let me out of the house," Verboom joked, signaling to me with his right thumb.

Spotting us, a woman approached. "*The Portland Rose Giant!*"

"A gentle giant, to be sure, mademoiselle," Verboom added, bowing slightly.

"Your speech was a divine proclamation!" she gushed.

"We read a lot of scripture in my youth, but those words were mostly improvisation, not entirely sure where that language came from. To be honest, I'm not entirely sure that I'm *well*, but I hate to see such tension in humanity," Verboom confessed.

"Sick times," she agreed. "Wall Street gets golden parachutes, and the rest of us get golden showers, plus this truck mob is getting a free pass to rock out with their Glocks out. They say they're protesting taxes, but the president lowered taxes in the recovery program."

"They do seem a sensitive lot," Verboom continued. "Just now, I learned that a simple box of donuts can put them on edge. Like Freud said, 'Sometimes a cigar is just a cigar.'"

Someone jogged up, camera aimed. Verboom raised his hand to shield his face, then spun and sprinted towards an alley. Zigging and zagging, he didn't slow until we reached Genevieve's building.

"No one's following us," I assured him, catching my breath.

"We can't let my image circulate in the public domain. *Code orange*! We'll need *orange gi*s. I'll wash them, press them, and hang them. I'll do all the laundry, but I can't do the shopping. It's the decision fatigue—you must know about the 'paradox of choice.'"

"Tired of hearing about it."

"We'll make orange my new professional wardrobe and take a tax deduction too! Orange will be a functional necessity, a reminder of our status."

"Which *is*?"

"*Code orange*! Lockdown! I almost forgot already! If I'm not wearing orange, how will I remember?"

We ascended the stairs to the top floor of Genevieve's building, where we found a stack of boxes outside our apartment door. Upon closer inspection, all the boxes were shipped from the same AV supplier in Los Angeles.

We carried the boxes inside, and Verboom arranged them into a makeshift pyramid before unpacking them, starting with the smallest box on top.

"It's like a Christmas tree," Verboom remarked, then sang a few lines of "O' Tannenbaum."

The first box contained black cables with gold-plated connectors; the second held two pairs of studio monitor headphones. The third box revealed two microphones, complete with stands, arms, and shields. As he unpacked each item, I arranged them neatly on the dining room table.

Also in the third box was a note from Genevieve: "Dear Pieter, I know you will find your voice. Within these boxes, you have everything needed to start your show. Remember: in my house, you are free to speak your piece. Blessings, Genevieve."

In the fourth box, we found an audio mixer and an extra display monitor to pair with my laptop. This box also contained a note from Genevieve's senior producer, which provided detailed instructions for setting up a VoIP number to receive calls, along with software recommendations for streaming and recording.

The largest of the five boxes contained several black acoustic foam tiles. Verboom stacked them into a precarious tower—like a house of cards. But as the pungent aroma of the synthetic materials filled the air, he sprang into action, flinging open the windows with the desperation of a skin diver surfacing for air.

"*The VOCs!* These puppies are off gassing like the airborne toxic event!" he exclaimed.

Once the room was ventilated, he methodically broke down the boxes, using his Swiss Army knife to score the seams. Gathering the flattened cardboard into a bundle under his arm, he shuffled toward the front door, barely squeezing through with the bulky load.

Returning, he went to the kitchen and poured himself a large glass of milk, then trudged to the couch to watch WNN.

While he watched, I made a first pass at setting up the studio in our dining room—a compact space with French doors leading to the living room and a small side door opening to the hallway, which connected to the kitchen, bathroom, and bedrooms. Through the French doors, the dining room offered a clear view of both the TV and the Puget Sound.

I installed acoustic foam on the two solid walls to improve sound quality. During a commercial break, I called Verboom over to help attach a few strips of foam to the ceiling. He didn't need a ladder.

Later that night, local news aired man-on-the-street interviews. One burly fellow wearing a red hat that said "JIM!"and holding a pink box queued up for his turn and quickly voiced his irritation:

> **PROTESTOR:** *See how we've been provoked, just for standing up for our God-given rights?*

> **REPORTER:** *How so?*

> **PROTESTOR:** *Here. See what's in this box? One dozen old-fashioned donuts. Look at this provocation!*

> **REPORTER:** *How are donuts a provocation?*

> **PROTESTOR:** *You don't see the parallel? They're*

old-fashioneds. We're the Old-Fashioned American Mob. They're calling us donuts—white, round, and empty in the middle! The giant clown in pajamas who left them for us didn't think we'd be smart enough to figure it out.

REPORTER: *What did he say when he gave them to you?*

PROTESTOR: *Enjoy!*

REPORTER: *Okay…?*

PROTESTOR: *It was a sinister tone.*

REPORTER: *How so?*

PROTESTOR: *Goofy, just plain goofy. He was obviously mocking us.*

REPORTER: *And who was he?*

PROTESTOR: *A big, tall guy with a beard and messy blond hair, wearing pinstripe pajamas.*

The reporter thanked the gentleman for his time and moved onto the next interviewee.

Verboom had been shaking his head slowly while listening, then finally interjected: "We can't get those orange *gis* here soon enough!" He sank back into the leather love seat with a groan. "I just can't party like I used to. All it took was two donuts to wreck my gut!"

"They *were* heavy donuts," I reminded him with a tickle of mockery.

"Yes, did you feel the weight?" He paused. "But that's not it. *I've* changed."

"Some guy preaching, 'change is the only constant' is the only constant," I joked.

"I'd say the chances are 50/50 you can make my persona funny. But don't make me laugh now, Santo. It hurts too much," he replied, trying to stifle a chuckle. "But there's an upside to this tummy ache. I don't have the oomph to get angry over my connection to this rally guy and his donuts."

"Wasn't sure you recognized the description."

"The pinstripe pajamas, he obviously meant my signature look. The orange *gis* can't get here soon enough."

"You mentioned that."

While he bellyached about donuts and uniforms, an email alert popped up. Jacqueline was curious about my writing and travel observations. She mentioned that the truck guys were holding rallies near her campus, causing regular disturbances. A few nights back, they knocked a student reporter to the ground, and despite a complaint being filed, no arrests had been made. Jacqueline noticed Kroes' campaign branding scattered through the crowd and wondered if his following extended to Seattle.

While there were no formal ties reported between O.F.A.M. and the Draft Jimmers, the two movements seemed to be merging before our eyes. Despite establishment pundits' refusal to take Kroes seriously as a contender, networks like ANN and WNN continued to broadcast all his public events. One salty analyst said, "The only thing making James Kroes popular is his popularity."

Though claiming to be a grassroots movement, *The New York Times* found that O.F.A.M. was bankrolled by billionaire-funded think tanks and political action groups, providing both financial and marketing support. For example, Ralph Chicory, an experienced

Arizona political operative who had worked with extremists like Barry Goldwater and George Wallace, leveraged his expertise in direct mail marketing from the 1960s to present, now supporting the Kroes and O.F.A.M. movements. Despite nearing eighty, Chicory had adapted to current tech and maintained significant influence through his extensive mailing list, originally started by hand.

According to *The New York Times*, in 2008 the then-future president had a substantial advantage in digital technology. However, by refining their tech for 2012, Conservatives and the adjacent Kroesters managed to bridge the gap, perhaps even surpassing the Liberals, who over-innovated with too many complex features on their action app.

Right-wing organizations opted for simplicity, creating tools that let users mass text their existing contacts effortlessly. Now, grandma could spam you with messages that might seem tailor-made. However, unless she typically called you "PATRIOT" in all caps and doted on you with dystopian anecdotes, it was clear she was forwarding propaganda.

While considering a reply to Jacqueline, Verboom remarked, "Just because billionaires promote religious and political doctrine, it doesn't mean the beliefs of the rank and file are insincere."

"But the 'grassroots' branding is phony; it's *astroturfing*. What's at issue is the 'halo effect,' big money putting on the veneer of 'regular folks.'"

"Did they break any laws?"

"That's not my point. They're duping people. Just like these trucking mobsters have polluted the American flag. Now the Stars and Stripes are a symbol of O.F.A.M. and Kroes."

"You're saying the American flag is guilty by association?"

"Well, I know what you'll say next: logical fallacy. *Ad hominem circumstantial.*"

"True. Despite my Germanic roots, I do love a Latin label!"

"I thought you were of Dutch ancestry?"

"Supposedly Dutch ethnicity mainly traces back to the Franks, Frisians, and Saxons—my family is mainly Frisian—but I was speaking about language. The Dutch language is considered Germanic." Then like a character in a mafia movie, he asked, "*Capisce?*"

"*Capisce,*" I confirmed. "But you forgot to mention the Romans and Vikings. Now, do you mind if I make my point?"

"*Alstublieft*. Please."

"The flag is now identified with the American Right, not the American Left."

"Let's take it back! We'll fly the Stars and Stripes high above our coordinates! We'll turn this road trip into a roving think tank for faith and flag! And for a name... *hmm*. How about the Institute for Tautology—or the Institute of Tautological Science? And along these lines, we should create an LLC, an umbrella for the new radio show and this new flag research—just in case you get sued."

"*Me?*" I asked, a bit surprised. "You're the one playing with other people's guns!"

"Yes, you." He shook his head. "Bayesian statistics, bias, and *blah blah blah*! We need to secure the advanced personhood of an LLC! A whole suite of benefits! Now again, what should we call this person of limited liability? Maybe the International Court of Tautology? Though O.F.A.M. won't like that international feel, it's just one click away from *globalist*, which is a dog-whistle for..."

"Why please that audience?"

"Bridges, Santo. *Bridges*! Maybe we should do an 'America Is America' chapter? And perhaps 'Exceptional Is Exceptional' pamphlets? Goodwill is vital in these polarizing times... Anyway, the institute is the institute."

"Fly the American flag and people will assume you're a

right-winger."

"A bit harsh, *ja*?"

"Perhaps premature." I gave a little ground. "How about a field experiment? We could walk around town with an American flag and observe the reactions?"

"Santo, you know I'm keeping a low profile."

"You've been in the news at least two days in a row."

"Indeed. It's dreadful. Let's just go with your gut on this flag thing. By the way, did we get the SEALs back?"

"Not yet, but a new hostage photo was released showing each soldier holding up a current issue of *The New York Times*. ANN claimed it's further proof of Liberal complicity."

He shifted restlessly on the couch, then his expression brightened as a thought struck him. "Good news! I've finally come up with a name for my *persona*!"

"What is it?"

"He's a virtuoso and so much more so! *Vincent Vermeer*: The coming of the Dutch Maestro!" he proclaimed, his fingers deftly twisting his mustache as if he were a method actor trying to stay in character. "Santo, pretending to be someone else is already doing wonders for my confidence!"

"Must be nice."

"Ever wonder why the Dutch were the great painters and the Germans the great composers?"

"Pieter Verboom is dead; long live Vincent Vermeer!"

He leapt up from the couch and darted over to the dining room studio. He slipped on his chunky headphones and, with a theatrical gesture, placed his right hand behind his ear to show off his new gear.

"I'm 'The Girl with a Pearlstein Earring.' You like?" He winked at me. "Ever wonder why the Dutch were the sublime painters, and the Germans were the sublime composers? Think it was Lutheranism?

Nope! *I've got it*. It's because the Dutch grappled with iconoclastic Calvinism! The canvas became their act of theological rebellion!"

"Maybe you should paint instead of doing radio?"

Pointing at his headphones, he said loudly, "I'm sorry, Santo. I can't hear anything with these earrings."

While I composed an email to Jacqueline, Verboom busied himself with the studio equipment—poking at the acoustic foam, unplugging and re-plugging cables, adjusting the mic arms up, then lowering them again.

Then the wood floors cracked and squeaked as he returned to the couch. He plopped down and switched to ANN.

"Viewpoint diversity," he mumbled.

However, it quickly became intolerable.

Unable to concentrate, I asked, "How can anyone watch this hyperbolic crap?"

"Basic drives, Santo. We must survive danger to reproduce, and ANN allows those who are already safe and past their reproductive prime to get off on a jag of danger!" he exclaimed with a sparkle.

"Media lessons from the guy who just tuned in."

"The real trouble with *hot media* isn't a simple Left-versus-Right; it's more like cocaine. Does a rat in a cage press the cocaine button?"

"Until it's gone. But comparing ANN and WNN is like apples and oranges."

"Sure, their flavors differ, but the psychological impact they wield is eerily similar; both are masters of the outrage stimulus. *Who do we include? Who do we exclude?* WNN might paint a truer picture of our world—liberal personality types require more nuanced titillation, but both *networks* manipulate the same *neural* pathways."

"The professor is not yet dead," I mused.

"Speaking of stimulation, I recall a pastor from my youth saying, 'Men are like microwaves, and women are like Crock-Pots.' Sexually speaking, of course."

"Slow live the slow cooker," I pronounced.

"The professor *is* dead, and *The Dutch Uncle* will take humanity to higher sleights! We'll use our knowledge of the natural world to transcend crude Naturalism. Instead of demeaning humanity with blatant propaganda, we will insult humanity with the truth!"

"Humor is the only way to truly reach everyone," I said. "But it seems Americans are forgetting how to laugh."

"Don't forget your mission! Teach Vermeer to be funny!"

As Verboom started humming chord progressions, pretending to warm up important vocal chords, I tossed a seat cushion at him in jest. He ducked, and the cushion landed on the worn wooden floor with a thud.

"Going back to the Institute of Tautology, perhaps we organize as a non-profit entity," he mused.

"A 501(c)?" I suggested. "Allows us to..."

"Avoid even more taxes!"

"More importantly, if a career in psychology doesn't pan out, I'll need some kind of organizational name to describe my work history in production. 'Driving Miss Dutchie' isn't going to cut it."

"I believe in you, Santo! You can still make it in academia, even if my career is swirling down the drain along with my hair."

"Your hair still looks thick."

"Because no one's tall enough to see the top of my head!"

"What's the institute's mission statement?"

"A public service to excavate theocrats." He smiled wryly.

He stroked his beard, displaying a mix of blond, brown, and red whiskers. "You do know that think tanks formed in opposition to FDR's New Deal. Instead of giving money to help people with food and medicine, wealthy folks could make tax-saving donations to support the untaxed propagation of their propaganda for reducing *their* taxes. Triple win."

"Wouldn't you rather go back to teaching?"

"Seems like I may be joining the exclusive club of terminated tenured professors."

"What's the cause?"

"Going to DC—*bad idea*. My study on sexual stereotypes in politics—*bad idea*. Perhaps once tenured, I indulged one whim too many."

"Don't underestimate yourself, your 'famous' study is more efficient than Wythe and Weirsma's four parenting questions."

"Come again?"

"Would you rather your child be *independent* or *show respect* for elders, rather *self-reliant* or *obedient*, rather *curious* or *well-mannered*, and rather *considerate* or *well-behaved*. Though I think asking questions about parenting pushes everything to the right—it brings out conservation," I said.

"Maybe you'd prefer to study with that metaphor guy down in Berkeley? The nurturing-parent and disciplining-parent models for each party..."

"We've got *three* parties now. Your research awaits you!"

"If Ella's still hunting for me once the sabbatical is up, that is, if I'm still on the lam, well..."

I sighed. "Spit it out?"

"Job abandonment is tantamount to quitting."

"Professors say 'tantamount' not shock jocks."

"*All jock and no shock*!" His mood instantly rebounded. "Maybe a tagline for Vermeer, *eh*?"

"I can't do this," I said to myself.

"Do what?"

"Teach you to be funny." I shook my head. "We've got to get you back on your feet before your sabbatical runs out."

"Giving up on your purpose so soon? You should talk to Genevieve."

"Corporations are people, my friend!" I read the words scrolling across the bottom of the television. Pointing to the screen, I asked, "Is this why you're considering incorporation?"

"I really want to be *somebody*, Santo!" he shouted theatrically, yet his gaze remained fixed on the TV.

That offhand remark about corporations being people was undermining the Conservative candidate. Until that ill-chosen statement, the most severe media criticism had stemmed from revelations that he had let his dog ride on the roof of his minivan during a family vacation. While his fondness for the investor class had already weakened his appeal with swing voters, something about his phrasing continued to gnaw at people.

Technically speaking, he was right about corporations. 'Personhood,' as a concept, had made everything from zygotes to xylophone manufacturing sacred—assuming you weren't a regular human adult, personhood rights had become quite expansive.

"I suspect 'radical personhood' is the core concept uniting big business and big religion," Verboom noted, his attention fixed on the screen.

"Maybe the candidate's got the wrong kind of religion too?" I asked. "Do Mormon's fraternize with First Brothers?"

"Here's an ode to a future institute," Verboom began, his voice rising with the flourish of a seasoned bard. "*Ahem*. O my tautologies are laughed at by Santo, but soon you'll see them most hallowed. *You will see! You will see!* A person is a person. A corporation is not a person; a corporation is a corporation. Speech is speech; money is not speech. Money is money, honey! And a frown is a frown, until it's turned upside down! *Say?* Is it time for a hamburger?" Verboom folded his arms and smiled.

CRACK!

I ducked.

Verboom sprang to his feet and ran to the window, then glanced back at me. "*Time*?"

Looking up from my phone, I said, "Six PM sharp."

"Boy o boy, you can set your watch to these boys!"

I glared at him.

"Perhaps, you would feel more comfortable ordering in?" he asked. "Besides, it's best for the Portland Rose Giant to stay in the building."

"How about pizza? Extra veggies."

"Veggie pie for you, meat-lover for me! Let's use the funds in my hip pack," he said, motioning toward the coat stand without taking his eyes off the TV.

As we waited on the delivery, I rearranged the studio while Verboom continued his media vigil. Every commercial break, he asked me when the food would arrive.

The pizzas were lukewarm when the delivery guy—a flustered young man in a lime green hoodie and a cap pulled low—handed them over and apologized. I asked about the mood on the street. He shook his head and urged us to check the local news.

After we each finished a slice during a long commercial break, the local report aired: "Sparks fly on Capitol Hill!" Someone had sabotaged the O.F.A.M. rally trucks, loosening the lug nuts from the wheel mounts of their front axels. Just after 6 PM when the convoy began, wheels slid off as the trucks cornered, metal scraping pavement. The footage looped again and again on the broadcast.

A reporter on the street gathered comments from witnesses until a broad-shouldered man wearing a green field jacket and red hat pushed into the frame, declaring, "We'll get justice!" The camera focused on his "Draft Jim" hat. Thinking fast, the reporter asked if he planned to go to the police.

"We *are* the police," he snapped back.

"What's your badge number?" she challenged.

Then the man shoved the camera aside and stormed off to his wounded pickup.

16

The orange *gis* arrived a few mornings later, and Verboom slipped on a pair and returned to the couch in his crisp new uniform. Fixated on the ever "breaking news," he could hideout in Genevieve's apartment, a safehouse between the O.F.A.M. lot and the protestors camping in the park.

Since the sparks flew, the tense mood on Capitol Hill had only worsened. The bank handed over surveillance footage from the lot to Seattle police, but they claimed no individual could be clearly identified as a perpetrator. Despite calls for its release, the footage remained private, fueling rumors of collusion between law enforcement and the bank. Although the bank strained to make clear that it did not endorse the sabotage, it also emphasized that it had not invited O.F.A.M. to use its parking lot. The men in trucks simply arrived early each morning, taking most of the spots and paying for their use.

O.F.A.M. responded by posting lookouts at all three corners of the lot and arriving even earlier in the morning. They also ran convoys around Cal Anderson Park at regular intervals, posturing as a kind of citizens' patrol.

"Santo, we're perched at the crossroads of American politics! Try on an orange jacket and show me the red light!"

I flashed my phone at him, confirming a recording in progress.

Through the first week in Seattle, Verboom's mental clarity improved mildly, but he continued to resist razor and scissor.

Thankfully he kept up with other forms of personal hygiene. While watching the morning news shows, he did pushups and sit-ups during commercial breaks.

"Fifty-nine, sixty..." he counted.

"Maybe some lunges?" I offered. "Don't get top-heavy."

In one week, Verboom went from zero cable news to watching several hours a day. In the hotel, he had mocked such foolish consumption—even unplugging the TV—but now he was hooked. When I called out this hypocrisy, he explained his behavior as "research."

It was hard to gauge the authenticity of the news-addled Verboom. Was he wrapped up in the delusion or cheekily playing along?

"Let's try out some taglines for the new show," he said, catching his breath after a set of pushups.

"Maybe you could riff on 'busting a Dutch?'"

"Indeed! Busting the Dutch Mafia."

"It's a reference to cannabis in cigar wrappers, finding your way to an altered state."

"To a boy with wooden shoes, everything's *gouda*!"

"Americans don't know anything about the Netherlands."

"*Nay*! People 'go Dutch' all the time."

"Your people-group is associated with cheapness and cheese—how exciting."

"Don't forget cannabis!" he giggled. "Hey Santo, what's better than roses on the piano?" Verboom tilted his head forward knowingly. "*Tulips* on the *organ*."

I shook my head.

"Now let's get some good bumper music! Lots of bass guitar, I want to reverberate in those big rigs out there on the freeway. Oh, and do you get it, Santo? *Two lips*? So, think my jokes are ready for broadcast?" he asked excitedly.

"There must be a study correlating the consumption of cable news with low testosterone," I said, looking up from my laptop at the TV.

"I'm awash in that ancient hormone. Let me know if you run short."

He dropped to the floor and did at least thirty push-ups.

I shook my head again. "All set there, but I'm hungry. Heading out for lunch, can I bring you back something?"

"All that takeaway packaging? No, I better join. Single-use plastic is a crime against humanity! Today the plastic wraps your lunch; tomorrow it's *in* your lunch! Perhaps, I still have another book in me: *Homo Plasticus*. A new species brought to you by big oil and the American need for convenience…"

"Have you *looked* at yourself?" I asked judgementally.

"*Code Orange*. You're right. This won't do."

He tied a purple paisley bandana behind his neck and then pulled the front of it up over his bushy beard and Dutch nose. He put on the aviator sunglasses and trucker hat from the gas station, then he followed me down the stairs and out of the apartment.

"The sun on my skin, that vitamin D, I'm high as a kite!" he exclaimed, almost skipping with glee down 15th Street as we approached Pine Street.

I noticed that only his hands and forearms were exposed to direct sunlight.

The park activists had taken the acronym D.D.P.—N.A.P.A.M. (Direct Democracy Participants—Not A Party, A Movement). Though it looked poor in print, their chant worked like an earworm:

> *D! D! P! [low tone]*
> *Nap'am! [high tone]*

Nap'am! [high tone]

During the day, the D.D.P. occupied five retail blocks in the Pike & Pine Corridor of Capitol Hill using human barricades to stop all vehicle traffic. At first the police chief and mayor had used force to restore vehicle traffic, but the D.D.P. reached a truce with the city. The mayor could choose between tear-gassing and zip-tying Seattle's protestors, or she could take heat for allowing nonviolent civil disobedience. She tried the first, then opted for the latter and took heat from everyone.

"They're calling this the 'Erogenous Zone.' Economic Radicals Occupying for a Green Economy Now. As far as I know, the 'ous' has not been enumerated," I said to Verboom as we walked through the zone.

One woman, who looked to be over eighty years old, conducted a teach-in with a scruffy but attentive audience. Verboom's bandana slipped off his face and hung around his neck. We passed a series of meetings, food vendors, and artists displaying work. Though I'd overheard a talk of "marauding vigilantes" and "opportunistic future capitalists" spoiling previous gatherings, in this moment it felt like a farmers' market festooned with political signs.

On the southern edge of the zone, a truck hauling home appliances idled at an intersection, waiting for the light to change. With the windows down Fritz Hearn's voice boomed:

> *Folks, these D.D.P. protest bums are conducting class warfare plain and simple. Don't fall for it! They're not hippies; they're hustlers! The rent is not too damn high. These people are too damn lazy! They don't want to work. They want to scream at people driving to work. The problem isn't lack of opportunity. It's the lack of effort. Don't fall for their lies.*

> *They want a war on the rich, but they're coming after your working-class paycheck next. While they're fooling around in the parks of America's Liberal cities, we... are... at... work...*

The truck rolled away, and the words faded until the deep bass of the Hearn theme song played.

At the Pacific Fish House on Pike Street, Verboom ordered fish 'n chips, and I decided on pulled pork. We ate sitting on barstools in the half-subterranean restaurant. Now confident in his anonymity, Verboom spun his hat backward and removed his glasses. While I jotted a few notes in my field book, Verboom unknotted his bandana, folding it neatly into a small triangle, then he looked my way.

"Now that you're liberated from the Neo-Freudian, have you succeeded with any reproductive activity?"

I stayed mum as the question was obviously rhetorical; I'd spent almost every minute in Seattle with him. Then he waxed ineloquent on the naturalness of reproduction and pleasure seeking.

"Lucky you weren't raised by Calvinists!" his voice soared. "They've found a way to take the satisfaction out of everything—except making money."

Verboom wiped his mouth and hands thoroughly with a thick white paper napkin, shook his bandana out like a magician and used it to polish his sunglasses, then he reapplied his disguise. He suggested we visit a record shop on 10th Avenue and "peruse some bumper music and a theme song."

Theme song. My life needed one, but one didn't come to mind.

With Jacqueline's challenge to redeem the trip through writing, Genevieve's encouragement to indulge the professor's self-realization, and my own childhood desire to be a documentarian, I found myself tangled in conflicting motivations that somehow still aligned.

And through all the mental noise, I heard my mother's voice: *Yes*. I saw her smile in my mind's eye. *Yes*. Say, *yes*. And with that, my inner tension eased. In saying yes to a wild but gentle man, I could observe, write, and ride along. I could learn. And I could stay out of Grand Rapids.

The shop only sold vinyl, and we didn't have a record player, so Verboom zipped open his hip pack, peeled off bills, and handed them to me. He turned his trucker hat backwards and raised his glasses, looking me dead in the eye.

"Do whatever it takes. If a person can ruin a presidency, perhaps a persona can save it." He paused, then added, "Please." He shook his head. "I seem to have lost my manners in the fugue. Forgive me."

Setting his glasses back on his nose, he zipped around the store manically.

"Now for music! Please pick something fresh! Pick something stale! Hot and cold! Sweet and sour! *Sa-sa-sa-salty*! Let's have something from every genre! Classy and eclectic... Sounds electric!" He pulled the purple bandana over the tip of his nose, then spun his hat forward.

I looked at him blankly.

"Mind making the choice? I can't make decisions," he pleaded, slightly muffled by whiskers scratching on his face covering.

The clerk helped me pick a few albums and a record player with an audio jack. Verboom pulled his bandana down and bellowed: "Vermeer can *hear*! Vermeer can *hear*! Bring the music to my *ear!*"

"Is he going to break something?" the clerk asked.

"He's already broken."

The clerk studied Verboom. "Is that a prison suit?"

"Karate," I replied.

"Who's Vermeer?"

"His imaginary friend."

"So you're like his babysitter?"

"We've been described as partners."

Though no longer the full-feathered free-thought zone of its low-rent heyday, in addition to the protesters, Capitol Hill had bohemian holdovers, who provided cover to a longhaired man dressed in orange, squawking about refinement.

With sunshine, fresh air, and enough fish and chips for two regular-sized people, I told Verboom about his next assignment. Genevieve expected him as a guest on her weekly radio program later that evening. It would be a chance to try out the new gear.

"*Verboom*?" he said. "He vanished in the canals of Venice. Didn't you receive the novella *Almost Amsterdam*? The fiction of the *self* becomes a fiction *itself*! It's a Platonic dialogue on the could-be's of what-might-have-been and what-never-was!" He plopped down on a public bench and tried to talk me out of it. Then, as he closed his eyes and drifted back to LA, he began to reminisce on "the holistic beauty" of his "consort," but I stopped him before it got gross.

"Verboom will do it," he said, after another moment of thought. "Just this one time. But no one can know from where he calls."

"Let's head back and test your mic."

"It must be the meds you got me on; I get lost in thought, and the next thing you know, the body betrays me. Let me sit here for a moment. Now, tell me again about the polar icecaps. We need to wreck the mood."

I had been through the apartment a few times over, cleaning and organizing, staying ready to leave as soon as possible. And unless he hid them in that fanny pack, there were no meds.

A few days earlier, I'd called Genevieve while out on a walk alone. She was convinced that Verboom was sane. "Likely as lucid as he's ever been, but his emotions are surging like the ocean," she said. "The moods crest, break, and recede, but the shore remains. History has caught up to him, but the storm will pass."

She didn't think he needed medication or hospitalization, just love and attention, like she'd said in person. She doubted Verboom found liberation in the "Liberal Consensus," saying that he simply moved onto a different but equally rigid set of ideas and maintained the same repressive habits. "He's plagued by a new puritanism—constantly self-censoring. Yet now, all these years later, he's becoming a free spirit. He still has half his life to live!"

This interpretation was more generous than mine, but Genevieve had seen more of life, and though I felt differently, she lifted my spirits. Perhaps he wouldn't need to be tazed and hauled off in a straitjacket during orange hour.

"In fact, I want him on my show," she added. "He needs to talk, but he still feels the need for a formal reason, a social or professional structure to express his thoughts. Let's give him the excuse he needs."

"Like a classroom."

"Exactly. Plus, it'll be a warmup for his *new* program."

"I don't think he'll go for it. After Portland, he's even more paranoid."

"You'll find a way to persuade him."

"Do you know why he went to LA?" I asked.

"He wanted to disappear. He said my voice brought him back, but it was you."

As Verboom sat upright in a wooden chair, digesting his fish and chips, I dialed Genevieve's studio, masking my caller ID with a simple *67 trick. Her producer answered and said we'd be on-air in a few minutes.

Verboom put on his headphones and pulled his mic close.

"Tracing this call?" he asked Genevieve's producer.

"Your number is blocked, and Genevieve's agreed not to mention your location."

"She won't bring up the mess in DC or my convalescence at the sanitarium?" he asked.

"Or their 'encounters?'" I leaned in on Verboom's mic.

"She practices radical honesty," Verboom said. "Kind-hearted as she is, you never know what she'll say. In fact, she observed that my left testicle is larger than my right testicle. No one's ever told me that before, not even my doctors. What if a caller gets wise and asks about our connection?"

"You'll discuss *Final Freedom* and what it means for progressive faiths."

"Could I pitch my seersucker *gis*?"

"*Geese*?" the producer asked.

"*Karate suits*. She has a big audience."

"Absolutely not. Now clear your mind and take a deep breath. It's time to speak with Genevieve," the producer said going into a calm whisper. "And if it's any consolation, my left foot is a half-size larger than my right."

Suddenly ear-piercing feedback came through the phone, then echoed: *wah wah wah.*

"Are we on speaker?"

"No."

"Check your plugs," the producer said. "We're going live in *five, four, three, two, one…*"

Verboom wiggled the jack to his mic and shrugged, then he looked at me with the eyes of a child lost at the zoo.

Genevieve introduced Verboom as a prolific author and the playfully literalistic mind behind *Tautology*, but today's appearance centered on *Final Freedom* and what it could mean to those left of center.

When asked about its origin, he said, "My closest colleague describes the event as a sarcastic tantrum after getting fed-up with authoritarians trolling my talk show." He disavowed the challenge as both *100% rhetorical* and *100% ironic,* and then he referred to himself in the third person: "Verboom is a loyal Unionist." His eyes closed as he spoke. Asked if he remembered the event, he said, "The body was willing, but the mind was in the gables."

Genevieve wanted to clarify, "You have no direct memory of the event?"

Verboom claimed, "I only know what I read in the paper," and asked why she cared, when it seemed to be a right-wing thing. Verboom was irritated that a sophisticated thinker like Genevieve Van Diest would give credence to *Final Freedom.*

She defended her stance by referencing Abraham Maslow's hierarchy of needs, arguing that a church should nurture the whole person—an approach that, in her view, could reduce reliance on the social safety net.

Verboom scoffed and riffed on the ancient patriarch: "What about the Abraham who nearly sacrificed his own son? The Abraham who impregnated his wife's servant? The same Abraham who let his wife be taken as Pharaoh's concubine just to save his own skin? *'Tell him you're my sister so I won't be killed.'* Yes, *that* Abraham!"

They went on to discuss the incentives for faith and church membership, the difference between "religious" and "spiritual," then the nature of Jesus and the nature of salvation, which led to discussing modern German theologians and great figures in the history of Western philosophy.

Verboom said, "Can you believe that the guy who taught my Modern Theology course didn't understand Hegel? *'The Absolute? The*

Absolute? I kept asking: What the hell is *the Absolute?'* Like Jonathan Kuiper asking where the bullets land, I never got a straight answer."

Genevieve asked where he hoped *Final Freedom* would go next.

"To the outhouse of *history*!" he bellowed.

Verboom squirmed in his seat as Genevieve pressed for an interpretation of his *Final Freedom* challenge, then he yelled: "Listeners at home, turn up the sound. There *is* a remedy for America: Tune into *The Dutch Uncle with Vincent Vermeer* tomorrow at noon Pacific Time! That's *The Dutch Uncle* at noon Pacific tomorrow! Get Vermeer in your ear! America's Dutch uncle will tell you what you need to hear!"

He pulled off his headphones and pushed away the mic.

"Help me to the couch," he said. "Pieter Verboom exhausts me."

He leaned on me like a man with a twisted ankle until collapsing into the cushions.

"The remote," he said like an elderly chieftain barely able to see, short of breath, reaching out his hand limply.

Once he held the remote control in his hand, he rested it on his stomach without turning on the set.

After a brief snooze, his arm went up, remote in hand, and he returned to the world of cable news.

James Kroes is holding a rally this evening in Tulsa, where he's promising to finalize his choice for a running mate. Analysts speculate as to whether he'll choose a retired general or an established political mainstay to balance his 'outsider' status.

Earlier today, Kroes repeated his attack lines on the president: failing to kill OBL and failing to rescue the captured SEALs. Kroes has also gone after the president's campaign

> *to rebuild the wall between church and state, referring to the president's definitive statement last February, when he said, 'America is the world's oldest secular democracy. The most influential founders were not puritanical Christians but pragmatic rationalists. They believed in a wall of separation between church and state—to protect both—and we must continue to build that wall.*

Irritated, Verboom dropped to the floor and did a set of perfect pushups to exhaustion. He counted aloud. Forty-six. He watched a commercial for cholesterol-reducing medication, and then he rolled onto his back and did a set of sit-ups. Sixty-seven. After resting on the floor for a moment he returned to the couch, eyes ever on the screen. The news continued:

> *Even with its high signature threshold, Kroes has qualified for the ballot in Florida, one of the toughest hurdles to clear. Having done so, even his staunchest critics concede that his candidacy has an outside chance. The reputable Gunther Survey shows Kroes at 17%, while the president is at 31%. The Conservative candidate is at 23%, which leaves 29% of the country undecided.*

"And uninterested," Verboom said.

I walked to the coffee table, took the remote and turned the television off.

"Only one hour tomorrow. We go live at noon. Thanks to your work on Genevieve's show, there may be a few listeners."

"Think I ruined my alias?" he asked.

"How Verboom is Vermeer? Enough difference, maybe no one catches on."

"The Nooner, Pacific Time. Tune in and let me turn you off!" he intoned, his voice dipping into a rich baritone.

"Vermeer's a morning zoo DJ?"

"What's a Dutch uncle again?" he asked.

"Criticizing every idea that's not your own," I reminded him.

"Just like every adult in my childhood! Shall I use a whistling Dutch accent or more of a halting style? English V's or Dutch V's?"

"You want to go with *Finchent Furmirror*?" I asked.

"Say it, don't spray it!"

"What shall we call your newsletter? That's how you'll build a subscriber base and..."

"Change the world," he said absently.

"*Charge* subscription fees. Somebody's got to buy protein for the baby," I teased.

"Vincent Vermeer: Sometimes your Dutch uncle is the only one who will tell you the stoned cold truth."

"The only one?"

"The Fritzers love that about their Fritz; he's their self-proclaimed one-and-only. He 'gets it,' and they get *him*. Efficient. Now the Left, they like those stacked-up puns and inside wordplays. *Stoned. Dutch. Amsterdam. Cannabis...* And 'the only one' stuff would be considered ironic."

"For your first essay?"

"Perhaps a Haiku?" He grinned, then closed his eyes to concentrate. "Now, if you need to run advertisements"—his eyes popped open—"maybe '*The Big Quake's Coming*!' Or '*The Great Pacific Shaker*!' Or '*The Next Big One*.'" He clapped his hands together. "I'm on a roll! Let's go all in! Let's hire your MFA friend to write our newsletter and bring home the bacon!" He howled in the delirious mania of his WNN appearance on *Hot Button Science*. "Let's make art out of culture war! Pay her whatever she wants! Give her the whole war chest!"

"Maybe she can refer someone more juvenile."

"Yes, we can't have too much talent," he said. "If it's too funny, people will know it's written by a liberal personality type, and we'll blow our cover. We've got to disguise in rigid, puritanical anarchy," he said.

"A *stoned* cold paradox," I pretended to muse.

Later that afternoon, I emailed Jacqueline: "Know a ghostwriter? Inexpensive and inexperienced preferred. Poor taste appreciated but not required."

She responded to my message but not my question, asking about the street rallies and protests in Seattle. After Portland, Seattle had the largest recurring O.F.A.M. rallies and reportedly the largest D.D.P. encampment.

"You could get that from one article in *The New Yorker*," Jacqueline wrote back. "As an almost-psychologist—a skilled observer—you must be seeing something more."

What could I see? The television over Verboom's orange clad knees slung on the arm of a leather couch. He'd changed the channel to ANN, and there was no shortage of insults for the perceived danger of the D.D.P. protestors.

"Please change the station!" I shouted. "There's no policy or context; it's only fearmongering. They're playing one burning trashcan on loop!"

"The burning trashcan has become the burning bush," Verboom said like a sleepy ghost. "If you believed these yahoos, you'd think hordes of America's youth were flooding the streets with Molotov cocktails, crowbars, and spray paint." He yawned. "Let's make a pot of coffee."

ANN moved to an image of a burning bodega and ran the title: *Your Home Next?*

"Good thing we don't live in a minimart," Verboom replied.

Thinking of something to share with Jacqueline, I walked to the window. There were more D.D.P. protestors than rally guys. D.D.P. held more territory but lacked hardware. In addition to their parking lot vigil, O.F.A.M. ran daily convoys through the city. The recurring street action consumed ten blocks and a park, and though Seattle is over 83 square miles—looking at the television—that sliver seemed to be all of Seattle.

Later that evening, Jacqueline and I ran another trial webcast, our third and final, to confirm the stream quality.

"Your voice sounds good, just wish you had something to say other than 'testing... 1, 2, 3,'" she said.

To meet her challenge, I channeled the forthcoming Vincent Vermeer and howled a pretend monologue.

When I finished, there was silence.

"Jacqueline? You there?"

"*Zzz...*" She snored.

"Jacqueline?"

"You mean 'caller.' Yes. I'm here." She paused. "When you write this up, make sure you cut that mock diatribe. It wasn't flattering."

"Impersonating a persona isn't easy."

"Style-wise: Turn down the whining nasal and turn up the gravelly gravitas. Content-wise: Does the professor really think politics boils down to personality type?"

"He makes a good case for it."

"But personalities need convictions."

"He says beliefs are acquired to reinforce the pre-existing personality, then one stays in a reinforcing tribe or finds a new tribe to reinforce the personality with better paired beliefs. Put it this way, your personality type predicts your politics better than economic class."

"What about people with mixed personalities?" Jacqueline asked.

"Blended personalities have blended ideologies and lean Right more often than Left, especially when activated by fear. Psychologically, Conservatives have an advantage in hot media," I concluded.

"*Psychologically*? I think it's time you go outside!"

Apparently Verboom could hear the conversation and cranked up the TV's volume, the sound flooding through the French doors, so we ended the call.

The TV boomed: "Has another attempt to free the SEALs failed? Find out more at 11 PM."

With the studio shutdown, I slipped through the French doors and told Verboom I was headed out for a bike ride. Even though the station was at commercial break, he waved without turning around to face me.

After descending the main stairs to the ground floor, I took a narrow stairway at the back of the building, leading to the laundry room. The air was thick with the scent of detergent and fabric softener, a manufactured freshness hanging in the humid air. The rhythmic clatter of zippers and buttons echoed in the dryers—a band of metallic drums playing as I spun the dial on my bike lock just outside. Six numbers. My ex's birthday. I could still picture the look on her face when I chose them at the bike shop, the way it fell when the clerk mentioned the combination could never be reset.

As dusk settled, I pedaled past the empty rally lot then cut through the hushed university campus nearby. I looped back down the Pike and Pine Corridor, where streetlamps and neon signs cast light against the maple and oak leaves. The wet pavement shimmered, as I passed bars and restaurants. Headlights flared, then faded behind me as I descended toward the waterfront, where a briny scent mixed with diesel exhaust.

At Pike Place Market, empty stalls stood dim as seagulls scavenged the last scraps. I cruised through the Olympic Sculpture Park, weaving past steel giants frozen against the Sound, then pushed on toward Elliott Bay Park. No protesters. No signs. No militia. No flags. Just me, my 10-speed, my legs strong, and my heart broken.

For more than two years, I lived with the knowledge that my mother would die young of cancer. But when it came, the horror eclipsed anything I had imagined, tearing through my sense of order, destroying my faith in the intelligible world. Both slow and sudden, expected yet shocking, I had been prepared, or so I thought. But as I held her hand, watching her final breath after hours of panting, the grief overwhelmed me in a way my agile mind couldn't predict—even after hundreds of days spent anticipating the inevitable. Until then, anticipation had steeled my nerves. When the pain came, I had always thought: that wasn't so bad. But losing my young mother was a terror beyond reckoning—a grief so singular and consuming it could keep a poet working for a lifetime.

When my mother took her last breath, I looked over to my grandmother, who sat on the other side of the bed. Her tears were silent, her eyes closed; she did not sob or scream. She sat like a weeping statue, holding her daughter's left hand.

I looked over to my mom's gaunt face, never to speak or smile again. I let go of her right hand. I saw a nurse standing at the foot of the bed, her eyes brimming with empathy. And then—my vision failed. My mind failed.

Before I knew it, I was running like a spooked animal down the hall, searching for an exit. Down the stairs. Across the parking lot. Up a cold, grassy hill. My feet slipped, but I didn't fall. My thighs burned. My arms shook. And at the top of the hill, I wailed like a caribou dying in the lion's teeth.

My mother died forty years before the standard life expectancy for an American woman in 2012. She had only slept with one man. She believed it was a sin. And from that single act, I was born—a son whose mother dedicated her life to preaching purity.

"What I meant for evil, God meant for good," my mom would say, when giving her testimony in a church sanctuary or in the gym of a Christian high school. And those conjoined intentions of good and evil played second base, earned a 4.7 GPA, landed scholarships, signed a minor league contract, made friends, found lovers, and tasted success—living like half a god, half a devil. And he hitched his hope to a woman who stayed not for love, but out of pity and cowardice.

I had lived in a conscious world, always one step ahead of other people—until that confidence shattered. My mother's last breath tore the veil guarding the Holy of Holies, and like the high priest cleansed by blood, I saw the raw terror of existence.

In the lowest gear, I pushed the bike to its highest speed, the wind drawing tears from my dry eyes. I shut them for a moment—until a voice cut through the rush of air:

"Watch where you're going!"

I swerved just in time to avoid a middle-aged man in a Draft Jim hat. He hollered an expletive, then a slur.

I squeezed both brake levers. The tires locked, and the bike screamed to a stop. I dropped it.

I ran at him, yanking off my shirt, fists ready.

He swung.

I ducked.

He was slow and stupid, and I told him so.

He swung again—missed again.

This time, I caught his wrist, twisted him around, and wrenched his arm up his back. I lifted until his shoulder gave a sickening pop, and his mouth let out a raw bellow, like a cow giving birth. With a final shove, I sent him chin-first into the concrete.

I pulled back my right foot, ready to drive it into his ribs...

"Oh, child, please *stop*." The voice was calm but firm.

I turned to see a middle-aged woman—small, exquisitely dressed—watching me with steady eyes.

As I walked back to my bike, the twisted man shouted slur after slur. His voice faded. He wasn't following me, so I didn't look back.

I rode shirtless through the city well into the dark hours, the wind cooling my skin and humming in my ears.

When I finally returned to the apartment, I dropped onto the couch next to Verboom. Without a word, he handed me an orange *gi*—pants and jacket folded neatly, a rolled belt resting on top.

"Freshly laundered," he said. "You were gone a long time."

The belt was made of three long stripes: red, white, and blue. I unrolled it, running my fingers over the fabric.

"So what rank am I?" I asked.

Verboom leaned in close, his voice just above a whisper, "You're going to take the flag back."

17

At 11:59 AM the next morning, I looked over to Verboom and held up an index finger signaling one minute to broadcast. He gestured like a megalomaniac directing lightning bolts, knocking his headphones askew—a response to the strong coffee consumed liberally on an empty stomach.

Even with the pitch on Genevieve's show, I didn't expect many listeners. Still, we sat ready for callers, both of us in chunky headphones, mics beneath our chins.

Earlier that morning, I'd bought two enormous American flags from an Army & Navy surplus store in Belltown and draped them over the French doors—ostensibly for soundproofing but mainly to block Verboom's view of the TV. He called our dim little studio "America's tomb."

As the noon hour approached, I held up one hand, all fingers up, and mouthed the countdown as I pulled down each digit. *Five, four, three, two, one...* He mouthed: *mushroom cloud.*

> **VINCENT VERMEER:** *Sound the trumpets for the Dutch demigod demolishing dainty dimwits! I'd pray for my enemies, but they'd still fail! So, Heavenly Dad, we will not take up any of your ear-time with our airtime. The masses must defend themselves—unaided—from the Dutch Maestro, the virtuoso, and the oh-so-much-more-so: Vincent Vermeer.*

> *Contrary to right-wing complaint, I'm convinced that the present-day Liberal is a most convenient opponent. I can sum up why in a single word: evidence. The Liberal believes presenting more and more evidence will persuade opponents to change their minds. However, they do so without evidence for the effectiveness of providing evidence; the Liberal holds to a standard, a fantasy, not at work in the real world of persuasion. Look at your own life. Ever find enough evidence to change a self-righteous mind?*

His seething mania was honed into an uncanny mental focus, as his persona crackled with bravado. Shocked, I rubbed my eyes and looked again. Where had this *persona* emerged from? Then he looked up at me and mouthed, "Callers?"

I shook my head.

> **VERMEER:** *Here's a secret! The remarkable but unspoken feature of our political tribes is how we're grouped by personality type. It's not ideology. We don't need verisimilitude. We need mood and attitude! Sure, we "reason" from a system of beliefs, a point of view, a view of the world, a weltanschuung—a German word, isn't it fun! But what's deeper than those systems of ideas? It's our temperaments! Style precedes substance.*
>
> *We're getting to the guts of it now, my fellow citizens. Sanguine about your future? Perhaps phlegmatic? Whatever your humor, I'm going to unveil your inner workings, whether you like it or not! I'm the only one who sees through it all. And what do you do when you're in the know? That's it! You get a show! So, so, so! Do you have the bile to be bilious? Are you sick*

enough to make a call? Don't linger with that finger. Don't dither and do come hither.

Verboom removed his headphones, swept back his long hair with a claw-like hand, and then slipped the headphones back on. He reached down to tighten the knot on his red, white, and blue belt. Continuing, he discussed the practical benefits of liberal policy, all while critiquing their naïve approach to communication.

VERMEER: *Liberals appeal to shrinking icecaps, while the righteous refer to the ancient book of Genesis and the Promise of the Rainbow. "God's not going to flood this world twice," they whistle, so drill, baby, drill. Now, as any bible thumper already knows, you must answer a statement of "revelation" with a theological rebuttal. And if you read the Bible, you'll see it has nothing to say about climate change. And look how generous I am. I'm spotting the Bible in advance, which I have no obligation to do! According to the Bible, God only promises to prevent "all life" from being destroyed by a global flood! That doesn't mean we can't ruin our coastlines and cut the human population in half. (And wouldn't Conservatives prefer our coastal elites be washed out to sea, like the Pharaoh and his chariots?) According to the Bible, God only needs to keep one life living, and voila! Promise kept. And don't you worry, Fritz Hearn: you will certainly float! How do I know all this, eh Lawrence? Drumroll please... Because I've read the Bible, the entire grande dame! Ask me, Lawrence, just ask for chapter and verse on how burning fossil fuel will not heat the globe and royally screw up the weather! Ask for it!*

But the sweet, loving Liberal dutifully "respects" the pre-rational and anti-scientific thinking of old-time religion, and then goes on quoting more research data. At least go the whole way! Ignorance under the mantle of revelation is still ignorance. One must break the spell of revelation with more revelation! Or better still: break the assumptions behind science denial! Now here's the real and scandalous revelation: one must do philosophy! The philosophy of science precedes science. You don't defend science by conducting science; you need philosophy to defend science!

Stop your heads from spinning and listen. When you allow your opponent to "argue" with pre-modern beliefs and think you can win the day with carbon reports, you're the fool in this formula! You need more than a body count of dead polar bears; you must go to battle with their philosophy of science, or in this case, their philosophy of anti-science. Someone gong these fundamentalists off the stage!

The closest Conservatives get to a scientific debate is declaring that the "science is debatable." When challenged with a "how so?" their typical response is, "Don't know, not a scientist." Moreover, when the work of scientists is actually examined, they assail the scientists' political motivations, diverting the discussion from the science itself to the scientists.

With such asymmetry, one might wonder why Conservatives fear Liberals. Here's why, my nephews and nieces: The "righteous" are terrified of anything that isn't "traditional." Their dread of new ideas, their fear of differences, their apprehension of all things "other" have made them overly anxious about even a modest competitor like the Liberal. For instance, conservative personalities are more easily startled. Don't believe me? Try blowing in someone's ear. A liberal type will be titillated, and a conservative type will elbow you in the nose!

As the last Liberal president holds office today, Conservatives are howling about his purported secret agenda to destroy America. "He's a wolf in sheep's clothing!" they cry. He's labeled a Socialist, a Marxist, a Communist, a brain-washer, a dictator, a tyrant, a terrorist, some even say he's demon possessed... If Conservatives truly have God on their side, why all the whining? Is their faith that fragile? Is their arsenal exhausted? Are their laser scopes shaky? They've got God, Guns, and Gold—and I don't deny it, I've seen the flags and bumper stickers. So now I'm asking, what more could they possibly need? A backrub? A pat on the bum? If God's on your side, shouldn't you at least be sweet about it?

Just tuning in? Question: Why do Conservatives act like their God is powerless? Because they don't act on faith, they react on temperamental fear. Conservatives perceive the world as fraught with danger. They are more sensitive to bitter tastes and irritated by new ideas—especially if those ideas are complex! If it involves a fresh detail about Liberals destroying America, well by golly, they can't get enough. Conservatives crave cognitive closure. They want to wash all the grey right out of their hair, opting for stark black and white thinking until the Holsteins come home—MOO!

There you have it! I've unraveled the paradox: the more

guns, gold, and God one has, the more fear they have! Lord, come quickly! The American political scene is so dull! The people who truly know things don't know how to talk to people. And the people who know nothing won't shut up!

[In a mock high voice:] "But not too quickly, Lord. My laser scope arrives Wednesday!"

Personally, if I had the three G's—god, gold, and guns—I'd have ice in my veins. Hell, I'd have an ice cream cone and just lick, lick, lick, lick, lick, lick! If your divinity is almighty, and your rifle so precise, then why all the whining? I'm bored with it. Take your Tonka trucks and go home!

The Bible commands: "Be strong and very courageous!" And yet there's constant complaining about persecution. But where, exactly, is the oppression? You don't know whether to say 'Black' or 'African American?' What a burden! (Have pronouns got you worried?) And now, a woman can marry a woman, taking two women "off the market" for patriotic red-blooded American men! Two men holding hands in public... it's like seeing the Hindenburg crash!

Seriously, folks, what about those famous words, remember them? "Pray for your enemies and love those who persecute you." Another quote from Karl Marx? ...uh-NO! That was Jesus "born in a manger" Christ! Can you smell the straw, man?

[Mock whining voice:] "Vincent, we're outraged by oppressive taxes."

Quit whining and stop paying them! Fly your "Come And Take It" flag and tell the feds to pound sand. Arrooooo! There's no courage in this whiney-pants patriotism. Remember: Outrage is not courage. Anger is not courage. Indignation is not courage. Sneering is not courage. Complaining is not courage. Courage is courage!

[In a whisper:] "Read Tautology."

[Mock whining voice:] "Liberal elites control Washington!"

Who are the liberal elites? The Emergency Conference of Scholars? We couldn't invent a better foil!

[Mock whining voice:] "Uncle Vincent, it's the liberal media."

ANN is number one in cable noise! Fritz Hearn tops the AM radio charts! And they say Liberals run the media? Please. Are they missing the forest for the trees? Absolutely! Obsessed with petty scandals and salacious sensationalism? Check. Understaffed and overheated? A thousand times yes!

[Mock whining voice:] "In a survey, over 80% of journalists identified as center or left of center."

As it should be! Journalism is a job for people who are open to new ideas! (And do no equate "the media" with proper journalism, the latter being only a small subset.) And consider this: for every journalist, there are four public relations agents.

> *Thorough reporting doesn't generate profit, because people want entertainment in the form of outrage. Which is exactly why you need to listen to The Dutch Uncle! I'm the only one who can make sense of it all. Without me, you would have to read a handful of independent news sources every day from across the political spectrum, then read a book or two a week that thoroughly explores one subject, a good old deep-dive, and then some energy and time to mull it all over. So, like I said, you need me. The American has always been an intellectual couch potato...*

Verboom continued in this manner, posing high-pitched questions and following them with impassioned diatribes. No callers interrupted his fiery monologue, which lasted until the show concluded at 12:59 PM Pacific Time.

At 1 PM, I asked, "Am I Lawrence?"

"Thought you might try on a new persona too," he replied, with a playful acknowledgment of the day's theatrics.

Wild-eyed, Verboom left the studio and headed to the kitchen to brew chamomile tea—two bags. After we wrapped up the show's business, I suggested grabbing some lunch. He wasn't interested. Then I proposed a walk, but he declined that too, expressing concern about being recognized on the street as the Portland Rose Giant. Instead, he felt he needed to stay on the couch to learn about the world watching WNN.

Alone in Capitol Hill, I observed my strained nerves and tight shoulders. Verboom's radio act was both impressive and revolting.

As I walked down Pike Street in search of lunch, a menacing caravan of pickups paraded by. The last truck had a thin man in a business suit, handcuffed and wearing a handwritten sign: "Guilty." It was unclear whether he was a willing participant or a captive. From the same truck the driver repeated a message over his PA system: "James Kroes will lockup Wall Street crooks and their government cronies."

After grabbing a slice of pizza and a cup of ice water, I heard the caravan moving back up the street, its message blaring relentlessly.

Holding my slice of pizza on a white paper plate, I wandered over to the quad at the university campus, just a few blocks away. There, I stumbled upon an event and was promptly handed a pamphlet titled "Mainstream the Marginal." An inclusive dance troupe performed, clad in differently colored bodysuits. They gyrated in color-coded teams, ranging from a white-clad inner circle to an outer ring of dancers in dark attire. The dancers scrambled and reassembled, eventually positioning the dark-suited dancers at the center and the white-suited dancers on the exterior. After another swirl of movement, a brown core formed. Each concentric circle spun in opposite directions. Then, starting from the outermost ring and moving inward, each dancer dropped to the ground, leaving only one person standing at the center—a dancer in a purple suit, a color I hadn't previously noticed.

"Doesn't leave much to the imagination," a guy next to me remarked.

"The message is clear."

"There's nothing underneath those leotards."

"Oh. Yes, plenty of private details," I said, pretending I'd only just noticed.

After a series of pirouettes, the performer clad in purple danced in a mock-drunk manner through the bodies lying prone on the ground. She then sprinted toward the chapel steps, bounding up the staircase in wide, side-to-side leaps. At the top, she executed another pirouette, then, fixing her gaze on the chapel's cross, extended her arms to form a T-shape. She held the pose for a moment, then suddenly began to shake—violently, like she was being electrocuted.

The dancer was still for a moment.

A premature cheer rose from the crowd.

Turning to face her fellow dancers, the purple dancer unzipped her bodysuit, removed a large cloth, and unfolded it to reveal a banner, though its words were unclear from my vantage point. Raising it above her head, she vigorously pumped her arms as the other dancers emitted sharp, warlike shrieks. In a dramatic gesture, she then produced a lighter from an internal pocket and set the cloth aflame. As it burned halfway, she tossed it down whereupon the other dancers quickly surrounded her, lifting her high and carrying her off the quad like a coach after a big win.

A young woman dressed in a black tee shirt, black jeans, and black leather boots handed me a pamphlet. It outlined a student-led boycott of the national bank allowing O.F.A.M. gatherings in their parking lot. After slipping the flyer in my shirt pocket, I took out my field book to jot down notes, relishing the anonymity of a campus not my own. No one knew me, and I felt at home.

Pizza finished, I called my grandmother. After exchanging a few brief updates, I brought up the letter from Ella, claiming knowledge about my father. She fell silent.

"What do you know?" I pressed.

"Your mother, rest in peace, made me promise never to tell you, no matter what."

"You know!"

"But I can never tell."

I had been angry with her before, but until now, I had never felt betrayed.

"She's gone, and all promises with her," I argued.

"My dear grandson, I must keep my word," she insisted.
As I was about to hang up, a thought struck me.
"What if I find out who he is, will you confirm it?" I asked.
She was silent again.
"Grandma! Are you there?"
"I was nodding," she finally said.

18

Verboom kicked off the second show with the same fiery bravado as the first. Again, he modulated his voice in an obvious manner, adopting a falsetto tone reminiscent of a Cub Scout or a choirboy. He posed high-pitched questions, to be batted down by the baritone Dutch Uncle. In one notable exchange between the Vermeer persona and the falsetto choirboy, he explained how a secular government was not only a historical fact but practical for the health of sincere religion.

> **VERMEER:** *When Christianity became the favored religion of the Roman Empire, church membership soared! But many of these new Christians lacked the moral discipline of the earlier generations. No costly virtue displays required—in fact, quite the opposite! There were now earthly benefits. So... You can see how St. Augustine's groundbreaking work on human depravity might be helpful? Doggone it, why have so many Christians gone wild?*
>
> *[Mock high-pitched voice:] "My roommate had that one on DVD."*
>
> *Augustine transformed the prevailing Roman ideal—from self-mastery through reason and virtue to a worldview rooted in depravity, moral weakness, shame, and dependence on*

divine grace. And you can't question Augustine's belief in human depravity; that horndog of a saint removed his God-given gonads to control his lust. I'm talking about castration! And Christians have been taking his advice on human nature for hundreds of years since! Now, I think Augustine's little fryers should be added to displays of the cross. But where should they go?... I've got it! Right at the base! Clang a cymbal! Gong the gong! I've wanted to say that out loud for twenty-five years! I'm drunk on free speech! Who will challenge me now?

*[**Mock high-pitched voice:**] "Oh how base... and debased!"*

Yes, right at the base. A shocking revelation, eh? It's true. And though the transgression of your totem angers you, and it's only a totem dear friend, I've said nothing about divinity, only God's self-proclaimed spokespersons. Now hear my words: if Christian Nationalists, also known as theocrats, insist on forcing their crosses into public spaces, they should be prepared to talk about them.

*[**Mock high-pitched voice:**] "If I were a liberal personality type, I'd say you've committed an ad hominem fallacy, attacking the castrated person instead of the castrated argument."*

Ever wonder why God doesn't speak to our talk shows? Presumably, God wouldn't need a phone! Now what's more offensive: a man claiming to speak for God or a man castrating himself and claiming to speak for God?

[Mock high-pitched voice:] "Look out! Your show will be struck with lightening!"

Our American founders thought emperor Constantine's merger of church and state ruined both. Madison said: "During almost fifteen centuries has the legal establishment of Christianity been on trial. What has been its fruits? In all places, pride and indolence in the clergy, ignorance or servility in the laity, in both, superstition, bigotry and persecution..." Goodness, I need a drum set to finish off that quote! The founders thought the best thing for religion was to keep it separate from government. In the debates over Article VI of the Constitution, the founders made it clear: they didn't want a church operated by the federal government or a government operated by a church. The authors of the Constitution left a record of their discussion about declaring the United States a Christian nation and the resounding consensus was NO!

[Mock high-pitched voice:] "What's the doggone point here?"

Like many of our founders, you can be a Christian without being a Christian Nationalist. Personal religious convictions should not mandate national policies! Buy this choirboy a copy of Tautology. The Constitution is the Constitution. The Bible is the Bible. The Constitution is not the Bible.

The studio was filled with the sound of rustling newspapers. Verboom hummed the opening notes of Rossini's "William Tell Overture"—famously used as the theme for *The Lone Ranger*—and readied himself to deliver a scathing analysis. But then, unexpectedly, we received a call from the outside world. I couldn't help but wonder if Genevieve had orchestrated this unexpected interruption, but then I heard the question.

CALLER 1: *Americans support a government based on the Bible. Like it or not, we are a Christian nation.*

VERMEER: *Even if that were true, you're arguing for a tyranny of the majority. Just what the founders feared!*

CALLER 1: *Heard your rant about the Constitution, but the Declaration of Independence clearly appeals to the Creator.*

VERMEER: *A creator is referenced, but that document is even less 'Christian' than the Constitution! Read Romans 13 and tell me how obedient Christians can rebel against the established government? As far as the 1770s go, devout Christians should have said, "Give unto King George, what is King George's." So, so, so! Tell me, caller, I'm on pins and needles, what is your denomination?*

CALLER 1: *Presbyterian.*

VERMEER: *Let's say the majority elects a Southern Baptist president.*

CALLER 1: *Why Southern Baptist?*

VERMEER: *Why? Because it's the largest Protestant*

denomination in the United States. Now, our new Baptist president is born an American citizen, as the constitution requires, and he's openly committed to remaking America as a theocracy. Now, most of us are comfortable connecting the T-word to Islamic countries, but when you accuse an American Christian Nationalist of doing the same thing, they say their approach is simply "Constitutional." But that's wrong. I'm going to make all you pious gangsters own up to your theocracy!

CALLER 1: *Hey Dutch guy, if you knew any American history, you'd know the Constitution is based on God's truth.*

VERMEER: *The Constitution is not a true or false document; it's a set of rules we agree to follow. It applies.*

CALLER 1: *You sound like a know-it-all professor.*

VERMEER: *Why wouldn't you want your faith to compete in the free market? Let the best ideas win!*

CALLER 1: *Religion isn't a business. It's got to be protected.*

VERMEER: *From what? Scrutiny?*

CALLER 1: *From secularism!*

VERMEER: *A secular government complements the sincere practice of religion, unless of course you want something like... theocracy! DING-DING-DING! Perhaps, you should spend more time reading the Bible and less time watching* *cable news. Better yet, read the First Amendment: "Congress shall make no law respecting an establishment of religion."*

CALLER 1: *It was already established.*

VERMEER: *The Southern Baptists?*

CALLER 1: *Christianity.*

VERMEER: *The Southern Baptists formed around slave-holders' "rights" in the lead up to the Civil War.*

CALLER 1: *I mean Christianity in general.*

VERMEER: *So, we'll include the Southern Baptists who formed around the endorsement of human slavery. What about Catholics?*

CALLER 1: *No, they're loyal to the Pope, not the Constitution.*

VERMEER: *JFK should not have been president?*

CALLER 1: *Exactly.*

VERMEER: *Let's say our hypothetical president outlaws infant baptism...*

CALLER 1: *No, Presbyterians baptize their babies.*

VERMEER: *You do know the pope is fond of infant*

baptism? Guess he got lucky on that one.

CALLER 1: *Can we leave the Catholics out of this; we're not talking about Mexico.*

VERMEER: *One out of five Americans is Catholic. On the Supreme Court it's two out of three! But let's say it's been a great couple of election cycles for the Southern Baptist and two thirds of congress is Southern Baptist, as well as five ninths of the Supreme Court. Now that infant baptism is outlawed, what should the punishment be?*

CALLER 1: *Christians can choose how they want to be baptized.*

VERMEER: *Babies don't choose to be baptized! But that's not the question, caller. What should the penalty be? A fine? Prison? Death?*

Hel-lo? What, he hung up? Hup! Hup! The Dutch Uncle dominates a duplicitous dummy! Lawrence, do we have any folk anthems in the queue? What's that you say? Time's up? Let's get out of here, I haven't been this hungry in months. Ahem. And so, I bid farewell to the intellectual couch potatoes of America. Tune in tomorrow for more titillating talk. Can you take a tweaking?

19

On the way to lunch I scolded Verboom for referring to his book, *Tautology*. He'd also provoked the gun-guys. And castration? He dropped his bandana and raised his sunglasses. He looked me in the eye and told me to check the historical record.

"Oh shoot!" He raised his brow. "Come to think of it," he added, putting his glasses down and pulling his bandana up, "it was Origen of Alexandria who did the self-castration thing. *Nuts*! We'll have to clean that up in tomorrow's broadcast. I'll pretend like it was a test to see how informed the listeners are. That sounds Vermeer, right? And the spirit of my point stands, Origen was one of the most influential church fathers, following Matthew 19:12. How is that for an origin story! In fact, one of Origen's main contributions was establishing the literal interpretation of scripture. Wow. Of all the verses to take literally!"

"Just because it happened, doesn't mean you need to talk about it."

"Perhaps you're right. In fact, I'm no longer feeling well."

As we neared the restaurant, he stopped, leaned on a tree, pulled down his bandana, and wretched. After a moment, he readjusted the bandana and muttered, "Maybe a brothy soup instead of fried food?"

The streets were unusually quiet. A man in an EAT THE RICH tee shirt strolled toward the park. Verboom did a doubletake, then yanked down his bandana, and puked.

"I just imagined that guy eating my rich uncle Mike." He gagged, then wretched a third time. "Okay, that's it. So, what are we cooking up for the newsletter?" he asked meekly.

I smirked. "How about something on the origin of the Radical Right."

"*Ja* jongen!" His vigor rebounded. "Who's got the big persona now! So, are you thinking Cain in the Garden of Eden?"

"Something more recent."

"Do you think my persona is working? Is the condescension both humorous and erudite?"

"Let's wait for the reviews."

We found a pan-Asian restaurant, where Verboom ordered a small bowl of broth and a side of white rice. I opted for Thailand's number one beer and Vietnamese imperial rolls.

From our seat near the window, I watched as a truck rumbled down the street. Three young men, dressed in green, sat in the back, wearing red hats and gripping rifles.

"With everything going on, should we get a gun too?" I asked.

He tapped my bicep. "You're already well-armed."

"Put the persona away. I'm talking to you."

"Well," he said, shifting into his *Ask The Professor* tone, "if you had called my last show, I would have said studies indicate you're more likely to hurt yourself or someone you know than defend yourself from a criminal."

"Other people are careless. We'd be careful."

"And most students think they're above average. If you get a gun, the most likely outcome is that you'll harm yourself—on purpose. The next most likely is that you'll hurt yourself—by accident. After that, you're most likely to shoot me." He gave a pointed look. "You can see where this is going. But hey, if owning a gun makes you *feel* safer, go for it. I'm not afraid to be shot—on purpose or accidentally."

"Have you ever owned a gun?" I asked.

"A shotgun. Gave it to my brother Willem."

"I've never fired a gun," I admitted.

"Just make sure you wear earplugs. And if you're shooting me, make sure I have earplugs too."

"I'm not going to shoot you."

"That's what they all say." Verboom shook his head.

"What do you think about Kroes' chances?" I asked, shifting the conversation.

"He's got a better shot than the folks on WNN think."

"That's unsettling."

"Not for those who score high on the Right-wing Authoritarian screener."

"Have you ever taken the assessment?" I asked.

"Can I give you some farmer-ly advice, Santo? This should be second nature to us psychologists, but don't forget the situation."

"You don't have to convince me of situation effects," I said.

"Of course, I do. You don't know what you're going to do in a situation until you're in the *situation*. Might surprise yourself."

"What situation are you talking about?"

"The more surprising the situation, the more surprising the behavior. When the *mest* hits the windmill, you may not act like you expect."

"Oh, you mean Situationism?"

"Isn't that what I just said?" he asked.

"You know I'm more into Interactionism," I said.

"That's a good one too." Verboom nodded.

"You think the rally guys and the campers are going to interact?"

"Beats me."

"Do you think they help or hurt their causes?"

"Depends on how they interact."

After lunch and a brisk walk around Capitol Hill, we returned to Genevieve's building. Verboom bounded up the stairwell, taking three steps at a time, and immediately collapsed onto the couch.

At commercial break, he dropped to the floor for push-ups and sit-ups. When the show returned, he watched from the hardwood floor, avoiding the rug—fearful of getting soft. He mumbled to himself, then stood up and started talking back to the pundits. He listened, then grumbled again.

While Verboom carried on with his WNN friends, I took care of some unfinished business—completing my bereavement form to defer the fall semester. To finalize the process, I needed to upload my mother's death certificate. My chest tightened as I located the file. A creeping panic set in. The document itself spooked me. The date. The time. The cause.

The idea of leaving school—even just for a semester—troubled me.

Writer? That was never my plan.

Documentarian? I'd buried that dream long ago.

At the next commercial break, he sprinted to the bathroom for a shower and rushed back to the living room with only a towel around his waist, arriving just in time to catch the next segment.

BREAKING NEWS: Kroes Picks Running Mate, Escalates Populist Uprising

REPORTER: *In a move shaking up the election, third-party firebrand James Kroes has selected Billy Henniker as his running mate, solidifying his insurgent bid for the presidency. We now go live to the Kroes event.*

> **KROES:** *The bigshots in DC are shaking in their shoes because they know exactly who Billy Henniker is. Billy came up hard, fists covered in oil and dirt. He started as a roughneck with nothing in his pockets and ended up running an empire. Already the most successful oilman in Texas, he next became the most powerful cattleman in the Lone Star State. He made his money the old-fashioned way—pulling it from the ground and dodging bureaucrats like a man swatting mosquitoes in summer. Thanks to men like Billy Henniker, America can fuel and feed itself—provided we get these traitors out of Washington.*

The crowd erupted, as Kroes paced the stage. WNN cut to wide shots of jubilant faces, red hats bobbing in the frenzied arena.

> **KROES:** *Billy knows there's no such thing as a good politician, which is why he's steered clear of politics his entire life—at least until Jim Kroes called him up. The folks of Texas tried again and again to get Billy to run for governor, but he always said the only job he'd take was President of the Republic of Texas.*

WNN cut to the crowd—stomping, shouting, fists in the air. The camera zoomed in on Henniker standing off to the side of the stage, arms crossed, nodding, his smile tight and knowing.

> **KROES:** *But out of concern for the good people of Texas, Billy has agreed to join my ticket.*

The cheers surged again. Kroes turned, motioning toward his running mate.

The arena exploded into a standing ovation. The camera followed Henniker striding toward the podium.

As Verboom edged closer to the screen, I grabbed my keys and slipped out for a ride.

20

On Wednesday, Verboom returned to form, using the high-pitched voice for another question-and-answer session.

Twenty minutes into the show, a caller asked about the "Dutch stuff." Verboom explained that his parents were from the Netherlands, then he pushed his microphone away. He turned to me and said, "When I was a kid, jokes about Poles were all the rage. The first time I repeated one to my mom, she got down on one knee beside me and said, 'We don't make fun of other peoples. If you must make fun of a group—*only the Dutch.*'" He pulled his mic back to his mouth.

CALLER 1: *Hello...? You were born there too?*

VERMEER: *Nay, nay, nay. I was born right here, in the greatest country in the history of all histories. Greater than every nation in every parallel universe! Greater than any country, real or imagined! A country so great, its very existence proves the existence of God! Folks, the USA is giving heaven a run for its money—and don't you dare say otherwise! But listen bub, if you prefer, call me a Nederlander, or the sad-eyed Laddy from the Lowlands.*

CALLER 1: *Don't you love America?*

VERMEER: *You want to know why I'm The Dutch Uncle? There are too many Americans bleating about "American Exceptionalism!"*

Verboom raked back his long hair with his left hand, then stood up. Grabbing the front of his *gi*, he gave it a sharp tug to straighten it. The microphone caught the crisp snap of the fabric.

VERMEER: *And besides, that old country is cute, innovative, non-hierarchical, grudgingly tolerant... They do massive agricultural output, second only to America in total farming exports. Can we at least say: Netherlands Second?! Holland number two! I'll send you a bumper sticker.*

CALLER 1: *Prostitutes, socialism, legalized drugs, euthanasia...*

VERMEER: *Look up the phrase 'Dutch uncle.' It's English. Do you read English? Are you a literate primate, or did someone dial the machine for you?*

CALLER 1: *How can you love such a godless country? There has never been a great power without God!*

VERMEER: *China. Russia...*

CALLER 1: *Godless!*

VERMEER: *Big, powerful, what's not great about that? Nukes, baby. They've both got nukes. Lawrence, where's that drum set we ordered? When I think nukes, I've got to* *make jazz.*

CALLER 1: *They didn't have God as their foundation.*

VERMEER: *Fine. Persia, Egypt, Greece, and Rome... They all had gods and were all pretty great. Perhaps, the more gods the greater? India, the most gods and the most people, and they have nukes too! I follow your logic now, caller! India's number one! IN-DEE-UH! IN-DEE-UH! Pour me another cup of tea, this guy makes me sleepy...*

CALLER 1: *False gods. Failing countries.*

VERMEER: *So you're saying: One: A great country must be founded by your God. Two: Your God did not found Russia, Persia, Egypt, Greece, Rome, China, Japan, or any other powerful country. Therefore, three: None of them are great nations. Wow. Suffocating logic. I apologize if you can hear me yawning.*

CALLER 1: *God is what makes this country great.*

VERMEER: *Isn't it the hardworking people, the creativity, the openness, the freedom, the resources, the infrastructure, the military—the polished black boot on the neck of secularism?*

CALLER 1: *Would you rather live in another country?*

VERMEER: *Liberals will know what my next question is: have you ever been to another country? Well?... Hello? Lawrence? Oh, he hung up? Get that caller a collar!*

[In a breathy voice:] While we wait for our next victim, I'm going to help our listeners out there. Today I offer a tool-kit any prophet, preacher, politician, or slick commentator can use. Just follow these simple steps.

[Switching to an infomercial voice:] Out of work? Unemployed or underemployed? Put Vincent Vermeer's techniques to work! It's a simple strategy, and I give it away freely.

[Singing an old hymn like a pious baritone:] "Freely, freely you have received! Freely, freely GIVE!"

So, here's the formula for you budding theocratic politicians. There's plenty of profit and power to be had in being right all the time. It's essential for any tribal leader! Now, regarding physical blessing or wellbeing, always keep these two premises in mind. One: If you like the recipient (she's on your side), then a good thing is a mark of God's approval, that is, a proper "blessing," so advise caution and gratefulness. Two: If you dislike the recipient (she's not on your side), then this good thing is ill-gotten gain and not a blessing but rather a theft and a set up for greater pain, so advise fear of reprisal and immediate repentance.

Keep these conditional statements in mind regarding physical suffering or lack of wellbeing. One: If you like the one suffering, it confirms their righteousness, for the evil world hates those who are good! Two: If you don't like the one suffering, then it is God's punishment for bad behavior. Do the crime, pay the fine!

Now, some people may not seem to warrant such harsh retribution, but fortunately, there's a category of sin designated as 'lack of faith,' something only observable by God or only intuited by the dear leader. Once you get a poor little fella' turned in on his own naughty thoughts, you'll keep him busy in self-loathing for hours.

Oh, brothers and sisters, when I think back on my tender days in the church, all those hours spent in tears examining my unworthiness and wondering if my faith was real—real enough to save—oh, it makes me shudder. All those hours wondering if I was really saved... What a waste of time! With all that energy, I could have really done something special, like invent the Windmere Clothes Shaver. Boy, that little puppy is handy on an old sweatshirt. Pays for itself in no time!

If anyone needs counseling, call in now. Call 88-DUTCH-UNC, that's 8-8-D-U-T-C-H-U-N-C! I move from politics to religion, just as comfortably as the theocrats do...

CALLER 2: *Vermeer, I don't know what kind of preaching you've heard, but the Gospel is simple: repent and believe, and you shall be saved.*

VERMEER: *What does it mean to sufficiently 'repent'?*

CALLER 2: *Being sorry for your sins.*

VERMEER: *A simple shift in attitude? You don't have to do anything different? I'm sorry I ate that Twinkie; pass me* *another Twinkie.*

CALLER 2: *If you're truly sorry, then you'll change your behavior.*

VERMEER: *So then caller, when you were "saved," you quit masturbating?*

CALLER 2: *Not answering that.*

VERMEER: *Then tell me about a sin for which you repented and then quit.*

CALLER 2: *I stopped taking the Lord's name in vain.*

VERMEER: *Never a slip-up?*

CALLER 2: *No.*

VERMEER: *You're not lying, are you? That's a sin too. Now, have you ever gone to a movie where actors take the Lord's name in vain?*

CALLER 2: *It's hard to avoid.*

VERMEER: *So you walk out of the theater if an actor takes the Lord's name in vain?*

CALLER 2: *I'm not responsible for what other people say.*

VERMEER: *But you did pick the film!*

CALLER 2: *If you insist that the world be perfect, you'll never leave the house.*

VERMEER: *Which is terrible! It's so hard not to masturbate once you have cabin fever! Now. What if you were to stub your toe? A bad one, say that toe is broken sideways and you let loose with a string a profanity that includes taking God's name in vain. Would that mean you're not in an adequate state of repentance?*

CALLER 2: *I'd confess, and God would forgive me.*

VERMEER: *What if you commit sins and fail to repent of them? You're not omniscient, right? Perhaps you missed a few.*

CALLER 2: *We're not saved by good works but by faith in Jesus.*

VERMEER: *So, you don't need to follow God's law? Sounds like we've got some anarchy cooking!*

CALLER 2: *You can never behave perfectly, that's why we need Jesus.*

VERMEER: *Of course, we are saved by grace through faith. But how do you know whether your faith is genuine?*

CALLER 2: *Read the Bible, attend church, pray, and you know, live a Christian lifestyle.*

VERMEER: *Lifestyle, hmmm... Aren't you referring to what psychologists call 'behavior' and what old time theologians call 'good works?' And as you've just established, a person is not 'saved' by good deeds. Care to reconcile the contradiction?*

CALLER 2: *"You will know them by their fruit," Jesus said.*

VERMEER: *What if you stop producing fruit?*

CALLER 2: *The fruit doesn't save you; it's the evidence of your faith.*

VERMEER: *Evidence! What are you, a Liberal?*

CALLER 2: *Of course not.*

VERMEER: *A dry spell is an absence of evidence. No evidence, no certainty of salvation.*

CALLER 2: *It's not proof; it's an indicator.*

VERMEER: *But your way of knowing that God's given you grace is by your faith, and the test of a sincere faith is good deeds, so the only way you can really be sure you've been saved is to behave well... Well, caller?*

CALLER 2: *Faith is not something you can see.*

VERMEER: *Sounds like you need faith in your faith. How do you know whether or not you have faith in your faith?*

CALLER 2: *By believing?...*

VERMEER: *Believing in your own believing is what faith is? So, what's to keep me from simply saying, "I'm saved, because I believe I'm saved"?*

CALLER 2: *You believe in the death and resurrection of Jesus for the forgiveness of sin!*

VERMEER: *Okay, so fruit isn't the issue; it's about believing the right doctrine!*

CALLER 2: *Good fruit is evidence of believing the right doctrine!*

VERMEER: *So how much fruit do you need to know you've got real faith in the right doctrine?*

CALLER 2: *God saves you; you don't save yourself.*

VERMEER: *What if you lose your faith, no longer believe in your beliefs?*

CALLER 2: *Then you wouldn't be saved, but you might believe again down the road.*

VERMEER: *So not having faith is not proof that I won't be saved in the future? And having faith in the present is not proof that I may forsake my faith in the future and thereby lose my salvation? Right now, caller, tell me how to know that I'm saved?*

CALLER 2: *Do you believe that you can be saved?*

VERMEER: *Yes!*

CALLER 2: *Then believe and be saved!*

VERMEER: *Now I can get on with my life and do whatever I want? Pass the Twinkies!*

CALLER 2: *No, you have to do what the Bible says.*

VERMEER: *Like, say, no masturbating?*

CALLER 2: *Following the law doesn't save you.*

VERMEER: *But why then do I have to try to follow the Bible's rules?*

CALLER 2: *Don't you want to? Faith changes you. You will act differently if you have real faith.*

VERMEER: *So how good do I have to be to show that it's not just lip service?*

CALLER 2: *You're saved by grace through faith!*

VERMEER: *The vultures are circling, like your logic. If the authenticity of your saving faith must be demonstrated with behavioral evidence, you are left to wonder if your behavior is good enough! Plus, you'll start to sound like a Liberal, looking for evidence! And we all know Liberals* *don't go to heaven!*

CALLER 2: *What if you saw a house on fire, wouldn't you want to go in and rescue the people inside?*

VERMEER: *Let's go deeper, right to your most basic and unexamined starting point and ask: what does it even mean to be saved? You're going to explain why some decent guy like me deserves to suffer in burning sulfur for an everlasting life of torture because I reject an incoherent doctrine? You believe it, but you can't even make sense of it! Come on. Call back tomorrow, I'm tired of this conversation. The Dutch Maestro declares you a dim...*

I put my hand up to remind Verboom that the caller was supposed to hang up out of frustration. He mumbled and shooed me away.

VERMEER: *Are you there, caller? It's me, Vincent. I know your weakness, why you've never been certain about your standing with God... Shall I say it? Masturbation.*

CALLER 2: *That word makes me very uncomfortable.*

VERMEER: *The word? It's simply the word that makes you uncomfortable? Or is it your uncontrolled behavior that makes you uncomfortable? The fact that you must go to a weekly support group to wallow with your brothers in self-hatred and grovel in prayer because you can't tame the beast?*

CALLER 2: *Stop being so crude.*

VERMEER: *I'll say the word again... But wait! There it is! I heard the click, the tone of disconnection. The poor caller is stuck in a Rube Goldberg mechanism of guilt resolution. Anyhow Lawrence, can we get back to politics? All this religion is tiresome. Do we have a headline? Let's try out that new microphone!*

In between callers, Verboom expanded on an article about global mercenaries, its headline stark: "MKG Commandos Eclipse 200K Globally." The Martin Koning Group (MKG) had more combat-ready troops abroad than the US Marines.

He mused about hiring an MKG commando for our security, given current political tensions. But the article put the price of an MKG soldier at nearly a quarter million a year—roughly twelve hundred bucks a day. Even with a Dutch Mafia discount—Koning was of Western Michigan stock—the rate was far out of budget.

Koning, the article detailed, had raked in several millions of dollars to help a Mideast nation develop an elite battalion. It could be deployed inside and outside the country to protect strategic locations from terrorist threats as well as put down activists and striking workers.

VERMEER: *Where's the outrage? It's reported in The Times, and no one gives a rat's ass?*

LAWRENCE: *Another headline for The Dutch Maestro: "Activists Pressure DC Prayer Breakfast to Ban Pro-Choice Congress Members." The article details efforts by religious hardliners to bar lawmakers who support reproductive* *rights from attending the high-profile event, arguing that their presence taints the gathering's moral integrity.*

Let's pair it with another story about the First Brothers' movement: "LGBTQ Activist Groups Push Politicians to Skip National Prayer Breakfast." Progressives are calling on congresspersons to follow the president's lead and boycott the next event, citing the organizations long-standing ties to Christian groups hostile to gay rights.

VERMEER: *He was the first American president since Harry Truman to rebuff First Brothers, and with that move became the most Christlike. "And when you pray, do not be like the hypocrites, for they love to pray standing in the synagogues and on the street corners to be seen by others. Truly I tell you, they have received their reward in full. But when you pray, go into your room, close the door, and pray to your Father, who is unseen. Then your Father, who sees what is done in secret, will reward you." This according to the Gospel of Matthew, chapter 6.*

LAWRENCE: *The president opted out as a conscientious objection to First Brothers' anti-gay agenda in Uganda and Romania.*

VERMEER: *I thought it was because some naïve professor convinced the president to build the wall between church and state...*

LAWRENCE: *Maybe you're thinking of James Kroes' comment: "When the president kicked God out of government, I* *decided to run for the office."*

VERMEER: *Let's stop there. No more airtime for that showboat! Now. Take a step back. If you listen to how politicians speak, it's as though their God can't do anything but get thrown around like a football!*

Remember, I'm simply analyzing language. I'm examining how people talk about God. I'm not talking about God directly. Even though the Bible describes God as almighty, Christian Nationalists claim we've "kicked God out of government" through the goalposts of secularism! And there you have it!

HELLO CANADA! Do we have any callers, eh? Our number works up there too, eh! 88-DUTCH-UNC, eh! Do we have a "contractor" who doesn't do construction? Let's get a theocrat on the line.

Can we take out an ad in Righteousness magazine? We cannot afford a commando, but surely, we can afford Righteousness magazine... Wait! I've just had a deliverance from the unconscious! We'll put advertising in fortune cookies! Real fortune cookies! Not the proverb cookies or affirmation cookies like "hard work pays off in the end." I mean a sliver of paper that predicts the future! Perhaps, "The end is near!"

The third caller attempted a flimsy argument for the United States officially being a Christian nation. Verboom dismantled it with ease, exposing the caller's lack of historical knowledge before launching into a lecture on the wild popularity of Thomas Paine's

Common Sense among the patriots of the American Revolution.

Things escalated when the caller dismissed Paine as "just one guy who signed the Declaration." Verboom practically roared: "Paine didn't sign the thing—but he was a flaming deist!" He went on, hammering home that many of the actual signers, including Franklin and Jefferson, were also deists.

Before Verboom could pivot to explaining how James Madison defended Baptists in Virginia from persecution by the Church of England, the caller bailed—hanging up mid-rant. Verboom grinned with manic glee, his eyes alight with the thrill of demolition.

> **VERMEER:** *Put the next caller through! I'm wild, Lorenzo! Wild with insight!*
>
> **LAWRENCE:** *The caller hasn't been screened...*
>
> **VERMEER:** *I fear no one! Connect the caller...*
>
> **CALLER 4:** *Hello, professor. I've got something to ask: why'd you leave me in Flagstaff?*

Verboom whipped off his headphones and bolted through the French doors. I cut the live stream and stopped the recording.

By the time I made it to street level, he was galloping down the sidewalk in his orange *gi*, a blur in the color of madness. Then, without hesitation, he grabbed an unlocked bike and pushed off downhill. The midsized BMX wobbled under his weight, but he pedaled hard, legs splayed wide.

Picking up speed, his red, white, and blue karate belt fluttered behind him—until it snagged in the chain. With one violent tug, it unraveled from his waist, setting his *gi* top free to billow like a battle flag. The belt coiled around the rear hub, locking the back wheel in an instant.

The tire screamed. Verboom soared over the handlebars.

For one glorious moment, he looked like a freshly minted superhero, cape unfurled, arms stretched wide. Then gravity intervened. His forehead kissed the concrete, and he skidded on his elbows and knees.

Silence.

Then from the heap of limbs and fabric, he groaned.

By the time I reached him, he had rolled onto his back and was staring up at the sky in dazed silence. A red circular scrape marked the center of his forehead. His chest had somehow escaped injury, but his arms were another story—blood ran freely from deep scrapes, pooling near his elbows. His pants were torn through at the knees, exposing road rash.

He shifted his weight, as if taking silent inventory of his skeleton. Then another groan, this one more existential.

"What if she's pregnant? I'm not capable of parenting."

"Are you sure that was Ella?"

"That smoky voice. Knowledge of Flagstaff. *Ask. Professor.*"

"Why are you worried about pregnancy?"

"I may be built like an oak tree, but I'm emotionally frail. My mind's whirled up and looping. How will I nurture a helpless child? The world doesn't need more farmers. We have engineers. We have machines." He winced, touching the raw scrape on his forehead. "*Oh Jiminy Christmas,* my head hurts. Where are we going to hide now?"

"You haven't given out our location over the broadcast. She doesn't know where we are, she only knows the show's number."

"How did she find our program?"

"You linked your personhood to your persona on Genevieve's show, and you won't stop talking about *Tautology*."

"A masterpiece is a masterpiece. I should've ended my intellectual life after *Tautology* and joined the merchant marines, smoking my pipe and pining for what's been and what never was. But now!" he bellowed. "I have a child! I'll die before he gets to high school. Who will teach him how to pretend to be tough?"

"You're 47, and you're going to live to 94 like your grandparents, that's 47 years. And, maybe she's a *she*?"

"So you're saying women aren't supposed to pretend to be tough? That's a dated form of thinking, Santo." He sat up with a grimace.

"What are you going to do?"

"Take a hot bath."

"About Ella?"

"What can be done, but to accept the hand I've been dealt?" He shook his head as if trying to clear water from his ears. "Onto practical matters, then. Let's get this bike back to where it belongs."

Verboom flicked open the large blade of his pocketknife and began slicing through the tangled fabric wrapped around the back wheel. After several deliberate cuts, he yanked the belt free. He slipped the knife back into his hip pack, then pulled out his money clip. Peeling off two large bills, he folded them neatly and tucked them between the brake cable and the top tube of the bike.

Without another word, he started up the street, walking the bike alongside him.

As we reached the stoop where he'd snatched the bike, he turned to me and said, "We better get an Ella-sized orange *gi* just in case she shows up. Studies show uniforms work on the mind. Let's make sure our interests align. And get one for yourself while you're at it. That is, if you wouldn't mind doing so. Forgive me for sounding bossy about pants."

Verboom paused, then straightened his posture with newfound dignity.

"Perhaps before my bath, Santo, we should stop by Linda's Tavern for a belt of gin. It's just down the block."

"A what of *what*? You made a vow about sacred cows..."

"I need the Dutch courage, if I'm allowed to use English euphemisms. Besides, my persona has already been playing target practice with sacred cows."

The neon sign at Linda's door cast pink and green light, its three-line message in all caps:

TOOLS

RADIO

TACKLE

Inside, a buffalo head mounted behind the bar stared down at us, as unamused as the bartender. Linda's had the feel of a rustic mountain saloon, with exposed rafters, tan lampshades, and wood-paneled walls. A black-and-white photo of cattle hung framed behind the jukebox, its glass glowing faintly in the dim light. A massive wooden beam cut through the center of the room, resting on thick, round timbers—tree trunks stripped of bark and sealed with a glossy finish.

"No TVs," Verboom noted, scanning the room. "Think the Portland Rose Giant is still a story?"

"Ask the buffalo."

He felt for the bandana around his neck, then patted the top of his head. "Hey, where are my sunglasses?"

"You left without them."

"A reckless move. My radiant green eyes are a dead giveaway."

He ordered two gin and tonics, peeled off a twenty, and left six dollars in change—a stingy tip by his recent standards. The bartender slid the drinks forward. Verboom grabbed both in one hand, snatched a few napkins with the other, and headed to a four-top beneath a wagon wheel chandelier.

As I pulled back my chair, he asked, "What are you drinking?"

I frowned. "Wasn't one for me?"

"Afraid not, Santo. As a large mammal, I must dose appropriately." He dabbed his forehead with a napkin, checked it, then grinned, holding up the results. "Technically, I'm still a red-blooded American."

"Want some ice for your forehead?"

"*Nay.* Save it for the drinks."

When I returned with a Manny's pale ale, Verboom was drumming his fingers on the table, waiting for the gin to hit.

"A belt of gin," he had called it, as if it might keep his pants up, or perhaps a boxer's championship belt—fittingly grandiose and ridiculous. Perhaps he latched on to the phrase because he'd lost his actual belt to a bike chain.

His frown had lifted. He looked up at the bitter buffalo and smiled.

"I see the gin's a' grinning," I said. "It's a beautiful day. Let's move to the patio."

"Linda's hasn't changed since '94." He radiated warmth and nostalgia. "I used to stop here on the drive up to visit my folks. The city's transforming, but inside, Linda's stays the same—a low-lit refuge."

"It's certainly dim," I said. "How about some sun and a burger on the patio?"

"My brain's hamburger."

"Two decades since your last drink. How does it feel?"

"Like another!" He pushed the empty glass away and reached for the full one.

I leaned in. "What are we going to do about Ella? Even if she doesn't find you here, she'll be waiting in Michigan."

"Playing ostrich as Vermeer won't work, eh?"

"No, it won't." I gestured toward a mounted elk past the jukebox. "You might end up on the wall with your long neck wrung."

"Oh no. I'm donating my body to medicine. Think how many people I could save. Liver—*one*! Heart—*two*! Kidneys—*three, four*!"

"One drink and you're already maudlin?"

"*Nay, nay*! Thrilled by the idea of making a larger contribution—sometimes the parts are greater than the whole."

We let that comment hang, as we nursed our drinks.

To catch up with the professor, I went back for another round. The bartender, busy fine-tuning his station, took my order without looking up. When he slid the beer across the bar, I asked a question I immediately regretted.

"Is this really the last place Kurt Cobain was seen?"

Still not looking up he said, "*Five*. Keep it open or close it?"

I respected his move to extinguish behavior by ignoring it. "Close it."

Back at the table, Verboom took another slow sip.

"The warmth is spreading—like an old furnace rumbling back to life." He exhaled, shaking his head, as if to help the alcohol along. "My brain's hamburger, and my heart's the coal," he muttered, watching the buffalo.

From across the room, a pool stick cracked against the cue ball, breaking a new game. Verboom flinched at the sound.

"While you're still lucid," I said, "let me make something clear. Ella's coming for you. She wants *you* so badly, she's messing with *me*."

"Let's think for a moment, what do we really know about her?"

He swirled the ice in his glass. "One, she likes cameras. Two, she has poor taste in men. I just don't get it."

"Never had a student get a crush on you?"

"As an ostrich, I only see sand."

"Since my head is above ground, let me tell you what's up. It's fatal attraction. She describes you like an object to possess."

"Oh, the whims of youth," he laughed, unable to believe that a woman would go psycho for him.

"She's thirty-six."

Verboom raised an eyebrow. "Really? Thought she was younger."

"Very little UV damage in Michigan."

"True," he nodded. "By California standards, we have the supple radiance of teenagers."

"So. What do you want to do?"

Verboom finished the second glass and circled his index finger for another round.

"We'll have to see what the situation presents, *ja?*"

21

The following day, Thursday, a box of white roses arrived at the apartment. The card inside provided Ella's travel details. She would arrive by Amtrak on the Empire Builder line the following Saturday.

Verboom wondered aloud if we should run, and I wondered silently why it would take so long as he would have plenty of time to flee temptation.

"We'll leave next Friday. She'll already be on the train," he said. "We'll reach Grand Rapids before she's back, then I'll grab a few precious things from my house and drive to Canada."

"I'm not ready for Grand Rapids."

"What happened?"

"My girlfriend—*ex*-girlfriend—is seeing other people. She dumped me, shortly after getting to Flagstaff..."

"*Flagstaff*! This is my fault. Instead of nurturing a romance, you got stuck helping me."

"No. It was doomed from the beginning." I paused. "Let's stay a bit longer."

"But now we're sitting ducks!" He deliberated. "Though come to think of it, when are you going to get free lodging in Seattle during the best time of the year." Then he was struck by a different thought. "Your *work*, Santo? You can't get stuck with me."

"I've filed the form to defer next semester."

"Please don't let me drag you down. I'm not your responsibility."

Though he'd convinced himself that a radio persona and a disguise provided sufficient stealth, it was clear Verboom was incapable of keeping a low profile. At this point, I had to accept that Ella would find us no matter where we ran—so why fight it? And what would she do with the video? More importantly, I could finally hand off the babysitting. Maybe Ella could succeed where I had failed—nudging Verboom back toward a saner brand of eccentricity.

Starting at Linda's, Verboom stayed "on the drip"—slow and steady gin from lunch until passing out. He became more assertive and even more prone to tangents, but without the focus to hammer his points home. He was, somehow, easier to be around. Perhaps the professor had finally been exorcised, spirited away in a tonic of gin, replaced by something looser, softer.

His new habits of booze and news glued him inside the apartment, giving me more time to bike through the city and swim at the Blaine Denny Park beach in the heat of the afternoon. Despite the gruff banter of Vincent Vermeer and his kooky callers, I could feel my mood lifting, my vitality returning. My appetite came back.

Eight days later, we drove to the train station well ahead of Ella's arrival. Since our last use of Verboom's truck, it had acquired its new slogan: GO BACK TO DIXIE, FASCIST PIG! Not the work of an experienced artist, but the long white pickup had provided an ample canvas for a rookie.

Preoccupied, Verboom never noticed the bold black letters—not when he climbed into the truck at the apartment, and not when he stepped out at the station. He simply slid on his sunglasses, pulled up his bandana, and strode ahead.

Inside, we located her arrival platform, and Verboom paced relentlessly for a half hour, stopping occasionally to loosen his shoulders, stretch his calves, and practice the delivery of prepared lines. I stayed put on a bench, notebook in hand, watching him burn off nervous energy.

When the train eased to a stop, Verboom shuffled to the edge of the platform.

Ella stepped off the carriage with effortless precision, dressed in a navy blue skirt that skimmed just above the knee, three-inch heels, and a white button-up shirt left tastefully open at the top. Her dark red lipstick was bold and deliberate, like war paint.

"What's that red circle on your forehead?" Ella asked as they stood face-to-face on the platform.

"Fate," Verboom said. Even after rehearsing his lines, it was the only word he could muster.

She didn't kiss him. Didn't hug him. Instead, she handed him her carry-on bag, then a set of luggage tickets. Without a word, he took them and hurried off to claim her suitcases.

For Ella's arrival, he had resurrected his 1930s archaeologist look. Though his scraped elbows were freshly gauzed, the tight sleeves irritated the wounds, causing them to bleed through the bandages and into the jacket.

"The guest bedroom is ready for you," I said, leaving my seat on the bench to join Ella. "I'll take the couch."

"I'll stay in Dr. Verboom's room," she replied, smooth and unwavering. "Sleep wherever you like."

"I'm putting in my one-week notice," I said firmly. "You two will have the place to yourselves." As much as I wanted to avoid Grand Rapids, seeing Ella had changed my feelings about staying.

I glanced over. Verboom was hustling toward us, a large leather suitcase in each hand, the smaller carry-on slung over his shoulder, glasses on, bandana up.

"We'll talk plans later," Ella said sternly. "Which way to the truck?"

Verboom reached us just as we started toward the exit, slowing his pace to match ours, falling into step beside Ella.

Then, after a few paces, she deftly slipped behind him.

"Remember these hands," she whispered.

She could barely reach the base of his neck, so he leaned back ten degrees to accommodate. They moved like that—one in front of the other—as she worked her fingers into his overgrown shoulders. Verboom adjusted his stride to short, *tap-tap-tap* steps, careful not to heel-kick her shins.

I faded out wide, letting a stream of travelers pass between us. When I looked back to the pair, I took in the full absurdity of the scene—Verboom lugging two oversized leather suitcases, his blazer soaked with blood at the elbows, his back arched for the massage, and a full-blown erection, the pleats in his pants being of great aid.

Having tamed her golden bear, Ella let go of his shoulders and slid up beside him.

We walked three across down the passageway, heading for the parking lot.

"So. I've been listening to your new show."

"Obviously," I said, sharing my annoyance.

"I'm surprised you make such a good jerk. I like the edge, but you're still lecturing. We don't want another professor, do we, *professor?*"

"Are you taking me back to Michigan?" Verboom asked.

"Let me help Vermeer first."

"Don't your agency standards prohibit sleepovers?" I injected.

Ella ignored me. "Instead of lectures, we need whistleblowers. A hotline for tipsters. People will tune in for revelations."

"Out the theocrats?" Verboom asked. "I've been casting bait in every direction."

"A hotline will only platform conspiracy nuts," I objected.

"What if they have the truth?" Ella countered.

"How can we verify their claims?"

She shrugged. "You're the scientist."

"An almost-scientist," I corrected. "At this point I'm only an advanced critical thinker. But if you hand the mic to anyone who can dial ten digits, all you'll have is a rumor mill."

"People don't want to be talked at like students. They want to feel like insiders, so bring them into the conversation," Ella said. "A hotline could be a pipeline for real leaks—government cover-ups, corporate fraud, illicit affairs."

"Let's reward the best dirt with a signed copy of *Tautology*." Verboom beamed.

"You'll never stay underground if you keep referring to your publications," I said.

"*Nay, nay*. Vincent Vermeer has clearly got a life of his own. My persona has full blown personhood—legally and psychologically."

"Where did you get this alias?" Ella asked.

"A deliverance from the unconscious! I'm the voice of radio anarchy—it's quite a rush. Like the mythical Samson, I'm tearing it all down. Somebody cut my hair!"

"Anarchism is just an act," I said. "A way to place Vermeer on the political spectrum, not an actual goal he's trying to accomplish."

"Indeed," Verboom added. "*Vermeer's* main ambition seems to be revenge."

"Against whom?" Ella asked.

"The folks who mocked the professor," Verboom answered as if it was already totally obvious. "The Vermeer persona is like an intellectual hitman, an enforcer delivering payback. Imagine having a platform in which you could slam every ass-wipe who ever spoke against you!"

As we stepped into the parking lot, we saw an army sergeant freshly reunited with her family. They fell into each other, sobbing, clinging, shaking.

Verboom's tweed tent collapsed.

As soon as we reached the truck, I slid behind the wheel. After seeing the graffiti and griping about the lawlessness of liberal cities, Ella took shotgun, adjusting the seat forward for Verboom, who sprawled across the second row. Though he'd kept his bloody elbows off us, he didn't seem concerned about the truck's interior. By the time we got home, it would look like a crime scene.

I remembered reading somewhere that rubbing alcohol gets blood out of fabric and tried not to dwell on the mess.

As we made our way to Genevieve's apartment, Verboom read almost every street sign aloud, calling out points of interest like a demented tour guide. Ella didn't react—no amusement, no irritation—just perfect posture, staring ahead.

Arriving at the apartment, I went straight for my bike. Though only a hundred pages shy of a Ph.D. in psychology, I was out here playing amateur anthropologist, or journalist, or writer, or chaperone, in Seattle's E.R.O.G.E.N.O.U.S. Zone. As ridiculous as it was, one thing was certain: I wasn't going to sit on the couch pretending to watch TV while Ella and Verboom reunited with biblical thunder.

After Ella scolded me for not wearing a helmet, I biked down to the ferry terminal and bought a walk-on ticket for the next ferry to Bainbridge Island.

As the boat rumbled away from the dock, I leaned against the railing and called Jacqueline. Right away, she asked about Verboom's wellbeing. I told her about the gin, Ella's arrival, and how I felt stuck—not wanting to be a third wheel, not wanting to go home. To my surprise, she offered to host me in Flagstaff.

"What about my writing assignment on Verboom?"

"Write a chapter on the clinic here. How could they lose such a large patient?" She laughed. "Hey, I heard you hooked up with one of the nurses. What was that like?"

"My mom's ministry—rest in peace—was preaching against premarital sex. It's not something I want to talk about."

"But I'm *all ears*," she said, channeling Ross Perot, circa 1992.

I chuckled. "You remember Perot? You were what—six?"

"Watched the debate in undergrad poli sci."

"Classic moment."

"Perot is top of mind. People on campus are comparing him to Kroes."

"Perot had a shot, not Kroes."

"My mom is convinced he'll win," Jacqueline said. "She's picked every race correctly since I was born."

"She studies the paper?"

"Dreams. She can feel the future."

"Does she play Lotto?" I asked.

"It's not like that, asshole. She's just... highly attuned. She feels the mood of things."

Since I didn't know what to say, I said nothing.

"If you come back, I'll introduce you to her."

Dating my ex for a year, she'd never made that offer.

The island's ferry terminal buzzed with summer energy, the sun glinting off metal gangways and shimmering across the bay. The air carried a mix of salt, sunscreen, and fried seafood.

Beyond the pier, sailboats speckled the water, their white sails sharp against the dark green coastline.

In town, I grabbed green curry at a Thai restaurant with a perfect view of Eagle Harbor and Mt. Rainier. Afterward, I rode to a waterfront park, found a shaded bench, and sat for a while thinking about my next steps.

A bike ride, a stop for coffee, and a slow browse through the bookstore filled the afternoon.

As the evening crept closer, I had an early dinner at a brewery, the crisp bite of a pale ale opened up my appetite.

Heading back across the Sound, the skyline gleamed in the low-angle light. The Emerald City in the Evergreen State, a castle between sea and sky.

Entering the apartment, Verboom was sitting on the couch, wearing only a white towel around his waist. His long hair, still damp, was combed back as he sat watching American News Network.

My serenity spoiled, I asked, "What are you *doing*?"

"I do what I do what I do," he replied, staring into the TV.

"*ANN*?"

"Viewpoint diversity."

"WNN provides different viewpoints."

"More difference here. And I must say, these folks do anarchy better than anyone I've seen so far! They should be advertising pitchforks at commercial break!"

I headed to the kitchen. Draped in an orange *gi*, Ella was cooking, her hair wrapped in a towel. As she turned to face me, her jacket hung open. With her hair pulled up, her strong jawline looked even sharper—and for the first time, I noticed her ears: small and delicate, in striking contrast to her commanding presence.

I reached in the refrigerator for a beer.

"You don't need to cook," I said, popping the cap off.

"But I love to, and you boys need some protein, getting skinny on all this Left Coast trail mix and dandelion juice."

"I'll do the dishes."

"*Yes you can*," she chanted. It may have been the first time she had ever fully smiled at me.

As I turned back toward the living room she said, "Take this to the professor," handing me a tumbler with a wedge of lime and a sprig of rosemary. Then she stopped me with a touch on the shoulder and topped off the glass with more gin.

"Cheers," I said, making a pivot to face her.

"Thanks, but I'm not drinking."

"How long will you be in town?"

"Let's get breakfast tomorrow while the professor sleeps it off."

Back in the living room, I handed Verboom his drink and sat down.

"*Hartelijk dank*." He tilted his glass toward me without looking my way. "The networks are obsessed with Kroes. On ANN the commentators say he's a buffoon, but a relatable buffoon; they barely mention the other candidates. He's become *the* story, even though he's dismissed as having no chance."

"A conservative pollster floated the idea of Kroes for president by slipping him into a likeability survey—just a popular cultural figure with no real political prospects. A way to measure how the expected frontrunners stacked up..."

"And, *ta da*, he came in first," Verboom finished the story.

"More likeable than any politician. Let's nail him on your show."

"So, it wasn't because I kicked God out of government —allegedly?"

"Glad your memory is coming back."

"*Nay*. Ella insisted we watch my segment on *Hot Button Science*. After biblical relations, I didn't have the strength to resist."

"Quoting scripture isn't working?"

"Ignored," he said, staring at an image of Kroes on ANN. "Like *he* must be ignored."

"What if someone calls your show with a scoop?"

"Nothing about Kroes—good, bad, or indifferent."

"Doesn't that reveal a bias too?"

He slurped then coughed. "Got the rosemary in my nostril." He set the glass on the table.

"You finished your gin in one slurp!"

"Kroes drives me to drink."

"Thought that was Ella…"

"*Not so loud*," Verboom growled in a worried whisper. "Not sure how to say this, Lawrence."

"*Santo*. I'm Santo. Let's put our personas aside. What is it?"

"It's Ella." He glanced over to the kitchen. "It's delicate."

"You want my blessing?" I frowned. "I'm not your son."

"She hasn't threatened me explicitly, but she made it clear that a camera crew can be here in less than five minutes if I upset her."

"Did you upset her?"

"*Do you see a camera crew?*" He jumped to his feet.

"No."

"The leash is tight," he said, dropping back to the couch.

"She doesn't want you to talk about Kroes?"

"No directions on Kroes, she just asked me to change the channel to ANN. But the channel doesn't matter so much anymore, with the entire media talking about Kroes as a spoiler, they're going to make him a spoiler. He's met every filing deadline. Even in North Carolina, which proves he was running before he admitted an earnest campaign publicly. They're saying California is the only state out of reach."

"'*They're saying*?' You're doing *they-speak* now?"

"Kroes says he doesn't need or want California. Says the state will slide off into the Pacific when the Big One hits. Then he laughs and says he'll win with the heartland, 'real America,' and he's looking forward to Arizona getting a beach."

"The next *Big One* is coming to the Pacific Northwest. He should revise his strategy. Even if he was right, that's not how the fault lines run... Wasn't he born in California? He should know better."

"Born in New Jersey, but he's spent most of his professional life in Arizona. Obviously, he's prepping for a loss. He'll claim the system is rigged. That way when he loses, he didn't really lose."

"What if he wins?" I asked.

"Then he wins."

"Sounds like he's playing God," I said.

Verboom leaned back in the couch and crossed his arms, smiling contentedly, then he said admiringly, "You learn so quickly, Santo."

I leaned forward to set my beer on the table. As I reclined, something alarming caught my eye. As he'd leaned back, his towel had unclasped. I stood up and walked down the hall. I returned to the kitchen with a pair of pants and asked Ella to sheath her manchild.

Returning to the living room, I made a point to professionalize our conversation.

"During your costume change, I skimmed a new paper online that complicates the left-brain right-brain model, so you can stop calling me 'the left brain.'"

"You read the article that quickly?" he asked with amazement.

"Only the methods and conclusion sections."

"Both my hemispheres are junk. You can be 'the brain.' Plus, it's safer not to be associated with the Left, even anatomically," Verboom mumbled, concentrating on tying up his pants. "Next thing you know, right-wingers will start calling anything under-handed '*lefthanded*.'"

"The brain is going to pack for Michigan. I'll show Ella how to push the buttons."

"*Ta da*!" His pants were secured.

"Dinner will be ready soon," Ella called from the kitchen.

"You may be the brain, but I am the *mind*! Now let me get on my *behind*! It's time for Jonathan Kuiper, that anchor-friend of *mine*." He changed the channel from ANN to WNN, then turned to me and put his index finger to his lips for a silent *shhh*... It was the monologue. He patted the sofa cushion next to him, inviting me to sit.

Later that evening while Verboom and Ella ate a late dinner of pork chops, mashed potatoes, and brussels sprouts, I decided to work in my bedroom.

Jacqueline had skimmed my first draft and suggested I establish Verboom's firsthand insight into the movement for theocracy.

Verboom's journey through Christendom was both heartfelt and cerebral—in turns nominal, mystical, devout, dogmatic, ethical, and finally, skeptical.

In high school, he devoured books on dominion theology by Theonomists and Restorationists. At first, I thought he was making up funny words to annoy me, but these political movements were real and growing, despite being dressed in friendlier language by schoolteachers and pastors. Names and labels vary, but according to Verboom, "gonzo Calvinists were the brains behind America's theocracy movements."

When he wasn't working on the family farm, he spent much of his childhood learning theology and growing flowers. If anyone questioned the masculinity of these pursuits, he'd simply rebrand them as philosophy and horticulture.

"I was a thinker, Santo. I wanted to know how things worked. By disposition, I wasn't a rebel—not in the least! But following the chain of cause-and-effect will put you at odds with the powers that be." And to illustrate how his cognitive style clashed with the dogmatic culture of his childhood, he routinely told me two stories.

In his teens, he read Albert Camus' *The Fall*, assuming it was an essay on original sin—as in humanity's *fall* into sin. Though not a classic work of theology, one minor idea stuck with him: Camus' narrator, a self-congratulatory, over-humble lawyer, speculated that Jesus *allowed* himself to be crucified out of guilt for "the deaths of the innocents"—the children murdered in Herod's hunt for the Messiah.

Verboom took the idea a step further. In a high school theology paper, he argued that "if the Messiah had a Messiah Complex," then by the same logic, St. Paul must have had a death wish—his guilt for executing the earliest Christians would drive St. Paul to become a martyr himself.

His instructor wasn't impressed. The "F" was written twice, pressed hard enough to bleed through the page.

The final break from Christendom happened in a college Apologetics course. He told me the story at least once a month in his office, so my report follows his self-report exactly.

Midway through the semester, the Apologetics professor opened the class: "Before we continue critiquing Freud's view of religion, let's start with a word of prayer: *Our Father in heaven, we gather here today as your children...*"

This was where Verboom lost it, like he would every time he told the story, howling with laughter, just as he had then. Wailing like a hyena during prayer was inconceivable to those around him, and his cackling escalated so wildly that the instructor quit talking to God and spoke to Verboom directly.

"*What's the meaning of this?*" he demanded to know of young Pieter.

"*Father!*" Verboom bellowed. "*Children!*" he gasped. Then laughing, he asked, "Don't you get it?"

"What's there to get about laughing during prayer?" the instructor growled.

"You're supposedly dismantling Freud's view of religion, and yet you start with 'Our Father' and call us 'children.' You're summarily confirming Freud's analysis!"

The professor was irate. "How can anyone laugh during prayer!"

But Verboom couldn't stop. The poignant irony of the situation broke something loose inside of him.

The professor demanded Verboom leave class, telling him not to return until he had "repaired his relationship with God."

"As you wish!" Verboom bellowed, doubling over.

He tried switching his major to Psychology, but it would have taken an extra year. In a parochial school, his Theology courses could be counted as Philosophy credits, so he took the latter for his degree, with a minor in Psychology.

"Apologetics—the study of defending the faith," Verboom would reflect. "If the answer never changes, no matter what the argument or evidence, you can see why a freethinker like me cracked up. Though it was a school slogan, 'thinking faithfully' was never my cognitive style. What I took from parochial schools? All pursuits rolled up into obedience. Sure, details were fine. Elaborating technical points could even be welcome—so long as everything lined up with what we already believed. The goal wasn't truth. It was making every activity obedient to whatever the head honchos decreed. And of course, they claimed to speak on God's behalf—but that, too, was just one more gimmick."

About his college days, he would lament: "I lost my faculty for prayer, but the urge was still there—too many urges! I didn't drink, didn't smoke. I was a virgin, technically speaking. Too restless to think sitting down, I walked the hilly trails by campus for hours a day. And I'm still a man without a home, no place to put my wooden shoes."

"Do you even have wooden shoes?" I asked him, after hearing his reminiscing one too many times.

"I'm speaking cosmically! The wooden shoe is a symbol—a relic of a hollowed-out culture. All that's left is pessimism and cheese! You're lucky to have escaped the doctrines of determinism. Every inch of experience must be brought to heel under God's *dominion*."

He tried to package his thoughts on Dutch American subculture as entertainment rather than a grim fixation. After unburdening himself one afternoon while still on campus, he shifted gears, attempting to lighten the mood, reveling in the marvel of human evolution.

"Well, in the end, we're all Africans," he concluded.

To which I clarified: "White folks are partial Neanderthals."

"Still not proven!" Verboom sang giddily, flailing his arms like a caveman. "Still not proven!" He knocked over his pencil holder, swinging his knuckles in slow, exaggerated arcs, his elbows locked, his arms like dumb logs. "Not entirely proven!"

At that moment, an undergrad walked into his office.

"What's not proven?" she asked.

"That I'm part Neanderthal," Verboom said, eyes twinkling.

"Of course you are," she said confidently. "Three new studies out. You're likely 5%."

Verboom froze in thought. Then, in a low, measured voice, as if contemplating an entirely new future, he said, "Think of the possibilities."

22

A hard knock rattled my bedroom door early the next morning.

"Let's leave in five minutes," Ella said through the door. "I'm not waiting in line for breakfast."

Already half-dressed, I rolled out of bed and pulled my head-phones through my shirt, the earbuds and mic dangling over my crew neck. Plugging in, I hit record, threw on my jeans, slipped my phone into my front pocket, and met Ella at the front door.

We walked to a diner on Union Street, a spot that had started as a burger truck before evolving into a brick-and-mortar shop. The exterior walls were large roll-up window-doors—now up in the warm air of summer, bringing the feeling of the outdoors in. With polished concrete floors, exposed steel beams, stained wood, and vintage vinyl seating, the place felt old and new, cozy and industrial.

We arrived early enough to skip the wait, sliding into a booth.

Ella ordered two coffees, and the server walked off without a word.

"I know you're dying to see this." She took her phone from her purse, unlocked the screen, pressed play, and slid it over.

I recognized the scene immediately and cupped my hands around the phone—like warming them around a candle—hoping to shield any curious eyes. In the video, you could see a naked woman straddling a naked man, but the light was low and the picture grainy.

"Wait until she turns on the lamp," Ella said. "Just about... now."

"How many times have you watched this?" I growled.

"Boy, those two are really going at it," the server said, suddenly standing at our table with coffee. "No tip jokes from me. I promise." He set the mugs down and gave a knowing nod. "I'll give you two more time."

With her phone in my hands, I considered deleting the video, but she certainly had backup copies. In a rush of clarity, I accepted that Ella would always have this on me, so I turned the phone over and slid it back.

"You don't want to see how it ends?" Ella grinned.

"Who are these people?" I asked.

"I'm just a friend showing you a video."

"There's no crime in this video. *The video is the crime.*"

"The professor must have told you about my letter?"

"How could you know who my father is?"

"A good source."

"The Dutch Mafia?" I laughed too sarcastically, revealing anxiety.

"That's a poorly chosen nickname for an insular subculture; it's not an organization."

"Verboom seems to think they pull every string in Western Michigan."

"Your father's family doesn't like publicity, which is why you don't know who he is."

"Don't make me wait for an omelet," I sneered.

"Our professor showed you the photos from the yacht, at the country club, in an evening gown..."

"You're a true beauty. Point made." I took an angry sip of coffee. "Next, you'll say we're siblings and should join forces."

"Your father is from one of the wealthiest families in Michigan, part of the Dutch Mafia, if that's what you want to call them."

"That's what Verboom calls them."

"The professor is a paranoid child in Tarzan's body." She paused. "Your father was a junior in high school when you were born, and your mom just a sophomore. I don't know what happened. I don't know if they loved each other. But the family, on whose yacht I've sailed, was not going to allow their son to..."

"*Marry out of his tax bracket!*" I banged on the table then exhaled, steadying my body and composing my thoughts.

"They didn't want him to miss college. In that community, there would be pressure to drop out of school and get a job to provide for the child and the mother, who *must* become his wife."

"No need to work. They're rich."

"It's not the money; it's the principle. During this party on the yacht, your uncle got overly drunk and... I didn't hear the whole story."

"Tell me what you know." The force in my voice surprised me.

Ella leaned back, exhaled slowly and silently. "I heard your uncle talking about your family." Then she leaned forward and dropped her voice. "About what to do with *you*."

"This is a tasteless joke."

"He was clearly drunk, but also upset—even worried."

"Didn't want his brother's sin smearing the family name."

"It seemed more like..." She paused. "Concern."

"*Guilt* is the word you're searching for."

"Your uncle spoke about how much they've already done but wondered if it was enough. I couldn't catch every detail. What was clear: your mother's death triggered your uncle's concern for you."

"Why were you there?"

"I know someone who works with your uncle."

"Why tell me this now?"

"It's too soon to go home. Stay with us through Election Day, and I'll tell you everything."

"That's November 6!" I leaned back in the booth, unsure of what to do.

"It's not so far off."

"Wouldn't you rather have Verboom to yourself?" I asked.

"He's too much for me alone. I can't listen to him talk all day the way you can."

"You want to keep me around like some kind of concierge?" I scoffed, then thought for a moment. "He doesn't need a babysitter anymore; he's got Jonathan Kuiper and friends."

"In a hurry to get home, Santo? I heard your ex has been…" Ella paused, her lips curling into a wicked grin. "Making the rounds."

"*Making the rounds?*"

"We've been in touch. Took her out for happy hour, and she really took advantage of the discount." Ella smirked, letting it hang before adding, "One thing I remember her saying: 'I've been making up for lost time.'"

"How can I know you have more? You're asking me to take a leap of faith—just so you can blackmail me."

"Do you know who funded your scholarships?"

"Earned them with baseball and my GPA."

"You have good grades; you're an all-star. But plenty of boys play second base and earn high marks. Why were those scholarships awarded to you and not someone else? And do you know how your mom paid her medical bills?" She held up a hand. "Take a breath before you say anything."

I inhaled, forcing myself to look away. Through a window, two men kissed on the sidewalk, standing close, carefree. I thought: James Kroes will never be president. I exhaled and turned back to Ella.

"Does it look like I'm lying?" She took a sip of coffee.

"Maybe I'll call my grandmother?"

"You must have done that after you saw the letter," Ella said.

Before I could respond, the server interrupted. "You folks ready to order?"

"Eggs *benedict* for her," I snarled.

Ella raised a brow. "Actually, that sounds good. Sauce on the side please."

"Bloody Mary. Hold the bacon."

"And to eat?"

"Lost my appetite."

The server winked at me.

After ordering, Ella kept up a steady stream of small talk, filling any gaps where silence might settle.

She didn't touch her sauce—why not just *hold* the sauce? She ate all the eggs and ham but left the English muffins untouched.

Before we left, she ordered three breakfast sandwiches for Verboom and paid in cash.

On the walk back to the apartment, our conversation turned to Vincent Vermeer. Ella sounded more like a fan than a concerned friend.

Halfway home, I slipped in a quick question as we walked, hoping to catch her off guard.

"Why'd you come to Seattle?"

She grinned. "Why, I'm the professor's publicist, of course."

23

Despite my initial reluctance to chronicle Verboom's life, my commitment to the recordings had become officially obsessive. It was my life too—my observations, my experience. Still, it seemed ethical to run the book idea past Verboom a second time, both to check his recall and to confirm his decision.

After he finished his breakfast sandwiches, after Ella left for a walk, and after I'd searched the apartment for bugs, I broached the topic with the professor.

"Just plain text, right? No cameras?"

"Correct. No video, no pictures—just the story of how politics ruined your life."

That sounded just grim enough for him to look away from the TV and study my expression.

"A cautionary tale printed in a pleasant font." I winked.

"My life was too easy, my capacities squandered by dawdling and doodling, with very little canoodling. I let my wheels spin, now I'm nowhere. You can find a better topic to write about."

"Take a more positive view of your life."

"Could never make a decision unless forced, and then I'd regret the force."

"But you study persuasion professionally."

"Because I can't persuade myself to do anything! You don't want a therapist who's had an easy life. She'll never understand your pain."

"At least you got to meet the president."

"Ruined his career, and now I'm ruining yours."

"The captured SEALs are ruining his career," I said.

"*Nay, nay*, it's his secular sensibility. The last president failed to stop the 9/11 attacks, but he got reelected because he called the terrorists 'evil doers.' Then he claimed to be God's chosen man."

"At least he didn't ban Muslims. He took great pains not to demonize an entire religion."

"Lucky to get away with that," Verboom said grimly.

"You don't think *Tautology* is making a difference?"

"It is what it is."

"Exactly."

"It is what it is," he repeated, like a mantra, and it *was*. "That was something a guy told me on a jobsite. My first day, he was training me. He'd describe a task—like stocking receipt tape in the server station—then say it could be done any number of other ways. He wasn't sure why it was done that particular way, maybe there was a better way, but... '*it is what it is*.' Then he'd shrug."

"What job was this?"

"Waiting tables in grad school. A tough gig to land in LA, with all the actors and musicians and what-have-you. But I was tall, tan, and well-mannered. I memorized the menu during my interview, then in a roleplay, I remembered twelve detailed orders without notes. So, they gave me a chance."

"Your life-philosophy is based on something some guy told you in a bar?"

"He was the supervisor. And it was a restaurant. With a bar area."

"And you turned that into a book?"

"*It is what it is*. I kept thinking about it. He said it like a slogan, a catchphrase, a punchline, a prayer... Must have said it twenty times. I couldn't get it out of my head. Every task, the same formula, the same conclusion. I'd never heard the phrase before. This was a long time ago, and I was new to the city. And I thought: You know, *that's true*. That's *always* true."

"You're confusing me."

"It's a tautology, Santo. A *equals* A. It's always true. There's no room for a false dilemma. There is no dilemma."

"You're talking about *existence*?"

"I have ideas, but I don't know how they touch the world."

"But... the world is the world?" I suggested.

"There is no apparent world. There is no ideal world. The world is the world. And you just have to let it be that."

"All it took was some guy in an LA bar to tell you."

"More of a restaurant. Full menu. And he was the supervisor."

"That's exactly the kind of anecdote I could use for the book."

"And the semantic analysis? All my words? You'll determine what condition my condition is in?"

"Should be clear soon enough."

Verboom hesitated, suddenly anxious.

"Hope it's okay," he said, "but I haven't told Ella about our recording project. Despite her wishes, I'm reducing my media presence, and I don't want to look like a hypocrite."

As I had hoped, we agreed to keep the project a secret.

"Now, I know you don't want pictures," I said, "but what about the cover? As a biographical sketch, the publisher's going to want an image."

"As long as you publish it posthumously—that is, *my* posthumous."

"I was thinking next year, while the election and your WNN appearance are still fresh. Maybe by then, *Final Freedom* will even be implemented."

He shuddered. "Well. If you don't buy a gun, and I'm alive next year, how about a seersucker book jacket?"

I placed my left hand over my fist and bowed. Then, with a smirk, I raised a single index finger to my lips—*shhh*.

That Sunday evening Ella reviewed her plan to makeover the show. She would become announcer and headline presenter, and we'd restyle things during the broadcast, like an organic revelation. Instead of squabbling with callers, *Vermeer* would provide a platform for callers to leak and listeners to learn about the hidden practices of big government and big business.

While *The Dutch Uncle* was getting reprogrammed, Verboom drank gin and kept an eye on cable news. The networks all ran commercials at the same time.

"Another example of organized capital," Verboom said to himself, flipping through channels rapidly.

Then he went on nodding and mumbling as Ella elaborated her strategy, but he was obviously distracted, so I stood in front of him, blocking the television.

"Do you agree?" I asked, hoping he would say no.

"Indeed. Just as you said, we are now The Pelican Committee." Seeing my blank face, he added, "Sure, I may look like a golden bear, but I've become a pelican, gliding along the culture, sucking up all the succulent morsels as they surface, sucking them all up into my giant beak. No beak is bigger! I've consumed it all! I'll bring it all to *you*."

"You want to change the name of the show?" Ella asked.

"The gin's got you ready for cable," I teased. "Are you a parrot or a savant?"

"Has your beak swallowed all the day's news?" Verboom continued. "A beak such as mine!" He kissed his palm with his thick lips and blew that kiss to the television. "We fly at the edge of the sea, Jonathan Kuiper and me! He and I, you and I, she and I..." he said, pointing as he listed. "We are *the we* of the Pelican Commit*tee*. We'll bring the baby home to roost! Speaking of which, look at that baby-faced Jonathan! So wise beyond his years..."

"You're the same age," I said.

Ella left for the master bedroom.

She returned a few minutes later with her purse and a light jacket.

"I'm going out to find curtains."

She pitched me a tape measure.

"Take the dimensions and text me. Be precise," she said and left the apartment.

I sat next to Verboom on the couch.

"We should call this puppy 'Laurels,'" he said, slapping the arm of the couch. "Just resting on my Laurels..." He exhaled audibly.

"Can you handle this much Ella?"

"Got my Dutch courage. Nerves are steady now." He rattled his cocktail glass. "Sky's the limit."

"Think it's safe out there this evening?"

"Ella's smart."

"But is she street-smart?"

"She's yacht-smart. Can't be much different," he said.

As I opened my mouth to ask if Ella had revealed my father's identity to him, he leaned toward the television, a signal that it was time to stop talking and start watching WNN at high volume.

Walking to the window for measurements, I heard the deep *crack* of a discharged rifle. A single shot. Reflexively, I crouched.

Verboom remained unmoved on the sofa.

The windows were open, and I could hear the folks in the park booing, jeering, and clanking their stainless-steel water bottles together. Their chant began:

D! D! P! [low tone]
Nap'am! [high tone]
Nap'am! [high tone]

While I stood on a dining room chair taking dimensions with the tape measure, Ella burst into the apartment. Leaning against the front door after closing it, she exhaled long and slow. Her white shirt was stained dark red. Verboom rushed to her.

"*My goodness! You've been shot!*"

Verboom put an open hand on her abdomen.

"I'm fine."

"*Santo!* Get the first aid kit while I apply pressure to the wound! *Call 911!*"

"It's paint," she said.

Since I froze standing on the chair, Verboom ran into the kitchen for the kit.

"Calm down. *It's paint!*" Ella yelled after him.

"*Paint?* I thought we needed drapes," he said, returning from the kitchen. "According to Stanley, the apartment is freshly coated. Don't like the color?"

"I was hit by a *paintball.*"

"The rally guys?" I asked from the chair.

"Someone in a big burgundy pickup approached with a few guys in the back. They were yelling at people on the sidewalk. Things started flying and then *pop pop pop...* Someone paint-balled us."

"Whose *us?*"

"The people. On. The sidewalk. Do you need to know the referent for every pronoun, Santo?"

Ella took off her shirt and handed it to Verboom. He held it up, looking for a hole. He sniffed the fluid. Then he looked at Ella, still standing in front of the door.

"There's a bruise forming," he said. "Where are my proverbial wooden shoes? I'm going to club those nincompoops!"

"Just get ice," she said.

From the park:

D! D! P! [low tone]
  Nap'am! [high tone]
  Nap'am! [high tone]

I closed the window in front of me to prevent commentary from Ella. Verboom hurried to the kitchen, while I stood on the chair with the tape measure, my eyes locked on Ella, and I lost track of time. She looked at me and put her arms together like she was returning a volleyball, then wiggled her shoulders at me.

"You ready for a burlesque?" she griped.

I turned to look out the window, still standing on the chair, the sunlight past its peak but bright, the leaves deep green and waving in the wind of a long summer evening. The D.D.P. chant went on.

24

On Monday morning, Verboom was up early, sporting an ice bag on the crown of his head. He claimed he'd been overthinking all night and needed to cool his scalp to prevent hair loss.

He'd made coffee, toast, and twelve scrambled eggs. Several newspapers were spread out on the table in the breakfast nook, a cozy media war room.

"Where's Ella?" I asked.

"Catching up on her rest."

"Kroes is on ANN tonight," I said looking at a front page. "*Big* interview." I set my coffee mug on his face.

"Seattle could use some law and order," Ella said, walking into the kitchen.

"Don't tell me you're a Kroester?" I asked.

"Don't like being hit with paintballs."

"If you're making a 'law and order' argument, keep in mind that the D.D.P. didn't paint ball you," I said.

Ella moved my mug to review the front page and added, "I'm looking forward to seeing Sheriff Kroes on ANN tonight."

"The only way to get rid of him is to ignore him," Verboom said.

"So, all the good Catholics and Lutherans of Germany should've ignored Hitler?" I asked.

"Absolutely! No attention, no following. No following, no power."

"Well, once he got in power, they had to do something?" I asked.

"It's not one man; it's a movement," Ella said.

"Kroes or Hitler?" I asked.

"Let's not be flippant!" Verboom growled. "My grandfather hid from the Nazis through the whole war, sleeping in barns and hiding in haystacks."

"The past is prologue to more people who can't learn from the past," I said.

Ella took her breakfast and *The Journal* and went back to the master bedroom.

At noon Ella, in her smoky voice, delivered the blustering intro of the "Dutch demigod demolishing dainty dimwits…"

Verboom sipped audibly from his gin as though it were hot coffee.

Ella read headlines: "Pennsylvania Lawmaker Prays In Jesus' Name Before First Muslim Woman Is Sworn In As Representative"; "Poland Bans Gay Public Affection"; and "Americans Consume 80% Of All Opioids—More Fatal Than Auto Accidents And Guns Combined."

Vermeer asked for more detail on the Pennsylvania congresswoman who repeatedly referred to Jesus as God during the swearing in of the state's first Muslim representative. The senior congresswoman also took liberties with the historical record, claiming that George Washington prayed to Jesus at Valley Forge and that Abraham Lincoln sought Jesus in prayer at Gettysburg.

"Myths, not history!" Vermeer interjected. Stories invented by the same writer who came up with the story of George Washington chopping down the cherry tree.

Discussion of the founders gave the opening to discuss Freemasonry and the contemporary parallel of First Brothers.

Vermeer did Verboom's usual rant, tying First Brothers to misogyny, big business, and theocracy. He repeatedly called for an insider to "rat out" the brotherhood, though "no one would give a rat's ass." Again, hoping to inspire callers, he called Americans "intellectual couch potatoes" and read out our toll-free number.

After flying over the handlebars, he'd spun a narrative of gin-drinking as the obsession of the Dutch and something he could do moderately as a connoisseur to embrace his heritage, something vital to being an on-air asshole. But the day Ella showed up in Seattle, all moderation went out the window.

Ella built on her earlier appeal for whistleblowers, framing the toll-free number as a hotline for leaks—an opportunity to save America.

Vermeer interrupted, wanting to keep focus on theocrats.

They went back and forth like a tennis match, volleying their pet preoccupations. With no calls coming in right away, they kept rolling—more headlines, more commentary.

Once Ella moved into the studio, I relocated to the other side of the French doors. One corner of the American flag curtain was pulled back, so we could see each other.

A call came in. The topic: the Ambassador-at-Large for International Religious Freedom, who reports directly to the Secretary of State.

"If you want an example of church and state mixing business, there you go!" the caller yelled—then hung up.

It wasn't a leak. The info was public, available on the State Department's website, established by the International Religious Freedom Act. The ambassador-at-large was the former governor of Kansas, Richard Kupchak. The Kupchak of the 'Kupchak Experiment,' who passed the largest state tax cut in Kansas' history, saying it would be a "shot of adrenaline" to the economy.

But the shot turned out to be a shot in the foot. The massive revenue shortfall led to devastating cuts to infrastructure and education. Kupchak lost popular support and legislative control in the next election and resigned to take the ambassadorship.

The talk show artist known as Vermeer zeroed in on Kupchak's membership in "The Brotherhood," his term for First Brothers.

Between Ella trying to shift the topic and Vermeer roasting Kupchak, they burned through the rest of the hour.

Ella noticed my frustration and confronted me later that afternoon.

I was tired of the Vermeer persona constantly referencing *Tautology* like it was scripture, and how he couldn't stop romanticizing Seattle—the coffee, the clouds, the cultural mystique.

She frowned, incredulous. "Who are you hiding from? I'm already here."

"First Brothers, O.F.A.M., D.D.P., and..."

"Afraid of D.D.P.?" she interrupted, then laughed.

"They spraypainted the truck."

"*They're* not going to do anything more than burn down their own neighborhoods."

"Do you know how that sounds?"

"You assumed it was the D.D.P. that tagged the truck. Have any proof?"

"Well, if I had to side with anyone, it would be those people."

"Did you just say *those people*?" she said shaking her head in faux offense.

"Some Kroester screamed a hat full of slurs at me a few weeks ago."

"What were you doing?"

"Riding my bike, but that shouldn't matter!"

"How do you know he's a Kroester?"

"He wore a *JIM* hat."

"What were the slurs?"

"Not repeating the words. Please keep Vermeer more discrete," I requested.

"Scared to stand up for the truth?"

"*Truth*? Verboom is having a midlife crisis on two-bit talk radio! He's fallen under the spell of a mysterious Michigan beauty queen, and for some reason that queen and I are enabling his on-air antics." I looked around.

"Don't worry," she said. "He's on the couch."

"He's lost touch with reality."

"By watching the news all day?"

"I don't know what he's watching, but I see the results on him. Maybe it's a scam to sell ads, or raw propaganda, or just the sugary infotainment Americans crave—the nonsense they vote for everyday with their remotes, but *it's not reality*!"

"Don't be hysterical, honey. How can a single man be so dangerous?"

"Because we're helping him," I said.

"Heard you're worried the professor's radio hobby will tank your prospects?"

"Not anymore, I'm leaving academia. I can't set up shop in some middle tier department for five decades and watch the world burn. I'm learning how to produce and podcast—how to tell a story—so I'd like some level of professionalism."

"'Watch the world burn?' Your research on conspiracies is getting the best of you. You need some distance... You need some *action*." Then she patted me on the butt like she did in Flagstaff and walked away.

After that conversation with Ella, I committed to finishing a final draft on Verboom before the year's end. Jacqueline was right—a book offered deeper redemption than simply learning to podcast or webcast. This whole crazy year had given me rich material.

I walked down to my usual coffeehouse on Pike. After ordering, I sat by the window, stared at my screen, then looked out at the street.

Verboom's demise didn't have to be mine.

My only crime was enabling eccentricity—something most graduate students end up doing anyway.

Paul Heitinga's book on the young Verboom would help make my case with a future publisher. Since then, Verboom had become a tenured professor, attended the E.C.S., had a nervous breakdown on WNN, launched a radio show, and blurted *Final Freedom* into a live mic. If you didn't have fame of your own, writing about someone else's was the next best thing.

Heitinga had been midstream in a stream-of-consciousness memoir when he met Verboom in Los Angeles. He found Verboom so odd that he ditched his own story and started a new manuscript about this bizarre son of a Dutchman, a condition they shared. He ended the book with a flourish: "He is Solomon. He is Samson. Will he write proverbs or gouge out his eyes?"

Fortunately for Verboom, he was accepted into a Ph.D. program before Heitinga's *A Theologian East of West Hollywood* hit the shelves.

Verboom used to joke with me back at the university: "If you ever get stuck doing a book about me, tell the people that I'm the last asshole in a long line of assholes predicting the end of the world."

After Ella's claim about my alleged uncle, we kept our conversations limited to the practical matters of the show—a show that was completely impractical. Her arrival did free me from babysitting, so I spent most afternoons writing at the coffeehouse on Pike.

Despite my run-in with the Jimmer, I passed by the rally lot every day on my way to and from the coffeehouse. The man who'd swung at me—*twice*—used such a bizarre mix of racist descriptors that I wasn't worried about being recognized.

I imagined his report to the police: "A man in his twenties... maybe thirties. Could be older. With those types, you never really know how old they are. He had all his hair. Was he Black? Maybe. Latino? Maybe. Pacific Islander? Possibly... I don't know, Detective, but he certainly wasn't white."

Though aloof at first, the coffeehouse regulars warmed up once I'd established my perch. Most days, I arrived in the midafternoon and stayed until dinner, averaging about a thousand words written, which I would then send to Jacqueline for review. She joked that I was getting an MFA in absurdism.

Each afternoon, on my way home, I made a point to pass through the E.R.O.G.E.N.O.U.S. Zone and Cal Anderson Park, taking notes in a way Verboom would have called "copious."

I owned up to my mixed motives—to be a loyal surrogate son, to be an observer of madness in a mad season, and to document in real-time the life of America's second-most-famous social psychologist—all while keeping an arm's length, just in case I returned to school.

There was another take, a deeper reason for avoiding my dissertation: Maybe I wasn't a specialist at heart. Maybe I was a generalist. And if I stayed in academia, I might end up like Verboom—myopic one moment, babbling about the cosmos in the next.

25

Not a single drop of rain fell in Seattle that August, and September offered only a trace—just 0.03 inches, barely enough to register. But in October, the skies opened. Seven inches of steady, soaking rain fell over thirty-one days—light rain all day, every day—a war of attrition on my happiness.

Despite the rain, D.D.P. campers stayed put in the park—drenched but defiant. O.F.A.M. kept their rally in the bank parking lot and caravanned unpredictably through town. Verboom told me people in Western Washington learn early in life not to let precipitation keep them indoors.

"Present company excluded," he added dryly, "as I'm in hiding from the local news crews and vigilante journalists."

The Portland Rose Giant was still at large.

That October the Rallymen, as O.F.A.M. members preferred to call themselves, wore rain boots and jackets, but never used umbrellas.

"Umbrellas are for city people and narrow-shouldered men," one Rallyman said to a local reporter. However, they did put camper shells on their trucks and strung up tarps.

The younger, more rambunctious rally guys circled the neighborhoods around downtown and Capitol Hill, still itching for a fight. It didn't take much—a tossed water bottle, a half-eaten apple lobbed at a truck—and suddenly there were shouts and shoves, but they always seemed to fizzle out before the police arrived.

Seattle had become ground zero in the national drama. Watching WNN or ANN felt like tuning into a strangely theatrical local broadcast—because the topic was the same: *Seattle Under Siege*.

The headlines scrolled: "Campers vs. Caravanners." "Tents vs. Trucks." "Green vs. Red." An endless contrast of spectacle, all style and tactics with almost no talk of ideology. That's where Verboom stepped in, like a theologian with a flare gun, firing wildly into the void: "Earth Mother vs. Sky Father. "Immanence vs. Transcendence." "Globalists vs. Nationalist."

"The consensus of liberal democracy and free-market capitalism is going up in smoke," he said to the television one night in October, ashing a pretend cigar with theatrical flair. "The American Dark Age darkens the door. Right on schedule," he remarked, tapping his watch. Then he put the wristwatch to his ear to see if it was still ticking. He delivered the lines with a grin, like a preacher who told a dirty joke at a tent revival and didn't get struck by lightning.

Given the city's centrality in the media, all three presidential candidates weighed in. The president reaffirmed his confidence in the governor and mayor (all from his party). The Conservative candidate called for the restoration of good order through "pragmatic policing." But James Kroes—the strongman—called for public humiliation, mass arrests, and purple jumpsuits, relishing the bygone era of stocks in the town square.

"These indolent punks should be sentenced to hard labor!" Kroes said in an interview. "If they like camping so much, I've got plenty of bunks in my jails!" These comments became applause lines at his rallies, but they sounded even more bizarre when quoted in the hush of public radio.

Polls showed Kroes leading among voters most concerned about crime. As a sheriff with national recognition, it was his home turf. He mused openly about harsh retribution and floated the idea of a federation of sheriffs—a unified, county-by-county constabulary, independent of federal oversight—should he be "robbed" of the election.

"A *confederacy* of sheriffs," Verboom said back to the TV as WNN ran the story.

"Someone needs to keep people in line," Ella replied from the kitchen.

The D.D.P. didn't officially renounce the president, because they didn't do things officially; however, they made it clear the whole system had to go and no candidate deserved a vote. All three were just different suits in the same rigged game, bought and paid for by the 1%.

At first WNN commentators scoffed at the D.D.P.'s "naive idealism," but as the fall wore on, pundits worried that the D.D.P.'s mood would dampen the Liberal party turnout, a rebrand that continued to be a bust.

On the second Saturday that October, we heard revving engines and squealing tires outside the apartment.

Out the window, I saw a chaotic exchange—what looked like the ConFas, a small but violent splinter group of the D.D.P., arguing with the Rallymen. From the shouting, I gathered that a ConFa member had knifed the tires of a truck stopped at a red light—the last vehicle in a Kroes-flagged convoy. Within seconds, three Rallymen pulled long guns. One ConFa raised a handgun in return.

Without thinking, I shouted out the window: "Your license plate has been recorded, and the police have been called! *Police en route! Police en route!*"

Then I bent below the height of the windowsill and crab-walked to the couch, heart pounding.

CRACK!

A gunshot shattered the window just one sill over from where I'd yelled. I heard trucks peel out and men shouting as they scattered in all directions. Then sirens.

"Where are you going?" I glared at Ella.

"I'm calling the police," Ella said sternly, picking up her phone in the kitchen.

"Did you see who did what?" I asked.

"You said the ConFas slashed a tire," she said, returning to the living room. "That's property damage."

"That's what the Rallymen claimed. I didn't *see* what happened."

"Well, which ConFa shot the window?" Ella asked. "They carry pistols, you know."

"Didn't see who took the shot, but the Rallymen carry rifles."

"So how do *you* know who did what?" She scowled.

We debated names and taxonomy—the blurry lines of membership and identity. We assigned blame, expressed sympathies, and tried to parse the chaos.

To carry a pistol in Seattle you needed a license, and if you had a license, the handgun could be loaded. Rifles were legal to carry in the city—but not loaded.

"Rallymen should stop cruising a neighborhood that's not theirs!" I finally yelled. "Their tourist thugs!"

"The roads are free for everyone to travel!" Ella snapped back.

"Those roads aren't free," Verboom muttered, emerging from his room. "Tax dollars. License and registration, ma'am."

"It's menacing. It's antagonizing. They shot you with a paintball," I said, voice rising. "And now a bullet through our window!"

"The paintball wasn't meant for me," Ella said. "Real men don't shoot women."

"And the bullet aimed at my head?" I shouted, then caught

myself and took a breath.

"It wasn't the Rallymen," she said flatly. "They wouldn't have missed."

"They didn't see which window I yelled from!"

Verboom broke in: "Let's ask Stanley to fix the glass. He can use the hip pack funds. Just did a count this morning—ample cash remains."

Ella glared at me.

"You think that bullet is *my* fault!" I protested.

"Where did the bullet land?" Verboom asked as if trying to redirect a toddler. No one took the bait, so he walked out of the room, studying the walls and ceiling.

"Why would you shout from the window like that?" Ella asked. "Trying to defend your people?"

"Who are my people?"

"The tire slashers, obviously!"

"*Alleged* tire slashers. I don't have people in this city other than Verboom—I don't even own a knife!"

Ella took a deep breath.

I turned back to the window. Broken glass covered the floor, so I walked to the kitchen for a dustpan and broom. Coming back, Ella stopped me in the hall, putting her hand on my forearm. Her anger seemed to have vanished.

"I'm glad you weren't hurt," she said.

"Me too."

"Maybe leave the glass until the police have a look?" She tried to smile.

Verboom sauntered to the window, stepping on the glass with thick wool hiking socks—as close as he would get to slippers. With four pushpins he put up a white pillowcase over the broken window. He'd printed a block letter message with a black marker on the white cloth, and it took me a moment to read it backwards as the ink bled through: THIS IS NOT A FLAG.

With the window address, Verboom collapsed back into the cushions with despair.

"Am I depressed, or is the world depressing?" he asked the screen.

The glass on the floor glinted with the light of the television. Pinned over the broken window, the pillowcase blocked the wind but let in the street sounds.

The three of us sat shoulder to shoulder on the couch, like it was just another night.

WNN reported on an Oakland man who, wearing a flak jacket under a Hawaiian shirt, had shot and injured two police officers in broad daylight to spark what he called "a bloody revolution." The kicker: the shooter was a radicalized police officer—still on the force, just off duty at the time.

Verboom began arguing with the broadcast. "Saying 'bloody revolution' is redundant."

"The word 'revolution' has been semantically bleached," I replied. "A senator from New England has been calling for 'revolution' for decades."

"I was talking to the television," Verboom muttered.

"He won't even start his own party," I went on. "Then complains about being treated like an outsider while trying to lead a party he refuses to join."

"He's a reformer, not a revolutionary. Reformers *reform*. Revolutionaries *revolt*! We should send every senator an embroidered copy of *Tautology*!" Verboom complained.

Then he folded his arms and went quiet, eyes locked on the screen, still hoping to hear some good news.

He turned up the volume as WNN's Rodger, of *Rodger and Rachel*, kicked off an interview with Dr. Evan Heidkamp, America's *number one* social psychologist. Or, "my nemesis," as Verboom called him.

Heidkamp launched into his thesis, one he'd been arguing since long before the major parties had realigned and renamed themselves: little C conservatives are "more moral" than little L liberals.

RODGER: *More moral? That's going to raise eyebrows!*

HEIDKAMP: *I'm not saying the Conservative party has better people, but those with conservative personalities show more moral sentiment across a wider range of moral dimensions. Liberal personalities tend to focus on three dimensions: Care vs. Harm, Fairness vs. Cheating, and Liberty vs. Oppression. Conservative personalities engage those dimensions too, but they also emphasize: Loyalty vs. Betrayal, Authority vs. Subversion, and Sanctity vs. Degradation.*

RODGER: *Let me get this straight. You're saying a conservative is twice as moral as a liberal.*

HEIDKAMP: *In terms of breadth, yes. Conservative types are more tribal, more hierarchical, and more reactive to perceived violations of purity or tradition. Of course, it's not binary—it's a matter of degree.*

RODGER: *An example?*

HEIDKAMP: *Sure. Take burning the American flag. A liberal-minded person might find it distasteful, even offensive—but still a valid act of expression. A conservative would see it as betrayal and desecration—the transgression*

| *of the sacred. The symbol itself is sacred.*

Verboom yawned, laced his fingers behind his head, and leaned back on the couch.

"What if someone burned the rainbow flag in front of a Liberal, eh Professor Wiseass?" he mumbled.

"Are you talking party or personality type?" I asked.

Ella jumped in. "Let me get you back on WNN. You've been watching for three months straight. Now you understand how TV works—this is your moment."

Verboom shook his head and clicked the television off. "No one wants to hear more from America's *second* most famous social psychologist."

"You boiled his dimensions down to WMD or XXX!" Ella said, as a compliment.

"From six dimensions to six letters..." he announced in the style of a news anchor, then let out a long descending whistle, the tone plummeting from high to low. The expression on his face said: *I don't give a rat's ass.*

"That study made you a sensation," she said.

"An irritation," he countered.

"Still a stimulus," I said.

There was a knock at the door. The police had arrived in response to Ella's call.

She welcomed them in, hosting their investigation of the scene.

I said as little as possible, while Verboom looked on, asking about the location of the bullet.

What Ella called the *WMD or XXX Study*, his grad students called the *Fist-or-Phallus Experiment*, which made him a recurring topic on university message boards and put him on the front page of the campus newspaper.

Naively, Verboom welcomed any interviewer who came calling. Fielding questions that were completely off topic, he spoke too freely about "adaptive" sex differences, unaware that any claim of difference would be taken as ranking. He mistakenly assumed everyone shared his understanding that an "*is* is not an *ought*." However, his tone-deafness to the cultural mood would soon become clear.

"Isn't the fact that your thesis includes the word 'phallus' all the proof we need of how you privilege men?" one student reporter had asked him.

"Should've gone with gonads. 'Gonads' would've been better," Verboom conceded.

Headline: "Professor Admits Pecker Privilege"

Cornered in another interview, Verboom defended himself by pointing out that he'd learned evolutionary psychology from a renowned woman professor in Santa Barbara. "The top mind in the field!" he was quoted.

Headline: "Fetishizing Females, Professor Longs To Learn Fascism"

Then came the protestors, who showed up to his classes, gathering in the back of the lecture hall. They held signs saying:

SEE ME, NOT MY ANATOMY

CAN'T HIDE HATE IN SCIENCE

SCREW SCIENTISM

At first, they stood silently. Verboom allowed them to occupy the back of his class and went on teaching anxiously, his brow covered in sweat. After a few days of silent demonstration, the shouting started, and the enrolled students shouted back.

Verboom, flustered, followed university protocol and called campus security. Then a woman rushed to the front of the lecture hall and shouted: "I AM MORE THAN EGGS AND A UTERUS!" She grabbed the crotch of her baggy romper and waved it like a flag.

Recoiling, Verboom replied, "I don't care about what's under there—I just want to teach my class."

Headline: "Professor Dismisses Student's Body"

Verboom's *Fist-or-Phallus Study* masqueraded as a test of motor functions, where subjects were tasked with stacking blocks. The stacking tasks were designed to frustrate and exhaust participants, promoting instinctive rather than reflective responses to the survey that followed. The survey included filler questions to obscure the study's true aim, which centered on the following question:

> *Which revelation about your adult son would be more challenging to discover? Circle A or B.*
>
> *A) While believing your adult child had been working on a cancer cure, your son had actually been working for a defense contractor to develop a weapon capable of annihilating biological life on an entire continent.*
>
> *B) Though seemingly living a traditional life as a suburban medical professional, your adult son had in reality become one of the most popular adult film actors, willingly appearing in hundreds of pornographic features.*

The study design was crass but meticulous, balancing the survey questions for daughters alongside those for sons, while randomly alternating the order of scenarios A and B. This method ensured a comprehensive analysis of parental responses, factoring in whether participants actually had children or were merely contemplating hypothetical situations.

Verboom predicted that fathers, when considering sons, would lean towards accepting a career in adult films, and a similar trend for mothers regarding their sons. Conversely, he expected fathers would prefer daughters to be involved in creating weapons of mass destruction rather than in adult films, arguing this preference aligned with survival pressures to protect female fertility.

For mothers thinking about daughters, Verboom anticipated a clash between modern egalitarian beliefs and evolutionary instincts, highlighting a potential conflict between cultural and biological evolution. However, the results revealed a surprising pattern: both liberal fathers and mothers, regardless of the child's sex, predominantly chose the adult film performer option, while conservative parents overwhelmingly selected the WMD-maker scenario. This outcome suggested that personality might have a stronger influence on such decisions than the sex of the child or the parent. This correlation emerged clearly as participants were also assessed through personality and ideology questions at the end of the survey.

With his work subject to campus scorn, Verboom began to question it himself. The external scrutiny turned inward, spiraling into morbid self-deprecation. A few days after the protests started, he confided in me as we sat in his drab office at the university.

"You know, Santo, I'm fresh out of fresh ideas. Maybe it's time to break me down for parts. The only thing that doesn't work is this big brain." He spanked his forehead with his palm. "Now, think how many people I could save! Liver—*one*! Heart—*two*! Kidneys—*three*, *four*!" (The same phrasing he would use at Linda's Tavern months later.)

He began working through a "thought exercise" on how best to donate every organ except the brain. He worried most of his body would be wasted unless someone alive managed the process. Then, slipping into a bizarre kind of cheerfulness, he cracked a joke: "Do you know how copper wire was invented? Two Dutchmen found a penny at the same time!"

As I provided an attentive audience, he seemed pacified at first, but as we crept toward the holidays, darker ideation surfaced: "An archery accident! You love the outdoors, Santo. Apples too! And you know, apple seeds contain arsenic. Nothing like fresh apple cider!"

"Now listen, I may be the 'phallus guy,' but I can do more than take a beating." He paused. "It's hard to admit now, but I should've built houses. Should've worked with my hands. Now I'm just a mangy quarter horse at a dog-and-pony show."

I tried to cheer him up with a review of his career, but he dismissed it all as due to *bias*.

"The only reason I have stature in the field is my *height*!" Then he perked up, eyes twinkling. "It's fall, Santo. Take me in for the harvest. Ready for apples and archery? Let's make the most of me. Sow a thought, reap a deed—indeed! And there's so much of me—reap it all!"

In this state, Verboom celebrated Christmas 2011. But before New Year's Eve, he received *the call*—a last-minute invitation to the president's Emergency Conference of Scholars. A gathering of thought leaders, thrown together in hopes of boosting the administration as it entered election year.

Verboom's study, presenting a novel yet controversial method for gauging political identity, captured the attention of DC strategists.

One pundit even posited that Verboom had distilled ideological screening to a single litmus test—"*dick or bomb*?" Its audacious approach was precisely what the president's Emergency Conference of Scholars was seeking.

26

Thanks to Kroes' notoriety, the hurdles for ballot placement were easily cleared. Fueled by his tough talk, high-profile stunts, relentless cable news coverage, and deep-pocketed backers, he landed on every state ballot—including the much-maligned California.

Pollsters claimed that California would never elect Kroes in a general election, but he used this to his favor, claiming he didn't want to be on the state's ballot. "My name is too good for it," he declared at a rally. After a laugh and a brief pause, he continued, "And come Inauguration Day, a coalition of willing states will bring California to heel."

Because of the situation in Portland, analysts believed Oregon could swing for Kroes. The city had seen insurrectionary anarchists, dubbed ConFas, setting fires, vandalizing federal buildings, and even ambushing a Rallyman, resulting in his hospitalization. The tension in Portland boiled throughout the summer and into the fall, with the Portland Rose Giant still at large.

Of special importance to Verboom, Western Michigan was all in for Kroes, who had the backing of the Koning family, of the Martin Koning Group, plus "the soap people and the garbage people."

With Bill Henniker joining the ticket, the extraction industry in Texas, and its neighboring states, threw its considerable weight behind the ticket. Jim and Bill had cash and charisma.

Election Day was a few weeks out, and Kroes ramped up his attack on the president for failing to kill OBL and "handing over the SEALs in a botched raid to take out that terrorist *c-nt*." He had actually used the whole C-word, considered the second most reviled word in America—unless used by a Scot in a charming foreign film. Responding to the controversy in a WNN interview, Kroes' campaign manager claimed the word had accidentally slipped out.

Jonathan, Roger, Rachel, and the entire team at WNN were convinced that Kroes had crossed a line this time. Though shocked by the crass word, their faces expressed relief, as if to say *he's done*. The October Surprise turned out to be a four-letter word that even stunned the pundits at ANN. Initially, a team of surrogates attempted to minimize the comment, dismissing it as a minor gaff during the "heat of the moment" in an "off-the-cuff" remark—simply put, it was "locker room talk." Surrogates urged the public to remember, "Kroes is a man of passion who shoots from the hip. He calls a spade a spade."

It turned out that the Kroesters were thrilled with the vulgarity and saw no need to sugarcoat the language. In fact, "BOMB THE C-NT" became a popular chant and appeared on top-selling tee shirts at Kroes' rallies, as reported by WNN. Major news outlets opted not to reprint or directly quote the offensive word. However, in live footage of Kroes' rallies, the chant was distinctly audible for those listening for it.

Kroes capitalized on the backlash to his offensive language by doubling down on the topic that resonated most with Americans: the hostages. "Sniveling Liberals are upset over four letters? What about our SEALs languishing in a desert cave? That's the real offense!"

The day after Kroes dropped the C-word, Martin Koning gave a rare interview. Seizing on the hostages' plight, he claimed to have the capability to eliminate OBL without a single American casualty. He implied that if someone else had been in the Oval Office, OBL would be dead, and the SEALs would be home. Koning also proposed that the American public should keep a daily count of the SEALs' captivity, pointedly noting, "Today is Day 106."

Kroes' rhetoric began to sound like a threat of secession, and WNN asked self-identifying Kroesters, "If Kroes loses the presidential election, will you take armed action?" Eleven percent said *Yes*, 41% said *No*, 29% said *It depends on Kroes' response*, and 19% were *Unsure*. The survey reached nearly 1,200 Kroesters with a margin of error of +/-3.5%.

As the leaves changed color, the air thickened with darker unrest. Liberal politicians campaigned on the need for civic virtue. A "stay the course" message was recalibrated to a "jackals at the gate" warning. In power, they couldn't call for radical change, so instead, they painted challengers as existential threats. Conservatives would hand the keys right back to Wall Street, and Kroes would turn the country into a police state. As the party of pragmatic competence, they were the true stewards of democracy.

But liberal intellectuals acknowledged the need to *understand* the impulses driving O.F.A.M. and D.D.P. "We must understand their appeal without caving into authoritarian tactics or conspiratorial thinking," the president said in a town hall meeting that October. Like Verboom in a lobby surrounded by free snacks, the Liberal party couldn't help themselves from feeling the pain.

Verboom grimaced while watching the town hall. "Liberals' empathy undercuts their claim of competence! His pitch is *it could be worse!*" Overcome with anxiety, he stood and loudly declared, "We've got to save the SEALs before November 6!"

"If he could do it, it would already be done," Ella responded.

"His best hope is locking down the base, while the other candidates split the remainder," I offered, though not fully convinced.

Conservatives touted "market-friendly deregulation" and

"traditional marriage" as the pillars of American dominance and pleaded with the Kroesters to come home.

And then, Conservatives seemed to get just what they needed. Kroes made his biggest gaff to date:

"Ronald Reagan is not my hero," Kroes said bluntly in an ANN interview—now a regular occurrence. The unforced error was sure to help Reagan's old party. But Kroes threw down the gauntlet like spiking a football. "I'm the kind of man Reagan could only pretend to be. He played the part in old movies—I'm living it, right here in real life."

27

I lived for Jacqueline's messages, which came throughout the day. She even offered to visit Seattle, if I agreed to camp with her in Cal Anderson Park.

Despite memories of boyhood camping adventures, the idea of braving the urban outdoors—with its relentless rain and thrum of noise—left me cold. But she was already plotting her route, a grueling twenty-hour drive over two days, her company being an audiobook and a backlog of calls. She aimed to arrive by the Saturday before Election Day, just in time for the last hurrah of the Rallymen. Her absentee ballot was on its way, as was mine, and we planned a subdued celebration of the president's victory.

But after the stray bullet struck Genevieve's apartment, I warned Jacqueline against coming. Unfazed, she rattled off a list of even grimmer tales from Flagstaff, making it clear she wasn't one to shy away from risk.

This would be more than sightseeing; Jacqueline said we could better finish the manuscript in person. She hoped the project would exercise his lingering influence and refocus me on my dissertation.

"It's not a commitment to a career in academia. A degree is just a degree," she reminded me, "not a life sentence."

Her wording perked my curiosity. Had she read *Tautology*? It turned out she had.

"Better than I expected," she admitted.

In anticipation of Jacqueline's visit, Ella, Verboom, and I agreed to go out for dinner on Saturday evening. Such excursions usually collapsed under the weight of Verboom's preferences—nursing gin and watching the relentless churn of cable news, while hiding from the public cloaked in a *gi*.

Ella occasionally managed to coax Verboom from the apartment—always in some kind of disguise—but these outings were rare and brief. His farmer-ly nature was hijacked by the idle outrage of soap opera infotainment, though he claimed—without a trace of irony—to be "analyzing the deep narrative structure of cable news culture."

With change in the air, I persuaded him to watch Public Broadcasting's no-nonsense nightly news program. It was packed with more content in an hour than an entire evening of cable, but Verboom grew restless.

"I need a hit," he finally grumbled and turned the channel.

"So, you understand."

"Santo, I may have gone mad, but I'm still a psychologist."

As we prepared to leave, I asked Ella, "Does the booze make him lazy?"

"No. He pleasures me after every show. Why do you think I want to broadcast seven days a week?"

I covered my ears.

"Is it hard to accept that a refined woman desires sexual intimacy?" she teased.

"I can't hear you," I protested.

Her smile widened as she tugged my left hand from my ear. "Go put on something nice. I'll do the same." And with that, she left for the master bedroom.

'Lazy' might have been too harsh a word to use with Ella. Verboom maintained a regimen of hundreds of push-ups and sit-ups each morning while glued to the TV, mixing in step-backs and bodyweight squats. His physical vigor was all that remained of his farmer's heritage. He began his gin during the show, finding a perfect balance of caffeine and alcohol for what he called "peak Dutch uncle performance," and continued imbibing until midnight.

In addition to his floor exercises, he kept busy during commercial breaks, running to collect laundry that he folded while seated on the couch. At the next break, he'd be off loading or unloading the dishwasher, then cranking up the volume to follow the program while sweeping and mopping the floors. His regimen also included running up and down the apartment stairwell seven times each day, a routine that initially alarmed other tenants, who mistook the thunderous pounding for an earthquake.

Under these conditions, he'd grown even heartier. By my tally, he consumed nearly 200 grams of protein a day. Breakfast typically included three large buttermilk pancakes, six scrambled eggs, sausage or bacon, country potatoes, and two slices of toast. Dinner, the second and final meal, was meat-heavy, typically made by Ella with recipes from a Betty Crocker cookbook. The self-dubbed Flying Dutchman bulked up while holing up, tilting at windmills from his couch, wearing an orange karate suit as a reminder to hide; he had become cinematically goofy as if directed by an eccentric *auteur*.

Looking around my bedroom, I opted for the black peacoat instead of the black hoodie. After swapping a black pocket tee for a black mock turtleneck, I put on a belt to finish off the look.

Back to the living room, I asked Verboom, "How are you getting so yoked as America's number one couch potato?"

He barely squeezed into his "Sunday clothes," the tweed suit, the blood stains removed, accessorized with a purple bandana and sunglasses.

"My cup runneth over," rattling his glass, "and it runneth out," he quipped, heading to the kitchen for another gin, while we waited for Ella to get ready.

Ella emerged, surpassing her usual high standards of style.

"Sorry for the wait, boys. I had to send a few work emails."

Despite all her time with Verboom, Ella still managed her other clients remotely, orchestrating media appearances, planning events, and managing crises. Under a veil of confidentiality, she shared scant detail about work but did mention that all her clients were based in Western Michigan.

With the professor entranced, Ella directed the conversation at me.

"Though, as you may already know, my real work is in the kitchen," she declared, letting the statement linger.

Then she pointed at me. "Your face! Wow, your ex really did a number on you." She chuckled. "What if I want to be in the kitchen, Santo? Not all women are radical feminists who want to be English professors." She shook her head, amused by my naivete.

Then Ella strutted to Verboom and pulled him off of the couch.

"And don't you clean up well," she said, playfully tugging on his lapels—the very ones he had pulled over his head on WNN's *Hot Button Science*.

Luckily, by this hour, the gin had tempered his sexual response.

Ella draped a raincoat over one arm and offered her other arm to Verboom.

After descending four floors, Verboom helped Ella into her ankle-length coat before leaving the building's lobby.

"You're becoming quite the gentleman," Ella noted. "One day

soon we'll get you into some true formalwear."

My stomach turned.

We walked toward the middlebrow French bistro near the corner of 12th Avenue and Madison Street. Ella led us past the Rallymen's parking lot, no longer concealing her fascination with big men and big trucks.

After the broken window, I had insisted we steer clear of the lot and its convoys, but my arguments lost their force when the bullet extracted from Genevieve's ceiling was identified as having been fired from a Glock 19 pistol—likely the model I'd seen a ConFa wielding.

After 6 PM, their shot already fired, I had hoped the lot would be empty, but the rally still lingered. One cluster of trucks blasted guitar-heavy music. At the lot exit, two pickups pulled beside each other, aimed opposite directions, so the drivers could talk at close range through their open windows.

We went behind the bank, crossed 13th Avenue, and skirted a brewery. The street sloped downward, and as we passed, it felt like the revelers inside floated up. After waiting a moment, the stoplight changed in our favor, and we began crossing 12th Avenue.

Halfway through the intersection, the sound of a roaring engine descended. Ella and Verboom quickened their pace through the intersection, but I sprinted across, reaching the curb first. Ella refused to run, opting for a brisk walk instead, with Verboom at her side.

As they hurried, a white pickup accelerated toward the intersection, flags flying, then someone on the sidewalk hurled a pizza box like a Frisbee at the truck. The driver slammed on the brakes, the wheels locked, and the truck skidded left, heading straight for Ella and Verboom in the crosswalk.

Trying to run, Ella's long rain jacket snagged beneath her feet, tripping her. In a swift, fluid motion, Verboom scooped her up and launched her into my arms. It was over so quickly; it was hard to tell if she had slid on her heels or hovered momentarily in flight. Struggling to maintain my balance, I managed to catch her with a firm hug and wrestle her up onto the sidewalk.

The squeal of tires grew louder as Verboom straightened up; he never looked to his right as the truck's ram bars struck him squarely, sending him flying off his feet. He landed a few yards from where he was hit, giving the truck just enough space to screech to a halt before it could run over his limp body. One moment he was standing, the next he was on the ground—I'm not certain I processed the part in between.

He lay there, certainly dead. In the misty darkness, the truck's headlights cast a harsh light over his body, the front tires just a few inches from his legs. I raced over to him. He was flat on his back, with a blank dead-eyed gaze into the sky.

"You okay?" I managed to squeak out, barely above a whisper.

Then his eyes slowly focused on me. "Never been so happy." He could barely exhale the last word. He took a shallow breath and exhaled faintly. "Just the way I wanted to go. Liver—*one*... Heart—*two*..."

"Don't talk, just breathe," I urged him.

The truck driver, now out of his vehicle, offered to take Verboom to the hospital. "Some *shitbird* threw something at my windshield," he explained, his voice tinged with frustration. "I couldn't see..."

"You were driving too fast!" Ella was kneeling on the pavement beside Verboom. "A reckless joyride on wet streets. What were you thinking?" she yelled, her voice breaking as she turned from the driver back to Verboom. A look of despair washed over her face, as she tenderly combed his hair with her fingers.

"It's so nice getting out of the house," Verboom whispered.

"Let's get him out of the street," I suggested anxiously.

"Don't move him! His neck could be broken!" Ella said sharply, her voice laced with panic.

Verboom took a labored breath, almost a gasp, and sat up. After doing so, he coughed violently.

"Stay down," Ella instructed.

Onlookers from across the street, who had dialed 911, reassured us, "The ambulance is on its way!"

"Did you throw that box?!" the driver shouted at them, seeking a culprit.

"Know how much a ride in that contraption costs?" Verboom grumbled, dismissing the idea of an ambulance as he wobbled up to his feet.

The passenger from the truck, a large man more round than tall, used both hands to stabilize Verboom.

"Not paying for that thing. I shall sashay to the place I stay," Verboom declared, attempting another step but falling into the man's embrace. The man wore a camouflage rain jacket and a red hat.

"Let's get him into the truck," the big guy in the red hat directed.

Verboom refocused his gaze, delirious, he climbed into the truck bed and slumped against the back of the cab.

"Sit in the front, big guy! You need to be more careful," the driver said.

"Don't want red liquid in the cockpit," Verboom mumbled. "Back here you can hose things down when I'm out. Like driving a heifer to auction. Used to haul 'em with *pakke* Dijkstra... Those milk-giving creatures seem so big when you're small. Now let's get to that place where we're going, before that other thing gets here and runs up my tab."

Verboom propped himself up in the corner of the truck bed, his arms resting atop the walls as if lounging in a hot tub, his gaze drifting and eyelids drooping.

The man in the red hat urged again, "Come up front."

"Don't think I can rise again," Verboom murmured, his voice fading.

"Just go to the hospital!" Ella yelled, climbing into the truck bed to sit next to Verboom.

The Rallymen hopped into the cab, their Kroes flags drooping, then lifting with the breeze. The truck's exhaust clouded the air, making me cough. The driver slammed his door shut.

"Come on, Santo. Get in!" Ella insisted.

I readied my hands to hop in next to Verboom.

"Stay out," the driver commanded abruptly.

"*Why*?" Ella demanded, her voice sharp with anger.

"*Jongen, jongen*, I must have serious head trauma," Verboom interjected, his tone bewildered as he pointed up. "This flag says, 'James Kroes for President.'"

"I'll go, Santo," Ella said, resolute. "Meet us at the hospital."

The driver revved the engine, letting the truck roll back slightly toward me as he prepared to drive away. I stared at him. He was close enough to strike.

"Don't leave me, Santo," Verboom whispered, his voice weak, blood and water dripping from his beard and hair.

"He needs a doctor, let's *go*!" Ella demanded.

As the truck rolled forward, the driver said to me, ice cold, "Even if you wore all white, I wouldn't let your kind of face in my truck." Then he sped off.

Speechless, I watched them go. Rage fueled me, and I thought of chasing them down. They were ten yards away, then fifteen.

Ella's scream pierced the air.

Verboom rolled out of the truck bed like a scuba diver off a dive boat, landing on his broad shoulders and rolling to a stop, lying motionless.

Ella pounded on the truck's roof in horror.

I sprinted toward Verboom and slid like a baseball player as I reached him. Once stopped, I crawled close, almost nose to nose.

"I'd rather die than go with those mammals," he whispered, just perceptibly.

"You just want to die," I said.

"*Nay*, my dear Santo. I would live, just to die for you."

The banging on the truck's roof continued. Then the screech of tires. The men had driven another full block before stopping. They tried to lift Ella out of the truck, but she'd removed her high heels and leapt out on her own. Landing gracefully on the balls of her feat, she ran toward us like a track star.

"Pieter!" she screamed. Then again.

Reaching him, she dropped to the concrete. "The ambulance is on its way. I can hear it. Can you hear it?" she asked urgently. Over and over, she whispered, "*I'm so sorry.*"

Verboom rested his head in her lap, then began to sing the country ballad "Angel Flying Too Close to the Ground," his voice weak, but filled with an aching sweetness.

Ella sucked in a sharp breath, the onset of a sob.

Verboom continued, his voice cracking as he crooned the tender country melody.

"You've got the song backward," Ella said, perplexed by his serenity. "I'm sorry for everything."

"I don't care about how many men you've slept with," Verboom said with spiritual indifference.

Ella raised her hand as if to slap him, but I caught her wrist.

Then he chuckled, before wincing from his injuries.

"What's so funny?" I asked, unable to see any humor.

"Huddled here together it looks like you two are in love," he said, a flicker of joy in his eyes.

I leaned away from Ella, while Ella leaned in closer to Verboom. "Not at all," I said firmly.

"Absolutely not," Ella echoed.

"*With me*, for a moment it felt like you both loved *me*. Must've smashed my melon, the gourd's gonzo, I'm seeing things—little things with wings—tales of fairies."

The ambulance drew closer, its siren escalating to a deafening roar that forced me to cover my ears.

Amidst the blaring sound, Ella bent down to Verboom, her face solemn, making a vow. Her words were lost to the noise, but I could read two words from her lips: "I promise."

28

The paramedics were quick to assess Verboom on the street. His pulse and breathing were stable. His long hair, matted with blood, made it difficult to see swelling.

One paramedic peppered Verboom with basic questions to gauge his mental acuity while the other readied the gurney.

"Sir, do you know where you are?"

"I'm right here," Verboom answered confidently.

"Do you know what day it is?"

"The sands of time... Each day is but a grain... Each grain is like the last."

"Please sir, the actual day?"

"*Ja*... I know this one. It's the day when the big trucks come. The one where they shoot a gun."

"Who is the president of the United States?"

"I see his face, a kind and intelligent face that's dear to me, as though I knew him once."

"Sir, do you know the president's name?"

"I see his face. Like he's right here with us. He's Black, and he's beautiful." Verboom's eyes welled up as he smiled. He blinked, and the tears rolled. Since the president was the only Black man ever to hold the office, the paramedic seemed satisfied and stopped asking questions.

The gurney was ready, but Verboom refused to get on it.

"This has been the best night of my life," Verboom said, his gaze distant, as if speaking to himself. "For a moment, I knew love."

"My wife is lucky if she gets *two* moments," one of the paramedics joked.

"Sir, we need to take you in for a better look," the other paramedic said.

"I had a moment of understanding..." Verboom went on.

"Let's get to the hospital," Ella pressed.

"It's gone now, the moment," Verboom said, his rapture fading.

"You'd help us do our job, sir, if you'd get on this gurney."

"I am 233 pounds and full of news. You'll never get me up there!" Verboom said, struggling to his feet. "See, I'm fine. If I walk to the place where I am going... There's no fee, *ja*?"

"We'll flip it into a chair. You can get on under your own strength," the paramedic suggested.

Verboom, fumbling with his wallet, tried to steady himself. He staggered like a drunk looking for his license. Then it occurred to me that he might be drunk.

"Look, look! Right here. I've got the sticker. I am a *mudder*, M.O.D.R.! Michigan Organ Donor Registry. Can you take my parts here? In this *province*? Or is it *providence*?"

No one answered.

"Do I have to be in Michiganland? It's all good stuff. Just a few bumps."

Ella wrapped her arm around his waist. "Rest up and get well," she said sweetly. "We don't want you donating banged-up goods."

"True. You don't want to give a guy a bruised kidney. Two guys! *One, two!*" Verboom put his left hand over his left kidney and his right hand over his right kidney, then his knees buckled.

The paramedic patted the seat of the gurney now folded into a chair.

"Look at those orbs for rolling," Verboom said, delirious, as he settled into the chair. "Now hold onto me or I'll roll into the... What's the name of all that fluid?"

"The Puget Sound."

"The part of my brain holding the handles-of-things may have been knocked out of business. Let's *not* donate that part." Verboom's head bobbed and teetered.

The paramedics eased him into the back of the ambulance, securing the gurney in a track with a click. Though both slight of frame, they maneuvered the Portland Rose Giant effortlessly. Then the paramedic who had cracked the poor joke climbed in with Verboom.

"Is he okay?" Ella asked the other paramedic.

"They'll run more tests, but his vitals are strong."

"They don't build 'em like this anymore," Verboom chimed in from the back of the ambulance, sticking a thumb into his chest. "Now, who am I supposed to be?"

The paramedic outside the ambulance shut the doors.

Ella and I squeezed into the cab's passenger seat. Her body was hot from running and worry, her hair cold and damp from the rain. The paramedic switched on the heater, which blew out musty air, like it hadn't been used in months.

As we drove to the hospital, the ambulance lights flashed, but the siren was off. While eluding a diagnosis, the paramedic said that situations like these could cause disorientation, but that hearty folks typically recover quickly. Then he added, "Bye the way, I'm not supposed to let people sit up here. But it's a strange night. I didn't want to leave you two behind."

"We're not leaving him," Ella stated firmly.

"It's okay," he reassured us. Then studying me, he asked, "Are you Filipino?"

"My grandma was born there."

"Cousin, like your grandma, I was born there too." He nodded with a steady bounce.

"I don't hear an accent," Ella noted.

I cringed.

"In the Philippines, I'm a doctor, but I make more money in the States driving this cart," he explained, steering us through the night.

Ella refused to leave Verboom's side, opting to stay with him at the hospital, while I went home to fetch the truck and grab a few hours of sleep.

When I called the hospital early the next morning, the nurse asked for my name. Upon providing it, she informed me that my "father" was ready for pickup. Once again, I found myself designated as next of kin.

As I pulled into the hospital entrance, Ella emerged, pushing Verboom in a wheelchair through the sliding doors. The truck still said GO BACK TO DIXIE FASCIST PIG across the passenger's side. And as they approached Verboom grinned and said, "Move over bacon, now there's something meatier."

During the brief drive home, Ella made sure we'd be present for an extra special Sunday dinner, the final meal of the week.

"The supper that comes last?" Verboom asked with a smile. "I'm nice and tender. Tenderized by the machinations of life... Whenever I say 'machinations' I see wheels and gears turn, big old farm machines turning in my mind, and then I sing to myself, *oh is it just my machinations...*"

"Glad to see you're almost back to normal," I said gratefully.

Arriving at Genevieve's building, I helped Verboom up the steps to the top floor.

"I feel so light," Verboom remarked, a trace of wonder in his voice.

"Not to me."

"Last night will live forever in my imagination," he continued, his words still tinged with a glow of concrete-cracked insight.

"You mean your *memory*," Ella corrected gently.

"That's the one!"

Once inside, he settled on the couch. Surprisingly, he did not reach for the remote control. Instead, he gazed out the window with a smile, looked around the room appreciatively, and listened contentedly to the sounds of Ella preparing breakfast. He seemed enveloped in a moment of peace, his eyes closed, his face content.

The family he always wanted, I thought, wincing with empathy.

After eating breakfast on the couch, he drifted off to sleep, the TV remaining off.

I remembered a youth pastor's advice after I had a snow sledding accident: "You shouldn't sleep with a concussion. You may never wake up." He wasn't a doctor but an experienced adventure guide. Although the nurse had assured me that my "father" didn't have a concussion, the warning echoed in my mind. While he napped, I sat next to him, watching his chest rise and fall. He slept for almost three hours as I replayed the previous day's events in my mind.

Then, he suddenly awoke with the startle of a first snore, exclaiming, "Who let the hogs out!"

29

Except for the sound-proofing foam, Ella and I restored the studio to a normal dining room for that Sunday evening, and we sat down to a feast: prime rib with horseradish sauce, buttery mashed potatoes, seared Brussels sprouts, and applesauce. With a rosemary shrub in front of the building, Ella used its sprigs to garnish just about everything.

My stomach growled impatiently.

"You can ask questions when I'm done," Ella said firmly.

"Better get a refill." Verboom rumbled off to the kitchen, each heavy step causing the wood floors to creak.

"Done with *what*?" I asked in a whisper, confused.

"Last night I promised to tell him the whole truth."

"Truth is, I'm hungry." I reached for the beef.

Ella slapped my hand away.

I heard the clink of ice cubes dancing in an empty glass, followed by the squeaky pop of a gin bottle opening, the crackle of the spirit hitting the ice, the fizzing splash of tonic, then a click, and Verboom was back with his drink.

After returning from the hospital, he switched back to a seersucker *gi*, which was so much easier on the eyes than orange, and, in my opinion, more dapper.

"You shouldn't be drinking," Ella remarked, her concern evident.

Verboom nodded slowly, his expression solemn as he puckered his lips to sip.

"Take a moment to collect yourselves." Ella paused, locking eyes with each of us in turn. "Any interruption, and I'll stop. I need you to grasp the entire situation. My conscience requires it. So, here it is: I work with Freedom's Clarion. Mark Sunderland recruited me to…"

I stood up, my body reacting before my mind could catch up.

"Interrupt me and you'll never get the whole story," Ella warned, her voice firm. "My resolve is fading."

Verboom appeared dopey, daydreaming, smiling vacantly with distant eyes.

"Mark hired me for Project Death Knell," she continued. "It's not a sting; you weren't doing anything illegal. We simply wanted to facilitate PR disasters for prominent academics and, by extension, the Liberal Party."

Stunned by her revelation, I sat down. She was a double agent—*a PR double agent*!

"Project Death Knell collects damaging statements from the Left, words that embarrass Liberal politicians and dampen voter enthusiasm. Some of our misinformed critics call the work 'disinformation,' but you've only said what you believe. We select assets *strategically*, but we're not interested in lies. We haven't put words in your mouths. We copy, cut, and paste.

"The project is co-funded by The Revelation Project, an organization affiliated with Professor Watch List, which is where Mr. Sunderland found you," Ella explained, fixing her gaze on Verboom, who sat in a dazed stupor. "With several complaints from students about your perceived gender bias, he initially thought you might be a natural ally. However, upon closer examination, we discovered that all those reviews originated from other departments. After following up with all seven complaints, it turns out none of the students had taken a course with you. Nonetheless, Mr. Sunderland recognized your knack for ruffling feathers—an 'accident waiting to

happen,' as he put it. He noted how receptive you were to my suggestions, including the idea of joining you in DC for the president's
Emergency Conference of Scholars. That's what changed everything. *Washington*."

She paused, her expression turning more intense. "You gave me a
key to your room, and when I brought your suit in before *Hot Button
Science*, I found you in the shower. You didn't see me, but I watched
from the doorway as you lathered and scrubbed your body."

Verboom appeared glazed over, his expression distant and
trance-like, eyes fixed on some faraway point. After all his lonely
years, he thought he had found a girlfriend, only to discover it was a
cruel sham.

"Even after WNN, when everyone thought you were finished,
Mr. Sunderland had a hunch you could accomplish even more on
radio, correctly guessing that you were only camera-shy," Ella continued. "Getting you on-air would be pure gold; you'd embarrass
the Left more effectively than any critic. And when you named the
show 'Ask The Professor,' we knew he'd made the right choice. His
idea was 'Scholastic Showdown.'"

Ella raised her brow.

"As the show progressed, we thought you might single-handedly
dismantle any remaining credibility for professors, as we amassed a
collection of humiliating quotes. But then you surpassed all expecta-
tion, daring the entire country to defy the federal government with
Final Freedom. It has become a thing-in-itself, complete with pins,
stickers, flags, public outrage, and civil action—you've seen it on the
street and in the news. That's all real, thanks to you. We gave you a
platform, but you took it to the next level. The more you talk, the
more your side loses. Your platform is a *gallows for liberalism*."

Verboom swallowed hard, his gaze piercing through the French
doors.

"And now, your latest show is a hotline for conspiracy and gossip. It seems you might have done enough to ensure this president only serves one term. Sure, Kroes deserves much of the credit, but you're like *his*..."

"*Prophet*," Verboom belched the word like a ghost, like the last bit of air from a deflated balloon.

"Yes." She paused. "And I wouldn't call it *accidental*."

Ella went on, "Working with you has been my greatest accomplishment—certainly, the most impactful. We nudged you, professor. Then, you nudged the world. There's just one problem..."

"You're pregnant," Verboom said with a wide smile and floating eyes, head tilting back.

"We've had a few close calls, but I'm not pregnant. The problem is..."

"*Your right-wing spy unit doesn't want you having sex outside of marriage!*" I yelled with a twisted, angry laugh.

"We do endorse that ideal, when possible, but it's not always possible," she said without shame.

"You've been screwing his brains out for propaganda!" I hollered. "This lonely guy is finally getting some action, and it's all a con!"

She shook her head. "I haven't put a single word in his mouth."

"So, what's the problem? Why are you telling us about your scheme now?"

My anger boiled over; I was ready to flip the table. While I had never trusted her—she was trying to blackmail me after all—I believed her schemes all stemmed from a fatal attraction, a need to control or even dominate, but not *politics*.

"The assignment is up on Election Day, and I need to go home for another project." Then turning back to Verboom, she said, "But I don't want this to end..."

"Even though you betrayed him, you've fallen in love with him! I don't believe it—even after last night."

"Santo, I'm not 'in love' with Dr. Verboom," she whispered.

"Worried about hurting his feelings?" I paused for a moment, then yelled: "*The secret's out!*"

"The professor isn't capable of a traditional relationship. Without your help, he can't really function in society."

"Take him back to Flagstaff."

"The problem is, Santo, and I know he's sitting right here, but he's not all *there*."

"You're saying you can't bring him home to your parents, so you'll have to leave him with me. You are a *black widow*!" I whispered angrily. "Knew the moment you walked into that Flagstaff brewery."

"I'm right here, Santo," Verboom said. "I'm perfectly fine." Still with the faraway look in his eyes.

"You're not clairvoyant, Santo. You didn't know anything," she said. "And since you're struggling to understand, let me make this as clear as possible—and I apologize in advance for how this is going to sound: Dr. Verboom has given me the best sex of my life, but he could never be my husband."

Verboom smiled like he was on drugs and gin.

"I thought the lust would subside," she went on, "but we've gone at it like..."

"Rabbits," Verboom said like a distant echo.

"It's a profound *chemistry* you couldn't possibly understand. Just the scent of his neck drives me crazy. And the fact that he's always trying to stop my advances, even as his member rises to attention while he quotes Bible verses about temptation, and then sings hymns of salvation after consummation... Santo, tell me where I'm going to find another man like this."

I opened my mouth to say something.

"It was a rhetorical question," she said terminally.

"You don't give yourself enough credit," I said to Verboom. "We knew she was up to something, but I was convinced it was some kind of psychotic romance, and you could use the affection. The simple story made the most sense."

"Shaved by Ockham's Razor," Verboom rasped. His mind seemed to drift in and out of the room, like he was rehearsing something. "My seed. I thought she wanted my seed. Since she wasn't getting pregnant, she just kept trying. I don't know how love is supposed to feel, but I do understand the reproductive drive."

"Why did you think she was trying to get pregnant?"

"She wouldn't let me flush the condoms." He stared into space, then blinked hard.

"They clog the plumbing," Ella said.

Verboom let out an "*Ohh...*" in slow motion.

"So how did *Ask The Professor* get so many calls?" I asked.

"The calls originated from the Clarion office..."

"No. I saw the numbers. They came from around the country."

"Staff used their own cell phones at first, so it looked like we had a wide range of national callers. After a while we patched through organic listeners but screened them in advance. If you remember our production meeting, we said our promotion team would ensure sufficient calls. The professor was worried about dead air. He needed the question-and-answer format to feel comfortable."

"You said you were honest."

"I never lied to you or the professor..."

"Maybe not *technically* in the most *literalistic* way."

Ella shook her head with a belittling smirk.

"*What?*" I yelled.

"*Literalistic,*" she scolded.

"So, The Revelation Project is funded by Freedom's Clarion

and your 'mission' is under the umbrella of 'Project Death Knell,' a partner of 'Professor Watch List?'" I was air-quoting like Verboom, which was almost as upsetting as Ella's revelations. "Your naming conventions are inconsistent." I stopped to groan. "But why Death Knell?"

"After we nailed A.C.O.R.N.—that was a sting—we began infiltrating Liberal campaign organizations, teachers' unions, and other leftwing political shops. While you Liberals..."

"Mixed," Verboom said like a drunk ready to belch. "I have a mixed-up personality."

Ella went on, undeterred. "While Liberals are doing comedy and late-night satire, we are getting inside access."

"Who's *we*?" I asked.

"Come on, Santo, you just gave me the flow chart."

"Is it true that someone stole the president's academic records?" I asked. "We never saw them."

"They weren't released."

"Didn't want to get caught?"

"The man earned A's in everything."

"So much for your commitment to the truth," I grumbled.

"All we really needed to finish off the culture war was academia," she continued.

"As if we're the last 'liberal' strong hold? What about arts and entertainment?"

"We are using the culture of the Left to defeat the Left. Your openness is our entrance."

"*Knock, knock, knocking on Death Knell's door,*" Verboom sang faintly.

"So, since Verboom saved your life, you feel obligated to confess! That's what you promised him last night."

"Yes. I promised to tell him everything."

"You're not worried about getting outed? After all, you converted *The Dutch Uncle* into a hotline for tipsters!"

"Give me some credit. I could barely sleep last night in the hospital, questioning all that I had done. I asked myself what I truly felt and wanted."

"I'll give you credit for an extravagant dinner. Where's the *poison*?" I poked at the mashed potatoes.

"Shall we eat?" Ella asked. "The food's cooling."

"*Wait*! What about *The Dutch Uncle*, is that part of your work?"

She grinned. "The professor is entirely responsible. I simply gave him a few suggestions to tune things up."

"How did you find us in Seattle?" I asked.

"I must protect my sources and methods."

"So, how is First Brothers involved?"

"It's a prayer club for men," Ella said.

"But they're coordinating behind the scenes, they're moving government secretly."

"And pasty Libs from New England play squash together. So what?"

"But they're secretive?"

"It's because they confess their sins to each other. They don't want all that hanging out in the open."

"But their control of..."

"Santo, they line up with their constituents. They're a network of pro-business Conservatives who pray."

"And Blankenship? He thanks Frank Fowler in his book."

"Frank may have helped land the professor on E.C.S."

"*Aha*! Another prayer answered," I said mockingly.

"First Brothers is just like any other influence group."

"What about that paper they made Verboom sign?"

"No idea," she said.

"You don't work with them?"

"It's a prayer club for *men*."

"Mind if we skip grace and eat?" I cut into the beef.

The meal was exceptional. Her love of cooking wasn't faked, and she must have put dinner on the table before the confession to make sure our conversation wouldn't go on long. Verboom would not touch the food Ella put on his plate. He just sipped and stared off into space.

As much as I didn't want to eat, I couldn't stop myself. I was an omnivore living with omnivores.

"We still doing a show tomorrow?" I asked with food tucked into my cheek.

"Ask the professor," Ella said. "It's his show."

"You said you had to see the show through the election?"

"When Verboom saved my life, when he rolled out of a moving truck rather than take help from that racist..."

"So you're *not* a Kroester?"

"I never lied to either of you. Only withheld."

"But you're saying something else. You care about his wellbeing."

"And yours. After last night, I felt the need—the conviction—to give you the whole story. I never spoke lies, but the arrangement is not fully *organic*."

"Why should we trust you now?" I asked.

"I'll erase your video."

"How will I know it's deleted everywhere? Aren't you worried we'll out your other *projects*?"

"Santo, I've heard you on the phone, lecturing your pretend girl-friend about how the media works. There's more to learn."

"You say that like a threat."

"Ready to mix it up in the press? Do you see how that went for your mentor? You'll only benefit my cause. Mr. Sunderland gave me approval to bring you into full knowledge."

"Even as a black widow, you need Sunderland's *permission* to bite?"

"If you have the guts to tell anyone, it will create a chilling effect. And Mr. Sunderland will raise more donations than ever. He believes we are going to win either way. Listen, I'm loyal to the movement, and now, I'm loyal to the professor too."

"The attraction is real. I know. Heard it. Seen it."

"Admiration too. Last night he saved my life. His mind may be mixed up, but he's got a good heart."

I scowled. "You only needed one egghead to crack. But Verboom is cherry-picked—a strawman."

"Scarecrow." Verboom puffed, then sang, *"If I only had a brain..."*

"You've betrayed us without so much as a technical—*literal*—lie. *Bravo*. Am I supposed to say *thank you*?"

"You're mad. I get it. You're probably thinking you can get me back. But I have all the leverage." She became irritated with my naiveté—as if I was supposed to applaud her gamesmanship. "Santo, maybe if you had this all recorded. If you could document the events and build a gripping narrative, then you might have a chance to change minds. But we're so far out ahead of you. It's like a Chinese finger trap; the harder you pull, the tighter our grip."

She didn't seem to know about my recordings. I looked at Verboom for a clue, but he stared out through the open French doors.

He finished his gin and set the glass down. Then he backed his chair away from the table with the sound of wood skidding on wood. An empty bottle wobbled on the floor next to him and came to a rest. He stepped away from the table and left the room without looking at either of us.

"Here." Ella handed me an envelope.

It felt thick with cash. I peered in, then looked at her.

"Pay down a student loan. Or you can make a down payment on a modest house—I hear downtown Muskegon is coming up. Consider it a grant from the organization."

"Which one?"

"Does it matter?"

"I earned scholarships. I don't have debt."

"That's right. All... those... scholarships." She folded her hands.

"Your *Projects* must have copies of the video?"

"Think for a moment. Think about all the time you've spent watching the professor, instead of getting on with your life."

"Since you're coming clean, how about the details you owe me?"

"We'll talk at breakfast before the professor wakes. I need to lie down. You don't understand what the last twenty-four hours took out of me."

While weighing the envelope in my hand, I heard Verboom wretch in the shared bathroom down the hall—that is, my bathroom. Responding to the sound, I leaned forward and looked over my shoulder, across the table, as if I could somehow see the mess around the corners. And in that moment, I had Verboom's view through the French doors during dinner. The TV was on but muted. He had been watching WNN the entire meal, reading the news ticker and closed captions with that dopey, distant look on his face.

30

The next morning, I grabbed a cup of coffee and joined Verboom on the sofa. He was up earlier than usual.

"How are you feeling about last night's revelation?" I asked.

"A diagnosis can be freeing," he said, focused on the screen.

"You're *happy* about this?"

"Not entirely good news, but now I know the truth."

"She doesn't love you."

"But…" He glanced over his shoulder, checking for Ella. "At least we learned she wasn't faking orgasms."

"Nice you could be so accommodating." I watched him, waiting for a chuckle.

"Big surprise today: Kuiper is doing a last-minute interview with Kroes."

"What about *Ella*?"

"She doesn't know about the interview yet; she's still in bed."

He dropped to the floor and began doing push-ups, fewer than usual. Wisely, he skipped sit-ups.

I moved to the breakfast nook and waited for Ella.

The morning stretched on, while I read the papers.

When she finally arrived it was almost noon, which left us no opportunity to step out for a private conversation.

The professor was adamant: "The show *must* go on!"

He was not going to let the Kroesters put him out of business, even though they didn't know anything about the persona.

After a quick reassembly of the broadcasting gear, we carried on with the program. As per usual, Verboom started drinking at high noon. The calls about Kroes kept coming in—allegations of corruption and hypocrisy.

Verboom had an extra twinkle in his eye, the kind you get when you've dodged death, felt true affection, and brushed shoulders with betrayal, all while glued to cable news. Whether it was a hangover or damage from the ram bars, something was different about him. It seemed like he might finally cave into the incessant talk about Kroes. Perhaps he'd planned something to redeem the whole operation, a masterstroke.

I handed Verboom an article from *The Arizona Republic* detailing the Kroesters' intimidation of election officials and local newsrooms, but he shook his head dismissively. Next, I showed him a piece from *The Arizona Mirror* that featured a deep investigation into Kroes' border posse. It included credible accounts of extortion involving human smugglers, known as coyotes, who allegedly coordinated with posse members to shakedown individuals on both sides of the border. Once more, Verboom just shook his head.

Toward the end of the hour, a caller with an Arizona area code, who was obviously disguising his voice, claimed to be Kroes' ex-boyfriend, sharing intimate details that only a lover would know. Sitting outside the studio by the French doors, I quickly scribbled a note on a white sheet of paper: "KROES' EX-BOYFRIEND. SOUNDS LEGIT." I pressed the note against the glass of the French doors. When Verboom didn't notice, I knocked softly with my other hand. He finally looked up, read the note, but his expression remained blank.

As I waited for Verboom to process this revelation, the caller went on to claim that he had been Kroes' on-again-off-again lover for three decades and possessed a trove of compromising details.

Verboom looked at me, then shook his head; Ella did the same. Realizing the direction this was heading; I removed the note from the glass and informed the caller that our host had decided to pass.

"Santo, it's Adam—from Flagstaff," he said unmasking his voice.

My note had triggered another sermon from "Vermeer" on the need to suffocate demagogues. "Attention is the air they breathe!" While the persona lectured on, Adam said Jacqueline mentioned the show at Haddit's. Since the polls were so close, he finally decided to call.

"Why not go to a reputable news outlet?" I asked Adam on a separate line, while Verboom continued to lecture over the broadcast.

"Don't want Rallymen shooting up my bar. But you all operate on the dark edges of media, though hopefully close enough for the mainstream to catch on. I'm hoping we can get the truth out while keeping my name safe," Adam explained.

I put the note to the glass again, they both shook their heads, so I turned off their mics and spoke into the broadcast:

"This is Lawrence, technical producer of *The Dutch Uncle*. Listeners, we have a caller from Arizona with intimate knowledge of the presidential candidate James Kroes. Please go caller."

Adam proceeded:

"As Kroes' boyfriend for almost three decades, I know things not even his wife does. I've seen it all. He's in cahoots with smugglers and traffickers, letting them operate for a cut—a 'commission,' he calls it. He plays both sides, taking kickbacks from his cronies and making high-profile busts on their rivals to boost his image. Plus, he's been peddling surveillance data to private security firms. Kroes isn't just a sheriff; he's running his office like a mob boss—a closeted mob boss."

Ella burst through the French doors and yanked the cables from my laptop, then slammed it shut. Next, she crawled under my table frantically pulling every cord she could find, while the host watched, dumfounded by the chaos.

No transcript can be supplied here, but Ella and I argued for a few minutes. Her point: we can't allow malicious gossip to be broadcast. My point: you wanted open-line policy when Verboom barred calls on Kroes, but one negative call on Kroes and you pull the plug.

"It's his show! You disobeyed his orders!" she finally roared.

"*Disobeyed*?" My eyes flashed with anger. "*Orders*?"

Then Verboom's laughter broke through the squabble, a deep rolling laugh stopping all further discussion. He pulled off his headphones and walked out of the studio-dining room. He casually picked up his bandana, tying it around his neck, and then turned to Ella, asking for the whereabouts of his sunglasses.

With Ella distracted, I bolted out of the apartment with my laptop and down to my coffeehouse, where I got online and secured the archive of Adam's testimony of the corrupt sheriff, who had cheated on his wife for three decades. Then, I updated our website to keep the click-to-call button live indefinitely, inviting voice messages from anyone with information on Kroes. The tipster line was now *fully* open. I exhaled deeply.

"*Santo!*" My name echoed through the room.

My cortado was ready.

I sipped the drink, espresso mingling with steamed milk; strange how caffeine could calm my nerves. Then I inhaled slowly.

I looked at the website's inbox. More and more messages. Was I really going to amplify this *gossip*? I couldn't factcheck the callers' claims. Despite the possibility of Kroes winning, I couldn't stomach pushing unvetted hearsay, but I left the line open.

My mom may have regretted the circumstances of my birth— her so-called sin—but she always told me I was meant for "God's glory." She never knew exactly what that would be, but nonetheless, she believed I was destined to play a significant role in the world. Perhaps most mothers feel that way. While the sentiment was sweet, it felt like a burden. But as the day unfolded, I wondered if the moment had arrived.

After finishing my drink, I reread Jacqueline's last email. More than ever, she was invested in my manuscript and offered ideas on next steps: "Pitch the book as a story of a mad but lovable professor who's an unconscious bundle of contradictions *studying consciousness and contradictions*! Or maybe, the journey of an odd couple on the run from their insecurities... and *fascists*. Hmmm... You may have a genre problem, but I've got some title ideas. Call me."

Stepping outside the coffee house, I dialed.

Before I could update her on Verboom's accident and Ella's betrayal, she jumped in, picking up from her email.

"*The Mad Professor and the Almost-Scientist* would be a wonderful stocking stuffer this holiday season." She chuckled.

"Let's not put 'professor' in the title of anything." I chuckled. "But seriously, did you hear today's show?"

"Santo, I hope you've mastered the production skills, but I can't listen along anymore. Though you know, the idea has occurred to me a few times: if Kroes' wins, your book on the origin of *Final Freedom* will be even more..."

"Marketable?"

"Relevant. Think you'll be able to pitch it by mid-November?"

"If you can help me with my genre problem."

"Deal. Now tell me about what happened on today's show."

"You've got to hear it for yourself."

"Wonder if Adam was listening?" she asked.

"What? How would he know about the show?" I played dumb.

"After you left town, I went back to see him."

"Why?"

"Tried getting him to spill the beans on you."

"What did he say?"

"Nothing I didn't already know."

"Good. I prefer to be the messenger."

"Yes. You have a flair for nuance. Unless it's your feelings," she said. "So, what do you think of Adam?"

"Not sure about his politics, but he's a good person," I vouched.

Jaqueline continued; it turned out she got along well with Adam, and they'd struck up a casual friendship. That's it, I thought. It was a *crank call*. I'd gotten played by my Flagstaff friend.

"You got to know him?" I followed up.

"He's an interesting guy with an interesting life—a lot of opinions too. I ended up taking his old school conservatism, modifying and moderating it, then slapped an anarchist veneer on it before delivering it to you guys for the 'newsletter.' My game was to make sensible working-class politics sound radical."

"You literally wrote Vermeer's newsletter from a barstool?"

"Yes. Quickly and with a buzz. I treated it like a writing exercise."

"Like some kind of improv?"

"The whole thing was a farce, right?"

"Wow. You really nailed the aging man's perspective—except they want to call their ideas 'common sense' not 'stateless anarchy.'"

"Did you know Adam had a crush on you?"

"Thought the free beers were because I tip so well."

"He let it slip, and that's how we bonded. The Santo Vera Fan Club of Flagstaff." She almost giggled.

"Not a very creative name for a writer and a gay cop."

"We're too busy pining, darling." She laughed. "We're pining over here."

"I'll send you a chainsaw."

"Flagstaff's Finest. Let's do a calendar!"

"We'd sell two copies."

"Don't sell yourself short. Adam owns two houses, plus the bar, one for every bathroom and his office—we're already in double figures."

"Do you get a free calendar for the newsletter screeds, or should I be thanking Adam?"

"No, I didn't need Adam, though I will admit he's creative, just a little rough around the edges. He didn't know what I was up to. Our conversations were only a springboard. But you know, he's been messing with me the last few days. Claiming he was Kroes' lover for almost thirty years. His details are, well, vivid. Obviously, he's just teasing. A playfully contentious rapport is important to a guy his age. Still, he sticks to his story about Kroes, says he may go public with it."

"Go to the website and listen to the show."

"Just tell me what happened."

"Listen to it. Then call me back. But before you go. The institute is newly flush with cash—a small emergency slush fund. We can get you on a plane. I don't think I can finish the book without your help."

"No, I'm looking forward to the drive."

Our goodbyes had become awkward. Clearly, there was fondness, but we never discussed what we were doing—beyond writing a book.

About to head into the coffeehouse, I caught sight of Verboom galloping down Pike Street, glasses on and bandana raised. He had taken a standard-sized white top sheet—identical to mine—and scrawled THIS IS A FLAG across it. The sheet was tied to our coat stand, which he brandished high above his head. A block behind, Ella followed in the pickup still emblazoned with the graffiti.

Though faster than Verboom, I chose not to follow along,

determined instead to hit my daily word count.

Walking uphill toward the apartment, Jacqueline called. "It's true!" she exclaimed, skipping any form of greeting.

"Think so?"

"Played it three times. He has absolutely no reason to go public except civic duty. How would this be any good for him? If he wanted publicity, he would have done it a long time ago, same with payback. He's freaked out. He must believe that a president Kroes will wreck the country."

"Maybe it's just his turn to mess with me?"

"He's put himself at considerable risk. Public concern is the only possible motivation. I'm going to Haddit's right now."

"But you said he was *messing* with you?"

"It was more like he was laying crumbs to see if I'd bite."

"An example?"

"Sure. He said something like, 'With all Kroes' over-the-top masculinity, do you think he might *prefer* men?' I replied, 'Of course he wants men in power. Didn't Kroes even say that women should be taken back to the kitchen?' Then Adam chuckled and said, 'Oh, I think he's *taken* more than a few men in the kitchen.' That last line is an exact quote. You can see where I thought it was a joke."

I laughed, more out of exasperation than amusement.

"Babe!" She stopped herself. "*Santo.* Have I not made the situation clear to you? There are Kroes-loving Rallymen prowling all over Arizona! If a revelation like this got out, Adam's in danger."

"He did tell me he'd be 'ready' for the gun nuts."

"Have you ever been behind his bar?" she asked.

"No. You?"

"Yes. He *is* ready."

"Holy shit."

"In person, I'll see the truth."

"Detectives are trained liars. Misleading suspects is part of their job."

"Am I a suspect?" she asked.

"Of course not, but maybe take a polygraph with you."

I imagined the polygraph pen, jittering and sweeping dramatically across the rolling paper. Each question about his amorous encounters with Kroes causing the pen to spike and dive, as if the truth could be etched in ink.

"But if it's true, what are you going to do, Santo? You said you would never publish caller gossip in your book."

"Did you know the ancient church father Origen castrated himself?"

"Seriously, what are you going to do?"

"Staying true to my word. I will not promote unvetted claims."

"But we *can* verify this one. That was the only objection you had to printing caller transcripts."

"So, the one tipster we can fact-check may get him hurt."

"Let me talk to him. You can decide later."

There was more to tell Jacqueline, not least of which was Ella's confession, but it seemed best to let her get to Haddit's, and I'd reached my destination.

31

Inside Genevieve's apartment, I found *Genevieve*. She was standing next to the shot-out window, along with the building manager. He had taken down the pillowcase and gave me a quick nod before measuring the frame's dimensions.

"Good to see you, Santo Vera. Where's the professor?" Genevieve asked.

"Saw him about an hour ago running down Pike with a sheet tied to a coat stand. You didn't spot him on the way in?"

"Afraid not." She smiled.

"About the window, we gave our guy Stanley $900 to replace the glass. Verboom insisted on overpaying."

"Received," Stanley said. "Work in progress."

"All's well, Stanley keeps me informed," she said.

"He's been watching us?"

"Only the building. He told me about the window, and I wanted to see what's been going on in the neighborhood. I'm on my way to a conference in Vancouver."

She walked over and hugged me, then she turned me toward the mirror hanging by the door, just above a skinny table with a catch-all on top. I studied her in the mirror for a moment, flowing denim on denim, with a cream wool sweater under her jean jacket, her wavy blonde hair down, no makeup; here was the crunchy guru I'd expected.

With one arm around my waist, she said, "Look at your face,

Santo." She paused. "You're on edge. When I saw you in LA, you were more sad than angry, now the reverse."

We turned to face each other, and she studied my eyes, one eyeball at a time with careful concentration, gentle hands on my upper arms, my body felt tranquilized.

I was jolted out of the calm as Verboom materialized at the front door, hands tied behind his back with a karate belt. Suddenly Ella prodded him forward with the coat stand. But once Verboom saw Genevieve, he stopped abruptly, the coat stand jabbing into his back. Ella, caught by her momentum, stumbled hard into its base. She groaned and dropped the stand, then collapsed to her knees, clutching her stomach, the wind knocked out of her.

Genevieve quickly untied Verboom and peeled back one side of his open *gi* top; she inhaled sharply, taken aback, and asked what had happened.

"Not going to ask about me?" Ella groaned, rolling from her knees to her bum.

Genevieve studied Ella, who was sitting on the hallway carpet, skirt hiked up her thighs as she crossed her legs.

After a moment, Genevieve walked away and returned with a small bag of ice wrapped in a cloth. Ella accepted the ice and pressed it against her stomach.

I introduced the women to each other, but neither offered a handshake.

"You have the legs of an athlete and the face of a small town beauty who can go anywhere she chooses," Genevieve said to Ella. "Your eyes burn with zeal... Your childhood was profoundly cruel, and yet you've worked so hard... You seek justice at any cost, but you cannot love."

Letting go of the ice, Ella leaned forward to stand up for confrontation, but then put her face in her hands, crying softly while sitting cross-legged. Genevieve walked away, and then came back with a glass of water for Ella, who accepted the drink.

Verboom's eyes darted from woman to woman; he appeared pale and ready to faint. Genevieve took the glass of water from Ella and handed it to Verboom, who drank it like a laborer on a Kroes chain gang.

"Help me up," Ella said to me.

On her feet, she walked to the back bedroom.

Dazed, Verboom hurried to the kitchen and poured out five gin and tonics, a wedge of lime for each, but no rosemary. He took three tumblers in one hand and two in the other. We met him in the middle of the living room, cool air blowing through the busted window. Genevieve, Stanley, and I took a glass simultaneously from the hand with three drinks, preventing a spill.

"Welcome home," Verboom and I said to Genevieve at the same time.

After touching glasses, Verboom left for the master bedroom.

Genevieve, Stanley, and I walked over to the broken window, unsure of what to say.

"*This is not a flag*?" Stanley read the pillowcase. "Strange."

Genevieve pointed to a small picture next to the front door. A reproduction of Rene Magritte's *This Is Not a Pipe*. The painted image of a pipe with *Ceci n'est pas une pipe* written underneath.

"Does the professor speak French?" Genevieve asked.

"Not sure," I said. "But he does refer to Magritte as 'Southern Dutch' as opposed to 'Belgian.' Since the Dutch are the only people he's allowed to insult, he tries to include as many as possible."

Genevieve raised her glass.

Before we finished the strong drinks, Ella and Verboom came down the hall with three leather suitcases, two large and one small. Ella didn't look over to us and went straight out the front door followed by Verboom with his *gi* top hanging open, sunglasses sitting atop his head and bandana at his neck. As he looked over to us his glasses slid from the top of his forehead to the bridge of his nose.

I stepped forward to follow, but Genevieve gently placed her arm in front of me.

Once the pair disappeared down the hall, Genevieve turned to me and asked, "Are you okay?"

"Giving my one-week notice. Hear that, Stanley?"

"You can stay as long as you like," Genevieve said.

"One week," I confirmed. "Thank you both."

"We'll have the glass replaced tomorrow," Stanley said to Genevieve.

She nodded.

"What about the big guy?" Stanley asked me. "How long is he staying?"

"He may already be gone."

I walked back to Verboom's room; his clothes were in the closet, and his hip pack sat on the bed.

"His stuff is here," I called down the hall. "Looks like he's planning to come back."

In my room, I opened the white envelope from Ella. Inside, a thick stack of hundred-dollar bills—an unexpected bonus. I removed the cash and counted it for the first time: $12,500.

Sitting at my desk, I pulled up the average price of homes in Muskegon and Grand Rapids, both hovering around $125,000. It *could* serve as a down payment for a house, like Ella suggested, like my mom had dreamed—if only I had a steady middle-class income to secure a mortgage. Holding one end of the stack, I waved it for a few moments as if it were a blackjack, then I riffled through it, like flipping through the pages of a novel too long to read.

I walked back to Verboom's bedroom and put the cash in his

hip pack. A voice in my head told me not to be so high-minded, so I unzipped the pack and took $2,500 back for emergency expenses.

As I reached the building's main entrance on the ground floor, I heard my name. Turning around, I saw Genevieve emerging from a guest chair in the office. Stepping into the hallway, she fixed her gaze intently on my eyes, once again studying me closely.

"Heading out to dinner, want to join?" I asked.

"Please, the gin's wearing off, and I'm hungry."

We walked just over five blocks to a café on 10th Street, the sun long since set, the streets well-lit and slick with rain, bustling with steady foot and car traffic.

Nestled in a brick building constructed in the late 1800s, the restaurant boasted high ceilings, tall windows, and vintage wood furniture. The servers, all svelte and youthful, moved gracefully around the space, and the bartender, sporting a waxed mustache, considered himself a beverage artist. He wore a clean denim apron, outfitted with several small pockets filled with small tools.

After a quick beer while waiting for a table, we were seated. Then without planning to, I found myself unloading my thoughts to Genevieve. She listened intently, as I poured out my burdens.

"Well, that's the worst of it," I said.

"The professor seems more troubled than I realized," Genevieve said.

"Since Los Angeles: drugs and alcohol were added to the formula."

"*Drugs?*"

"Cable news. We call it cocaine."

"At least there are treatment programs for powder substances," she lamented.

"Maybe you can start a new ministry for cable news addicts?"

"You think there's a need?"

"I need to go home."

"And you must," she said without hesitation. "After I finish the conference in Vancouver, I'll come back to check on the professor. It's time for you to move on."

"Weird timing for a conference. Right before Election Day."

"It's in Canada. There's a whole world beyond our borders." She thought for a moment. "After dinner, I'll finish the drive so I can check in tonight."

"Not going to stick around?"

"Better to give him space."

"What if he got on a plane or train with Ella?" I asked.

"He won't."

"What you said about Ella. You can see all that?"

"Years of practice."

"Do you believe in God?" I asked, finishing my second beer just as the food arrived. It was another thought that slipped out unplanned.

"Not sure what you mean?" She smiled as the server set the food down.

"Okay," I sniffed, as if gearing up to throw another pitch. "Do you have 'spiritual gifts?'"

She smiled, her expression free from fear or pretense. "If I tell you I believe in a god or am connected to divinity in a special way, you'll put me on one track, and if I say no, you'll put me on another, like an engineer with a train set. You usually foresee what's next, predicting people's words and actions as if you scripted them yourself. It's something intelligent people do, but maybe you can take a break from forecasting and just let things unfold."

She glanced at my plate—steak frites—then speared a beet from her salad and placed it beside my fries. "Good for the liver."

She observed that the restaurant was housed in the Odd Fellows

Hall and complimented my choice of venue.

"Hope it will be spared from the developers," she said.

"And the Big One," I added. "Can you predict the future?"

"Geology isn't my strong suit." She smiled.

"Who preaches when you're out of town?"

"I join remote. Same with radio."

"Maybe I could spend a day with your production team."

"Anytime, but first go home and see your grandma. Put your house in order. And by the way, thank you for keeping the apartment so clean—it's sparkling."

"Verboom's work, he cleans for hours a day—one of the few things he can do while following the news."

"Y'all are leaving it better than you found it."

"You may be down a pillowcase and top sheet," I said.

"But who's counting threads." She grinned.

"What's your convention about?"

"It's the Mind Body Spirit Conference. In this group, I feel a bit old fashioned, but it's good to feel conservative a few days every year."

"You're not a plenary speaker?"

"A humble attendee. Surprised?"

"*Yes.*"

"Feels good, doesn't it?"

A dessert arrived, raspberry sorbet, compliments of the host, who'd recognized the minister. Genevieve took a quick spoonful, savored it, and said, "Delectable." She nodded to the host watching from her stand.

"Tell my darling professor that I'll see him soon." She took another sip of black coffee and stood up, eager to get back on the road. Reflexively, I stood up, and she hugged me, then I plopped into my chair.

"Gonna sit a while," I said with a smile.

After the sorbet and an apéritif, I readied myself to see the apartment. Before my chair pushed back, the host sat down in Genevieve's spot.

"My shift's over, can I buy you a drink?" she asked.

My knowledge of Genevieve was exhausted by the end of one round, and I grew antsy about Verboom.

The host seemed better informed on Genevieve than me, but not disappointed. Her parting words were, "Come back and see me."

Walking down the hallway of the top floor, I noticed the apartment door slightly ajar. On reaching the threshold I listened.

"The only way to secure your financial future is GOLD!"

I pushed the door open and saw Verboom draped across the couch like the Messiah in Michelangelo's *Pieta*. As I turned the volume to zero, he popped up: "Where is *she*?"

"Which one?" I asked.

"*Genevieve.*"

"She drove to Vancouver."

"Washington or B.C.?"

"British Colombia. Where's Ella?"

"On the Empire Builder. She's got to change trains in Chicago for Grand Rapids. Watched her board, but she didn't look out the window for me. I was so sad, I milled around downtown for a few hours."

"The Dutch Mafia didn't have a private plane available?"

"*Nay*, poor Ella is a foot soldier, a pawn."

"At least a rook, I'd say. What did you talk about on the drive to the station?"

"She condemned Genevieve as a progressive, then a socialist, then a Marxist, then a Communist."

"Bolshevik or Leninist?"

"As we waited for the train," Verboom sighed, "she said I'd wasted my talent hiding in Seattle and should be making more of myself."

"Maybe if you improve your status, she can look past your quirks. Think of all the protein you could provision as a cable news political analyst…"

"And all those free munchies in the studio!" His eyes sparkled.

"If she's gone, why are you watching ANN?"

"*Ja, ja*… Must be missing her."

"Thanks to Genevieve, you know Ella cannot love, so don't take it personally."

He closed his eyes and exhaled.

"All these commercials on ANN—gold, catheters, motorized carts, home security, pillows…" I stopped listening to think, then continued. "Well, it's…"

"Surreal," Verboom said. "But perhaps hyperreal if your over sixty-five years of age. Last commercial break was prostate supplements, adult diapers, big-button cellphones, gutter covers, and a few medications for lifestyle diseases."

"Wouldn't you rather go outside? Ella's gone, so no one's trying to put you on TV."

"The amateur video journalists are everywhere. You've heard the WNN call for civilian video. It's not safe for my likeness to leave the house. Even major newspapers are calling for tipsters. Plus, you just outed James Kroes. Say, do you think anyone's listening to the show? Or is it all a hoax?"

"It's amateur, but real. We own the means of production."

"How many people listening?"

"We're about to find out."

He shook his head. "Better I stay in."

"The locals have probably forgotten about the Portland Rose Giant. But just in case, what if you left your likeness at home?" I handed him the bandana and glasses.

He knotted the bandana and set his shades on the top of his forehead. Then he slid into an extra *gi* jacket and re-tied his belt, which reminded me of the way he came home earlier that day.

"How did Ella get you tied up? Did you pass out drunk?"

"I ran my flag all the way down to the Space Needle, and when I tried to climb one of its legs, the security arrived immediately. Ella jumped in and said, 'You get down here right now, you've been a very *bad* boy.' The guards were taken aback, but then she winked at them. She said, 'Mama's gonna take you home for a good spanking, let's go Pieter.'"

"And you followed orders?"

"The situation afforded two options: go with the guards or go with Ella. She cranked on my ear and bent me over. All the men laughed as I groaned. Then she untied my belt to more hoots and hollers, grabbed me by the wrists, and tied my hands together. The men all cheered like it was a vaudeville act. Then she loaded me in the truck and took a bow to the men's applause."

"You eat dinner?" I asked.

"Meal planning isn't a strength of mine."

"It's 10 PM. Let's get you a burrito. *Carne asada, carnitas,* or *pollo?*"

"One of each, let me grab my hip pack."

The coat stand had been returned to its home near the door, and as he lifted the pack from its hook, he paused for a moment.

"Feels heavier," he said. "I must be weakening from lack of protein."

Halfway through his second burrito and third horchata, Verboom's eyes focused over my shoulder. Turning around, I saw a pickup with fat tires and a lifted suspension idling at the intersection. The rear bumper sported a "Get'em JIM" magnet, obscured slightly by tailpipe exhaust, and on the other side, a "Save the SEALs" sticker. From the cab flew an American flag alongside a white flag, its message hidden within the tangled folds.

"Told you they hijacked the flag," I said and returned to my tacos.

"The white one, what does it say?"

"Can't read it," I said, my words muffled with food tucked in my cheek.

He squinted, straining his eyes for a better look. "If it says, *Final Freedom...*"

Without another word, he tore out of our booth and sprinted up to the passenger side of the truck. He knocked on the window, which then rolled down halfway.

"What does your flag say—the white one?"

"*Final Freedom*, we're taking the country back from the feds."

"May I buy into your cause?" Verboom asked like a politician, perhaps channeling a touch of Vermeer's showmanship.

A car behind the truck honked, and the driver waved him around.

"What do you have in mind?" the driver asked, lowering the window all the way.

"I'll give you all the cash in my hip pack for that white flag."

"Mind removing your sunglasses? I want to see how high you are."

"It's a good faith business opportunity," Verboom said, removing his glasses. "Here." He held up the hip pack. "Whatever I have is yours."

Then out came the down payment on a house in Muskegon. Verboom was surprised, then seemed happy to know his sense of weight was still intact.

"Deal!" the driver yelled, eager to forestall a change of heart.

He climbed out of the cab and into the truck bed, detached the flag, and held it out to Verboom, then a simultaneous exchange. The driver fanned through the cash and Verboom folded the flag neatly.

As the driver rolled forward, Verboom asked, "Say? Where did you acquire this artifact?"

"*What?*"

"The flag."

"Hearn is selling them for $59.99, with the attachment stand."

Another car caught behind the idling truck honked, so the flag-seller dropped his rig into gear and spun out over the wet concrete, fishtailing around the corner and heading downhill.

"What's he going to do with all that money?" I asked Verboom.

"Well, if he's a 'good Christian,' I presume he'll help widows and orphans."

"Does anyone ever claim to be a 'bad Christian?'" I asked.

"Only the good ones," he said.

The truck revved, accelerating through the next intersection toward downtown.

"What will you do with the flag?" I asked.

"Burry it in the back of the closet."

"Do you want to know where all that money came from?"

"*Freely, freely, you have received. Freely, freely give! Go in my name, and because you believe, others will know that I live!*"

He belted out the hymn like he sang in a church choir, beginning with the chorus, his voice deep and resonant, then singing the first verse before returning to the chorus. As he looped from the second verse to the chorus, we reentered the restaurant for the rest of our food. Still singing, he gestured for more drinks, and I refilled our horchatas. It seemed as though he couldn't stop himself from singing until the rice milk was back in hand.

Once he had his drink, he stopped singing and guzzled it down in one shot. A loud belch escaped him, like a frat house partygoer, and he apologized profusely.

"You better get me home," he said, embarrassed.

32

The next morning, Jacqueline called. Her mother's dreams continued to predict a Kroes victory, despite him trailing in every poll. Jacqueline wasn't convinced by the dreams, but she worried that a Kroes loss would ignite violence.

I offered to fly in and drive back out with her, suggesting we could stay in Seattle for a few days and then do the return drive together.

"You're a pretty-boy almost-scientist, not some kind of soldier of fortune. Don't get the wrong idea," she responded. "It's not just about my mom's dream; my absentee ballot hasn't arrived, and I can't leave without voting. We'll meet up after the election. Let's hope my mom's wrong."

"When can I call you Beatrice?" I asked.

"That's my middle name. Not until you know me."

"Even that guy working at the Spotted Owl called you Bea."

"He's my ex."

"If he's your ex, how can you keep going there for pancakes?" I joked, though a hint of jealousy tinged my voice.

"Lately, I'm too anxious to eat breakfast. We can't even let Kroes win his home state. If he does, he'll probably try to..."

"Secede?" I chuckled awkwardly. "You sound spooked."

"Another rally in Flagstaff last night. They beat up a student reporter, who's now in ICU. Yes, I'm *spooked*. On Tuesday I'm going to be the first person in line at my precinct."

"Who are you going to vote for?"

"What a dumb thing to say right now."

"You're pretty hard on the president."

"I admit it. I took his centrism for granted," she said.

"Verboom blames himself for the president's drop in the polls."

"There are *Final Freedom* flags in AZ, but without you, I may not have noticed. The real problem is Kroes! He's giving wannabe tough guys permission to bully the rest of us."

"Well, Verboom still blames himself." I sighed. "He needs another clinic."

"Delusions of grandeur?"

"Gin."

"Why not bring him back?"

"Without his radio persona and Ella, I don't know what he's going to do."

"Does he like being Vermeer?"

"There's no curing a wild man. He comes from a long line of wild men. Some of them loved Jesus. Some of them loved the jug. Some of them loved both."

"Start the book with that line. It's not art, but..."

"He's estranged from his family. He has no close friends, and while there're two women in his life, one's a honeypot and the other a spiritual guru."

"Santo, this is already a better narrative."

"Maybe I'll change my name too. You know it's short for Crisanto? Sounds like my mother couldn't choose between Christ and saint. Said she always liked the name Travis, after we watched *Old Yeller* one Saturday night, but she worried folks would expect me to be a redneck. Looked the name up, turns out it's French."

"You know rednecks were the good guys, right?"

"Maybe in high school I did."

"*Old Yeller*? Sounds like a description of Kroes."

"It's like 'yellow' not 'yelling.' Hard to believe that was a Disney movie. Do you remember what Travis does at the end?"

"Never saw it."

"Has to shoot his dying dog."

"What are you talking about?" she asked.

"Names. Vera isn't my father's name."

"What's in a name?"

"'Would a rose by any other name smell as sweet?'"

"You'd smell the same, handsome," she said, her voice becoming tender. "But you sound so sad."

"My mom. I'm not getting used to her absence, just missing her more and more. It's been longer since I've seen her." I took a breath. "Time heals nothing."

"That's the saddest thing you've ever said."

"When she passed, I went through two years of phone bills, worried that I didn't call enough..."

"But you called her every day."

"Almost." I exhaled hard and disconnected the call. Even by phone, I felt disgust with showing grief.

After filling my water bottle and grabbing a jacket, I circled down the stairs, unlocked my bike, and rode toward the Sound. Along the water I worked all the way up to the West Point Lighthouse, then east across the Ballard Locks to Fremont, where I ordered a lager and a club sandwich at a brewery. With the tall glass of beer finished well ahead of the sandwich, lightheaded, and a little dizzy, a smile formed as I looked out at Lake Union.

A woman walked by, looking vaguely like my ex as she waved at a man next to me. I may be the only person who would see a resemblance, but I saw it.

I felt sharp pain in my sternum.

I opened my phone and began reading through my thread with NEVER CALL. Every text still there, unlike my lost voicemails. Reading the messages, my arms didn't feel like mine, my shoulders imposters, the vision of my mind's eye someone else's, and the pattern was clear: NEVER CALL was always dragged along. The invitations came from Santo Vera. The accepts and rejects came from her. She wasn't old fashioned; she was disinterested. I knew about her cold feet, but now it was clear she didn't even *like* me.

The sandwich and beer number two arrived; I ate the long dill pickle, chugged half my lager, and deleted the text thread. I called my grandmother, planning to ask her about NEVER CALL, but once we connected, her delight with the sound of my voice tamped down the questions.

Riding home through Queen Anne, the drizzling rain returned. I noticed a small group of full-size pickups converged to box in a small hybrid hatchback like a policing move. Stopping ten yards away, I turned my smartphone camera on the men.

"What did he do?" I hollered. "*Speak up*, I want to make sure your answer is recorded clearly!"

"This beardless chump shot us the bird."

"The middle finger?" I called back for clarification. "You're saying he flipped you off?"

"Yeah."

The middle-aged man in the small car was scared. He took his hands from the steering wheel, picked up his phone, and trained his camera.

"You've got flags, bumper stickers, hats, patches, and pins—but I don't see a badge," I yelled. "If this is a citizen's arrest, what's the crime?"

"*Who are you? What does your hat say?*" A man hollered from another truck.

I'd been wearing Verboom's trucker hat backwards, I took it off my head and turned it around: DON'T BLAME ME I VOTED FOR WILLIE.

"Willie *who*?" The first guy yelled.

"The only Willie who matters," I said.

A medium sized SUV—headed the opposite direction of the trucks—came to a stop, and the driver lowered his window. Then the back windows came down, revealing a full bench of passengers. A phone popped out—camera aimed at the trucks.

"Are you helping this guy with a tire?" the SUV driver asked, with a sense of knowing, more playful than sarcastic. He smiled like a decent guy who'd been treated well most of his life.

A sporty station wagon stopped behind the SUV, a stylish mom jumped out and spoke to the driver blocking the path.

With jovial authority, the SUV driver said, "This nice lady needs to get her kids home and needs me to move. Are we done here? I think Mr. Hybrid is ready to go too."

The hybrid driver gave a thumbs up, and the mom went back to her car. The lead truck rumbled off, and the other trucks followed. The SUV rolled forward, driver offering a nod, and the station wagon drove on.

I recorded until the last pickup was well up the street. The hybrid took a U-turn, the bumper and back hatch covered with progressive slogans. I turned Verboom's hat backward and rode up beside the car. He lowered his window and said thank you, still moving slowly.

"Did you really flip them off?"

"I sure *fucking* did." Then he sped off with a wave.

Looking over my shoulders, the trucks were no longer visible. I rode fast through the city for several miles, wondering what made me so bold—the lager, the heartache, or the fact I was leaving town.

After a few hours, I pulled up to Swinging Richard's in Capitol

Hill and ordered a burger for myself and three for Verboom.

Verboom was dusting the windowsills when I opened the door, he'd muted the television, which showed an ad for a high-performance walking cane.

"You eat?" I asked.

"Like a pelican."

I sat next to Verboom on the couch, planning to disconnect from my feelings with a burger, a few beers, and a long session of WNN political panic. An *almost-reality*, the outrage would titillate and paralyze us. And like rats in the lab, we'd push the button. After eating, I fell asleep on Laurels.

When I woke, Verboom had the volume at a whisper. As soon as I leaned forward for my water, he turned the volume up. An ad from the president ran, he said: "Now, you may disagree with me, with what we're doing and how we're doing it, but the economy is growing, financial markets are stable, and the unemployment rate has dropped every month of my presidency. Let's continue the work of restoring America."

"But the bankers are still free and making more money than ever while the SEALs are stuck in the desert getting skinnier than ever," Verboom lamented.

I looked at the time and considered what to do. I felt the need to get out and see people. After months without a date in Seattle, I had no real human contact, other than a time at Linda's Tavern when I let a woman put her arm around me, and a few demeaning pats from Ella. No touch of a woman but the womanly touches of our furnishings and décor—I'd sunk to rehashing Verboom's dad jokes. Despite my exhausted legs, I couldn't spend more of life inside with the bemused Samson, dumbstruck with gin and infotainment.

The ancient book of Judges reports that the Philistines put Samson in bronze shackles after gouging out his eyes, and they sentenced him to walking in circles, grinding grain while bound in chains. Here now was the professor, shackled to his sofa.

"*Let's go*! We need fresh air!"

"But Kuiper has Kroes on tonight, America's Toughest Cop!"

"You can't watch that! Live up to your own boycotting principles."

"Jonathan will make him look so foolish, and Kroes will be caught in his web of lies. When America finds out who Kroes really is, he's through!"

"If you've taught me anything, that's not going to happen. No offense to Mr. Kuiper."

"None taken," Verboom said in Kuiper's voice with an uncanny impersonation.

Instead of putting on a jacket, Verboom put on a second *gi* top.

After walking a few blocks, we were inside the E.R.O.G.E.N.O.U.S. Zone, which still felt like a farmers' market and street fair, though heightened with the mood and messaging of political unrest. While Verboom loved their spirit, he feared for their outcome.

"It's you!" a stranger yelled. "The *Portland Rose Giant*! Haven't seen you in months, but I heard you ran a fake surrender flag through the city! We're with you. We've missed your nonsense—true Dadaism."

"You're too kind," Verboom said like he'd accepted an award he didn't deserve but wanted anyway, removing his bandana and glasses. "But please be careful, this war of abstractions is becoming concrete. Even by accident, you can get trucked down by these truc-ulent truckers."

"*Preach*," another stranger chimed in.

"Now listen, only just a few days ago..." He stopped. "Well, let me show you..." Verboom untied his belt and opened his jackets, revealing his bruises. Someone shined a flashlight on him.

"*The rally goons?*"

"I should've been wearing orange," Verboom said regretfully.

"The rally boys ran him over!" another stranger yelled. "*That's attempted murder!*"

The flashlight trained on Verboom's ribs, as a small group gathered.

"Let's get you to the speakers' soapbox. Tell us what happened," a woman said.

The small group escorted us a half block to a few stacked crates, screwed together with side braces and a half sheet of plywood on top.

"*Listen up*! The Rose Giant has a message from the edge... a near death experience. He saw the light—*two big headlights*!"

There were a few tepid cheers and some polite clapping.

"*Everyone!* This is the guy who stuffed a white rose in that rally goon's gun down in Stumptown! He served old-fashioned donuts to the Old-Fashioned American Mob! *And they are a mob*, like the Klan and the Brownshirts. He landed a rose in just one barrel, but it stood for all guns, for all hate! In Portland, they beat him with boots and fists. In Seattle, they rammed him with a *truck*!" Then looking at Verboom, he said, "We've seen your commitment, give us a few words."

The man pulled Verboom onto the platform with him. It crackled and creaked under their weight.

"They had guns down in Portland, but yet they used their hands to strike me. Think of the progress!" Verboom exclaimed, though it seemed as if no one could hear.

"Listen everyone, the Rose Giant was run over and left to die on the street like a *gigantic blond dog*! But here he is. Still standing. Show us your bruises again."

Verboom complied, removing both jackets, standing topless on the crates. The stranger stepped off the platform and shined a flash-light on Verboom's torso. There was a corporate groan of disgust as the light hit Verboom's discolored ribs. Despite his indestructible milk-fed bones, he bruised badly, yellowing purples and blues. The unsteady flashlight occasionally danced light up Verboom's bearded face, casting ghoulish shadows. I clenched my teeth as Verboom closed his eyes and spoke.

"I have for you a verse, written on the roof of my hearse:

Ahem.
I wrote the story of the world's richest man.
I have no paper; it's all in my van.
The richest man lived in Seattle.
He wined and dined in his castle,
While the streets were pitched in battle.
He made more money than many small gods.
—His tithing was toothless.
—His critics were ruthless.
He laughed off their whines drinking Napa vines.
Then in the middle of the middle of life,
He took some direction from his decent wife.
In a crisis of scruples, he shared his dough.
Let this make *the people* go...
And go...
Then it turned out,
Coming out like a spout,
He could not get enough of the sharing,
Those faces of gratitude for his caring.
He had to share more of his bank full.
The dough made everyone so thank*ful.*
He *rolled it out, rolled it out*—baker's dozen,

He even gave cash to his despicable cousin.

He *rolled it out, rolled it out*—thick and thin,

He couldn't believe the joy it let in.

Ahem.

They said when he had too much dough he was selfish.

They said when he'd given it all back he was foolish.

He was being fooled and fleeced by the lying,

Making the lazy lazier when they should be dying.

But when the richest man in the world had given it all away:

He was never happier up to that day.

He was never more lov*ed*.

He was never more respect*ed*.

Wherever the richest man travelled—though without
dough,

He had a world of friends in rain, sleet, and snow.

There was always a bed for him.

There was always a meal for him.

There was always a doctor for him.

Always a glass of wine—even gin!

Ahem.

And when the richest man lay on his deathbed,

Reporters and family gathered around.

They said, 'Hey richest man in the world, what's one thing
you regret?'

The richest man said, 'I do not regret emptying my tank,
I made the most and I gave the most, my only regret
is that no one can feel the joy like me—the joy of such
quantity.'

The pastors hissed!

—Does this man think he's divine? Is this man not sorry
for all his crime?

But I say, hey? Didn't Jesus *say* to give it *all* away?
The capitalists hissed!
—Let the people work and buy their own bread... The
   bread they make for us, so we can sell it back to *them*!
The Communists hissed!
—Does he think he's better than us? Above the rest? A
   class of a class, unto himself, all to himself? If he hadn't
   pillaged and plundered with his machines, we wouldn't
   need his fatty breast to solve our unrest..."

"No man, that's *bullshit*!" a guy from the crowd yelled. "Fuck that guy!"

There were cheers.

"No handouts, no cash—lets catch the dude and roast his ass!" another man yelled.

It quickly became a short-lived chant, though some seemed reluctant to join. Perhaps they weren't sure who 'the dude' was or how they felt about rump roast.

"Let the Rose Giant speak!" the original stranger yelled as the chant fizzled.

The crowd booed Verboom as he postured to speak again.

"You know, my mother always said, you catch more flies with honey than vinegar. So, what do you say? Would it be so bad to ask the fattest cat of the fat cats, to help you with his biggest vat?" Verboom paused like it was a meaningful question and he expected a thoughtful reply.

"Who is this giant Dr. Seuss?" a woman yelled.

"He's got a screw loose!"

"Kick his caboose!" someone shouted with a laugh.

"Yo, Giant, the rich aren't gonna help us, they're building spaceships!"

"It's a pissing contest to see who can colonize the moon."

"And build a penthouse on Mars!"

"They're ditching the planet!"

"There are trillions of dollars of *minerals* up there!"

"And 'no homeless,'" a man grumbled and air-quoted in judgment.

"Going to *space*, instead of saving the human *race*?" Verboom replied sincerely.

"They're building survival bunkers and space-bound rockets... You're barking up the wrong tree if you want anything fixed here on earth! They're vampires!"

"You shall know them by their fruit," Verboom said.

"They're ripe and ready to eat!" a woman yelled.

"Now, in terms of persuasion, and I'm only speaking psychologically, not ethically or economically: would you want to help someone who was threatening to roast you?"

"We're hungry!"

"What if you made a concerted appeal to the rich as siblings in a shared humanity, as fellow humans? Help them see you as a partner! Offer them an *excellent opportunity* to share the love—instead of putting on a space glove."

"Time's up!"

"But businesspeople just love *opportunities*! Pitches, not pitchforks, *eh*?"

The crowd booed.

"Again, I'm only speaking psychologically. In fact, I have a slight update for one of your favorite slogans: how about, *fudge the police*?"

"Oh, *fuck* no!"

"Get off the soapbox, man."

"Your head's more bruised than your ribs!"

"Praise works better than punishment; it's proven scientifically,"

Verboom continued. "Why not offer an officer some fudge?" Verboom asked sincerely.

Someone squirted water on Verboom. He opened his mouth, catching only the last few drops of the stream, thirsty from his crowd-slammed poetry.

I pulled him down from the crates.

"I'd have preferred a sponge with vinegar, offered on a stick," Verboom said landing next to me.

"You're lucky it was water." I towed him up the street.

"Let's go to that bake sale just up the way. There are so many people I need to *fudge*."

Up the block, a woman offered home-baked goods from a few large woven baskets.

"How much for your entire inventory?" Verboom removed cash from his fanny pack, replenished after his flag purchase.

"We're cashless, friend. Anything to trade?"

Verboom neatly folded his *gi* tops and put the cash inside, while discrete, the vender could see the large bills.

"What can I get for two high quality *and fashionable* tops?"

"It's the end of the night. Take it all."

She dumped the contents from one basket into the other. Verboom set his tops in her empty basket and took the full one.

Verboom strolled back to the soapbox and set the basket on top.

"Thank you for listening!" he bellowed. "An audience deserves its desserts."

A young man in a rain poncho dug into the basket filled with plastic wrapped items, then yelled, "*Special brownies*!"

Verboom didn't know what made brownies special, and he was confused by the crowd's vibe shift. As his blood-alcohol level dropped, his mood shifted from exuberance to paranoia, so we took a few extra turns and entered the apartment through the back alley.

By the time we got home, fixed our drinks, and returned to the couch, WNN was only a few minutes into *re*-airing Kuiper's interview with Kroes:

KROES: *When the voice of the people is heard, we will bring back America's greatness.*

KUIPER: *What's wrong with America now?*

KROES: *A bloated Liberal establishment. Identity politics. Political correctness. Godlessness. Washington is a cesspool. We all know it. They've lost sight of real people.*

KUIPER: *Is it possible that one party has stopped the productive work of government, because that's in their interest? To jam the gears of government, to make it ineffective, and then blame the other side for nothing working? Isn't that more like sabotage?*

KROES: *We all know you're talking about Conservatives, Jonathan. I'm not a Conservative; I'm a sheriff.*

KUIPER: *If elected, would you govern like a sheriff?*

KROES: *That's the essence of the job.*

KUIPER: *Patrolling the streets?*

KROES: *We need a leader to cut through the BS.*

KUIPER: *What's the BS?*

KROES: *A swamp of corrupt lobbyists, crooked environmentalists, secular academics, and other traitors.*

KUIPER: *Traitors?*

KROES: *People who care more about the world than the people of this country.*

KUIPER: *You're an isolationist?*

KROES: *The man occupying the White House has gone country to country, apologizing for America.*

KUIPER: *Quick fact check: the president has never 'apologized' to any leader of any country on behalf of America.*

KROES: *He needs to apologize for those mom jeans.*

KUIPER: *Yes, we've heard your repeated attempts to unman the president in the most childish ways. Wearing a bike helmet while riding a bicycle instead of riding a large motorcycle in a leather vest, licking an ice cream cone instead of drinking warm whiskey, not wearing a flag pin every time he steps out of the house... These jabs at the president's masculinity and patriotism are juvenile.*

KROES: *If it wasn't a problem, we wouldn't be talking about it.*

KUIPER: *How would you be different?*

KROES: *How much time do you have?*

KUIPER: *You know this interview is scheduled for twenty minutes, and you're wasting time on cheap shots.*

KROES: *Did the man wear mom jeans? Yes or no?*

KUIPER: *Our time is running.*

KROES: *Where's the fact check now, Jonathan?*

KUIPER: *Yes, we've seen the pictures. So far, you've managed to make your case on mom jeans. Care to add some substance?*

KROES: *Jonathan, do you think it's okay for a man to dress as a woman?*

KUIPER: *It's figurative. Those jeans are literally made for men.*

KROES: *I want to make sure we've got the right figure in office.*

KUIPER: *There are those on the Left who consider these insults a form of dog-whistle racism. Some of your critics have called you an outright racist. How do you respond?*

KROES: *That question is racist. I should have known that appearing on WNN would turn into a big boohoo about race.*

KUIPER: *Is there a problem with racism in this country?*

KROES: *Jonathan, the matter was settled decades ago.*

KUIPER: *So, racism is not a problem in America?*

KROES: *WNN is stirring discontent, throwing out accusations, making everything about race and sex—and who gets to wear pantyhose. All this PC crap, that's the real problem with America.*

KUIPER: *So, why'd you come on my show? To promote dad jeans?*

KROES: *To show that I can't be bullied, even by 'the great' Jonathan Kuiper.*

KUIPER: *Fifty-five percent of white Americans think that they face discrimination for being white, and just over a third say that whites face more discrimination than any other group. Are these your sentiments, sheriff? Are you the 'white grievance' candidate?*

KROES: *Media and government have turned on straight white men.*

KUIPER: *The media and the government are dominated by straight white men.*

KROES: *Which shows the insidious nature of real racism, it produces self-defeat... weakness.*

> **KUIPER:** *Are you implying that it's harder to be a white man in America than a person of color?*
>
> **KROES:** *I believe in hard work and individual responsibility. Full stop. And we'd all be in a better place if we'd quit crying about the sins of the past.*
>
> **KUIPER:** *So, you admit there were sins? Because you've described yourself as an 'ardent believer in American Exceptionalism.'*
>
> **KROES:** *You're playing a gotcha game. I'm not playing that game with you.*
>
> **KUIPER:** *Asking about your outlook on the past isn't a trick question. You're running for president. Answer the question.*

Here Kroes took off his cowboy hat and set it on his kitchen table. It wasn't clear if he had all his hair, but he had enough to make it look full without obvious tricks. He was doing the interview from his cozy Southwest-styled home in Arizona.

> **KROES:** *No one loves this country more than I do.*
>
> **KUIPER:** *Does the president love this country?*
>
> **KROES:** *He loves saying what's wrong with it.*
>
> **KUIPER:** *You don't think he loves America?*
>
> **KROES:** *Doesn't act like it. He's left our boys to be tortured*

in Pakistan.

KUIPER: *In rallies, you've said that you will hire the Martin Koning Group to drop a proprietary missile on OBL instead of sending in Special Forces. Aren't you worried about the loss of innocent life? About being able to identify the body? What about the SEALs who may be nearby?*

KROES: *The Koning group has the know-how. The government can't keep up with private market innovation. They have tools the president refuses to use, and I have the will the president lacks.*

KUIPER: *Are you saying the Koning Group is more capable of defending the United States than the American military?*

KROES: *I will get the job done, and the president can't.*

KUIPER: *If president, you would outsource our nation's most important work to a for-profit security outfit?*

KROES: *As president, I will get things done. Whatever it takes.*

KUIPER: *Including the bombing of innocent civilians?*

KROES: *That's what they did to us.*

KUIPER: *As sheriff, you supported, some say even led, a vigilante group called Border Hunters. Can you explain to me why, as sheriff, you would encourage a group of vigilantes* *to interfere with federal jurisdiction?*

KROES: *This so-called president refuses to close our borders and protect the American people. He's given an open invitation to any criminal looking for new victims. The citizens in my county are picking up the slack.*

KUIPER: *You're an elected sheriff with official county personnel, and yet you still direct a vigilante group preying on residents?*

KROES: *There are people who believe the county sheriff is the supreme law of the land.*

KUIPER: *I take it you do too. So, how will you direct the Rallymen if in office?*

KROES: *Stay ready to defend American freedom, as all true patriots must.*

KUIPER: *You're not going to tell them to go home? Quit the rallies, stop the gunfire, and end their thuggish intimidation?*

KROES: *What is it about freedom that intimidates you, Jonathan?*

KUIPER: *Why are you running for president—a federal office—if you want to maintain a militia?*

KROES: *I will set our people free.*

KUIPER: *How are they not free?*

KROES: *We've got three of our boys in Pakistan who aren't free.*

KUIPER: *Some say you've based your entire campaign on a machismo image, that when you're in office you'll change your tone. If your fans call you 'America's Toughest Cop,' what would they call you as president?*

KROES: *The man who put WNN out of business.*

KUIPER: *Are you threatening me?*

KROES: *The lying press will be shut down.*

KUIPER: *You don't believe in a marketplace of ideas? Free enterprise? Millions of Americans choose to watch us. Millions have tuned in to see you, which is why you agreed to appear on my show.*

KROES: *What you do is libel. One hitjob after another.*

KUIPER: *Then why are you here?*

KROES: *So those watching could see a real man for a change.*

KUIPER: *What the hell does that mean?*

KROES: *We all know your tastes, Jonathan. What you like* *to do in the bathhouse...*

KUIPER: *There's nothing wrong with public bathing facilities, but I'm a known germaphobe—you would never catch me going barefoot...*

KROES: *You mean bareback?*

KUIPER: *That term, especially with your pejorative intent, has fallen out of favor! Your insinuations are out of touch. You're indicting yourself.*

KROES: *Oh, I don't know about that. I can wrap up this election win right here by simply calling you a ****** on WNN. America's been begging for it.*

The word was censored for the interview's replay, but you could still read Kroes' lips and hear the first half of the 'F' sound before the bleep interrupted.

KUIPER: *Sheriff Kroes, maybe in your demented fantasy world that's a winning strategy. But you've just lost this election using that word.*

KROES: *Can't take the steam, get out of the bathhouse, Johnny.*

KUIPER: *You're an ignorant bully. America has seen enough. This interview is over!*

KROES: *WNN is through!*

| **KUIPER:** *Cut his feed.*

"Turn it off!" Verboom yelled as the replay of the interview went to commercials.

"Now we've got a November Surprise to match October's," I said in astonishment.

The initial broadcast of the interview, which aired live, along with its two immediate rebroadcasts, made the highest nightly ratings in WNN's history, even surpassing ANN that night.

"Maybe he's trying to get ahead of news about his own preferences," I said, still astonished. "But that was beyond the pale."

"Or is it just what the pale wants?" He paused. "Perhaps you thought Ronald Reagan was the far Right, but next to Kroes, he seems like a polite centrist. The spectrum isn't simply between FDR and Reagan. As America's second most popular social psychologist, I should've been more alert to their inevitability."

"Who's '*they*?'"

"Fascists, Communists, and Anarchists. The let-their-heads-roll revolutionaries! Jacobins! Puritans! Radicals!"

"You're not an anarchist anymore?" I asked, trying to smile.

"*I am a dissenter, and I dissent*! When I was sincere, it backfired. When I was ironic, it backfired. I thought maybe being sincerely ironic would work, but that too has backfired. I'm ruining the world, one *word* at a time!"

"Maybe you have nothing to do with this?"

"I long for that to be true!"

"We could amplify the testimony of the whistleblower who called your show. I know the man, he's legit. You can reveal Kroes' hypocrisy."

"Don't care who he loves, I'm not talking about him!"

"He's a grifter abusing his power!"

"Got a better idea. Going to set those Rallymen *straight*! If they knew their manifesto was only the childish taunt of a washed-up *professor*, well, I imagine they'd drop their guns and go back to the suburbs from which they came."

"They'll just go home and turn on ANN, where another asshole will be talking apocalypse."

"They must know the origin story—I'll give them an excavation in bad ideas!"

I stayed put on the sofa.

Verboom swiftly donned three fresh orange *gi* tops, slipped into his orange size thirteen sneakers, secured his fanny pack, and rushed out the door.

Curious about what WNN would do next, I turned on the TV and headed to the kitchen for a beer. From the open kitchen window, the sound of chanting drifted in from the park, and I pictured Verboom facing off against the Rallymen at their gathering spot. I thought he'd be safer without me.

I froze at the thought.

I'd let that Rally goon's words get into my head.

After wrapping a steak knife in a thick cloth napkin, I tucked it into my jacket pocket and headed for the door.

As I left, WNN aired a Kroes campaign commercial: "When I'm elected, I'll buy every Communist, Socialist, Liberal, Atheist, Muslim, and Anarchist a one-way ticket out of America. If they're scared of flying, they can take a train to Canada or a boat to China. ANYONE who doubts America can take a hike. Love it or leave it. I'm James Kroes, and I wrote this message my damn self."

33

In the center of the lot, Verboom gesticulated wildly with his large wingspan, confronting a small group of lingering Rallymen.

Someone was playing the Kroes-Kuiper interview over a loudspeaker, but once closer, I could hear Verboom's plea.

"*Final Freedom*! You got that backward idea from me, *a professor*! I was angry and sarcastic—two things we shouldn't mix! Regardless of my standing, you need to understand that *Final Freedom* was purely sarcastic! Remember how *The New York Times* mocked your literalism?"

"We're literate, asshole."

"I'm America's second most popular social psychologist." He was circling now, as if everyone was nearsighted and needed a closer look. "Does 'Professor Phallus' ring a bell—Pavlovian or otherwise? *No*? Well, even worse than academia, I worked for the president—the guy who wants to 'get God out of government.' Supposedly that was my idea!"

"Take a hike!" a man shouted, his hand ominously resting on the heel of his holstered revolver.

I reached into my pocket for the knife, holding it there.

"Maybe you know me as the Portland Rose Giant. Your comrades in Portland beat me up, because they're scared of flowers!"

"You can't fool with someone's gun, dipshit."

"*Aha*! So you *do* know who I am! I'm the spewer from the radio sewer. I announced *Final Freedom*. That's me! You're marching to the words of a discredited professor. *Look!* This guy over here's flying the flag right now!"

"Put your glasses on, professor. It says 'Freedom First.'"

I moved closer to Verboom and pulled his arms down.

"You've been duped! But now it's time to go home!" Verboom pleaded.

"We don't care who you are, get your ass off our lot!" a bear-like man growled.

"I'll give you all the proof you need," Verboom took off his three *gi* tops. "See these bruises, your friend over *there* ran me down—knocked me straight to the ground!" Verboom pointed at the man and demanded, "Tell them all what happened on 12th and Pike!"

The man shrugged.

"Your pickups—all festooned with ram bars, floodlights, and flags—are putting the people of Seattle in danger. Look, my hips and thighs are scraped too."

Verboom dropped his pants to reveal the evidence. The men standing closest to him recoiled, so he chased after them, leaving his pants behind. After hounding each man for a closeup, he wound up standing next to me, wearing only his orange sneakers and his fanny pack. His beard past his collarbone and his hair past his shoulders, he swayed as he lectured on:

"My brothers, you've misunderstood the ravings of a madman!"

"Put that *thing* away!" A guy handed Verboom the *gi* bottoms, but they fell to the ground.

"Don't believe what you see? I shall march around you seven times, until the scales fall from your eyes!"

Like the ancient Israelites circling Jericho, Verboom briskly strode around the lot. Despite the cold, the professor's phallus thwacked from thigh to thigh as he looped around them.

When he reached me, after the seventh loop, he began jogging in place, hyperactively.

A man shoved Verboom: "Get out of here, *fucking pervert*!"

Then a second guy shoved him. Unaware of the curb, Verboom stepped back awkwardly and lost his balance. He fell onto his side. I looked down at him, sprawled on the ground. He was manic, joyless, and confused.

"*Let's go*," I pleaded.

His eyes lit up with rage as he looked over my shoulder, becoming fierce like a grizzly.

"The Flag of Treason!" he bellowed in a guttural exhalation of disgust.

I looked over my shoulder to see a man holding The Stars and Bars.

"Honest Abe put your insurrection down. I can no longer be kept on the ground!"

Verboom rolled forward, leapt to his feet, and roared, "*Give me that flag!*"

He pounced on the man holding it. From fear of Verboom's nakedness or fear of his strength, none of the Rallymen moved against him. Verboom took the flag. He snapped its staff in half like kindling. He tore the flag free. The flag's owner lunged at Verboom.

"*Stay back!*" Verboom fumed.

The man stepped back, lost his balance, and fell.

"Shame on you! Shame on you all!"

Then Verboom did maybe the last thing that could still surprise me. He jumped out into a basketball player's defensive stance and held the flag up with both hands at shoulder height.

"*See here, see here—the end is near!*" Verboom bellowed.

Then he swung the flag up and through his legs and pinched it with his inner thigh. He tucked the flag into his hip pack strap from the front and then into the strap at the back. The giant now wore a starred-and-barred diaper.

"Nobody moves, or I'll soil this flag from here to kingdom come!"

I dialed 911.

"Go home ye babes, ye sucklings, ye suckers! Go home unto your mothers' teats! Or I'll soil your sacred sheet—*you gosh darn creeps*!"

Then he raised his large arms like a bodybuilder in a pose down. He curled his fingers into eagle's claws, as though seizing an invisible titan. His biceps, triceps, deltoids, pecs, lats, core, thighs, and calves all flexed in sequence. He bore down, maintaining the statuesque posture for a moment before screaming like a jet engine. Then he studied the faces of the nearby Rallymen before looking at me. A flush of embarrassment colored his cheeks.

Dropping his arms, he turned his back on the Rallymen and strode up Madison Street with long, determined steps. He had taken about twenty strides when...

"No!" a man yelled.

I turned to see another man load his rifle with a single bullet; it was the same man who had been stripped of the treasonous flag.

"*Pieter*!" I screamed.

Verboom turned around.

The man lifted his gun.

CRACK.

The rifle fired.

Verboom brought his hand to his head and closed his eyes.

I braced for his collapse.

Then he gingerly felt the side of his head, opened his eyes, and looked at his hand smeared with blood. He touched the side of his head again.

"That little traitor *shot my ear off!*" Verboom yelled. "That was a perfectly good ear you've wasted!"

Blood ran down Verboom's neck and spread across his chest as he marched downhill toward the Rallymen.

"Right here, right here, shoot me right *here*!" Verboom shouted, slapping his forehead with the palm of his hand.

With his head tilted forward, he strode down the street, back to the men. Again, he spanked his forehead with his palm, causing a splatter of red droplets. He marched right up to the edge of the Rallymen, but no one moved.

"Shoot me right *here*!" He spanked his forehead again. As he breached their cluster, they parted, clearing a path like boys in a game of tag.

The sounds of sirens cut through the air.

"Take the shot, you cowards! Finish your treason, you men without reason!"

He stood in the middle of the parking lot, yet no one aimed at him. As he stomped and lunged, the flag, tucked into his fanny pack, came loose in the front; it now hung like a cape for his asshole, and the thwack came back as he chased the men.

One by one, they climbed into their trucks and drove off. The traitorous flag-holder was the last of them, and from behind the steering wheel his gaze locked on Verboom.

Verboom slapped his forehead one last time.

The traitor floored the gas pedal, and Verboom glared back, unmoved. The truck accelerated, swerved around Verboom, jumped the curb, and sped down the street.

The professor stood in the empty parking lot, drawing heavy breaths. The flag fell from his backside, as the sirens closed in.

The paramedics soon arrived and managed to stop the bleeding from Verboom's ear, though the top half was now missing. After applying bandages, they handed me extra gauze and tape in case it was needed later. Despite the gravity of the situation and the persistent inquiries from the police, Verboom stubbornly refused to file a charge against his assailant.

"Nothingness happened here, officer," Verboom declared.

"Sir, you're saying 'nothing happened?'"

"That's what I said, *nothingness*."

"Sir, the top half of your ear is gone..."

"May I take what's left of it and go home?"

"We could write you a ticket for indecent exposure, do you mind covering up?"

"Pass me a flag," Verboom said without sarcasm.

I handed Verboom his pants.

"We need details for our report," the detective pressed.

"How's this?" Verboom stated. "We could call all these behaviors incidents of accidents."

The officer was visibly frustrated with Verboom. She glanced down at her notepad, then back up at the shirtless professor, his beard gummed up with blood, his ear heavily bandaged, and medical tape wrapped around his skull like a headband. She handed him a business card: "Call me after you get some rest."

Heading back to the apartment, Verboom walked wide-legged, almost stomping. His manic energy present but waning. He went to the kitchen and grabbed a half-empty liter of tonic from the refrigerator and topped it up with gin. Then he marched to the master bedroom for a bath.

I retreated to my room, sinking into the bed with a heavy sigh. As I lay back, I felt the wrapped knife in my pocket. My thoughts whirled. My gaze settled on a prominent crack in the ceiling plaster, snaking its way from the corner. Studying the crack, I guessed at the age of the building, imagining the history it had endured and how it might have shifted with the settling earth.

About ten minutes later, I heard the tonic bottle drop on the tile floor of the master bathroom.

I rushed in to find Verboom asleep. His arms were out of the water, his head leaned back against the wall tile. His legs were so long, there was no chance of him drowning, but I pulled the plug anyway. The sound of the draining water didn't wake him. I threw a bath towel over him, and he didn't stir. Then I took the wool blanket from his bed to add a second layer.

I dialed Jacqueline's number and left a voicemail detailing the night's chaos, then a delirious smile broke through my weariness. Soon this would all be over. The president in office for a second term and me back in Michigan—the thought brought a sense of relief amidst the fatigue. I collapsed into bed and quickly fell into a deep sleep.

Hours later, I woke in a panic. I had forgotten to check if Verboom was still breathing. I sprinted back to his bathroom, where I found him snoring peacefully in the tub—his breathing loud and steady. The crisis had passed, at least for the night.

34

First thing in the morning, I went to check on him. He had moved to the bed and was sleeping on his back, the wool blanket pulled up to his chest. Dried blood was visible on his forehead, and his bandages needed changing.

Midmorning, Verboom sauntered into the kitchen, mumbling something in Dutch. Clearing his throat, he declared, "Tonight, *boerenkool met worst*!"

"What's that?"

"*Stamppot*! Potatoes mashed with kale and a sausage on top, a classic farmer's dish. Perhaps some pickled beets on the side. *Lekker!* Well, I'm off to the market!" Verboom said like a happy homemaker from 1950s TV. He put on his sunglasses and bandana—his usual hat didn't fit over the bandages, so he draped a kitchen towel over his head like a shawl—and sauntered out.

After a few hours, he burst through the front door singing, "*Food*, glorious *food*!" He had one brown bag under his left arm, and he held a bundle of kale in his right hand.

"Guess where I got it?"

"The grocery store?"

"*The park, the park, I got it from the park*!" he sang. "Freshly grown in the community garden!"

"Thought they found you unsavory?"

"Just my thoughts on asking the rich for help politely, framing it as an *opportunity* rather than a guilt trip. Otherwise, they're quite receptive, especially after they found out about my ear. It's like the more I get beat up, the more these folks warm up to me. Go for a walk, dear friend. Get some fresh air. I have dinner under control."

"You're suspiciously jolly. Drinking already?"

"*Drippity drip*! Now save some room for dinner, *jonge*!"

"Still need lunch."

"Did you know that my father was the number one potato peeler? Even with thick fingers, he was agile like a tailor."

"When are you seeing the folks?"

"When the time's right."

"Think they've seen you on television?"

"Oh no, they may have poor taste in politics, but they're too smart to watch TV. And if they did flip on the old tube, they wouldn't be interested in my point of view."

"Why not?"

"My father told me with his Dutch accent that I was the 'single biggest disappointment of his life.' And he's lived a tough life."

"Thought he was hearty and good-spirited?"

"You better get out for some air; these potatoes aren't going to peal themselves."

"But why would he say that?"

"You know how fathers are..." He stopped and looked carefully at me. He gave a pained smile and went on as if I was owed an answer. "He thinks my whole life has been a waste."

"You were—*are*—a top mind in your field."

"He thinks I'm an ignorant Liberal doing liberal nonsense. 'Corrupting the youth,' I think he said. It was in Dutch at that point. Maybe I mixed up the words. But he did say in English, 'We didn't come all the way to America just for you to play with words.'"

"Does he know how much money you've made in book sales? That Canada's biggest hip-hop artist wants *Tautology* in every hotel nightstand instead of Gideon's Bibles?"

"Of course not, Santo. That would be bragging."

As I walked to the park, I considered whether Verboom's challenge had triggered this upheaval, or if events would have unraveled this way regardless of what any one person said. When Verboom confronted the Rallymen, his words fell on deaf ears—then they literally shot off his ear.

From the park, I dialed Jacqueline's number. When she picked up, I tried to summarize the cascade of events, guessing again and again at their causes.

She quoted Macbeth in reply: "Life's but a walking shadow, a poor player that struts and frets his hour upon the stage and then is heard no more. It is a tale told by an idiot, full of sound and fury. Signifying nothing."

"Who's the idiot?"

"Verboom isn't the first person to experience futility."

"Do you ever feel that way?" I asked.

"No. I have plans."

Despite the terrible sounding words, the *boerenkool met worst* satisfied, comforting as any comfort food, but Verboom hardly ate. He mostly drank beer, what he called "taking it easy." No longer jolly, he was in a funk.

"You probably can't tell, but I'm in a foul mood. In case you notice, I don't want you to think it's your fault." He closed his eyes, then sighed. "I apologize for indulging my feelings; it could be worse, right? It could always be worse, but here I go feeling sorry for myself. Forgive me."

"I forgive you."

"You are the only person who can tolerate me."

"What about Ella?"

"She was only in it for the sex."

"And the espionage, it turns out."

"Let's move to my couch, Laurels, the only place I can rest."

Verboom patted Laurels lovingly, like a prize cow.

"Been thinking," Verboom said. "I want in on the book."

"Book?"

"Will you let me speak to your future readers?"

"Shoot."

"Okay. I'm going directly to the people now. *This is the present.* In fact, Santo, if you don't mind, let's call this section *The Present.*"

I held up my phone to reassure him. "We're rolling."

"I, Pieter Cornelius Verboom, with Santo as my witness, do hereby testify as to how the culture war ended," he declared, then hiccupped. "This is no longer speculation. It unfolds before us—you only need to look up and see for yourself. Do you have the eyes to see?"

"I'm right here looking at you."

"Santo, I'm talking to the readers. *Ahem.* Please note, *Verboom* is a real surname from the Netherlands and not an attempt to have a cute end-of-times rhyme with *doom* or *tomb* or *gloom*. Besides, when you pronounce the name in Dutch, it rhymes better with *throne* and *bone*.

"Don't be alarmed. Despite what you may have heard, I'm only a humble observer and not a prophet. I'll be reading the events back to you—and perhaps by the end, along with you. You know what I say about hindsight?"

"You say: 'Hindsight isn't 20/20, it's 100% confirmation bias.'"

"If that rhymed, I might believe you were quoting me." He laughed but had no mirth in his eyes. "Our president said, 'In anxious times folks cling to their guns and religion.' But I tell you the American people have always clung to their guns and religion. What's changed is their willingness to shoot! Santo, perhaps you can include a photo of my taped-up head? But please don't show my face. Or my thinning crown... I'm on my way down, soon to leave town, like a clown, in a nightgown. Say, is it the *orange hour*?"

"Your next point."

"My fellow Americans, if you want to know who wins this battle of words we call 'the culture wars,' you only need to ask the right questions: Who has the guns? Who views the other party as invaders rather than rivals? And who frames the present in the revolutionary symbols of the past?" He paused. "Santo, maybe you'll make this the prologue? Back in my school days I learned that the prologue is the most important part of a textbook! It's where writers reveal their *intentions*. The preface helps you sniff out the author's motives. And if we've learned anything in two thousand years of Christendom, it's that nothing really counts as right if you have the wrong motives and nothing really counts as wrong if you have the right motives. As senator Hesse said recently on ANN, 'A tax cut isn't a tax cut if it's proposed by a Liberal.'"

"Jacqueline says you're like a holy fool from Dostoevsky."

"My crowning achievement!"

"'Heavy is the head that wears the dunce cap,' if I may quote you?"

"Please. I've worn many hats: teacher, philosopher, psychologist, cognitive scientist, professor, E.C.S. fellow, talk show host, talk show host again, and finally a ripe-and-ready reverend."

"When did you get ordained?"

"A few weeks ago. Ella filled out the forms."

He handed me a document, a printed email he'd pulled from his hip pack.

"She ordered formal business cards too. Something I can keep in my wallet, right behind my license with the donor sticker."

"Finish your proclamation."

"The Apostle Paul said his message is foolishness or blasphemy, depending on whether it's Greek or Jew who's listening; however, it's 'the power of God to those who believe!' And so, brothers and sisters, the power of my argument reduces to a question: *do you believe?* If my experience tells me anything: it's not *you* who chooses the conclusion, the conclusion *chooses* you."

"You know that humans *are* highly reasonable when dispassionate."

"But *passion* is all we have left!"

"You're using reason to deny reason."

"Where is sanctity? The terror of the holy? Our Liberal brothers and sisters have been outclassed in the categories of outrage. They can't compete in a holy war!"

"You mean culture war?"

"St. Paul argued that if you disagree with him, it's because you're evil. Question his authority to call someone evil, and he says, 'hey-buddy-it's-not-me-talking-here-it's-God, so take up your argument with the Almighty!' Now whether the saint is full of hot air, you must admit it's a cunning way to cover your backside. But St. Pieter need not cover his bum, because The Kingdom is coming upon us. Just look out your window!"

I looked toward the window.

"The readers, Santo! Please watch the recorder."

Verboom took a big sip of his gin and tonic.

"We heirs to the Enlightenment believed research and education could bring about a better world in which things are fair, while missing the demonstrable fact that the righteous ideologues have declared total war. We fiddled with nuance but neglected the straightforward *declaration* of truth! Sadly, it's more important to *say* something is true, than *show* something is true. Believe me. As we say in the old country: don't bring a book to a knife fight."

"Ever been to the old country?"

"Amsterdam may be the most progressive city in the world, but those Old-World farm boys and girls out in the Low Countries are as right-wing as any. I went to school with the children of these immigrant farmers, and I still recall Bill Van Landt bragging about castrating and dehorning calves; this was somewhere in grade three or four. These kids were marked with scars and missing tips of fingers. They were sharpshooters by the age of ten. They operated tractors before the state allowed them a driver's license."

"We're out of tape."

"Santo, you may want to start your book with a series of questions: *Who has the guns? Who views the president as a foreign invader? And how large is this gun party?* We need not be prophets to understand this pickle."

"You're pickled!"

"I avoided the word 'truth.' I preferred to say things like 'accurate,' 'the evidence seems to support,' 'approximate,' 'indicates,' and 'this would lead me to conclude provisionally...' *yawn*. I avoided 'truth' because our analysis was so fine-grained and specialized, it didn't make sense to employ the term. I avoided saying 'truth' because the word was so often used in the absence of understanding. Most of all, it seemed to me that when you said something sensible, you didn't have to add: *And that's the truth, assholes!* But I finally realized that if the people who know things won't bark *truth, truth, truth*—then only the assholes will! If two thousand years of Christendom teaches us anything, it's that 'truth' is a special word."

He looked at me for a moment, unsure of what to say next.

"Well," he concluded, "this asshole is going to bed."

Verboom set down his drink and retreated to his room, locking the door behind him.

<h1 style="text-align:center">35</h1>

The next morning, I was jolted awake by insistent knocking at the front door. Peering through the spy hole, I saw four police officers in full uniform, accompanied by a woman dressed in plain clothes. Taking a moment to collect myself, I stepped back from the door.

"We can see your shadow," one officer called out.

I hit the record button on my phone and opened the door, keeping the chain lock connected.

"It's the Seattle Police. We'd like to talk to Dr. Pieter Verboom."

"One moment, please," I responded.

I quickly walked back to the master bedroom and banged on Verboom's door.

"Cops are here."

"*Kroes?*" Verboom's voice was groggy.

"No, the regular cops."

"Did they find my ear?"

I heard a creak as Verboom rolled out of bed and a thud as his feet hit the floor. He opened the door and emerged, tightening his orange *gi* bottoms with a quick tug of the strings.

"Why didn't you let them in?" he whispered.

"You *never* let the police in without a search warrant," I whispered back.

At the front door, Verboom unchained the lock and swung it open.

"Pieter Verboom?" the plain-clothes detective asked.

"The *Reverend* Doctor, freshly ordained and ready to solemnize!" Verboom declared with a dramatic flourish, giving me a wink. "*Here* about the *ear*?" he asked the detective.

"It's been reported that you've damaged property, incited a riot, threatened lives, and committed a hate crime. We're going to need to take a statement from you," she informed him with a stern tone.

"*Hate crime*?" I blurted out, incredulous.

"Are you a witness?" the detective shot back.

"I watched this man get attacked by armed men with trucks. *They* shot *him*! What injuries do they have?"

"You can invite us in and talk us through what happened, or we can take this conversation to the station," the detective proposed.

"The station?" I repeated, a sense of urgency creeping into my voice.

"You have a problem with that?" The nearest officer eyed me suspiciously.

"Without more information, we may have to proceed with charges," the detective added firmly.

"Let me put on a pot of coffee!" Verboom interjected, swinging the door wide open. "*Mi casa es su casa*. I'll have coffee ready in a jiffy. Santo, please amuse our civil servants."

We settled into the living room, and the sounds of Verboom bustling in the kitchen filled the air—pots clanging, water running, coffee percolating. As I narrated the events, I smelled the fresh brew and heard the last gurgle of the percolator and a hiss of steam. Then silence.

"Maybe you can check on him?" the detective suggested after a pause.

He wasn't in the kitchen or my bedroom. He wasn't in the master bedroom, but the window was open. He was *gone*. I returned to the kitchen with the coffee pot and the mugs Verboom had set out.

"You don't have permission to search, but he left. Out the back window," I informed them.

After pouring the coffee, we dove into the details again. The detective read her notes back to me, and I confirmed the accuracy of her recorded facts. She nodded once, her expression unreadable.

"That should cover it," I concluded.

Bang. The front door was abruptly kicked open.

The officers instantly drew on Verboom, who walked in, nonchalantly carrying a pink donut box. "Feel that weight," he said, offering the box to the detective. "You know it's the good stuff."

Taking the coffee pot, still a quarter full, Verboom went around offering warmups. He then sat down on the TV console, crossing his legs casually. He held court for over an hour. No one had been that interested in listening to him since their grade depended on it. Though he went off on painfully long tangents, he managed to extract a few chuckles.

"Those ruffians kept staring at my *gonads*!" Verboom exclaimed, bursting into laughter.

The officers couldn't help but grin; however, there was more work to be done, and they'd "be in touch."

Once they had left, I couldn't help but scold Verboom for his earlier disappearance, but his charm with the police made it hard to stay angry.

"When they accused me of a hate crime, I dysregulated. I had to get out. If I went berserk, they would've arrested you."

"*Me?*" I asked, surprised.

"Us. I shouldn't have left you. I apologize," he said, looking sheepish.

"The donuts?" I asked, still puzzled.

"To see if they were Rallymen. They all ate one. So, I think we can conclude they're regular people," he reasoned.

"You ready to go back to the show?" I probed.

"Let's take it easy today. Tomorrow the world may end."

"No more show?"

"Screw it," he sighed, a weary smile on his face.

"Screw it?"

"*Every single call* is about Kroes, right? Screw him. Screw them. We're all screwed," he declared.

"I left your number open. Anyone who calls can still leave a message."

"Many calls so far?"

"A steady drip," I replied.

"Could we hear a few?" he asked, his interest piqued.

"Interesting anecdotes, but not verifiable data," I cautioned.

"More fakes from Ella's projects?" he guessed.

"She would say that the questions were real, and you gave your honest answers."

"Let's call them *staged*."

Perhaps eager to avoid another visit from the police, Verboom suggested a day trip to San Juan Island to clear our heads. With the leftover donuts and a thermos of coffee, we jumped into the truck.

"My mom and aunt took me to the islands when I was in junior high," Verboom reminisced as we drove north out of Seattle. "I wore a jean jacket back then—denim on denim—that jacket was the only thing about my appearance I liked."

"It couldn't have been that bad," I replied, trying to lighten the mood.

He shook his head as if I couldn't possibly understand, then opened his wallet and pulled out an old school portrait from the eighth grade, handing it to me. I waited until we reached a stop, then I studied the boy in the photo while the truck idled. He was a handsome kid, with unblemished skin, green eyes, sandy blond hair, and a bit of baby fat giving him chubby cheeks and a slight double chin.

"Looks like a regular kid to me," I commented after a moment.

"Since the day I turned thirteen, I've felt like something's wrong," he confessed.

"Puberty can really change a person."

"Good one! Put that in your book," he chuckled, then reached into his pocket and pulled out a flask. "You want a hit?"

"I'm driving," I reminded him gently.

"My apologies for blubbering. With the booze, I just let it all out," he admitted.

"Ever try moderation?" I suggested, half-teasing.

"Moderation just makes the wrongness of the world more unbearable. I find it easier to be fully committed one way or the other. But today, I'll be moderate in my excesses," he said with a deep inhale. "You are a good person. You deserve better." He exhaled slowly. "I asked Ella to review all the paperwork—before I found out that she's a spy—but if the documents are done right, you'll get everything. You deserve so much more. Some have the Midas touch... me, not so much."

"Should I be worried about you?" I asked, concern creeping into my voice.

"Sorry, got distracted here at the crucible," he replied vaguely.

"The crucible?"

"Where the roads meet," he explained.

"Oh, you mean the intersection."

He reached over and squeezed my shoulder. I glanced at him; his eyes were watery. Then he looked ahead and nodded. Up and down the highway, we saw trucks and SUVs flying flags.

"If I hadn't vowed to keep my mouth shut, I'd note that many of these vehicles flying Kroes flags are Japanese makes," Verboom remarked. "So much for nationalism."

As we approached Anacortes to board the ferry to Friday Harbor, Verboom suggested playing the voicemails left for Vincent Vermeer.

Making a quick stop, I pulled up our site on my laptop, connected a jack to the truck's audio system, and hit play.

The first caller's message played through the speakers: "If Kroes wins, I'm moving to Canada before Inauguration Day." The second caller echoed the sentiment, opting for Mexico, while the third chose Portugal. Verboom nodded, then chuckled, "No one said the Netherlands?"

As the messages played, the callers covered voter intimidation, political sign stealing, the accuracy of polls, and a lot of guesses about the coming election.

"Sounds like cable news," Verboom muttered as the last caller's voice faded and we rolled into the Anacortes ferry terminal lot.

"The callers sure seem unhappy." He paused in thought. "You know, back in church, they told us that 'happiness' is a choice, even though they didn't believe in 'free will.' If you weren't happy, that's one more thing you messed up! But that's progress, Santo! Real progress. Calvinists were putting happiness on the table!"

"You lost me."

"It's like bigots, they don't want to be called *racists*. We've made progress!"

"Isn't a 'bigot' a 'racist?'"

"All racists are bigots, not all bigots are racists."

"Leave taxonomy to me," I said.

"At four years old, I feared hell," he went on. "A little lamb, just barely on my feet, but already bracing for eternal fire! Of course, I didn't know what the word meant entirely, but I heard the tone—the dread—and I was scared shitless. *Hell.* And then I learned that God wouldn't forgive without the shedding of blood. God will kill *anyone*, even God's own son. It's surprising that evolution hasn't eliminated my type of sensitivity from the gene pool." He took a sip from his flask.

Onboard the ferry, we each grabbed a cup of coffee and took seats at the forward-most bench on the lower deck. For a moment, in the early afternoon, the sun broke through and everything shiny shimmered.

On the island, we ate wide hamburgers and skinny fries at a charmingly weathered café. True to his word, Verboom kept himself in check—no sermon, no spectacle. I only caught his eyes watering once.

After lunch, we wandered through town, past quaint storefronts and Victorian homes painted in coastal pastels. A few political flags flapped lazily from porches, but nothing like the jacked-up chaos back in Seattle. Friday Harbor felt like a place still living in peacetime, free of the marauding trucks and barricaded streets.

Off the return ferry, we found a note stuck under the driver's side windshield wiper: "Please don't leave for Dixie, we need hard working men to keep us strong."

Verboom read the note twice, then folded it neatly and slipped it into his hip pack like it was something sacred or absurd—possibly both.

Driving through Mt. Vernon with the ferry behind us and the lowlands stretching wide, I asked if he wanted to swing by the family farm.

He shook his head, firm and slow.

"Where is it?"

He pointed north.

"How far?"

He took a breath. "What if they're flying a Kroes flag? I've got too much Dutch courage right now."

"Wednesday I'm heading home. Can I take you to your folks before I go?"

"*Ja*, Stanley asked about my plans. Said you'd given notice."

"When did you talk to him?"

"Day the glass got fixed. We had a chat. He mentioned Genevieve would be back in town soon, so I might stay a little longer. See if she has a diagnosis for me." He paused, then added, "At this point, you can probably see that I need help."

"Did you give him your notice?"

"Said I'd put myself on notice to get him a notice."

Arriving at Genevieve's apartment, he turned up the drip and began pacing the living room with restless anticipation.

"The sun has set; the day is over, and the media fast may be broken!" he declared with theatrical flourish, before flopping into the couch, draping an arm over Laurels, and patting her like an old warhorse.

He flipped on WNN just in time to see Jonathan Kuiper grilling the president. The questioning was relentless—about faith, about OBL still at-large, about why the SEALs were still prisoners. Then came the question Kuiper had clearly been saving: "Do you think the false rumors about your birth are racist?"

The president kept his tone calm, his face placid.

"I don't know what's in another man's heart," he said. "But those accusations are categorically false."

"Yes. Just say *YES!*" Verboom shouted at the screen, throwing a hand in the air.

"If he calls them racists," I said, reaching for the remote, "Kuiper gets his headline, and ANN has another week of outrage bait. Then the Right says he's *playing the race card.*"

I clicked off the TV.

Verboom's frown deepened.

"He's still going to win," I added. "He's obviously the most competent candidate."

"We'll see tomorrow," Verboom muttered. "Unless it's another year 2000 mess. Then we'll see in December."

Verboom left the sofa, then turned for the hallway, wobbling slightly, and looked back over his shoulder.

"Thanks for being my designated driver," he said. "I hope they serve hamburgers in The Kingdom."

36

I woke up on Election Day and went straight to Verboom's door. I paused, expecting the familiar rumble of his snoring—but heard nothing. The silence knotted my stomach. I turned the knob slowly, started to push the door open, then a noise came from the living room.

He was on the couch, watching WNN with the volume low.

I smelled coffee and bacon. For a moment, I was back in a booth at the Spotted Owl, waiting for a girl who might not show.

"Confessing straight away that I'm drinking Irish coffee!" he shouted. "Don't judge me, I'm on edge. If I lose this election for the president, I won't be able to live with myself."

"Then live as your *persona*," I griped.

"Vermeer is here." He tapped his finger into the temple opposite his missing ear.

"What do the exit polls say?"

"Each party claims early signs of victory. But the experts say POTUS has a comfy lead."

"Kroes' team polls?"

"Say he's pulling support from both sides, sweeping up independents, and drawing a flock of first-time voters. The Kuiper interview may have helped him more than the captive SEALs."

I crawled back into bed, hoping for a few more hours of sleep. Just as I started to drift off, my phone buzzed on the nightstand—Jacqueline.

"Rallymen are at every precinct in Flagstaff," she snapped. "Guns, Kroes flags, the whole show."

The Rallymen handed out ominous pamphlets packed with misleading information and warnings of stiff penalties for voter fraud. They stayed just outside the seventy-five-foot buffer zone—far enough to skirt electioneering laws but close enough that every voter had to pass through a gauntlet of armed men to reach the polls. Local news ran wall-to-wall coverage of the antics; though critical, the effect was chilling.

"By warning people, they're scaring people!" Jacqueline fumed.

Even though she'd arrived early, she still waited over three hours in line. She got her ballot in but missed class. We traded predictions about the day ahead, but I was teetering between sleep and waking, my nerves worn thin by weeks of rising tension.

With no show to prepare for, I drifted into a half-sleep. My phone buzzed. I ignored it. I stayed under the covers until the light in the room had shifted to late afternoon gray.

When I finally stepped out, Verboom was perched on the coffee table, hunched too close to the TV—like a kid mesmerized by cartoons, except the screen showed a muted news anchor mouthing doom. I rattled my keys and mumbled a goodbye. He didn't flinch, fixed in place, as if he'd turned to stone while I slept.

Winding down the back stairs, I made my way out through the laundry room to the bike rack. After deleting my NEVER CALL text thread and reminiscing on my U-lock's combination, I had trashed it and went to a local bike shop and bought the thickest chain lock available. At three and a half feet long, it weighed almost fifteen pounds. I set the code with my mom's birthday.

Once I freed this new lock, I put the chain over my head and wore it like a sash.

I popped through the side gate and zig-zagged through cars

stuck in traffic. These bike rides had preserved my sanity and swollen my thighs, making my straight-leg jeans snug.

Seeing a neighborhood on foot is so much richer than by car, but the bike allowed me to cover a large swath of the city while still slow enough for the finer details. My routes changed, but I tended to ride the same circuit, first downtown and to the water's edge, then SODO, from which I shot north along the water, all the way to Ballard, then over to Fremont and Wallingford, through the University, down across Montlake Bridge, and back into Capitol Hill from the east side, roughly twenty miles.

Ending this loop for the last time, I stopped in at the café on 10th and used the emergency funds to buy a beet salad and three orders of steak frites plus a double side of grilled vegetables. My favorite host didn't appear, but I didn't ask about her. Three glasses of ice water and a pilsner drained, the food was ready, and I walked the feast and my bike up to Genevieve's apartment.

"*A hate crime*?" Verboom snorted, shooting up from his slumber on the couch late in the evening, as I opened the door.

From the open window, I could hear the chant from the park: *A FALSE CHOICE IS NO CHOICE*. It went on and on in a medium-low tone.

"*A hate crime*?" he repeated, louder this time.

"It's tactical. The charge gets them donations. They've got a legal fund the size of a campaign war chest. You should go after them for attempted murder."

He scoffed. "Rather burn my money."

"The best defense is a good offense."

"Let me talk to the book again, my final testimony."

He popped up and went to the kitchen. The squeak of a gin bottle opening, ice hitting glass, crackling, fizz, another splash, then he came back and sat down next to me with a full pint glass.

"There's more to know than can be known, and the people who know the most don't believe you can know anything *truly*. We've got skeptics and know-it-all know-nothings!" he hollered. Someone in the apartment below banged on the ceiling.

"Could you do this next bit in the form of a knock-knock joke?" I asked.

"*Point one*: Truth over tribe."

"Pieter Verboom: *Truth Firster*."

He sipped his gin. I swallowed my beer.

"More than *firsting*, we need falsification. You must be able to spell out a scenario in which something could be demonstrated false."

"Care to give your readers an example?"

"If candidate X has a fourth affair while his third wife is pregnant, then he cannot be considered a 'family values' politician. So, candidate X has had a fourth affair while his third wife is pregnant; therefore, candidate X is not a 'family values' politician. Hey. Am I slurring? My S's sound funny, don't they?"

"You're getting a Dutch accent."

"Let's see if Ohio's been called," he said, looking for the remote. I fetched a beer from the kitchen.

"*Gin please*!" he called after me. "Hear that lisp?"

"Ever so slightly."

"*Two*! A parliamentary government. We need five political parties: Left. Center Left. Center. Center Right. Right. No Nazis. No Communists. The president will be chosen by a multi-party coalition—cooperation required."

"What about Socialists?"

"To participate in democracy, you must believe in democracy and act accordingly. No more purists, parties shall only have a 'working' philosophy for governance. In fact, let's reduce a step further to *personality*. All citizens should be aware of their personality type.

Let's put our psychologists to work! We can still get you a job, Santo! Personality shapes your moral hierarchy and cognitive style, just look at First Brothers..."

"What was the deal with Hesse?"

"The senator's kid sent a thank-you card. Turns out I signed a letter of recommendation. His kid wants to go to my alma mater."

"No kidding?"

"It's a puppy mill for theocratic middle managers."

"Right, the puritans."

"Purity is the death of democracy and the death of knowledge. Purity is the language of revolution. And revolution, if it means *revolution*, means *violence*! Purity is not righteous; it's the persecution of others with an attitude of self-righteousness!"

I poured Verboom a finger of gin; he topped it off with tonic. I'd decided to drink him to sleep.

"*Three*! No money in politics. Money is not speech. Speech is not money. Money is money. Money exchanged is a payment. A payment is a bribe. Let's put *Tautology* to use!"

"As a corollary, no tax exemptions for propaganda—religious, political, or otherwise," I added.

"*Four!* A proportional senate. The Dakotas get one senator combined. California gets eleven. The District of Columbia is given statehood. No taxation without representation!"

"You ready to talk about statehood for Puerto Rico? Its population is greater than the Dakotas, Vermont, and Wyoming combined."

"As a sidenote, 'In God We Trust' should be struck down as the national motto—a slogan anathema to the founding spirit and not officially adopted until 1956. Instead, we go back to: *e pluribus unam*."

"*Latin*? You can't get the professor out of you."

"Now, if I were mayor, I would ban loud motorcycles and tailpipe enhancers, but that's not one of my national pillars. At a state level, I would ban Daylight Savings Time. No more falling back and springing ahead, the time is *The Time*. Mark it down, Santo: I'm saving time. But these are small ideas. You've caught me killing time now. *Has Ohio been called?*"

"I'm going to transcribe these for your last newsletter. Jacqueline quit. She thinks mixing satire and politics might be as bad as mixing religion and politics."

"Sidebar: What do you think of compulsory military service for all eighteen-year-olds? Service can be deferred until after your B.A. or trade school, but not past the age of twenty-five. We're too soft. It's not good for us to be this soft; we're becoming *crueler*.

"*Five*! Everyone must take four philosophy courses to graduate high school."

"Those classes would be?"

"Logic. Ethics. Metaphysics. Epistemology. In that order. Logic should include a bias supplement. Ethics should provide historical context. Metaphysics should have a dash of world religions. And epistemology should include cognitive science. Philosophy is more important than dissecting an earthworm, for goodness sakes!"

"Bye-bye, biology. Hello, philosophy!" I said. "Sounds like we're ready for another round."

"My brain is a receptacle for world-saving knowledge that no one gives a rat's ass about. What I would do for just one rat's ass of concern... I tried, Santo. But in the end, I'm just another guy resting on his Laurels." He petted the couch like a beloved pet before being put down. "With Ella, I thought all the sex would help me relax, but I am only more depressed."

"Do you love her?"

"As has been established, no woman has ever loved me."

"What about the hurdler back in high school?"

"Too young to know any better."

"Surely your mother?"

"*Nay*, she was mad at me for 'wrecking' her body. I've always been big-boned—even as a fetus—but she had a good sense of humor about it."

"Let me know when you need to be burped."

"Let me add to the parlimentary pillar: to vote for war authorization, senators and house members must have a child or a spouse in the armed forces who will be in harm's way. *No kin, no skin, no war vote*."

He finished his gin; I finished my beer.

"Well, there you have it, Mr. Santo Vera. Five pillars to bolster democracy, from *America's Number One Intellectual Couch Potato*!"

"You need to let me know when you're speaking from expertise and when you're just talking."

"As a public intellectual, I no longer make that distinction."

"I'll send your pillars to everyone on the mailing list, and then we let D.D.P. burn this building down, and O.F.A.M. can run us over as we flee..." My head wobbled. "I must be drunk."

"My theses may sound paltry, Santo, but I want to make a difference."

"Please don't hiccup. Then I'll hiccup. My stomach already hurts."

"We'll call this *The Final Lecture*, an antidote to *Final Freedom*. And to clarify, perhaps we do a draft. Not to combat, but to national service. This might be our last chance to stop the youth from falling into their screens forever!"

"The old folks have already fallen into their TVs and are fully out of their minds for a sheriff who runs a militia!" I shouted. Another knock on the floor from the tenant below.

He covered his mouth like he was deciding between a burp and a hiccup.

"Is this what you'd want for your kids?" I asked.

"You're my son on paper, what do you think?"

"Philosophy for all is hereby declared. *The Final Lecture* is complete."

"Now push the button, Santo. Turn on the TV. Just a wee flush of pleasure-laced dread. Push it, man."

WNN aired a commercial for a medication to treat high-blood sugar.

"I'm making coffee," Verboom said. "You'll never stay awake for the results."

With the volume muted, I slumped into the couch, my stomach turning. A few minutes later Verboom came back to the living room with a large gin and tonic, a small beer, a pot of coffee, and two mugs. I turned up the volume.

KUIPER: *Though California and Oregon remain too close to call, The Associated Press projects Washington State for the president. But now, in a stunning shift, the AP has called Pennsylvania, Michigan, and Wisconsin for Kroes—three decisive swing states once thought to form the so-called Blue Wall. It appears that wall has collapsed.*

And now more news just in, the AP is calling Arizona for James Kroes, which almost brings him to 270 Electoral College votes. Kroes continues to wildly outperform all credible forecasts. However, absentee and provisional ballots remain uncounted in many districts, and the full and final count can take days—weeks in California. Any conclusion reached tonight is provisional; yet, as it stands now, James Kroes looks poised to be the first third party candidate in modern history to win the presidency.

Interference hissed through the speakers—a warped, woofing sound that sometimes broke in when the TV was on, the same distortion that occasionally crackled through our streaming broadcasts. The screen stuttered, flickered, then blinked out entirely. A moment of blackness. Then static. White snow danced across the glass, accompanied by a low hum.

After a minute or two, the picture returned. Jonathan Kuiper sat still at the news desk, blinking under the studio lights, dabbing a tear with the back of his hand.

> **KUIPER:** *I'm told that ANN has declared James Kroes the winner of the 2012 presidential election. According to that network, Kroes has taken all but one of the Southern and Midwestern states: Illinois. While other networks race to crown a winner, WNN will standby until the last vote is counted.*

"I finally *did it*!" Verboom screamed. "I ended the presidency of the president!"

My head throbbed. I chugged what was left of my beer.

"In your next life, stick to milking cows," I said.

"But why is WNN reporting on ANN's call?" he asked.

"News about the media."

"Maybe some of these states will flip back with the late-counted votes, a 'Blue Shift.' If the president can get Pennsylvania or Michigan back..." Then my optimism gave out.

Verboom walked to the kitchen. I heard ice go into an empty glass. I heard a squeaking *ploop*, high-pitched and shallow, a new bottle. I heard ice cracking as it met room temperature gin.

"Bring me a beer!" I called.

The screen flashed, distorted, and turned to silent snow. Then I saw "BREAKING NEWS" through pixilation.

After three big swallows of cold beer, I felt woozy and leaned back into the couch.

"The picture is scrambled... Okay, now at the bottom it says, 'White House Lawn,'" Verboom read. "Did you mute the tube?"

The recording caught the TV's flickering, then the sound of static. Then silence.

"The picture is back. There's a man in a white robe on the White House lawn... Now it's fuzzy again!" Verboom hollered.

Someone thumped on the ceiling below to quiet Verboom.

A warping, woofing distortion came through the speakers. An oscillating *wah wah wah...*

"I'm going for more tonic! The flashing light is nauseating," Verboom groaned.

The recording captures the sound of a plastic tonic bottle cap hitting the kitchen floor and rolling a few feet. Heavy footsteps return to the living room.

"What's wrong with the television? It's just big blocks of rainbow colors!" he whined. "Now it's all snow and fuzz! How will we know what's happening in the world?"

The recording picked up another *wah wah wah...* Then silence.

"The picture's coming back! I can read 'BREAKING NEWS' through the snow. Come on, baby! Okay, here we go. A clear picture. Look at *this*, Santo! Kuiper's sitting next to the man in a white robe! What on God's green earth is this?" Verboom yelled. "The volume's all the way up, but I can't hear Jonathan!"

Wah, wah, wah... the speakers shrieked with interference. A moment of silence. Then...

KUIPER: *You were just at the White House and now you're already across town? How is this possible?*

THE BEARDED MAN: *Look at my cloak, my beard... my transportation is not of this world.*

KUIPER: *I don't know if I should get on my knees or ask what took so long?*

THE BEARDED MAN: *God collects all sound, like a quilt of words laid down every moment of the smallest moment. It takes a word many uses to capture the conscious awareness of God; a pattern must present itself. When God heard the word for God's name and the word 'Jesus,' interchanged, and interlinked, well, "God listened." God wound through all the word-quilts to find my beginning and brought me back to life, or I should say: a facsimile of Jesus to life. I have a photographic memory, I need only three hours of sleep a night, I live on olives and grapes and water alone—though I'm excited to try the avocados of the Americas! I can read at lightning speed, and I've been tucked away, deep in the bowels of an ancient castle outside Rome, reading the worlds' books, and in a sense, God has read them through me. You see, while God may be everywhere, as theologians say, God's conscious mind, to be a conscious mind like all conscious minds, can only attend to one thing at a time.*

KUIPER: *How can we believe you?*

JESUS: *The world has expected my return. Have you not heard of the power of belief?*

KUIPER: *Respectfully, you're not the first person claiming to be Jesus.*

JESUS: *I'm a facsimile. I see your technical crew is running "Jesus" under my image, and while I appreciate the speed, we should have more precision. Okay. Thank you for updating my description so quickly.*

KUIPER: *We've got the best in the business at WNN. Now. Why has God sent you to America?*

FACSIMILE OF JESUS: *America is exceptional. Exceptional at taking God's name in vain.*

KUIPER: *So, God is really listening?*

FACSIMILE OF JESUS: *Imagine the Almighty is trying to make a nice cup of tea in some other corner of the cosmos, and all God hears is "mom, mom, mom, mom, mom, mom, mom!" I speak in the euphemisms of your time and understanding, but tell me, how is God supposed to focus on anything with such constant beckoning? Does God indulge God's children, or does God ignore them?*

KUIPER: *On this show, I ask the questions.*

FACSIMILE OF JESUS: *I have come to take God's name back. God is getting out of America once and for all. Humankind can use words they do not understand. This can be harmless, but this can also be dangerous. More importantly, it really annoys God. "Mom, mom, mom..." like a jabbing finger.*

KUIPER: *Can't God just ignore us?*

FACSIMILE OF JESUS: *God's ready to get out of America. You make a mockery of God's being.*

KUIPER: *But even in your analogy, take away the word 'mom,' and a child can still bug the bejesus out of his mother with a different name.*

FACSIMILE OF JESUS: *Indeed. The entirety of the human mind must be addressed. Not just words, but the propensity to produce words for things beyond the possibility of knowing.*

KUIPER: *Then how can you speak for God?*

FACSIMILE OF JESUS: *I have capacities you do not have. God warns humanity once and for all: Stop using God's name to justify your ambitions!*

KUIPER: *Are you even real or more like a hologram?*

FACSIMILE OF JESUS: *Imagine if king Solomon had never died. Imagine if a talented, charismatic philosopher-poet was on a cocktail of performance enhancers and lost all interest in concubines—that whole system was so messed up by the way—imagine if he read every book written and learned the world's languages! ...I know the structure of data beyond human capacity. BELIEVE!*

KUIPER: *Are you claiming divinity?*

FACSIMILE OF JESUS: *I am a being like no other, a*

category with only one instance. Now, I can see you lack faith, Jonathan. Come. Feel me. We can touch knuckles. You will be the only man to have touched the coming of the Facsimile of the Christ.

KUIPER: *Weren't you just at the White House?*

FACSIMILE OF JESUS: *I spoke briefly with your president.*

KUIPER: *What did you tell him?*

FACSIMILE OF JESUS: *I said, "You were fit for the job, but the country wasn't fit for you."*

KUIPER: *Can you clear up one thing for the record? Is the president a Christian or a Muslim?*

FACSIMILE OF JESUS: *When the president saw me, he was humble but not embarrassed. He told me that he had lived life prepared for such a moment.*

KUIPER: *Not sure that answers the question.*

FACSIMILE OF JESUS: *Now. As the control room has informed you, this broadcast has been picked up by all the transmissions of transmitting devices. The world is listening.*

KUIPER: *We appreciate that ratings bump, Lord. You're welcome to come again.*

FACSIMILE OF JESUS: *With humanity tuned in, I will give you one last moment with your God-names, the words used to sooth and torture. In a moment, God will take 'God' back for good. In all languages and in all minds and in all texts and in all records.*

KUIPER: *That will mean anarchy! How will we know right from wrong?*

FACSIMILE OF JESUS: *Theology has nothing to do with morality, other than making God look bad. God was never needed to know right and wrong; the Buddha and the ancient Greeks knew this before the original Jesus arrived. Admittedly, there is correlational evidence that belief in God promotes ethical behavior. The likely mechanism is belief in surveillance, but we have gizmos for all that now. And yet Jonathan, take a step back, is behavior motivated by fear of punishment truly good?*

KUIPER: *Our listeners are going to think you're pandering to Liberals.*

FACSIMILE OF JESUS: *God has weighed the benefits of surveillance effects against the crimes committed in God's name, and God opts out.*

KUIPER: *What about civil rights movements influenced by spiritual leaders?*

FACSIMILE OF JESUS: *I speak of theology, not spirituality. Spirituality is recognizing the wonder of existence* *and the sacred essence of your fellow beings. You don't need theology for that!*

KUIPER: *You're spiritual but not religious?*

FACSIMILE OF JESUS: *Humanity is in the bad habit of saying, 'Hey, I have the right to do this because the big boss upstairs told me so.' And I am telling you, Jonathan, that the big boss absconds! The boss says no more! You cannot fake God's signature on your checks any longer. The checkbook is empty. No more saying 'because God told me so!' No more holy wars. Just wars. No more fear of God, just fear.*

KUIPER: *How can you speak for God, and say God can't be spoken for?*

FACSIMILE OF JESUS: *Many have claimed to be God's messenger, but Jonathan, let me save you the follow-up questions. And I will put aside the fact that I am only a Facsimile of Jesus, and not actually claiming to be Jesus. Let us be clear: Your flag and cross insult God. God is sick of being slandered. This shall end now! And so that you may believe, I will show you signs and wonders.*

KUIPER: *What's this? You're rattling the earth! How do you have this power as a mere facsimile?*

FACSIMILE OF JESUS: *I am in the eye of the storm. The divine bestows unique power upon me. The world shakes darkened minds!*

> **KUIPER:** *I feel terrible. Like I'm going to faint.*
>
> **FACSIMILE OF JESUS:** *It's because you're trying to think about God. Stop thinking about God.*
>
> **KUIPER:** *Oh no, that made it worse.*
>
> **FACSIMILE OF JESUS:** *To think on God truly, is to make your brain a burning bush! From now on and forever, when a human forms a word referring to God, that human being will faint under the weight of Ultimate Being. For no human can know the true God!*

"Santo! Open your eyes! What's wrong with the TV? *The building is shaking*! My goodness! And what's this? Kuiper is slumped over his desk. The cameras are bouncing and spinning, one's aimed up at the ceiling, like its operator's passed out, or maybe the director is searching for a clean shot—shot to shot to shot, boom, boom, boom... Now pixilation. Static. The Facsimile of Jesus has risen from his desk chair and is walking on the electric snow! It's all white now. White static fuzz!" Verboom howled.

Wah, wah, wah twisted through the speakers. The glass of ice rattled. The furniture scraped and squeaked.

"Santo, the television's gone black! The lights are out! We're in the darkness, pure darkness! This must be *oblivion*."

37

When I came to around 3 AM, the TV stood askew on the console. I sat up and looked to the door. The coat stand lay on its side. The Magritte had slipped from the wall.

"I've been waiting for you to wake," Verboom said, his voice light with relief, his eyes alert, full of focus.

He pulled me to the windows.

Buildings sagged where they once stood proud. Smoke and dust coiled from the street. Down the block, alarms rang in stuttering bursts.

"*The Great Pacific Quake*, Santo, just as you predicted! Turns out *you're* the asshole!" he shouted over the chaos.

My head throbbed. I could barely stand.

"Good thing you didn't get a gun. One of us would be dead already," he added.

"Close the windows. It's too loud."

"They're stuck. No longer plumb!" he hollered over the street noise. "The building shifted."

From a window, Verboom studied the scene outside.

"They're pulling rubble from the lot two doors down. The building's half collapsed."

He turned from the window and looked at me, his green eyes now electric. No longer the clinic eyes, or the eyes behind the microphone, or the eyes floating on gin, but radiating emerald globes. He darted to his room and returned with fanny pack, socks, and shoes.

He put on a second *gi* jacket and tied extra belts around his waist, then pulled up his socks and began tying his orange running shoes. As he finished his laces, I staggered to the kitchen and then back to meet him at the front door with two open beers.

"Hair of the dog," I offered. "My head hurts so bad, I can barely stand."

He waved off the drinks. "Now that you're awake, I must go."

"I'll load the truck," I said.

"May you be blessed," he said with a magnetic twinkle.

"You've lost your Dutch accent."

"Gin's worn off."

He bolted through the front door, then veered for the emergency stairs—reachable only through the tall double windows at the back of the building. He muscled one window open and climbed through.

I leaned out the window and watched him descend the four floors of metal framing and pull-down ladders. The last one didn't drop, but he was almost tall enough to span the length, dangling for a moment before letting go.

After hitting the concrete, he sprinted toward the collapsed building two doors down and began clearing timber and broken brick.

In the dark, with the streetlights knocked out, nearby cars were parked at odd angles, their headlights aimed at the rubble. Dust curled in the beams of light, swirling with the mist—each particle suspended and flickering.

I collected my clothes, computer, production gear, and external hard drives, but left the acoustic foam and curtains. With bags packed, I searched the apartment with the flashlight from my phone to see if anything was left behind.

In the medicine cabinet of Verboom's bathroom, I found

an envelope marked 'Santo' in Ella's script. I folded it in half and jammed it in my back pocket. At the front door, I dropped the building keys into the catch-all and turned to take one last look at the place. I was surprised by pangs of sentiment. The feeling passed as my eyes found the television.

After dropping my bags in the truck, I headed toward the wreckage, scanning for any sign of Verboom. I described him to onlookers—tall, broad, wearing orange—but the closest thing to a lead came from someone who said, "Maybe he went in?"

I stared into the partially collapsed building. Flickering beams of white and yellow cut through the haze. There were desperate cries. Shouts for help, sobs, groans of pain. Then, through the thick murk, I caught two green dots glowing faintly. Then they vanished.

I squinted. My eyes stung, then watered, loosening the grit. Somewhere inside the wreckage, a woman's voice tore through the clamor: "Here! We're here!"

Beams of light trained on the sound of her voice.

Then a titan's groan.

Wood and steel shifted. Dust swirled, and then from the debris, something moved toward me. A hulking figure emerged, backlit and blurred, a silhouette. For a moment, it looked monstrous—cross-shaped and heaving. Flashlights darted across its face, and the illusion shattered. It was Verboom. In the stark headlights of a parked car, he stepped onto the street, soot-covered, cradling a mother in his arms. The mother held an infant to her chest, wrapped tight.

"My dear Santo, take these wounded creatures to the hospital. I'm going back."

"No. Come with us!"

Then seeing my indecision, he placed his large hands on my shoulders, squeezing them painfully tight before softening his grip.

"Your work is in Michigan. After you leave the hospital, please leave Seattle. I can borrow a truck from my brother, and Genevieve will check in on me."

In the past months, his eyes had dulled—murky with depression and gin, drifting somewhere far from the rest of us. But now, they blazed with a startling clarity: the focus of a predator and the joy of an angel.

The baby let out a long, piercing wail. The mother, pale and smeared with ash, cooed back with astonishing calm. Her leg was twisted unnaturally, but she stroked her child's cheek as if she were sitting in a sunlit room, humming lullabies.

"Please go," Verboom said, his voice low and resolute. There was no plea in it—only certainty. Then, without waiting for a response, he turned and went back into the dust and rubble.

Most buildings had held firm through the quake, and I found a snaking path to the hospital, where floodlights lit the driveway in a sterile wash of white. The baby wailed, locked in her mother's arms. They were lifted onto a stretcher. The staff moved with urgency and calm, running triage in the open air, assessing vitals, applying pressure, wrapping limbs.

Once well clear of the city, I pulled off the freeway at a gas station glowing like an oasis in the dark. I filled the tank, then stepped inside the minimart, the automatic doors hissing behind me. I grabbed a cola and a water from the cooler, then scooped up bags of trail mix, dried mangos, and salted almonds.

At the counter, I paid in bills from the emergency stash. As the clerk handed me my change, my eyes caught the magazine stand by the register. A tabloid screamed in block font: "SEALs SNUBBED." The photo beneath it showed the president mid-speech, mouth open, hands frozen, shoulders in a defensive shrug.

Farther down the freeway, just before 6 AM, my phone lit up. Genevieve's voice was steady but tight with fatigue. She'd been in touch with Stanley and was headed to Seattle. No preamble, no small talk. Just the facts, like a pilot radioing in coordinates mid-flight.

Near Salt Lake City I called Jacqueline, and we arranged to meet. Scanning the dial, I found NPR:

> *At 11:58 PM Pacific Standard Time on Election Day, November 6, a massive 8.9 magnitude earthquake struck the Cascadia Subduction Zone—buildings crumbled, power grids failed, and flash flooding swept across the Pacific Northwest. Experts had warned of this for years, with seismologists forecasting a 15% chance of a megathrust event in 2012.*
>
> *Despite its tectonic inevitability, prominent evangelists and satirists have already begun to moralize on the event's significance, as either a demonstration of God's activity in America or the gullibility of God's people in America...*

The broadcast drew a comparison to another catastrophe that struck America on a day heavy with meaning. A megathrust quake rocked Alaska on Good Friday, 1964. With a magnitude of 9.2, it was the most powerful ever recorded in North America. Lasting over four minutes, the ground rose, sank, divided, and liquefied. Buildings danced, collapsed, and caught fire. A 27-foot tsunami killed half the residents of a small coastal village, and 1,400 miles south, in Seattle, the newly constructed Space Needle swayed.

In 1964, between Good Friday and Easter, a radio host in Anchorage named Genie Chance became Alaska's de facto public health officer and emergency relief coordinator. With infrastructure destroyed and the power out, she informed and advised over the radio, the broadcast fueled by her good will and gas-powered generators. She told folks how to purify water and where to find food and shelter.

"A true story," the NPR reporter said with a slight chuckle in his voice. "And her last name really was *Chance*—although by way of marriage."

The story was detailed and well-written, I thought they must have had it waiting in the can like an obituary for Jimmy Carter. With that, I turned the radio off and drove to Flagstaff in silence.

A caravan of Rallymen passed heading north, Kroes flags snapping in the morning air, but otherwise, the freeway was quiet.

When I arrived in Flagstaff, I found Jacqueline in a back booth at the Spotted Owl. She rushed out and pulled me into a hug, her arms tight, her strength startling me. When we leaned apart, she silenced me with a look, a quiet command in her gaze. Then she guided me through the dimming streets to her apartment, just a few blocks away.

The next morning, we tried piecing it all together. Election night and my escape from Seattle was a blur—hazy from too little sleep and clouded by alcohol. I couldn't recall the sequence of events clearly, so we played my recording. It captured Verboom describing the TV's strange behavior—its picture flickering, the sound warping, the signal cutting in and out.

The recording captured the rising storm outside the apartment—engines revving, protesters chanting, tires squealing, counter-protesters shouting back. And then, focused on the TV, Verboom described a man in a white robe on the White House lawn, then claimed to see the same figure appear beside Jonathan Kuiper at the WNN studio.

"Kuiper's voice sounds a little off," I said to Jacqueline as the recording continued to play.

"Ya' think?"

I listened closely for a few more lines. "*What*? 'The Facsimile of Jesus?'"

Jaqueline frowned with confusion.

"Oh shit, it's Verboom!" I exclaimed.

In the remaining audio, we listened to Verboom mimicking Kuiper and creating a different voice for the mysterious bearded man, supplying both sides of a conversation.

"So, you don't know what happened at WNN?" Jacqueline asked.

"I guess not."

"Before any network made a call, ANN aired footage of Rallymen gathering outside the WNN studios—then breaking in. A local ANN affiliate here picked up the feed, and I saw it live. When I switched over to WNN, their cameras were still rolling from inside the studio, but the audio was gone. Only a picture."

I blinked. "A *break-in*?"

Jacqueline nodded, eyes intense. "The Rallymen stormed the studio. Armed men flooded into the frame. And there was one man in a white robe. They surrounded Kuiper on set."

"A robed man?" I repeated, struggling to keep up. "It wasn't Jesus? I mean, some guy pretending to be Jesus? A *facsimile*?"

"After he pulled down his hood, he may have looked like a Sunday School Jesus—full beard, piercing blue eyes. He looked straight into the camera, like a preacher on meth. Then you could see Kuiper yelling—arms subdued. And the shot back and forth between Kuiper and the robed man."

"They took Kuiper *hostage*?"

"The Rallymen forced an interview, but there wasn't any audio.

Kuiper's mouth was moving in an exchange with the robed guy. But you couldn't hear a thing."

"This is when Verboom and I tuned in," I said, "right after he gave *The Final Lecture*."

Jacqueline narrowed her eyes. "The final *what*?"

"I tried to drink the professor to sleep while he gave a lecture on how to save America, but I guess he drunk *me* to sleep." I shook my head. "But how did the bearded guy get from the White House to the news studio so fast?"

"A different guy with a matching robe and beard... The Rallymen tolerates a hooded order."

"*Jesus Christ*," I swore. Then I felt woozy.

"Despite the loss of audio, WNN let it play because..."

"The breaking news *broke in*. The Rallymen mobbed WNN on Election Night, and Verboom supplied the missing voices!"

We were silent. I sat down on her love seat. Lightheaded, I leaned back and closed my eyes.

"Verboom's voice-over is awe-inspiring," she said, standing over me, a gleam in her eye. "*That's it!* That's how you end the book."

"The Facsimile of Jesus was actually some kind of Klansman, and Verboom was stone drunk on the couch filling in words, adlibbing and mad-libbing while I was passed out."

"But it happened. You have the recording." She stopped. Her eyes widened. "Maybe he was *lipreading*? We don't know yet."

"And the TV's strange behavior?"

"God's intervention?" she suggested with a wry smirk, then squinted like she was experiencing the start of a headache. "The Cascadia earthquake happened around the same time. A sign from God!" She grinned, her face beaming, her eyes dazzling, then pained with a further thought.

"What about all the static with the TV?" I asked.

"Probably someone using an old microwave in the apartment below," she guessed.

"Let's check WNN," I suggested.

"They're not re-airing the footage from Election Night."

"*Why*? Ratings would be higher than the Super Bowl."

"Maybe they want to promote calm, showing the attack will raise tension."

"Now's when they choose to be *responsible*! They rebroadcast the Kuiper-Kroes interview at least three times."

I turned on Jacqueline's TV and found WNN.

It was coverage of Kroes' win, nothing about the studio raid. I turned it off.

"What about Kuiper?" I asked. "They still have him?"

"I heard the Rallymen plan to keep him until Kroes takes office."

"So that's why they're not showing the footage... they don't want to air scenes of a crime while still in negotiation."

"Maybe WNN isn't showing the footage because Verboom was lipreading accurately." She grinned, a bit mocking. "As a secular network, they don't want to amplify Jesus' message," Jacqueline said then winced.

"*The Facsimile of Jesus*," I corrected.

"I'm getting a migraine," she said, steadying herself on the couch's arm. After catching her balance, she looked at me.

I frowned back with concern.

She reached for her phone and pulled up current headlines.

"You're right! Kuiper is still being held prisoner inside the DC studio!"

"So, their suppressing Election Night video as part of the negotiation?" I mused.

"God only knows if Kroes is running the militia or if the militia is running him!" She stopped. "*Damn*, my head hurts."

"Mine too."

"*Wait*! Stop right there! Ella left Seattle before giving you the whole family story!"

"She left a letter."

"What does it say?"

"It's in my back pocket."

She leaned over me and grabbed it.

"It's still sealed. You haven't read it?"

"Ella can't be trusted."

"Then what's the harm in reading it?"

"It is what it is."

Jacqueline opened the letter. She read it silently. Then handed it to me.

I handed the note back to her.

"It says, 'Mark Sunderland can put you in touch with your paternal uncle, Martin Koning. He's ready to talk about your father and can bring you into the family. There are things that only he knows about your mother and father...'"

"*Martin Koning*!" I said. "Founder of America's largest private army?"

"They're mercenaries, Santo. Call them mercenaries. It's not an army. But why is she talking about your uncle? He's obviously a big deal, but he's not your dad..."

Jacqueline continued reading. Her face troubled.

"Did you ever catch Ella in a lie?" she asked.

"Not a false statement, but she misled us."

"You got misled. But did she lie? About facts?"

"Maybe not literally."

She looked back at the note.

"There's more?" I asked.

"Your father never held you. He was forbidden to see your

mother. He went to college after you were born, but..." Jacqueline went silent. She looked at the floor.

"Tell me."

"Didn't she say at the diner that your father was part of that Dutch American community?"

I nodded.

"One of the richest families in the state. And, well..." Her eyes widened.

"*What?*"

"You look... *Oh shit*! *You're Dutch*!"

She opened her phone and pulled up a picture of Martin Koning. Her eyes moved between me and the image. Her stunned grin dropped into bewilderment.

"There's resemblance," she declared.

"Why is Ella talking about my alleged uncle? Because he's more famous than my alleged father?"

"Santo, the letter says your dad died in a car accident his freshman year of college. Jacob Koning."

Within seconds, Jacqueline found his obituary in *The Grand Rapid Gazette*. Which she skimmed, mumbled a few lines, then held the picture up to me.

The resemblance increased.

My stomach turned. I felt like I might never escape Jacqueline's couch.

She handed the letter back to me.

From my front pocket, I removed my phone and made the call.

My grandmother picked up on the second ring.

I gave her the names and facts as presented in Ella's letter.

I asked, "Is Jacob Koning my father?"

Nothing.

I checked the phone to make sure we were still connected.

"Grandma! Say something!"

Then I heard her sniff, sniffing like she could vacuum up all the pain, confusion, and sin. I waited for her to speak, but there was nothing.

I looked at the phone again. Still connected. Then I put it back to my ear and asked the question again.

"Thank you, Grandma. I'll be home soon."

I exhaled. Then hung up.

"What did she say?" Jaqueline asked.

"She said, 'I was nodding.' The silence. During the silence, she was nodding."

"There's a phone number in the letter. What are you going to do?"

"I'm done with Dutch uncles."

"God, Santo." She winced, still standing in front of me. "You should get to know your real uncle before the book is out."

"Oh my God!" I jumped to my feet. "You're right. I need to meet him before anyone reads it."

"Maybe, he'll have enough material for a sequel." She smiled, then squinted, wrinkled her nose, and sneezed hard.

Without thinking, I said, "God bless you."

"*God*... not God again."

She wobbled. Her shoulders went slack.

"*Jesus*! Jacqueline, are you okay?"

Her eyelids sagged. Her eyes rolled back—nothing but white. She fainted, collapsing into my arms, and together we sank into the couch.

www.ingramcontent.com/pod-product-compliance
Lightning Source LLC
Chambersburg PA
CBHW030330120726
47901CB00007B/1740